STAR QUALITY

STAR QUALITY

JENNIFER HALL

DONALD I. FINE, INC.

New York

Copyright © 1993 by Jennifer Hall

All rights reserved, including the right of reproduction in whole or in part in any form. Published in the United States of America by Donald I. Fine, Inc. and in Canada by General Publishing Company Limited.

Library of Congress Cataloging-in-Publication Data

Hall, Jennifer.
Star quality / Jennifer Hall.
p. cm.
ISBN 1-55611-346-3
I. Title.
PS3558.A3688S73   1993
813'.54—dc20   92-54468
                                                          CIP

Manufactured in the United States of America

Designed by Irving Perkins Associates

10 9 8 7 6 5 4 3 2 1

This novel is a work of fiction. Names, characters, places and incidents are either the product of the author's imagination or are used fictitiously. Any resemblance to actual events, locales, organizations or persons, living or dead, is entirely coincidental and beyond the intent of either the author or publisher.

*To my mother,
who gave me my love of books*

Special thanks and mention are due to the following exceptional people:

To my agent, Harvey Klinger. Thank you for your support, encouragement and tireless enthusiasm;

To my editor, Sarah Gallick, for wanting to buy *Star Quality*. Thank you for liking my book;

To Joyce Andes, a very classy lady;

To Nancy Bush and Susan Crose, my two favorite Oregonians;

To Lisa, who is always willing to listen to my sweet whining;

To John, who provides my inspiration;

And lastly, thanks again to my agent, Harvey Klinger. I know I keep saying "thank you" over and over, but *thank you* for everything, especially for giving me back my confidence.

PROLOGUE

HOLLYWOOD 1965

THE WOMAN WAS angry.
She paced the bedroom like a caged animal, constantly checking the time on her wafer-thin gold Piaget watch.

Where the hell was he?

She gave a mirthless laugh, chasing away the thought. She knew where he was—where he always was. With his mistress.

Her high heels dug deep furrows in the plush carpeting with each furious step taken. Then she stopped before a full-length mirror, surveying her image.

She was a beautiful woman. Men were constantly complimenting her, always lavishing praise and trying to catch her eye—hoping to entice her into stepping beyond the boundaries of her marriage. She never did.

She had never taken advantage of their offers. She had never paid the men any attention. Unlike her husband, she had believed in the sanctity of their marriage vows.

No more.

Her ivory silk dressing gown fell to the floor. She stepped out of it and reached for a sequined chemise with a dramatically low-cut back that she had purchased earlier that day at Neiman-Marcus. The dress was scarlet red, a definite contrast to the sedate colors she normally wore.

She slipped into the dress, savoring the way it clung to her body. Admiring herself before the full-length mirror, she took pride in her appearance, marvelling at the difference a change in color and style made.

Next came the cosmetics. She dramatized her pale beauty and

within minutes her face was startlingly intensified by the savage slashes of color she had applied.

The woman raised her chin determinedly as she added the last few finishing touches on her appearance. Another laugh escaped her throat, this time low and sarcastic.

Two could play at the same game.

The child pressed an eye to the closet crack, stifling a giggle. Wouldn't Mama be surprised when she opened her closet door and looked inside!

Hide and seek was the child's favorite game, but no one ever wanted to play. Nanny was always too busy and Papa was never home. Only Mama would play the game and playing with her was best because when she found you she would give you big hugs and lots of kisses.

Mama looked so different tonight. Where was she going? Mama never left the house at night the way Papa did. Papa was always gone for the longest times but Mama never went anywhere. She could always be found when needed.

Why was Mama taking so long? When was she going to finish?

The child released a sigh of impatience, then bounced on its knees with eager anticipation, waiting to be found.

There was the sound of approaching footsteps. Then the bedroom door opened.

The woman finished applying a coat of ruby red lipstick. After capping the lipstick she reached for a silver-backed hairbrush engraved with her initials, giving her long dark hair a few quick strokes. She didn't bother acknowledging her husband.

"You look like a whore," he growled.

At her husband's words, she turned. "So you're finally home. What's the matter, darling? Disappointed that your Madonna is gone?" She didn't mask the fury in her voice. Closing the distance between them she rubbed against him seductively. "Isn't this the way you like your women?"

He pushed her away. "Get out of that dress and put on something decent. We have a dinner to go to. And take that crap off your face."

"No." It was the first time in their marriage that she had used the word. Uttering it thrilled her. She moistened her lips with the tip of her tongue. "I'm all ready." Her eyes gleamed with determination, awaiting his challenge.

"Don't push me," he warned. "I'm not in the mood."

"You're never in the mood," she snapped aggressively, ready to begin the confrontation. "You're never in the mood with *me*. Only with *her*," she spat out, her face twisting with hurt and outrage. "You never give any thought to me. You never give me any time except when you want something. I'm sick of being your ornament, pulled out of this house only when you want to show me off."

"Are you saying I don't love you?" he demanded. "That I don't take care of you? I give you only the best that money can buy. You've got cars, furs, clothes, jewelry. What more do you want?"

"It isn't enough!" Suddenly she felt like throwing a tantrum. He didn't understand. He didn't know how she felt . . . he didn't *want* to know. And that infuriated her. "I want to be loved! I don't want to be some object in your life."

"Baby, you *are* loved, and this is the best you're gonna get." He pointed a stern finger at her. "You better get used to it."

She looked at him coldly. "I don't *have to* get used to it. I don't *have to* do anything you tell me to do. Not anymore."

He gave her an amused look. "Why's that?"

"Because I'm divorcing you. You're not man enough for me. You never were and you never will be."

He released a mocking laugh. "That's rich! You're hardly the voice of experience. When we got married you had nothing. Everything you have is because of me. You wouldn't even know how to take care of yourself if you were on your own."

She gave him an assessing look. "Really? I wouldn't be so sure. I'm a beautiful woman. Men desire me." Her voice rose with confidence. "I don't need to take care of myself. They'll take care of me."

"That would make you no better than a whore."

"Yes, just like your mistress," she angrily hissed, suddenly wanting to hurt him as much as he had hurt her after all the years of neglect. She didn't care how she did it. "I've taken a lover," she lied.

Her words didn't have their desired effect. Instead he remained cool and unruffled.

"Didn't you hear me?" she demanded. "I said I've taken a lover."

His voice was low and steely. "No man would dare touch you."

"But they have," she triumphantly purred, glad he had taken her bait. "Why wouldn't they? You're not as powerful as you'd like to think." She moved closer to him. "Bedding me is a challenge. My lovers always compare themselves to you and I always tell them how much better they are. *Always.*" She gave a malicious laugh, deciding to carry out her charade as far as it would go. "We never bother with hotel rooms. We always come here." She sprawled languorously on their bed. Her hand sensuously caressed the bedspread as she looked up at her husband from beneath lowered lashes. "Using *this* bed for hours on end."

His reaction was unexpected. Suddenly his hand whipped out, slapping her face. She fell off the bed onto the carpet. Before she could even get up he wrapped his fingers through her waist-length hair, dragging her to her feet as he shook her with a monstrous ferocity.

She started to struggle, but her efforts only infuriated him more. Looking into his face, the woman felt the first twinges of fear. Her husband's face was mottled red and his notorious temper had been unleashed. She had pushed him too far.

"Please," she begged, desperately wanting to undo what she'd done—to untangle her web of lies before it was too late. "Let me explain."

"Explain? What's there to explain? No one makes a fool of me!"

Releasing her hair, his hands clamped around her throat. Squeezing with all his might, he lifted her off the floor and slammed her to the wall. His eyes bulged from a face gone mad as he continued to squeeze.

The woman's feet twitched uselessly in the air and her fists bounced effortlessly off his chest . . . until finally they hung limply at her sides.

The child gasped, falling back into the darkness of the closet.

What was going on? Why was Papa hurting Mama?

At first the child couldn't move, frozen by fear. Then, inch by inch, the child returned to the closet crack, pressing an eye forward.

Papa was gone, but Mama was lying face down on the carpet. Pushing the closet door open, the child raced out.

"Mama?" It was a tentative whisper. The child knelt before the woman, giving her a gentle shake. "Mama? Mama, wake up." The next shake was stronger and more insistent. "Wake up. *Wake up!*"

Why wasn't she moving? Mama always woke up when called. And why was her hair covering her face? Mama's hair was usually worn piled on top of her head with loose curls dangling down the sides.

The child pushed away the long dark strands covering her face. The sight unloosed a shriek.

The woman's eyes were bulging and unseeing. Her tongue was swollen and protruding. Around her neck there were ugly red bruises.

The sobbing child backed away from the sight, scampering back into the closet and hiding in the farthest corner.

Hours later the body was gone. Moonlight streamed through the windows, illuminating two lovers engaged in an act of passion.

It was the man and his mistress.

Both were greedy lovers, consumed by an insatiable carnal hunger. Their bodies were drenched in glistening sweat and the air was heady with the smell of sex and perfume. They concentrated only on satisfying themselves.

"Did you really do it?" she asked in her seductive purr. "Did you really take care of things? Did you do as you promised?"

"Have I ever broken a promise to you?"

"Never," she passionately avowed.

"And I never will." He reached beneath his pillow and removed a gold necklace with a twenty-carat emerald surrounded by diamonds, lovingly draping it across her neck.

"Ooh!" she squealed, rubbing the cold gems over her skin. "You spoil me so!" She brought her lips to his as she greedily fingered the necklace. "Are you sure we're safe?"

He gave her a passionate kiss. "Don't worry. It won't even look like murder."

The child was still in the closet, but no longer hiding. Instead the child's eye was back at the closet crack, watching the two lovers with rapt attention. Burning hatred was the only emotion evident on the child's face.

PART ONE

JANUARY TO JUNE 1990

CHAPTER ONE

Drew Stern had made up his mind. He was going to star in *Long Journey Home*. As one of the year's hottest bestsellers, the novel had Oscar written all over it. He'd have to be crazy to turn down the role.

He got on the phone with his agent, Travis Sawyer, and delivered the news.

"Travis, tell Mark I'm in."

"Not only will I tell *him*, but every other person in the industry. Drew, this is the smartest move of your career."

After a few minutes of business talk with Travis, Drew hung up. He started pacing his Malibu beach house with mounting excitement. Already he was visualizing himself as Vietnam veteran Matt Thomas, protagonist of *Long Journey Home*.

He stared at his image in a mirror, assessing himself. Matt Thomas was going to be a definite contrast to the pretty-boy roles he usually played. Here was his chance to display a wide range of emotions and prove to the critics that he *could* act.

Usually his performances were panned, although the critics' opinions never affected box-office receipts. Drew was the hottest male star at the moment, edging way ahead of Tom Cruise and Patrick Swayze. Yet would the critics give him a chance or would they see him only as *People*'s "Sexiest Man Alive" and the face that almost every woman in America adored?

Until Hollywood Drew had never been acutely aware of his looks. Glossy black hair and ice-blue eyes were common fare. And the classic bone structure of his face wasn't at all unusual. Yet Drew possessed *something* that the camera loved and it drove women wild—they could never get enough of him. Whenever he made a public appearance he was stormed and in popularity polls he always rated number one. The demand for magazine interviews never diminished and he was a favorite with many talk show hosts, often appearing regularly on the "Tonight Show" and the "Arsenio Hall Show."

The tabloids found him boring. He lived a quiet life and was never seen on the party circuit unless he absolutely had to be. Female companions were rare, but there was no questioning his sexuality. His work was what he lived for and when he was given a part he threw himself into it with everything he had until the last frame was shot.

Yet despite Drew's life being an open book, he was still an elusive figure. Drew Stern was an enigma. No one knew what put him together.

Neither did Drew.

He supposed a lot of it had to do with the way he had been brought up. He had been born in New York in 1960 after being conceived in the back seat of a Buick on the night of his mother's senior prom. When his father wouldn't marry his mother or pay for an abortion, she'd had no choice but to confess all to her parents. They promptly threw Debra Stern out into the street.

With nowhere else to go, Debra moved in with her Aunt Sally, a wealthy widow who generously took care of the expectant mother. After the birth of Drew, Debra stole all of her aunt's jewelry and was never heard from again.

Despite his mother's abandonment, Drew's early years were happy. Aunt Sally doted on him and he was an adorable child, charming all those who crossed his path.

But the happiness ended for Drew at age eight when Aunt Sally died of cancer. When his grandparents refused to take him in, Drew entered the world of foster homes, shuffled from one house to another. The families were always clear about their intentions: Drew was only a way of supplementing their meager incomes.

The situations were always the same. Lower middle class incomes; families with too many children; a room in the basement or attic; secondhand clothing; no friends; exclusion from family events because he "wasn't one of them." The families never mistreated him, but they were hardly loving. They were indifferent and any sense of security in the young boy disappeared. As a result Drew became shy and withdrawn, often spending hours alone in his room, losing himself in the books he loved to read. It was the only way he could escape the world around him . . . just for a little while. And it allowed him to forget the way his foster families made him feel. He felt he wasn't good enough . . . he wasn't good enough to be loved.

For years Drew carried around these feelings, pushed to the farthest corner of his mind. He wouldn't allow himself to feel sorry. Instead he kept burying himself in his books. Then when he turned fifteen he found another way to escape.

He discovered acting.

It all started when he was cast in *Romeo and Juliet*. He'd gone to the auditions as a lark because he'd had nothing better to do, thinking he'd get a job as a stagehand. Yet not too many of his male classmates had turned up for the audition. The next thing he knew a copy of the play was put in his hands and he was center stage. He surprised everyone, including himself, by proving he could not only remember his lines, but deliver them with conviction.

It hadn't been the applause that had gotten to him. Rather, it had been a revelation during the opening-night performance. Upon delivering his lines to Juliet, Drew realized that he actually *was* Romeo. His thoughts and actions were all those of his character. For a short time he had escaped from being Drew Stern. He was no longer unwanted and unloved.

It had felt wonderful.

In order to keep that feeling, Drew continued to audition. It didn't matter if he didn't always get the starring role. As long as he was up on stage, immersed in another persona, he was happy.

The idea that he might want to spend the rest of his life acting didn't come to him until some time later. One of his teachers directing a play asked if he was going to make acting a career. The question threw Drew off guard and he didn't have an answer. He'd never thought of acting as a career or as a way of making money. But when given some thought the idea seemed highly plausible. Why not make a living doing something he enjoyed? Why not find a way to forget his pain?

After making his decision to become an actor, Drew worked toward his goal with an all-consuming passion. In school he took as many drama-related courses as possible. Workshops and seminars were attended religiously on weekends and during the summer.

He was a willing student, able to take criticism well. Mistakes needed to be pointed out and corrected. How else could he perfect his craft?

Whatever money he made at part-time jobs was saved. Once he

turned eighteen and graduated from high school he was heading to California and he knew he'd need every available cent to achieve his goal.

After receiving his diploma Drew packed his bags, emptied his savings account, and headed out to California without even bothering to leave behind a farewell note for his newest set of foster parents. Why bother? They'd made it perfectly clear that once he turned eighteen and the checks for taking care of him stopped coming in, he was on his own.

The early years were lean ones for Drew. At first there were only bit parts. Walk-ons in movies. One-liners on soaps. An occasional episode on a sitcom. To supplement his meager earnings he took a string of jobs ranging from lifeguard to chauffeur to gardener, and of course, waiter.

Throughout that time Drew managed to be patient. Acting classes and seminars made up his evenings. Connections were made with other actors and actresses. Auditions were always attended.

Drew's face soon became familiar as he made the rounds and he kept getting called back. His first big break came when he was cast in a low-budget slasher movie. The audition had been open so the cast was made up of unknowns. As one of the next-to-last victims of the killer, Drew was constantly on the screen. Though the pay hadn't been great and the two months of filming in Oregon had been horrendous, Drew finally got what he wanted: exposure.

Death Blade made a small profit at the box office. Its success came at a time when slasher movies were at their peak and Drew was cast in three more. All were box-office hits.

Producers and studios started to take notice. Pictures featuring Drew Stern brought in more money than their competition in the same genre. Was it a fluke or did Drew Stern possess some sort of appeal? Surveys were taken at preview screenings. Females were infatuated with Drew's looks. Males thought Drew possessed a hard edge they could admire.

It was then that the offers started rolling in. Drew, who had been starving for roles, now had his pick. He was very selective, taking a number of factors into consideration. Ultimately he had to like the character he was playing. With Travis's guidance he starred in a western, two thrillers, and an adult comedy. But his big hit came in 1985 when he starred in *Vendetta*. *Vendetta* was the story of Cal Parker, a private detective who combs New York's underground world of prostitution and pornography after his fifteen-year-old niece is abducted in a plan of revenge. With his Colt .45 filled with silver bullets, Cal Parker manages to save his niece and at the same time pull in one hundred million dollars at the box office. Two successful sequels did the same.

After the two Cal Parker sequels, Drew became even more selective about the roles he chose to play. He didn't want to get pigeonholed and he could afford to take his time. He'd managed to save quite a lot of his salary.

Drew was always looking for his next project. He read everything he could get his hands on. Three months ago when he had finished *Long Journey Home* he knew he had found his next role.

There wasn't a doubt that *Long Journey Home* would be made into a film. The only question was how could he become a part of the project? Mark Bauer had bought all dramatic rights to the novel and would be producing and directing. When Drew heard this he urged Travis to do all that he could to express his interest in the film. He'd do whatever was necessary to work with Mark.

Drew met with Mark a number of times. He read not only for the role of Matt, but Matt's younger brother, Patrick. When Mark asked if a cut in salary was a problem, Drew told him it wasn't. Mark told him that he was considering other people, such as Matthew Broderick and James Spader, but would stay in touch.

An hour ago Mark had called Travis, offering Drew the role of Matt. And Drew had accepted.

At last he was making a "real" picture. With Mark Bauer helming the project, the picture was a guaranteed success. Maybe he'd be nominated for an Oscar. Maybe he'd even win. Drew stared at the mantel of his fireplace, envisioning what it would look like with an Oscar for Best Actor. It would be nice not to be alone . . . to have something to come home to . . . something to signify acceptance and belonging.

Grabbing his Ray-Bans and copy of *Long Journey Home,* Drew headed for the beach, leaving his ghosts behind him.

CHAPTER TWO

"I LOVE PINEAPPLE, don't you?" Gabrielle Fontana Moore murmured as she added another pineapple slice to her co-star's erection.

Her tongue moved deftly over his shaft as she nibbled through the fruit. "Mmm." She licked the hot, sticky flesh before taking him in her mouth. "Pineapple suckers are my favorite."

Frost Barclay groaned at the skillful manipulation of Gabrielle's tongue. He clutched at her long raven curls, drawing her closer.

"Easy, lover!" she coaxed, pulling away her mouth. "Take your time. Save it for the good part." Gabrielle straddled Frost, drawing his erection into her moist center. "I'm not going anywhere."

Gabrielle Fontana Moore and Frost Barclay were two of the stars of "The Yields of Passion," daytime's number-one soap opera. Gabrielle starred as villainous Serena Taylor while Frost played corporate lawyer Chet Archer. Both characters were immensely popular with fans of the show, resulting in hefty salaries for both Gabrielle and Frost.

Frost had just finished his first year on the show and next month marked Gabrielle's third anniversary. Although Frost was perfectly content with his career at the moment, Gabrielle was unhappy with hers.

She couldn't wait to get off the show.

The reason was simple. Gabrielle wanted a *film* career. She had no intention of spending the next ten years playing Serena. Other soap stars had made the leap to the big screen. Kathleen Turner and Meg Ryan were two shining examples.

Now it was her turn. She'd waited long enough and now the perfect role had come along.

It was Olivia Thomas in *Long Journey Home*.

So what if the novel hadn't particularly thrilled her? So what if Jodie Foster and Geena Davis were interested in the role? So what if Mark Bauer wasn't returning her agent's phone calls?

None of that mattered. The role of Olivia Thomas was *hers*. Guaranteed.

From the time she had been a little girl, Gabrielle Fontana Moore had always gotten what she wanted. Her father, Paul Fontana, never denied a request. All she had to do was ask. Usually she'd ask nicely. If asking nicely didn't work, then she'd throw a tantrum. In the end she always won. Tonight would be no exception.

Daddy was flying in from his casino in Las Vegas. The reason for the trip was business. Daddy had gotten involved with Trinity Pictures. And Trinity Pictures was making *Long Journey Home*.

Gabrielle returned her attention to Frost. He continued pumping within her and she met his thrusts, choosing to ride the wave building within her.

"Let's hurry up," she urged. "We're due back on the set in fifteen minutes."

Frost brought his lips to her mouth and pressed his tongue forward. Gabrielle sucked at it while clutching at him furiously. He was all muscle covered by tanned smoothness. His green eyes, cold as emeralds, bore into her own dark ones.

"Ready for the grand finale?" he boasted.

Gabrielle found Frost's ego staggering. He thought he was God's gift to women. Please! She'd had better in the past and was sure to have better in the future. Maybe it was time to break things off with Frost. After all, she'd be leaving the show soon, and who needed excess baggage?

Gabrielle gave in to the climax engulfing her and collapsed on top of Frost.

His own climax was approaching. "Is it as good as this with Harrison?" he managed to ask between gasps.

Gabrielle laughed mockingly, tossing her long curls over one shoulder. "Are you kidding? My husband doesn't even know how to satisfy a woman."

"My God, Harrison! You're fantastic!"

Grace Warren shook her short cap of blonde hair, still charged from her lovemaking session with Harrison Moore.

She lounged comfortably against the fine linen sheets, relishing their coolness against her flushed body. She sipped from a fluted glass of champagne, offering the glass to Harrison. "Want a taste?"

He shook his head, leaning over her as he grabbed for a breast. "I'd rather have more of this," he stated, giving her a kiss.

Grace met his lips hungrily, then tore hers away, finishing off the rest of the champagne before bouncing from the bed. "You're not tempting me again. You've already thrown me off schedule."

"The day is still young." He gave her a mischievous smile, slipping the sheets away and unveiling his new erection. "Come back and join me."

"No way," Grace adamantly refused. She slipped into a black mini-skirt and white silk blouse, stepping into her high heels. "Gabrielle left me a million things to do."

At the mention of his wife's name, Harrison rolled his brown eyes. "What's the she-devil want done today?"

Grace fluffed a few stray locks off her forehead. "What *doesn't* she want done?"

"What's the occasion?"

"Don't tell me you've forgotten. Your father-in-law is flying in."

"Oh yes," Harrison sneered. "The esteemed mafioso."

"Gabrielle is planning a dinner for tonight. I've got to run around Beverly Hills in search of almost every Italian delicacy known to man."

"How do you put up with working for her?"

"How do *you* put up with being married to her?"

Harrison sighed. "You know the answer as well as I do. Let's not get into this again."

"No fights," Grace promised. She returned to the bed and gave Harrison a kiss. "Promise me you'll work on your screenplay?"

Harrison slumped into the mattress, pulling the sheets around him. "Yeah, sure. Right after I take a nap."

"*Now*, Harrison," Grace insisted, prodding him in the back. "All you have to do is sit yourself in front of your computer. The rest will be easy."

Harrison tossed back the sheets and sat up. He playfully swatted Grace's behind. "Go on. Get out of here. I'm up."

Grace rumpled Harrison's tousled brown hair. "I love you, Harrison. I know you can do it."

"I love you, Grace." He gave her a lopsided grin. "I won't let you down."

The moment Grace left the bedroom Harrison collapsed back onto the mattress.

Driving along Sunset Boulevard, the wind whipping through her hair while Eric Clapton blasted from her dashboard, Grace was deliriously happy. The reason for her happiness was Harrison Moore. He was everything she wanted in a man and more. The only problem was that he was married. Not that that should make a difference.

Gabrielle didn't love Harrison. That had been obvious from day one six months ago when she'd been hired as Gabrielle's personal assistant. The bitch was nothing more than a spoiled Mafia princess who had Harrison in her web and was destroying him bit by bit with each passing day.

Grace had never intended on starting an affair with Harrison. When she had first started working for Gabrielle she had tried not to cross paths with him, knowing he was a writer and would probably want his privacy. However, as she set about completing the tasks Gabrielle left for her, often he would stop what he was doing and go out of his way to start up a conversation. Soon he was bouncing story ideas for screenplays off her and asking her opinion. She readily offered her input and soon they moved onto other topics, discovering they had a lot in common.

After that they became lovers and Grace realized she had fallen in love.

Though Grace loved Harrison and knew he had talent, she also knew he was undisciplined and lazy. He could tell a story in the most marvelous way, but when it came to transforming his images onto paper, it took him forever! Yet Harrison would do it— she knew he would. After all, the first screenplay he'd written five years ago, when he'd only been twenty-three, had been nominated for an Oscar and had been made into a successful film starring Paul Newman. Sure, he'd lost his touch after that first film and Hollywood forgot all about him, but that was all in the past.

All Harrison needed to do now was finish the screenplay he was presently working on. She would handle everything else once he completed it. When Harrison saw he really could make money again, *lots* of money from his writing, he would regain the confidence he'd been lacking all these years. They would be on their way and Harrison would have no qualms about leaving Gabrielle. She knew the only reason Harrison stayed married to Gabrielle was because of her money—there was lots and lots of it. But soon, with her help, Harrison would no longer have any need for Gabrielle's money. He'd have his own. She would see to that. She was determined that she and Harrison would one day be leading their own lavish lifestyle. And she was prepared to do whatever was necessary. She was getting tired of having to share Harrison with his wife. She wanted him for herself, twenty-four hours a day and not just when he was able to steal away for a few hours.

Grace pressed down on the accelerator, thriving on the speed as she whipped past the other cars. Harrison had better hurry with his screenplay. All of her life she had dreamed of finding the perfect man to spend the rest of her life with. Now that she had found him, she was determined to make her dreams come true.

Harrison stared at the ceiling, knowing he should be sitting in front of his computer, but unable to move a muscle.

It wasn't that he didn't have a story—he did. He just had a problem re-creating the visions in his mind. Thus, instead of even attempting to make an effort, he often gave up after an hour or two, choosing to spend the rest of his day sunning, swimming, or just making love with Grace.

Thoughts of Grace filled his mind, making him feel guilty. She had such confidence in him and he was letting her down. She believed in him—believed in his talent. Unlike Gabrielle.

Gabrielle never missed an opportunity to knock him and she was one to criticize—she couldn't act to save her life! Granted, she did a capable job playing Serena, but a good deal of that success was due to her smoldering sexuality. And Serena was a bitch; Gabrielle didn't really have to stretch herself in *that* department.

Marrying Gabrielle had been such a mistake. Yet at the time it had all seemed so perfect. Five years ago they had both been starting out. They met at a party and formed an attraction. Sex followed, but never love. Not that it mattered.

Gabrielle was the one who suggested they marry. At first he refused her proposal. He knew she was supporting herself on her father's monthly checks. He was barely making ends meet on his own. There was no way he could support a wife. And what if she accidentally got pregnant?

Gabrielle hadn't accepted his refusal. She told him that if they married he could spend all his time writing and not have to worry about working because her father would be more than willing to support them. He could write screenplays and then she could star in them. Her theory was that together they would rise to the top.

The offer had been too good to refuse.

Almost immediately the problems started. Hot off the success of his first Oscar-nominated screenplay (which sold days after his marriage to Gabrielle), Harrison started having difficulty with his writing. Ideas that burned in his brain suddenly fizzled on paper. But the studios were still hungry for his screenplays, though Harrison knew they were nowhere near as good as his first.

Then when his screenplays were turned into films, and the films bombed despite big budgets and big names, the studios stopped calling.

Gabrielle, impatient for a role, started needling him. What was his problem? She had read material of his from when he was a film student at UCLA. Those scripts had been infinitely better than the crap he was churning out now. What had happened? What was his problem?

Harrison didn't know, though he suspected he had become overwhelmed by all the attention he had been given. Everyone had been watching . . . waiting to see what he would do next. For Harrison, his writing was something personal and private. It always had been. It had been something he'd done for *himself*. But with that gone, he suspected he had lost his inspiration and the creative spark that enabled him to do what he had done so well had dimmed.

Gabrielle fumed when she realized her personal scriptwriter wasn't producing product and went back to attending auditions, ultimately landing the role of Serena Taylor (though Harrison suspected that his father-in-law had pulled a string or two).

Next came the lovers. Harrison hadn't been surprised. Anything male that looked good had to be sampled by Gabrielle. It was then that he realized why she had married him. She was using him as a smokescreen. If Daddy got word that his virginal princess was sleeping around, there'd be hell to pay. But if Gabrielle had a husband, and her husband remained with her despite the rumors, then her father could hardly have cause for action.

Harrison allowed Gabrielle her flings. He really didn't care. Gabrielle knew this and it provoked her bitchiness. But why should he give a damn? He was being well compensated for remaining her husband. And he'd had his share of lovers.

Yet none had mattered to him as much as Grace.

He rose from the bed, deciding to take a cold shower. Maybe that would perk him up. Then he would hit his keyboard. He owed it to Grace and he owed it to himself.

Passing by the window he saw it was a beautiful day. The sun was shining and the blue water of the pool beckoned.

Harrison inspected his tan. Kind of fading. A few hours under the sun would intensify his bronzeness. Later this afternoon he'd come back inside. His computer wasn't going anywhere.

CHAPTER THREE

Hollywood was Diana Halloway's town and for more than four decades she had been its queen.

Her first screen appearance had been in 1945 at the age of five opposite Mickey Rooney. Her screen presence was immediately recognized by the studios and she was signed to a contract at Warner's. As the years went by her roles grew. So did her popularity. No matter what role Diana Halloway played her fans flocked to the movie theaters in droves. In the fifties she was the number-one box-office draw.

No other actress had been able to dominate a movie screen like Diana Halloway. With her elegantly beautiful features, soft pouty lips, bright violet eyes and mane of honey-blonde hair, she had projected an alluring, yet untamed, sexuality.

She'd worked only with the best. Among the male stars there had been James Dean, Rock Hudson, and Marlon Brando. Among the female stars there had been Lana Turner, Elizabeth Taylor, and Shelley Winters.

Diana had always outshone them.

Her realm had extended beyond Hollywood. She'd performed on Broadway and showcased in Las Vegas. There had been numerous television appearances. The praise and accolades only continued, resulting in two Emmys and a Tony.

Diana made sure she reaped the rewards of all her endeavors, pampering herself with a lush and lavish lifestyle. Money was never an objection. There were apartments in New York, Paris, Milan, London, and Monte Carlo. A beach house in Jamaica and a chalet in Switzerland.

None of the material trappings of her success really mattered to Diana. Though she liked pretty and expensive things, often buying cars, designer clothing, furs, and jewelry in excess and solely on whim, all of it was for show. Diana's Tony and Emmy awards mattered. They were proof that she was an actress—that she was the best in her field. An Oscar mattered. Although one wasn't in her possession yet, she planned on having one.

Her desire for an Oscar was what drove her in her early days. She informed her agent, Jinxie Bishop, to keep her apprised of any projects that were possible Oscar contenders. He did as requested and in 1961 Diana landed the role of Marla Ryan in *Destiny*. She played the childlike mistress of a ruthless tycoon, played by Kirk Douglas, who was obsessed with her. By the film's conclusion, he'd killed her. Although Diana did gain an Oscar nomination for Best Actress, she lost to Anne Bancroft in *The Miracle Worker*.

In 1963 Diana's Oscar quest was forgotten when Adam Stoddard entered her life.

The two met in New York when they were both performing in *Twelfth Night*. Adam, a stage actor considered to be the next Olivier, was going to be returning to Hollywood for a film career. Would Diana mind showing him around?

Friendship quickly turned to romance and then marriage after three months together, with the press dubbing them the new Olivier and Leigh. The marriage was wonderful, their careers continued to flourish, and there was even a baby.

Then after two years of bliss Adam died on a stormy night when the brakes in the car he was driving failed and he crashed into a ravine in Laurel Canyon.

For weeks Diana was grief-stricken, becoming a virtual recluse and ignoring her baby daughter. Liz Taylor, who knew exactly what Diana was going through, tried to console her; it helped.

After her mourning Diana threw herself back into her career, working nonstop. Yet the gilded age of Hollywood that Diana had grown up in was over. There was a new Hollywood, and actresses like Diana Halloway no longer fit in.

She tried to hold on for as long as she could. The seventies managed to keep her employed, but the eighties locked her out. Most of her work was now on television; her last big screen role had been in 1979. Now at the age of fifty Diana Halloway had fallen on hard times.

The nighttime soap she had starred in for nine years, "The Cantrells," had just been cancelled. Her career, which had propelled her through forty-five years, appeared to be at a dead end. She needed a hit. Desperately. She had to get herself back on a movie screen. It wasn't because she needed the money. She was still able to afford the lifestyle she had accustomed herself to. No, it wasn't the money. She needed to be in the public's eye. She craved the attention and glory. My God, even the tabloids had forgotten about her! That had never happened to dear Liz, though she was sure Liz would be panicked if it ever did.

A comeback was possible. Very possible. All it would take was the right vehicle to showcase her talents. She was still beautiful and had her legions of fans. But that was it.

There came a knock on the bedroom door. "Ms. Halloway?"

Diana emerged from her thoughts. "Yes, Esmerelda?"

The Mexican maid entered, placing a tray on Diana's lap. "Your tea."

Diana made herself comfortable against her pillows while inspecting the breakfast tray. "Where's the strawberry marmalade for my scones?"

The pretty young girl blushed in embarrassment. "I'm sorry, Ms. Halloway. I forgot to buy another jar."

Diana sipped at her tea, giving Esmerelda a cold look. "Be sure we have some for tomorrow."

"Yes, Ms. Halloway." Esmerelda began backing away. "Will that be all?"

Diana didn't bother looking up, reaching for a hardcover novel on her bed. "That's all."

Esmerelda stopped at the bedroom door. "I'll be going to the market in an hour. Is there anything special I should get?"

"Just my marmalade."

"But don't you remember, Ms. Halloway? Today is the day Kelly comes home."

"I have more important things to worry about than my daughter's return home," Diana snapped, eyes still glued to her novel. "We haven't seen her in almost six years. Today is no different than any other day."

Esmerelda didn't question her mistress, dropping the subject and scurrying out. Diana added a dollop of clotted cream to a scone and began nibbling at it while she flipped through her copy of *Long Journey Home*.

When Jinxie had first mentioned *Long Journey Home* she hadn't known what he was talking about. Despite the book being a bestseller, she hadn't read it. Her reading list consisted of Jackie Collins, Judith Krantz, and Sidney Sheldon. However, at Jinxie's urging she had bought the book and read it.

She hadn't fallen in love with the role of Ellen Thomas.

The last thing she wanted to play was a worn out, frazzled-looking farm wife. Whenever she appeared on television or film she always looked dazzling. She wasn't going to allow her fans to see her looking *old*. She went to enough trouble trying to keep up a youthful image.

Diana dropped the hardcover on the floor. When she met Jinxie for lunch later that day she'd tell him to forget all about *Long Journey Home*. Not even his talk of the project being Oscar material was going to change her mind.

CHAPTER FOUR

PAUL FONTANA radiated power.
Striding through LAX with his bodyguard to the black limousine waiting for him, he was an imposing figure. He stood over six feet and was impeccably dressed in a well-cut navy Armani suit. His body was fit, his aquiline features tanned, capped by a full head of gleaming silver hair. He looked at least ten years younger than his fifty-five years.

Yet his eyes were his most striking feature. Dark and hooded, they were the mirrors to the soul of a man who had seen and done it all in his rise to the top. Without any regrets.

They were the eyes of a dangerous man.

But today Paul Fontana's eyes did not look dangerous. Instead they were bright and eager. Paul Fontana, head of one of the largest crime families in the U.S., was staking out new territory. Hollywood was the prize to be won. Like a beast on the prowl for new blood, he had found what he was looking for and was ready to attack.

Stepping into his limousine, Paul once again went over his plans. Then he gave his driver instructions.

Mark Bauer would be his first victim.

"Jinxie, my decision is final," Diana stated firmly. "I *do not* want you talking to Mark Bauer about *Long Journey Home*."

The scene was Morton's. Diana, dressed in a peach linen suit, was lunching with her agent of thirty years, Jinxie Bishop.

"Doll, listen to reason," the diminutive agent pleaded, pushing his thick black glasses up his nose. "*Long Journey Home* is destined to become a classic."

"It can become a classic without me."

Jinxie waved that day's edition of *Variety*. "Have you read this?"

Diana looked bored. "Should I have?"

Jinxie pointed to the front page. "Drew Stern is signed, sealed, and delivered to star in *Long Journey Home*."

Diana was aghast. "I will not play Drew Stern's mother. My God, what would my fans think? I have an image to uphold."

"At least let me feel out Mark."

"No!" Diana snapped. "I don't want you talking to him. I've already told you what kind of role I'm looking for. I want a glamor role with a big budget and lots of perks. Mark Bauer is a notorious tyrant when it comes to his films. He keeps count of all the pennies."

"Mark Bauer is considered a genius," Jinxie corrected. "He's the next Steven Spielberg." A crafty look came over the agent's face. "Rumor has it that Vanessa Vought is interested in the role of Ellen. Mark's already had a meeting with her. Plan on losing another Best Actress Oscar to her?"

Diana's eyes grew cold at the mention of her rival's name. She and Vanessa had started their careers at the same time but at different studios, and had often been pitted against each other for coveted roles. While Diana was now considered to represent the glamor of old Hollywood, Vanessa still represented the talent.

"Don't you dare mention *Manipulations!*" Diana growled. "You know how much I wanted to play Katerina. The network wouldn't give me the time off. Those bastards!"

In 1984 Diana had been offered the role of Katerina Hamilton in *Manipulations*, a moody melodrama of murder, wealth, and passion in the tradition of *The Postman Always Rings Twice*. When Diana had had to turn down the role, it had been given to Vanessa. The film was nominated for ten Oscars and won six, as well as giving Vanessa her second Best Actress award.

Vanessa's nomination had left Diana furious; Vanessa's win had left her vengeful. When it came time to renew her contract in 1986 at the height of the success of "The Cantrells," Diana had made the network pay through their teeth; they paid—without her there would have been no show.

Diana arched an eyebrow. "Don't tell me Vanessa has jumped into bed with Mark Bauer. Has she given up boy toys?"

"Have you?" Jinxie knew how far he could go with Diana. He

wasn't too sure how wild he was about the current affair she was involved in.

"Graham's in New York doing an off-Broadway play. Something in the Village." She closed her menu. "He won't be back for a week and I'm still deliriously happy. Shall we order? I'm going to have the grilled salmon steak with champagne and caviar sauce."

Jinxie decided to press the issue one last time. "Are you sure you don't want me talking to Mark Bauer?"

"Absolutely," Diana was adamant. "My mind is made up and my decision is final."

Mark Bauer felt like he had a noose around his neck. The reason was the man sitting across his desk.

Paul Fontana held all the cards. Mark knew that and there was nothing he could do. Not when he owed Paul Fontana two million dollars.

Mark's boyish good looks were marred by worry and he kept nervously pushing back his sun-streaked hair.

There was no one he could blame for this except himself. He knew that. Despite being able to manage the budgets of his films, sometimes in the untold millions, Mark Bauer was unable to handle his own money. He spent more than he had and lived beyond his means. He had three ex-wives to pay alimony to, along with child support payments. Mark also liked to gamble and his gambling had led to this predicament.

Mark had never been able to resist the allure of Las Vegas. It was the only place in the world where you could take a stake and transform it into something more. Tax-free.

On his last visit to Las Vegas, Mark had gone to the Fountain, Paul Fontana's casino. As a regular visitor he had been given the privilege of unlimited credit. Poker was Mark's weakness and he instantly found a big-money game.

At first Mark played cautiously, as he usually did. Then, as he started winning and having drinks, he changed tactics, playing recklessly as he doubled and tripled his bets, not paying attention to the stakes.

At the end of the evening, or more precisely, six A.M., Mark owed the Fountain two million dollars, although at the time he didn't know it.

Mark would never forget how he learned the news. How could

he? From that moment on, as a result of his gambling, his world had turned into a living nightmare.

There was an insistent knocking on the door of his suite.

Mark, still in his rumpled tuxedo, tie loosened and top button undone, had thrown himself across his bed with a wet washcloth draped over his forehead. He had the beginnings of what he knew was going to be one hell of a monster hangover. He cursed himself for not keeping track of the number of drinks he'd had. Yet the sexy cocktail waitress with the ample cleavage and short dress had kept coming back, taking away his empty glasses and bringing back filled ones, which he promptly made empty again.

The continued staccato on the door combined with the growing pounding in his head. All he wanted to do was sleep.

"Go away," Mark called.

The knocking continued.

"Go away," Mark repeated, this time in a louder tone of voice. "Come back later."

The request was ignored. There came another knock and then Mark heard the click of an electronic key as it was slid into place. The door to his suite opened and two burly men clad in dark suits loomed in the doorway.

"Hey, what is this?" Mark protested, flinging his legs over the side of the bed as he tried to get up. The suite started spinning and Mark fell back down on the bed.

"Mr. Fontana wants to see you," the taller of the two men said.

Mark sat up again and took a deep breath, removing the washcloth from his forehead and rubbing a hand over his face. "Sure. Why didn't you say so in the first place? Let me jump into the shower. Tell him I'll be up in an hour."

The second man spoke. "Now."

"Okay. Let me just shave and toss on a fresh shirt."

"*Now*," the first man repeated.

Mark saw there was no arguing with the two men. Though he tried to ignore it, a faint cold fear was beginning to stir in the pit of his stomach. Mark quickly squashed it, knowing it wouldn't do him any good. Showing fear would be a disadvantage—a lethal mistake.

"If you say now, then now it is," Mark conceded, heading out of the suite.

On their way to the private elevator that would take them to

Paul's penthouse, the two men flanked Mark on both sides. He knew he was being led, no longer acting of his own free will.

When the elevator doors opened the two men remained inside the car, leaving Mark to continue on his own.

"Mark," Paul greeted, turning from his panoramic view of the approaching morning as the lights of Las Vegas dimmed out. "Come join me."

Mark didn't want to. There was something predatory—almost bloodthirsty—in Paul's smile. The man was out for blood, ready to strike and make his kill. And Mark instinctively knew he was the prey Paul had chosen.

Somehow Mark made his way over to Paul, not wanting to yet unable to stop himself from taking the steps, knowing the last thing he wanted to do at this point was to displease Paul.

"How are you feeling?"

Mark effectively masked his panic though he was unsure why he should feel that way. He mustered a normal tone of voice. "A little under the weather."

"You had some night last night. Too bad you couldn't have been a winner."

Money. This was about money. Mark's panic ebbed as he reached into his jacket for his checkbook. "Paul, I know there's a debt and I'm more than willing to settle my account."

Paul waved away Mark's checkbook. "Put that away. You don't even have enough there. Come, let's head out onto the terrace where we can talk. I had some coffee made. You look like you could use a cup."

Mark tried not to gasp. What did Paul mean? How much money had he lost last night?

Expecting regular coffee, Mark was less than enthusiastic about a cup of demitasse. Yet he accepted the small cup and saucer offered, declining the lemon wedge and shot of anisette, forcing himself to sip the bitter black brew.

"This is my favorite time of morning. I'll bet it's yours too. Isn't this when you can get the best shots?"

"Natural lighting is always the best. I prefer working outdoors as much as I can."

"Yes, I remember reading that somewhere in an article about you. *Premiere*, I think it was," Paul mused. "Or *American Film*. Surprised at my interest?"

Mark wasn't surprised. Paul Fontana was a major shareholder in Trinity Pictures. The once-near-bankrupt studio was on its way back to the top. Paul and his associates were the power behind the scenes—buying up shares of stock, orchestrating a hostile takeover and, once in control, pouring their dirty money into studio projects. It was scary the way they had taken over in less than a year, but Hollywood didn't seem to be upset by the mob's invasion. Blood money seemed far more palatable than the way in which the Japanese were taking over everything.

"You're good at what you do, Mark. Very good. A hot property is what I think you're called. Hot properties are what Trinity needs. *Long Journey Home* is also a hot property."

Mark licked his suddenly dry lips, wanting a drink, but knowing more liquor was absolutely the last thing he needed. What he needed was a clear head. He forced himself to concentrate. *Concentrate. Concentrate, goddamn it!* He managed to find his voice. "Yes, *Long Journey Home* is a hot property." When the novel had first been published Mark had jumped on the dramatic rights, purchasing them outright. Then he had begun shopping the property around. All the studios were interested, but it was Paramount, in the wake of the Don Simpson/Jerry Bruckheimer debacle and desperate for a hit, that was making him the most lucrative offer. When he got back to Hollywood another round of talks was scheduled, but it looked like he and Paramount had a deal. "The project will be getting under way soon."

"Yes," Paul agreed. "Trinity's looking quite forward to it."

"What?" Mark exclaimed, immediately alert and clearheaded.

"You heard me, Mark. And you know the reason."

"How much do I owe?" he asked, knowing it would be an astronomical amount.

"Two million. If you have the money, I'll be more than happy to take it."

Mark felt like he had been punched in the stomach and was struggling for air. "Two million? You know I don't have that kind of money."

"I didn't think you did."

"Can't we work out some sort of payment schedule?"

"If that's what you'd like. But Mark, at five percent interest a week, you'll never get out from under."

In that instant Mark knew there was no way out. Not until Paul Fontana chose to let him out. Apparently making *Long Journey Home* for Trinity would be that way out.

"I'll do it," he hoarsely agreed, mustering up as much dignity as he could. "If we're finished I'd like to return to my suite." Mark had to get off this terrace. Though he felt like jumping off just to spite Paul, what he really wanted to do was push him off.

Paul gave Mark a sly smile, finishing off his demitasse. "Don't let me keep you. We don't want to extinguish that creative flare of yours. Our business is finished for today but don't worry. We'll be talking again in the future."

Mark didn't bother with an answer. All he wanted to do was get away from this man until he had to deal with him again. He couldn't wait to start on *Long Journey Home*. For once the film was finished he'd never have to deal with Paul Fontana again.

Mark cleared his throat. "Your visit is an unexpected surprise, Mr. Fontana."

"Call me Paul. I'm only out here to check on things at the studio. How's *Long Journey Home* coming along?"

Mark relaxed. He was most comfortable when it came to his projects. "Drew Stern has agreed to star. I've got a few ideas for the rest of the cast. Vanessa Vought was expressing some interest."

"Excellent. I'm sure you'll do us proud with *Long Journey Home* and in the years to come."

Mark didn't know what to make of the last words. His stomach tightened as Paul reached into his attaché case, pulling out a sheaf of papers.

"I'd like you to look these over," Paul said.

Mark reached for the pages offered. "What are they?"

"A five-year agreement in which you agree to work exclusively for Trinity Pictures."

"What?" Mark nearly jumped out of his chair. "You can't be serious!"

Paul's voice was deadly. "I can, Mr. Bauer. You seem to forget that a debt exists between us."

"But I agreed to make *Long Journey Home* for Trinity. I thought after that our debt would be settled. That's what you said."

"You thought wrong, Mr. Bauer. I never said such a thing. You see, Mark, you're Hollywood's golden boy. When it comes to making films, you have the Midas touch. Trinity Pictures needs a string of hits to re-establish itself and you're going to provide them. Don't worry about salary. You'll be well compensated for your talent, and at the end of five years your debt will be paid and forgotten."

Mark glumly stared at the contracts. "You can't do this to me."

"Yes, I can, unless you're able to pay your debt in full. Are you?"

Mark shook his head.

Paul closed his attaché case, preparing to leave Mark's office. "Then I'd say we're in business together."

CHAPTER FIVE

GRAHAM DENNING couldn't believe his eyes. The most beautiful woman he had ever seen was headed his way.

She stopped before him, eyes shining with friendliness. "Excuse me, is this Two-C?" she asked, pointing to the empty seat next to him.

"It most certainly is," he answered, offering a smile.

"Thanks." She returned the smile while putting her carry-on bag in the overhead hatch. Then she took the empty seat. "Hi, I'm Kelly Stoddard," she introduced.

"Graham Denning."

"Nice to meet you, Graham. How come you're heading out to L.A.? New York not your kind of town?"

She seemed genuinely interested. Why not strike up a conversation? It might lead somewhere. "For the moment I live in L.A. I've got some unfinished business to take care of. How about you?"

Kelly blushed, smiling self-consciously. "I just landed a part on a daytime soap, 'The Yields of Passion.' Have you heard of it?"

"Who hasn't? It's the number-one soap on TV. I'm impressed."

"It's my first real acting job and I'm a bundle of nerves," she confessed. "I just graduated from NYU's Tisch School of the Arts."

"Have you done any television?"

"None. This is my first big break, although I did a lot of summer stock and some off-Broadway."

"Really? No kidding. Me too!"

"Are you an actor?"

Graham was modest. "I've dabbled a bit. Some television. One or two movies. Nothing memorable. The theater is my first love, although it doesn't pay as well. Right now I'm performing in Sam Shepard's newest play at the Actor's Playhouse."

Just then the stewardess interrupted from the loudspeaker, instructing passengers to fasten their seat belts.

"I'm glad this is a long flight," Graham said, buckling up.

"Why's that?"

"Because I intend to learn all I can about you."

Laura Danby raced through the terminal, her auburn hair billowing out behind her.

"Hold that plane!" she cried. "Hold that plane!"

Struggling with her luggage and boarding pass, Laura shoved them all at the ticket taker, running for her flight to L.A.

"Whew!" she sighed, reaching the door of the plane in the nick of time.

After taking her seat Laura concentrated on catching her breath and straightening her appearance. She smoothed out the wrinkles of her mint green dress and ran a hairbrush through her shoulder-length auburn hair. Pulling out a compact, she dabbed away at the few beads of perspiration dotting her forehead and touched up the mascara highlighting her emerald eyes.

"At least I'll look like I belong out there," she muttered, twirling the mascara cap shut.

Once again Laura Danby wondered what she was doing flying out to Hollywood. This had been such a spontaneous decision and she wasn't the spontaneous type. If anything she was cautious, planning out her every move and questioning her every decision. But maybe that was the problem. She had gotten herself into a rut and was becoming too old before her time. After all, she was only twenty-seven. Why not start living it up and having some fun?

Relocating to California was just what she needed to shake herself up. She wasn't going to start doubting herself. She'd made her decision and was going to stick to it. If things didn't work out she could always start over.

Anyway, she was going to have the help of her college friend, Grace Warren, when she resettled. Although they hadn't seen each other since their college graduation, they had kept in touch over the years. Grace's letters of life in sunny California had intrigued Laura and she was determined to have a new life out there. She was a survivor. She knew what to do to take care of herself, and no one would ever make her a victim again.

* * *

Nico Rossi paced his jail cell relentlessly. His eyes were drawn to the calendar taped to the wall. Only six more months. Just six more months and then he'd have his freedom. The feeling was so intense, he could taste it.

For three years he had been in Nevada State Prison. The crime had been the hijacking of a Wells Fargo truck, resulting in the death of two men. Although Nico had been fingered as the driver of the getaway car, his two accomplices had gotten away and the state had been unable to pin the murders on him. And Nico had been unwilling to talk; he'd done the smart thing and kept his mouth shut.

No one crossed the Fontana crime family.

Nico was a handsome man, on the order of Mickey Rourke, but his looks were marred by a cruel savageness. His dark eyes were hard and penetrating; his lips always wore a mocking sneer and his cheeks carried small gouges, remnants of battles won. There was nothing he enjoyed more than invoking fear and pain in others.

The first thing he intended on doing when he was released was getting a decent shave and haircut. Then he was going to the finest Italian restaurant he could find and order all his favorite dishes. Afterwards he would smoke a Havana cigar and find some female companionship.

Nico unrolled the photo he held grasped in his hand, staring at the face he had hated for three long years.

After he pampered himself there was only one other thing he had to do before getting on with his life. All he had to do was track down Laura Danby. It was her fault he was locked behind bars. She had turned her back on him when he'd needed her the most and as a result had helped put him away. When he found her he was going to make her pay for her betrayal.

Graham studied Kelly's profile as she slept. He still couldn't get over her beauty.

Her hair was the color of caramel and fell past her shoulders in cascading waves. Dark lush lashes rested against closed eyelids; when opened her eyes were a warm cobalt blue that glowed with warmth and enthusiasm. And her lips possessed a yielding softness that he ached to taste. An aura of innocence surrounded her and Graham realized that unlike most beautiful women, Kelly seemed unaware of her breathtaking features. The way to describe her would be *sweet* and Graham was suddenly glad he had decided to break things off with Diana Halloway. Kelly Stoddard was someone he wanted to get to know.

His affair with Diana had been a mistake. From the moment they had gotten involved she'd tried to run his life, setting him up in a new apartment and paying his bills, telling him what he should and shouldn't do. At first he'd been flattered by all the attention. Then he realized she was trying to change him—trying to make him into something he wasn't and expecting him to be at her beck and call twenty-four hours a day.

Diana made all the rules. She was explicitly clear about the two of them being seen together in public—it just wasn't done. However, when they did meet in public, Diana chose the when and where. Usually it was at night at an out-of-the-way place. Diana would invariably turn up late and be dressed as inconspicuously as possible. At first Graham had found her games fun. It made their relationship exciting—even forbidden. Then he realized he wasn't the one in control of their relationship; she was—she called all the shots. When he realized this, he also realized something else: he had become a kept man. The only thing he provided Diana with was sex—that was it. He had become nothing more than her personal plaything. Yet that wasn't how he had felt in the beginning.

When they'd first met during the filming of a made-for-TV movie, he'd been intrigued by her. Here was the legendary Diana Halloway, mesmerizing all those around her, including him. When she'd started spending time with him during their breaks, offering advice on his performance, giving pointers and discussing the script, he'd been flattered. How could he not be? He was a young actor just starting out and here she was, taking him under her wing.

And when she'd made the first move, he'd been amazed, willingly accepting what she had to offer—doing her bidding without thought.

But it was only a matter of time before he woke up to reality and learned the truth. Diana Halloway existed only for one person: herself.

When it came to her appearance, she was obsessed. No one could match Diana Halloway's vanity and she fought desperately to hide her age. She kept her body in perfect shape with personal trainers and stays at exclusive spas. Liposuction and skin peels removed excess pounds and wrinkles. Hours were spent in front of her mirror for every personal appearance, talk show, or interview. She had wigs galore and spent thousands of dollars on cosmetics and beauty aids.

Now with her series cancelled, Diana was even more demanding of his time and more obsessive about her looks. She'd even mentioned the possibility of his moving in. No way. His career was gaining momentum and starting to take off. He wasn't going to sabotage it by remaining attached to Diana Halloway. She'd suck him dry if she knew how good things were going for him, waiting to become part of the package.

Graham gave Kelly a fond look. He and Diana Halloway were history. Hopefully he and Kelly Stoddard would have a future.

"Can I give you a ride?" he offered once they landed in L.A.

Kelly politely shook her head. "I've got a few errands and then I've got to drop by the studio."

"Can I give you a call?" Graham blurted, not wanting to lose contact with her.

Kelly reached into her quilted white Chanel bag for a pen and paper. "Tell you what. Since I don't have a phone yet, why don't you give me your number and I'll give *you* a call."

"Deal!" Graham readily agreed, writing out his number and handing it to Kelly. "Promise to call?"

Kelly waved the slip of paper he'd handed to her before zipping it away. "Promise."

Graham hailed a taxi. "Then I'll talk to you soon."

Kelly nodded, watching him step into the taxi. "Talk to you soon."

What does he see in me? Kelly wondered as she watched Graham's taxi disappear from sight. Why would such a good-looking man be interested in her?

Kelly took out the slip of paper with Graham's number, debating over whether or not to call him. Tons of women were probably interested in him. And why wouldn't they be? With his broad shoulders, straight jet black hair, smoldering gray eyes and killer grin, which emphasized his adorable dimples—well, there was no other way to say it, Graham Denning was *sexy!* And not only that, but he'd been fun to talk to. But what chance did *she* have with a man like Graham Denning? He was too good for her. She didn't deserve a man like him.

Taking one last look at the slip of paper, Kelly crumpled it into a ball and dropped it into a trash basket. There went one less problem to deal with. Now it was time to deal with the next: her mother.

At the thought of Diana, Kelly's stomach twisted into knots. She was dreading this return home.

If there was one thing Diana Halloway *wasn't*, it was a loving mother. For years Kelly had been the object of her mother's indifference. When she was growing up she was kept at a distance—first with nannies and expensive boarding schools. Then in the summers she was sent away to camp. Rarely did she spend more than six weeks with her mother during the year.

Only the slightest interest was shown in Kelly's life, but only because it was expected—the "right" thing to do. Then when she went away to college a greater degree of noncommunication was forged between them until Kelly finally gave up trying to get close to her mother.

As a child she hadn't known the reason. As she got older she put the pieces together. Kelly suspected the reason her mother ignored her was because she looked too much like her father. When her mother looked at her, she saw the husband she had lost. And Diana had never gotten over the loss of Adam Stoddard.

Kelly knew she and her mother had to work out their differences. After all, they'd now both be living in L.A. Their paths were bound to cross—if not as mother and daughter, then as fellow actresses.

As always, Kelly was the one making the first move.

She so wanted to make things right between herself and her mother. Despite her unhappy childhood, she did love Diana. How could she not? An aura surrounded her mother—an aura of glamor and something else—something magical. Growing up she had noticed the way people flocked around her mother and noticed the attention her mother gave to them. As a child she had so desperately wanted that same attention and, if she was honest with herself, still did.

She was going to try as hard as she could to become a part of her mother's life—to feel as though she belonged. For once she belonged, once she fit in, her mother would love her. Her return home was going to be a new beginning for the both of them.

Kelly took one last look at the crumpled slip of paper in the trash basket, fighting off the urge to retrieve it. Instead she searched within herself for the confidence she knew she had—the confidence that somehow always deserted her whenever she was with her mother.

CHAPTER SIX

"You're still a tigress in bed," Paul Fontana commented.

Diana gave Paul a look of disinterest, nestling against her satin sheets as she lit a cigarillo. "My motto is have fun, no matter who you're doing it with."

He caressed her shoulder. "You really don't like me, do you?"

"Darling, you've caught me on one of my bad days." She blew a smoke ring at the ceiling. "Let's just say you're no longer my cup of tea."

"But you're mine," he whispered.

"Only when you're in town and too cheap to spring for a whore."

Paul released a hearty laugh. "There's more than business between us, Diana. Admit it."

"Maybe years ago, but I'm not as naive as I once was, Paul. You can cut the crap." She reached for the remote control, flicking on the TV while taking another puff of her cigarillo. "How much longer are you staying?"

Paul trailed his lips down Diana's neck. "I thought we could have a little more fun."

"Damn!" Diana cursed as an image of Iris Larson filled the TV screen. "They're doing another film tribute to that bitch."

"Well, it has been twenty-five years since her death."

"And she's just as popular now as she was back then. Even more so!" Diana fumed.

Other than Vanessa Vought, Diana's only other main rival in her early days had been Iris Larson. Of the three, Iris had been considered the one with the most talent—the choicest roles had been offered to her first. Often the roles she had turned down had gone to Vanessa and if Vanessa had then turned that role down, it trickled down to Diana. Iris had never let Diana forget this.

Great things had been predicted for Iris Larson. Yet with only ten films to her credit and a Best Actress Oscar, Iris Larson had died at the age of twenty-five after accidentally drowning in her swimming pool.

Like James Dean and Marilyn Monroe, Iris had become a legend after her death. Memorabilia could be found everywhere and tons of books had been written about her. Diana's rivalry with Iris was always mentioned in these books, along with her loss of the leading role in *Banquet* after she'd become pregnant with Kelly. *Banquet* was the movie that had given Iris her Oscar.

Then too there was mention of Iris's affair with Adam Stoddard during the filming of *Banquet*. Even though Adam had returned to Diana, his liaison with Iris was still a sore point.

Diana's blood boiled as she watched Iris's face fill the television screen. The woman had always been smirking, on screen and off. She'd been such a smug bitch and Diana had hated her with a passion. She still did.

"You're so tense," Paul stated, massaging her back. "Let me loosen you up."

Diana stubbed out her cigarillo, clicking off Iris's face. She gave herself to Paul's embrace. "Anything would be better than watching Iris Larson. Even this."

Graham bounded up the stairs two at a time. He'd been through every inch of Diana's Beverly Hills mansion and hadn't found a sign of her. He really wanted to get this over with. All he kept thinking about was Kelly Stoddard.

The door to Diana's bedroom was closed. Without even thinking of knocking, he walked in. Then he froze in his tracks, wishing he had knocked. Diana was in bed with another man.

Initially he was shocked. Then the shock washed away. He shouldn't be surprised. Hell, it had probably happened before. Diana had never been one to deny herself anything.

Graham cleared his throat. "Don't let me interrupt," he dryly commented.

Paul and Diana pulled apart and Diana clutched the pink satin sheet to herself, covering her exposed breasts.

Her tone was icy, without a trace of guilt or embarrassment. "I thought you weren't due back for another week. What are you doing here?"

Graham lounged in the doorway. "Don't bother with any introductions. I don't intend on staying long. In fact, after today you'll never have to see me again."

"What are you talking about?" Diana gave him a surly look.

Graham tossed her the keys to the apartment she had rented for him in Westwood. "It's over between us."

"You can't be serious."

"I made it on my own before you walked into my life. I'll do it again. It's been fun, Diana, but we're wrong for each other."

"You're making a mistake. Think of your career. I can help you."

"Look, I appreciate the offer, but isn't it kind of late for you to be making it? I've got everything under control. My career is in good shape." He gestured toward Diana. "I'll leave you two alone."

"You can't do this to me!" Diana shrieked. "This relationship isn't over until *I* say it's over!"

With nothing left to say, Graham turned his back on Diana and walked away.

"You bastard!" Diana screamed at the top of her lungs, on her knees in the middle of her bed, cheeks flaming red. "No one walks out on Diana Halloway! No one!"

Paul joined her in the middle of the bed, wrapping an arm around her as he whispered in her ear, "Marvelous theatrics, darling, but as you can see, he just walked out of your life. How long did this one last? Looks like you're losing your touch. I remember a time when you were knee-deep in studs. You must be getting old."

"Shut up! Just shut the fuck up!" Diana spat, storming from her bed.

"Why would you want a boy like that when you can have a man like me?"

Diana struggled into a violet silk dressing gown trimmed with black marabou feathers. "Don't flatter yourself, honey. I'm not one of your Vegas bimbos."

"No, you're one of my Hollywood bimbos," he replied evenly.

Diana glared hatefully at Paul. "Get the hell out of my house!"

"My, aren't our claws sharp today?" Paul got out of bed and started dressing. "I see you want to be alone so I'll leave. But before I go I want you to take a look at these." He reached into his attaché case and tossed her a sheaf of papers.

"What is it?"

"The real reason I stopped by to see you before we got sidetracked. In case you've forgotten, it's time to re-sign your new performing contract with my casino."

"How could I have forgotten?" she stated sarcastically, flipping through the pages, searching for the clause pertaining to her salary.

"Don't bother looking," Paul said. "Nothing's changed. The terms are still the same."

Diana threw the contract to the floor. "I don't believe you! After everything I've done for your casino, you're still a miser. I'll bet you've still got the first penny you ever earned."

"Watch your mouth, Diana," Paul warned, shooting her a dark look. "I've tolerated your temper all afternoon." His voice turned silky. "You still have a long way to go before our debt is settled." He turned to a mirror, straightening his tie. "Tell me, how's Kelly? How old is she now? Twenty-four? Twenty-five? I'll bet she's grown up nicely. She must be beautiful." He sent Diana a wink. "Just like her mother."

Diana gritted her teeth, holding open the bedroom door. "I want you to leave."

Paul held up his hands in surrender, giving Diana an amused look on his way out. "Calm down. I'm going. But why don't we all get together for dinner soon? My son Peter would be a good match for Kelly. I know you want the best for your little girl, just like I want the best for Peter. It's time he settled down."

Peter Fontana cruised into West Hollywood in his red Ferrari, checking out the male action.

Beneath his sunglasses, Peter's blue eyes darted from left to right at the male figures offering their bodies for a price.

Peter's blood started racing and he gripped the steering wheel tightly as he grew excited. His heart thudded furiously and his stomach twisted with nervous glee. Each time he went cruising he experienced the same exhilarating rush. He couldn't wait to find someone. All he wanted was to feel another man's touch—to have a pair of strong arms wrapped around him as he was being pleasured.

For as long as Peter could remember, he had been attracted to his own sex. He didn't remember when he had first realized it, only that it was true—an unalterable fact.

More than anything else, Peter wanted to come out of the closet. Yet to do so would be fatal. He'd be incurring his father's wrath and Paul Fontana would never, *ever*, accept his son's homosexuality.

So Peter lived in a world of shadow, frequenting gay bars and clubs; cruising for hustlers and paying for escorts. Anonymous sex with the necessary precautions was all he would allow himself. Though the release he found was satisfying, the satisfaction was only temporary. He wanted something more. Yet no matter how much he wanted it, he couldn't risk a relationship. If his father ever learned the truth—he shuddered to think of the consequences. He couldn't put someone else's life in danger. There were no limits to how far his father would go if angered enough.

No one knew his secret. Over the years he had done an effective job of keeping his tracks well covered. After graduating from UCLA, he'd gone to Europe, backpacking from city to city for two years. When he'd gotten back to the States he'd done the same thing until finally settling in New York, as far away from his father as possible. But after a year in New York he'd been unable to remain. The Village was a lure he'd been unable to resist. He found himself taking risks, seeing people more than once, doing whatever he could to erase the loneliness eating him up inside.

The loneliness was the hardest part. It had always been with him, even when he was a child. He'd always felt so alone! He desperately wanted someone in his life. It had started when he was a child. After his mother Marina's suicide, his father never had time for his children, too obsessed with his businesses. Then Peter and Gabrielle had been shipped off to boarding schools and Peter had felt even more isolated.

Leaving the Village had been the hardest thing he had ever done. There he'd been accepted for who he was and given a sense of belonging. But he'd had to leave. He'd been becoming too secure in the lifestyle he so wanted to lead. Gabrielle's invitation to L.A. had arrived at the right time.

Peter slowed down the Ferrari. A figure approached and Peter stopped the car, lowering the window on the passenger side. A dark head with a dimpled grin stared in.

"Looking for some action?"

"Maybe. Why don't you hop in?"

The door opened and the man slid in, wrapping an arm around Peter. "Hi, what's your name?"

Peter swallowed, unable to find his voice, enjoying the feel of the man's touch.

"Are you a shy one?" the man coaxed, his lips descending onto Peter's.

Peter's erection was throbbing, straining against his zipper. "My name is Peter," he gasped.

"Nice name. I'm George." His fingers trailed down Peter's chest, brushing his Polo insignia. "What would you like to do, Peter?"

"Whatever it is you usually do," he whispered.

George gave Peter a wicked smile. He brushed back Peter's ash blond hair, giving him a long, lingering kiss. "Great. You're my kind of guy. Let's head back to my place, Peter. I'll give you an afternoon you won't forget."

Peter pulled away from the curb, tires squealing, as his foot pressed down hard on the gas.

"What a place!" Laura raved, following after Grace through Gabrielle and Harrison's Beverly Hills mansion.

"Isn't it though? It's way too big but Gabrielle says she has an image to uphold." Grace rolled her eyes. "If it wasn't for her father's monthly checks, she wouldn't be able to afford this place."

Laura viewed her surroundings with wonder. "Doesn't she make good money playing Serena?"

"Sure, but she's no Susan Lucci." Grace led Laura into a kitchen surrounded by a butcher block counter, hanging plants and gleaming white tile. "Why don't we have a drink on the terrace? I have to check up on a few things here. After I finish we'll head over to my place."

"Thanks for picking me up at the airport. And thanks again for the offer to let me spend a few days at your apartment until I find a place of my own. I really appreciate it."

"Don't even give it a second thought." Grace brought a pitcher of lemonade and two chilled glasses out onto the terrace.

Laura accepted a glass of lemonade, settling into a wrought iron chair, admiring the pool and hot tub through vines of flowering jasmine. "What does Gabrielle's husband do?"

"He's a marvelously talented screenwriter," Grace raved, "and he's working on something stupendous."

"I know one of his screenplays was nominated for an Oscar, but anything since then?"

"None of his newer projects have been developed yet, but trust me, Harrison Moore's name is going to light up many movie screens again."

"Sounds like you think pretty highly of the guy."

"I do."

Laura looked at Grace shrewdly. "Anything going on?"

Grace gave Laura a shrewd look of her own. "Maybe."

"Maybe? I'd say definitely. It sounds like you're pretty hung up on the guy. Just be careful. He's a married man. I'd hate to see you get hurt."

"Don't worry about me. I'm a big girl. I can take care of myself."

"Yes, I know that," Laura reminded, "but I also know you lose your head when you fall in love. Don't idolize Harrison, Grace. He's not perfect. No man is."

"I'll remember that," Grace promised.

"I still can't get over this estate," Laura said as she changed the topic of conversation, admiring the lush gardenia bushes and fruit trees around them. "How many acres is it?"

"Twenty. One day I'm going to have an estate just as grand as this one," Grace confidently stated.

"You'll probably get it," Laura agreed. "You always went after what you wanted."

"Yes, I did," Grace softly uttered, sipping from her glass. "There are only a few problems that need smoothing out. But they say the best things come to those who wait." She brightened. "Anyway, enough about me and the people I work for. Tell me about yourself. You look fabulous!"

Laura laughed. "Get real! I look hopelessly outdated. You're going to have to take me shopping. I need a totally new look."

"Deal! I love spending money. Any ideas on what else you want to do now that you're out here?"

"Besides getting a job and finding a place to live?" Laura closed her eyes, tilting her face to the sun. "A tan was on my list."

"Be serious! You've been very mysterious all these years. I know we didn't keep in touch much after graduation, but you just dropped out of sight those first two years."

Laura sighed. "Grace, there's nothing to tell. I did some traveling and then I decided to teach at a private school in New York. It wasn't for me and I decided I needed a change. You always did have an overactive imagination."

Grace gave Laura an assessing look. "Why don't I believe you? Why do I think you're holding back?"

Laura laughed nervously, taking another sip from her glass and deliberately avoiding eye contact. "Would I lie to you?"

"You used to be the most honest person I know."

Laura tossed her head back. "And now I'm not?" she countered lightly.

"I didn't say that. You've never lied a day in your life. You're still the most honest person I know and in this town, honesty is a rare thing. So if you say you need a fresh start, I'll buy it." She finished the rest of her lemonade. "Let me check with the caterer one last time to make sure Gabrielle's dinner arrives on time and then we'll hit the road."

After Grace disappeared, Laura rolled her empty glass between her hands, struggling with her guilty conscience. How wrong Grace was. Lying came easily to her. She'd learned how to do it without any qualms and she'd keep doing it. She had to. She'd almost lost her life to Nico Rossi. She never wanted to think about him or her past again. The memories were too painful.

What harm could a few white lies do?

CHAPTER SEVEN

K ELLY STARED at the oil painting of her father, wondering, as always, what it would have been like to have known him.

Her fingers traced the swirls of color as she admired him, staring into his eyes, which were identical to her own. She always felt such pride when she thought of her father. Adam Stoddard had been a dashing, handsome figure. It was no wonder he had become a star, captivating millions . . . including her mother.

Kelly's gaze fell on the framed photographs lining the mantel. There were photos of Adam and Diana, separately and together. Both looked exceptionally happy. There were photos of Diana as the years went by, at galas and premieres, posing alone and with other stars. Oddly enough, there were no photos of herself. Unlike most children, she had never been subjected to a camera lens. Of course, there had been publicity photos of herself and Mother, but not even those had been displayed.

Kelly picked up a silver-framed photo of her mother, admiring it. Whether captured in a photo or frozen on a movie screen, Diana always looked beautiful . . . mesmerizing . . . captivating. If there was one thing her mother knew how to do, it was create an image.

Kelly smiled wryly. If anyone knew that, she did.

Replacing the photograph, Kelly left the library and began walking from room to room. Being back in the house she had grown up in gave her a suffocating feeling. The memories starting to return were not pleasant. The walls felt as though they were closing in, getting ready to smother her with their secrets . . . secrets that had never been revealed.

What would Diana's fans think if they knew the truth? Would they still be as adoring or would their adulation end? If that ever happened, Kelly knew her mother would die. Diana couldn't function unless she was in the limelight. Kelly knew she was being harsh, but it was true . . . Diana had sacrificed being a mother for being a star.

Kelly fought back the bitterness. Her mother loved her. Everything her mother had done had been for her. To give her the best.

Her mother had *always* told her that.

"There you are! I've been looking everywhere!"

Kelly whirled at the sound of her mother's voice. Standing at the top of the sweeping staircase was Diana, dressed as impeccably as always in a two-piece suit of aqua silk crepe, every inch the star.

The sight of Diana stirred excitement in Kelly, overruling her nervousness. After six years there was Diana, still looking as beautiful as ever. Kelly remained rooted in place as her mother glided down the staircase.

"Don't just stand there! Let me have a look at you," Diana instructed once she'd reached the bottom. She took a step back, scrutinizing Kelly from head to toe. "What have you done to yourself?"

The words were spoken softly, inquisitively, yet Kelly was swallowed by panic. What was wrong with her appearance? She thought she looked presentable . . . even attractive. The black off-the-shoulder dress she was wearing, lit by a flash of violet on its off-the-shoulder cuff, was definitely flattering. Or so she had thought.

"What's wrong with the way I look?"

Diana laughed merrily. "Calm down. Don't get so jittery. God, you were always a bundle of nerves. I could never make a comment without you quivering. I can see that hasn't changed." She inspected Kelly's appearance again. "You've done something different with your hair."

Kelly nodded, tossing her head back. "I've let it grow longer and I've layered it."

Diana peered closely at Kelly. "You've definitely changed. New clothes, new hairstyle. And it looks like you're wearing makeup. I've never seen you looking so sleek."

"Does that mean you like it?" Kelly bubbled. Suddenly she felt like a little girl again, desperately seeking her mother's approval.

"Darling, it's your money." Diana adjusted a canary-and-white diamond drop earring. "Like I always said, once you start paying the bills you can do whatever you want."

Kelly winced at the uttering of that once familiar phrase. How she had fought with Diana for the clothes she had wanted to wear and the things she had wanted to do! Her mother had never budged an inch, maintaining control until the day Kelly had gone away to college.

"Yes, but do you like it?" Kelly persisted.

Diana gave an offhand wave. "If you like it, fine, but I never would have chosen that look for you. You don't carry it off very well."

"You always were to the point, Mother. By the way, mind if *I* bring up a point?"

"By all means."

"Where were you? I waited for over an hour at the airport. You said you were going to send someone to pick me up. I finally had to grab a taxi."

"Do stop whining, Kelly!" Diana snapped, heading in the direction of the library. Once inside she went to the bar and poured herself a straight scotch, no water or ice. She didn't ask Kelly if she wanted a drink. "I'm sorry to have inconvenienced you, but Paul Fontana dropped by on a business matter. I lost track of the time and your arrival slipped my mind. Besides, it's not like you're a child. You're here now, so let's just forget it."

"Doesn't surprise me," Kelly muttered daringly.

"Don't take that tone of voice with me!" Diana warned, slamming down her glass. "I've apologized. You always had to see how far you could push me."

"I'm sorry," Kelly said, hating the fact that this scene had been played before and once again *she* was the one apologizing. They hadn't even been together for ten minutes and already they were in their traditional roles: Diana as the aggressor and Kelly as the defender. She wouldn't even mention her disappointment at Diana's no-show at her graduation. All along Diana had planned on attending the ceremony, and Kelly had planned on sharing her news about the soap. But then, on the day of graduation, her mother sent a dozen peach roses, along with a note explaining that she was needed to reshoot some scenes on a mini-series she had wrapped and was unable to make the ceremony.

"I didn't forget you were coming," Diana said. "I instructed Esmerelda to air out your old room."

When Kelly didn't answer, Diana gave her a puzzled look. "Is there something wrong with that?"

Kelly forced herself to remain calm. She blocked out visions of her hated bedroom—her prison when she'd been growing up—where she'd spent hours on end punished for the slightest infractions or was sent to when she wasn't allowed to do the things she wanted with her friends.

"I'm not moving back in. I've gotten an apartment in Westwood. I can take care of myself, Mother. I've been doing it for six years. Thanks for the offer, though."

"How do you intend to pay for this apartment?" Diana asked haughtily. "Have you gotten a job or are you relying on the trust fund your father left you? That money isn't going to last forever."

Kelly knew she had offended her mother, but the news she was about to share would make amends. "I'm going into acting," she enthusiastically revealed. When her mother heard her news she was going to be thrilled. Now there was a common ground between them and hopefully they would be able to become close.

"Lots of luck," Diana commented somewhat flippantly. "Don't expect any help from me, though. If you want to make it in this business you're going to have to do it on your own. Don't come turning to me when the going gets tough. This isn't a business for favors; it's a business for talent. Once you see how difficult it is, you'll change your mind."

"No, no, Mother, you don't understand!" Kelly was bursting with excitement. "I've already landed an acting job. I don't need Daddy's trust fund and I don't need your help. I've done it all on my own!"

Only a month ago she had been a senior in a drama production written by one of her classmates. After the performance a producer had come backstage, asking to see her. After he'd found her, he gave her his business card and urged her to give him a call. He liked what he had seen that night and if she was interested there might be a future for her in daytime. His show was looking to cast a new character and she just might fit the bill.

Interested? Kelly instantly decided to call the producer the next morning while her best friend and roommate, Jill Kramer, listened in on the other line. Even if she didn't get the part, the audition would be a valuable learning experience. Kelly hadn't actually believed she had a chance at getting the part, but she got it!

Diana looked at Kelly skeptically. "What kind of an acting job?"

"Next week I start on 'The Yields of Passion.' It's the number-one daytime soap."

Diana breezed from behind the bar and embraced Kelly, although it was only a touching of the upper arms and a brushing of cheeks as the air was kissed. "Darling, I'm so very proud of you. Tell me, when did this all come about—your desire to act."

"Well, I've always wanted to do it," Kelly gushed, "ever since I was a little girl, but I was too shy to tell anyone. Then, when I got to NYU, I transferred to the film school in my third year. Because I had credits to make up that's why I graduated so late. The rest is history."

"But you never mentioned a word of it in your letters. Why so secretive?"

Kelly shrugged. She didn't know why. Some instinct had warned her *not* to tell her mother her true ambition and so she hadn't. "Like I said, I was too shy."

Diana stared at Kelly intently. "Why didn't you call me when you were in town to audition?"

Kelly tried to answer flippantly. Once again, she hadn't wanted Diana to know what she was doing, somehow fearful of incurring her disapproval. "I was so nervous, all I could think about was the audition. If I got the part I wanted to surprise you. I didn't want you to be disappointed if I didn't get it."

"Well, you've definitely surprised me! We must celebrate this good news soon," Diana promised, "but not tonight. I have an appointment this evening and I'm running late. Why don't we have dinner one night next week?"

Kelly was a bit disappointed that Diana hadn't kept tonight open for her—after all, it *was* her return home—but she hid her true feelings. "I'd like that. Well, if you have an appointment I'd better be on my way."

Diana gave her daughter a smile as she left, but as soon as the front door closed, her smile disappeared and her eyes narrowed into two tight slits. Storming to the phone in the hallway, she snatched up the receiver and dialed her agent's number.

"Jinxie, it's Diana. I've just changed my mind."

"About what?"

"*Long Journey Home.* Talk to Mark Bauer. Tell him I want in."

"But at lunch you said you didn't want any part of the project," the agent sputtered. "Why the sudden change of mind?"

"Just do it, Jinxie!" Diana barked. "That's what I'm paying you a commission for. Give him the hard sell. Promise him anything. I'll do whatever Mark wants as long as I get a role in *Long Journey Home.*"

Diana's gaze was riveted on the front door Kelly had left

through. "I'm prepared to destroy anyone who enters into my territory."

"My, don't we look virginal." Harrison's tone was biting and sarcastic. Much to his disappointment, Gabrielle ignored him, refusing to be baited. "Find that in the back of your closet or did you buy it specifically for Big Daddy's visit?"

Gabrielle wore an ivory dress trimmed in lace and her wild mane of long curly hair was tamed into a sedate french braid tied with a white ribbon. Quite a contrast to the plunging necklines, tight skirts and leathers she usually wore.

Harrison moved further into their bedroom. He flopped onto their bed in his wet swim trunks as Gabrielle inspected herself in a mirror.

He wanted to laugh. Who did Gabrielle think she was fooling? She had gone to the most extreme lengths to give herself an innocent quality . . . trying to transform herself back into Daddy's little girl. Harrison grinned wickedly, sipping from the glass of bourbon he carried. If Paul Fontana knew how his little girl had grown up!

"What are you asking Daddy for tonight?" It galled him the way she had her father wrapped around her little finger.

"Besides a real man for a husband?"

He ignored the barb. "Knowing you, it probably involves only yourself."

Gabrielle stared into the mirror at her husband while fastening her pearl drop earrings. "How right you are."

"What new toy do you want this week?"

"What any good actress wants. A good role." Gabrielle flushed with excitement. "I've finally found it."

"But has it found you? Where'd you ever get the idea you were a *good* actress," Harrison scoffed, "let alone an actress?"

Gabrielle smiled sweetly. "Where'd you ever get the idea you were a *good* screenwriter? You haven't produced a screenplay in years. Do much writing today? Or did you spend the day in your usual fashion—on your ass?"

Harrison suppressed the urge to wipe away the smug look on Gabrielle's face. "I did a few pages," he lied.

"What's a few? Two? Three? Surely no more than five?" she gasped mockingly.

"We'll see how funny you think things are once I finish my

screenplay. It's gonna be hot and once you read it you'll be begging me to let you star in it."

"The first time we had sex you said it was going to be hot. You don't see me coming back for seconds." Gabrielle patted Harrison's cheek on her way out. "Grand illusions are divine, but I'm not holding my breath. You? Finish a screenplay?" She laughed. "Dream on, honey."

After checking to make sure all was in order in the kitchen, Gabrielle headed for the living room, where she was thrilled to find her brother waiting. "Peter, you came!" She raced to give him a hug. "Been waiting long?"

Peter hugged his sister back. "No, I just got here."

"Sit down. I'll fix you a drink. What'll you have?"

"Mineral water is fine." While Gabrielle fiddled at the bar, Peter admired the room. "This is some place."

The walls of the living room were painted peach while the drapes were a rich cream. The sofa and side chairs were upholstered in violet silk and arranged around a glass coffee table. A pair of tin palm trees were in opposite corners and the fireplace was adorned by a framed monster-sized poster of Gabrielle.

"Isn't it marvelous?" she raved. "We've got ten rooms, a swimming pool and outdoor hot tub. As soon as I saw the place I had to have it." She handed Peter his drink. "When I told Daddy he instantly bought it."

Peter cut her off. "Dad bought you this place? Why doesn't that surprise me?"

Gabrielle sighed. "Peter, please. Let's not get into this again."

"Damn it, Gabrielle, when will you ever learn?" Peter gestured at the surroundings. "This is all guilt money. Paul Fontana wasn't around when his kids were growing up. He was never there when we needed him and he can't face that. His business dealings always came first," Peter spat out, "and now he's trying to buy our love."

Gabrielle instantly came to their father's defense. "Will you lay off him? Daddy was only doing what he had to do. What he thought was best."

"Yeah, placing his dirty money before his children."

"Stop it!"

"Come on, Gabrielle. Open your eyes."

"Whatever Daddy's done, he's done for us. He wanted us to have the best."

"No!" Peter's voice was angry. "The only person Paul Fontana has ever thought about or cared about is himself. Money and power are all that matter to him. That's why Mom is dead."

"Don't say that! Don't ever let me hear you say that again!" Gabrielle harshly ordered. "Daddy didn't push Mom to suicide."

Marina Fontana's suicide was a topic neither Peter nor Gabrielle ever liked to discuss. Both had been small children when their mother had hanged herself in the bathroom of their Beverly Hills home. There had been no suicide note.

"Then who did?"

"It wasn't Daddy!" Gabrielle flared. "I remember how it used to be between them."

"I remember certain things, too," Peter said.

"How could you? You were too young. Only three. Daddy loved her, just like he loves us." Gabrielle reached for a silver-framed photo from the coffee table, handing it to her brother. "Look what he sent me last week."

Within the silver frame was a photo of Marina. She was a beautiful woman with dark coal eyes and shimmering black hair. Peter's finger outlined her image.

"I miss her so much, Gabrielle."

Gabrielle sighed. She knew how hard their mother's death had been on her brother. "I know. I miss her too. She was so wonderful and I loved her so much. I don't know why she did it. She had everything she could possibly want."

"Tell me what she was like." Peter's memories of Marina were fuzzy. "I can never remember her."

"She was special. She spent all her time with us. I remember when she brought you home from the hospital. She made me so proud to be a big sister." Gabrielle smoothed Peter's hair. "Despite what she did, she loved us, Peter. You must believe that."

"I do. I've never doubted it."

"And Daddy loves us just as much. Please try to get along with him tonight," she begged. "It's only one dinner. Before long he'll be back in Las Vegas."

Peter returned the photo to his sister, unable to look at it any longer. "I'll try."

* * *

"Daddy, you sit at the head of the table." Gabrielle held a chair out for Paul. "I've gotten all your favorites. There's baked clams, stuffed mushrooms, hot sausage, lasagna and veal scallopini. For dessert I've gotten napoleons and cannolis."

Paul kissed Gabrielle's cheek. "How my little girl spoils me!"

"I should be so lucky," Harrison muttered under his breath.

Gabrielle started passing around dishes while Paul turned his attention to Peter. "How long has it been since we last saw each other?"

Peter shrugged. "Two years?"

"And you're still at loose ends."

"What's that supposed to mean?"

"Garlic bread, anyone?" Gabrielle asked, sensing the mounting tension.

"What I mean is that you're twenty-eight years old and you haven't done anything with your life. When I was your age I had a wife and two children."

Peter controlled himself. A wife? Children? No chance of that ever happening to him. "We're two different people, Dad. The things I want aren't necessarily the things you want."

"You don't know what you want, so I've done something about it," Paul announced.

"Like what?" Peter stared at his father suspiciously.

"I gave Mark Bauer a call this afternoon. Let's just say he owes me a few favors. Monday morning you report to him. I've gotten you a job as his assistant at Trinity Pictures."

"I don't believe this!" Peter raged, slamming down his napkin. "How could you do such a thing? How could you go behind my back and make a decision like this without consulting me? I'm not a child anymore."

"Peter, I have a vested interest in Trinity Pictures and I'd like someone I can trust on the inside. You've made it abundantly clear that my other businesses don't appeal to you. You'll learn plenty from Mark." Paul gave his son a stern look. "All I'm asking is you give it a chance."

Peter inwardly fumed. He *had* been toying with the idea of finding a job in the movie industry. Working with Mark Bauer wouldn't be bad—it'd be a golden opportunity. But he didn't like the way the job had come about. Knowing his father, he had probably put some pressure on Mark and Mark probably thought he was some spoiled rich kid who made his father play the heavy so he could get what he wanted. Plus, Peter *hated* giving in to his father.

"I'll think about it," he stated noncommittally.

"Speaking of Mark Bauer, I hear he's heading up an exciting new project for Trinity," Gabrielle innocently stated. "Is that true, Daddy?"

Paul nodded, slipping a forkful of veal into his mouth. "Delicious."

"I'm sure *Long Journey Home* is going to make a wonderful movie. The book was fabulous. I read it twice. Olivia is such a marvelous character."

Paul shrugged, too consumed with his veal. "All I know is the public is buying the book. Let's hope they fork out for the movie. Though with Bauer at the helm, I'm pretty sure they will."

"They will, Daddy. They definitely will. The public loves Mark Bauer's films. His last two made over a hundred million at the box office. *Long Journey Home* is going to be a hit." Gabrielle buttered a slice of garlic bread and handed it to her father. "You know, Daddy, I'd like to be a part of *Long Journey Home*. I think it would help my career immensely . . . you know, have me taken more seriously as an actress. I know I could handle the role of Olivia. She's such a wonderful character. Do you think you could talk to Mark, Daddy? I know he hasn't cast Olivia yet."

"Darling, are you sure *Long Journey Home* is the right vehicle for you?" Harrison smiled sweetly at his wife, playing with the burnt heel of garlic bread she had left in his plate. "It's a dramatic piece. Not a comedy."

Gabrielle tuned out Harrison, continuing her pitch. "Daddy, this is a break you can't let me miss. If you talk to Mark you'll be helping me with my film career."

"Lord knows her career needs all the help it can get," Harrison ventured to say to himself.

Gabrielle glowered at Harrison before returning her attention to her father. "Please, Daddy. Will you talk to him?"

"I'll talk to Mark and see what I can do," Paul conceded.

"Can you send me a script, Daddy? Last week you told me there were finished copies."

"There are?" Harrison choked out.

Gabrielle sent her husband a triumphant look, enjoying his surprise. "There are."

"Sure, no problem," Paul agreed. "Now enough talk about business. Let's eat."

Gabrielle jumped from her seat, throwing her arms around Paul. "Thank you, Daddy. I knew you wouldn't let me down. The role of Olivia is practically mine. What possible competition could I have?"

Heather McCall was a star—a very rich star who had decided it was time to parlay her talents into a legitimate film career.

The role of Olivia Thomas in *Long Journey Home* was going to help pave the way.

At the age of twenty-five, Heather was the queen of B movies, having successfully dethroned both Linda Blair and Sybil Danning. Among Heather's many hits were *Caged Women, Leather Vixens, Mafia Playmates,* and the infinitely successful *Slutzoids from Hell* series.

Although Heather's films rarely made it to movie theaters, they were big hits on video. And she'd made tons of money, resulting in a condo in Hollywood Hills, a Mercedes, and a nice stock portfolio. Pretty impressive for a farm girl from Ohio who had shown up in L.A. at the edge of seventeen.

Heather's first year, living in West Hollywood, had been the hardest. Pimps and porn producers had been after her and the offers they had made had been tempting. Yet Heather had held out, refusing their offers, knowing they were users who would toss her to one side once she had nothing left to give. She wasn't going to get sucked up by Hollywood's dark side. She was going to become a part of Hollywood's glitter.

She found a number of odd jobs to support herself and kept up with her acting lessons. Soon the parts started coming in. Unlike Linda Blair and Sybil Danning, Heather wasn't super jiggly or statuesque. She was an attractive blonde with a peaches-and-cream complexion reminiscent of the girl next door, though she could look quite sexy whenever she wanted—it was an appealing combination. She also happened to look sensational in leather and wet mud, her costume in *Wrestling Babes,* the movie that launched her career in B movies.

Now after five years, Heather was ready to remove her crown. She was bored with the parts she played. She was honest with herself—she'd only done them for the money. The scripts were garbage—any idiot could bounce and squeal in a few scraps of leather and lace. Heather wanted to challenge herself as an actress

—she wanted to put her talents to the test. She knew she could do it.

Months ago she had told her agent, Jinxie Bishop, of her plan. At first he'd tried to dissuade her, but she'd been insistent with him, telling him to keep his eyes open and do as she asked, otherwise she'd be looking for representation elsewhere. Jinxie wasn't the type to give up a lucrative meal ticket and so he'd done as Heather requested, sending over whatever he thought might tickle her "artistic" fancy, as he referred to it. Today he had messengered over another script and for the last two hours she had been unable to put it down.

The role had everything. Tenderness, vulnerability, sensuousness, determination.

It was the role of Olivia Thomas in *Long Journey Home.*

Heather hugged the script to her chest. She didn't want to let it go. She had to have this part. After playing Olivia Thomas, her career would be set. She'd be able to do any kind of film she wanted—no more of the shlock stuff she was chained to.

And she'd finally be able to keep her promise. Heather would never forget all that her mother had done to help make her dream of becoming an actress come true. With six kids to feed and a husband who was too lazy to work (but not too lazy to cash his unemployment checks and spend the money on liquor to swill all day) Norma McCall had somehow managed to save enough money from her housecleaning jobs to buy Heather a bus ticket to Hollywood and give her a small sum to tide her over until she found work. Though she hadn't wanted her daughter to go, Norma had known how important Heather's dream had been to her. And she had wanted better for her daughter—better than she had done for herself.

Heather would never forget the pride in her mother's tired face as she had kissed her goodbye.

"I'm gonna do you proud, Mama," Heather had promised. "I'm gonna become rich and famous and you'll never have to scrub floors again. I'm gonna buy you a house of your own and you'll have your own maid to order around! And when you go to the movies with your friends you'll be able to point to the screen and tell them that's your daughter up there."

"All that sounds wonderful, honey, but remember, I want you to be happy. That's what matters most to me."

Heather had hugged her mother fiercely before climbing on the

Greyhound bus. "Thank you, Mama. I won't let you down. I won't forget my promise."

Norma had run along the bus, waving goodbye to Heather for as long as she could. It was the last time Heather ever saw her mother alive. Six months later, Norma, along with Heather's six brothers and sisters, were dead. Her father, stinking drunk, had fallen asleep in bed with a lit cigarette and their house had gone up in flames. No one had had a chance to escape.

At the funeral, sprinkling her mother's coffin with the first handful of dirt before they buried her, Heather remembered her promise and vowed that one day she would keep it.

All she'd have to do now was convince Mark Bauer that she was right for the role of Olivia. All she wanted was a chance. If he gave her a reading and screen test, she'd knock his socks off. After that she'd be on her way to a *real* acting career.

And she'd have kept her promise to Mama.

"You said you were going to talk to your father about my writing the screenplay adaptation for *Long Journey Home!*" Harrison angrily reminded Gabrielle. "We discussed this weeks ago."

Gabrielle stepped out of her ivory dress, leaving it in a crumpled pile on the floor. "I don't recall that conversation." She reached into a drawer for a swimsuit, heading into the bathroom.

"You're full of shit! Your father has Mark Bauer by the balls. You know how much this meant to me. It would have been the easiest way for me to get myself back into my writing and revive my career."

"Darling, I've got a news flash for you. Your career is so dead it needs more than reviving." Gabrielle emerged wearing a one-piece midnight blue swimsuit. "Besides, when have you ever known me to make anything easier for you? Any advantage I come across will be used solely for *my* career. Not yours. There's no way I'm going to let your star rise before mine. No way."

"God, you're a bitch."

Gabrielle shoved her face into Harrison's. "And you're nothing but a has-been," she taunted. "You haven't written a thing in years. Your days of glory are over, darling. Frankly, I'm getting sick of looking at your face." She left the bedroom, waving her fingers over her shoulder. "Maybe I'll get rid of it."

* * *

After Gabrielle left, Harrison panicked. The bitch had been serious. Why not? If she got the role of Olivia, she'd be set. Once she had a film, especially a prestigious Mark Bauer film, under her belt other film roles would surely follow. Then what would she need him for? Gabrielle would no longer have to wait for him to custom-write a role for her. His usefulness would be over.

There was no way he was giving up his Hollywood lifestyle. He'd gotten too used to it.

Harrison headed for his den. If Gabrielle wanted a screenplay, then that was what she was going to get.

He sat himself in front of his computer, turned it on, and started to type.

CHAPTER EIGHT

"Let me take a look at daytime's new star!" Daniel Ellis exclaimed, embracing Kelly in a hug.

Kelly's heart warmed at the sight of her godfather and she hugged him fiercely. It was so good to see him. Growing up, he had been the only bright spot in her life.

Daniel Ellis and Adam Stoddard had been best friends. After leaving behind the coal mining town in West Virginia where they had grown up they'd started out on Broadway in the late fifties and then came out to Hollywood together. While Adam had been a serious dramatic actor, Daniel blazed his own name in a series of thrillers and melodramas. But stardom had come for Daniel Ellis when he was paired with Vanessa Vought in a Rock Hudson–Doris Day-style romantic comedy. Afterwards, Daniel's career skyrocketed and he and Vanessa followed up with a number of similar films, giving Rock and Doris a run for their money.

In the seventies there was TV for Daniel. Teamed once again with Vanessa, the two starred as a modern-day Nick and Nora Charles in "Murder Afoot." The show ran seven years and garnered Daniel and Vanessa two Emmys each for their portrayal of Trey and Chloe Alden.

With the eighties there came the advent of nighttime soaps. The Ellis-Vought formula worked again and for another seven years they starred as Lucas and Jayne Shepherd in "Bel Air." Every week they beat out their competition, "Dynasty," and left "Dallas" and "The Cantrells" in the ratings dust.

Now Daniel was doing the mini-series circuit and had just wrapped up a role in an upcoming Judith Krantz adaptation.

In his thirty-five years in show business, Daniel Ellis had never faded from the limelight. The blue-eyed, sandy-haired actor was still in great shape for his fifty-five years and audiences still loved him. They thought he was real. Believable. Without falseness or pretense. And this was true. Daniel loved to act, but he didn't see himself as a star. He saw himself as a professional. When he was on a set he was working with other professionals and the goal was for everyone to give their best possible performance. Woe to those who didn't! Daniel wouldn't tolerate second best in a project he was involved in. And when it came to his fans Daniel was always willing to sign an autograph, pose for a photograph, or, if he had time, chat with them for a minute or two. It was the least he could do.

He despised stars who expected the royal treatment. Like Diana Halloway. She'd traded in her talent years ago—what little she had, anyway—to play the everyday role of star. Daniel had never catered to Diana. In fact, he hadn't even masked his dislike for her. When Adam had announced his plans to marry her, Daniel had tried to dissuade his best friend. He could see what Diana was: a user. Marrying Adam was only a way to elevate her status in Hollywood. Adam hadn't wanted to listen and so he had married Diana, with Daniel as his best man.

After the wedding it had been all-out war between Daniel and Diana. She snubbed him whenever she could, often having him dropped from party lists and not inviting him to her own parties, making up one excuse or another to Adam. It hadn't been hard for Diana. Daniel's homosexuality had been the perfect tool for her to use against him.

Daniel Ellis's homosexuality was well known in Hollywood circles, although he tried to be as discreet as possible. Lovers who moved in were called assistants or secretaries. Vanessa was always glad to be his escort to events and even went so far as to pretend that an affair existed between them. Many of their fans still expected them one day to tie the knot.

Diana's vendetta succeeded only with those people who disliked Daniel. And her reign of power had been limited. After Adam's death, her status in Hollywood dropped. But their feud remained alive, still existing to this day, simmering beneath the surface of congeniality, ready to explode at any moment. And the fact that he was Kelly's godfather, something which Adam had insisted upon, didn't make things easier.

Despite his feud with Diana, Daniel had made sure he was part of Kelly's life. He owed it to Adam to watch over his daughter, and he loved Kelly dearly. Whenever he'd been able to, he had spent time with Kelly, taking her out and spoiling her. It had been hard when Kelly was a child, because Diana had always kept the visits short. But as Kelly grew older she found ways to sneak around her mother, much to Daniel's delight.

As a child, Kelly had been sweet and innocent. Now she was a beautiful young woman with a promising career ahead of her. If Adam were still alive, he'd be proud.

"Sit down," Daniel urged, allowing Kelly to slip into their corner booth first. "We've got lots of catching up to do, and what better place to do it than over lunch at the Polo Lounge?"

Kelly laughed. "You haven't changed a bit, Uncle Daniel. I'm so glad."

"Tell me all about your first month in Tinseltown."

"I'm loving every minute of it. The show is great and I'm having a blast."

"I just got back from London last week when the mini-series wrapped up. I haven't been able to watch the episodes I had taped. Fill me in on your character."

"I'm playing Melissa Duke and she has amnesia. I've just arrived in Spring Falls and I'm slated to have an affair with Frost Barclay's character. He and I and Gabrielle Fontana Moore are going to be the show's hot love triangle."

"How deliciously complex. Sounds like there's lots of possibilities."

"Months from now they may write in a family for me when I get my memory back. It's all so new to me. I'm at the studio at least twelve hours a day either blocking, running lines, taping, or having wardrobe fittings. You should see my clothes. Fabulous!"

"It's good to see you so happy, Kelly. I've missed you while you were away."

Kelly clasped Daniel's hand. "Thanks for all the letters and phone calls and visits when you were in New York. It meant a lot. You've always been there for me. You've always made me feel special . . . loved."

"What's that mother of yours done *now?*" Daniel instinctively asked. "'Fess up. I can hear it in your voice."

Kelly didn't want to get into it. In the six years she had been away at school she hadn't heard from Diana at all, except for an occasional phone call or a card on her birthday and at holidays. And now that she was back in Hollywood, things hadn't changed at all. It was as if she hadn't even returned.

Her first week back Diana had arranged for the two of them to have dinner together at L'Orangerie. Yet with the frenzied pace of the show and fifty pages of dialogue to learn a night, she'd had to cancel. Her mother had been cool on the phone, but suggested they meet another night. The night of the second dinner Kelly was left waiting at the restaurant. Her mother never showed. The next day at the studio she got a message from her mother saying she'd had to meet unexpectedly with her agent. There was no apology.

Since then she'd tried meeting with her mother again. Yet Diana kept snubbing her. She never returned her phone calls and last week she'd had a party, not even bothering to invite Kelly. That had hurt and she'd written her mother a note, which Diana, surprisingly, had responded to. She told Kelly that she hadn't invited her because she knew how "inflexible" and "unpredictable" Kelly's schedule was and she just couldn't play jeopardy with her seating arrangements. All this because of one cancelled dinner!

"It's nothing," Kelly said. "I haven't seen much of her. She's been busy. Did you know she's gotten a part in *Long Journey Home?*"

Daniel looked amazed. "How interesting."

"What's next for you?"

Daniel gave an absentminded wave to Joan Collins as she passed. "I have a project in the works. I'll fill you in once I have more details."

"Big stuff?"

"Let's just say I'm looking forward to getting this part." He handed a menu to Kelly. "Why don't we order?"

After ordering warm scallop salad with basil sauce for both of them, Daniel steered the conversation back to Kelly. "So how's your love life?"

"How's yours?" she countered.

Daniel thought of his muscular, dark-haired lover, twenty years his junior. "Jaime is still in the picture."

Kelly didn't comment. Of all of Daniel's lovers over the years, Jaime was the one she liked least. She didn't think he cared about Daniel at all except for what he could get out of him. When it came to his lovers, Daniel was exceedingly generous, giving them charge accounts at all the stores he shopped at. Then too there were the gifts of jewelry and cars, along with hefty cash allowances. Jaime was probably doing quite nicely, but Kelly strongly believed that for Jaime, this still wasn't enough.

"Promise me you'll be careful with Jaime," she asked. "I don't want to see you getting hurt."

"Don't worry. I'm a big boy. I can take care of myself. Now tell me about the interesting prospects that have crossed your path."

"I have my work, Uncle Daniel. It's enough."

"No, it isn't," he refuted. "You're beautiful, Kelly and you shouldn't be alone. You deserve someone special. Isn't there anyone?"

Kelly thought of Graham Denning. Whenever she least expected it, he popped into her mind. How could any woman forget those dimples when he smiled? She should have kept his number instead of throwing it away. She'd lost her chance. "No one special," she admitted somewhat regretfully.

Off in another corner of the Polo Lounge another lunch was taking place, this one between Mark Bauer and Paul Fontana.

"Have you had a chance to take a look at Gabrielle's tapes from her show?"

"Yes, I have," Mark answered. "She's a capable actress."

"She's got talent," Paul corrected. "She'd be a fine addition to *Long Journey Home*, wouldn't you agree?"

Mark blinked, unsure if he'd heard correctly. He also wanted to be careful with his response. "Excuse me?"

"For the role of Olivia," Paul added.

The reason for this lunch suddenly became clear to Mark. Paul Fontana was getting ready to put the squeeze on him again. First he forced him into working for his studio, then he made him hire his son (though he had to admit Peter was an unexpected asset), and now he was expecting him to give his daughter one of the plum roles in his film. Where was it going to end?

It was time to make his position clear. When it came to his films, Mark was a perfectionist. Only he could transform the visions in his mind onto film. He was going to make *Long Journey Home* his way and Gabrielle Fontana Moore *would not* be a part of it.

"Let me get this straight. You want me to give Gabrielle the role of Olivia?"

"That's right," Paul affirmed.

"No way," Mark snapped, pushing away his poached salmon.

"In case you've forgotten Mr. Bauer, I'm the one calling the shots," Paul reminded, a dangerous glint coming to his eyes.

Mark swallowed his fears. If he didn't make his stand now, the next five years would be hell and his career would be down the tubes. "And in case *you've* forgotten, I'm the one making this film.

I'm the one tied to Trinity for five years. I'm the one you're expecting to bail you out."

"What does this have to do with anything?"

"A lot! It's *my* vision! Even though you strong-armed me into making this picture for Trinity, I'm going to make the best damn picture I possibly can. I'm not gonna make a piece of shit." Mark decided he would compromise with Paul, even though his decision concerning Gabrielle was pretty much final. "If Gabrielle wants this role she's going to have to audition like any other actress. I'm not going to hand her this role on a silver platter just because you tell me to. If she's the best, she'll get the part. If not, there'll be other roles, other projects. All I want to do is give you the best, Mr. Fontana. We're going to be working together for five years. This is the way I am. Can you accept that?"

Paul was silent for a moment. Then he raised his wine glass to Mark. "I can accept that."

"Why haven't I been given an appointment to see Mr. Bauer?" Heather demanded.

"I've told you before and I'll tell you again," Peter patiently explained from behind his desk, guarding the door to Mark's office on the Trinity studio lot. "Mr. Bauer looked at the resumé your agent sent over and he doesn't think you're right for the role of Olivia. There's nothing more I can do."

"There's plenty you can do," Heather insisted, sliding a tape across the desk. "Have him take a look at this."

Peter slid the tape back. "He doesn't have the time."

"Look, you're my only chance. Even my agent doesn't think I'm right for this part, but I know I am. You're Mark's assistant. You can find a way for him to look at this."

Peter waved the tape at her. "If I did that for every actress who came in here looking for a part, we'd never get any work done." He handed back the tape. "I'm sorry, Ms. McCall."

Heather snatched the tape and sat herself down on a sofa. "I'm not leaving until Mr. Bauer gets back and I get to see him."

Peter picked up the phone. "Look, I'm running out of patience. If you're not gone in five minutes I'm calling security. I'm busy and I've had enough of your games."

"Fine," Heather huffed, flinging back the glass door of the reception area as she stomped out, "but you haven't seen the last of me."

* * *

Walking back outside to Melrose Avenue, Heather started plotting. She hadn't gotten as far as she had in this business by being a quitter. There was no way she was going to let the role of Olivia slip through her fingers. Somehow she was going to find a way to get a screen test with Mark Bauer. Her instincts told her Peter Fontana would be that way.

Actresses! Peter thought. What wouldn't they do for an audition! Had Gabrielle ever gotten that obsessed over a role?

Maybe he should have kept the tape. He could have taken a look at it himself. If it had been good he could have passed it along to Mark.

Working for Mark was actually a breeze. A lot of his time was spent answering phones and setting up appointments, but he also got to read scripts and write reports on them. Peter was enjoying himself and learning a lot about the film business. At the moment Mark was deeply involved with *Long Journey Home.* Location shots were being taken in Nebraska for their six weeks on location and sets were already being prepared. Casting was winding down, music was being experimented with and publicity was gearing up. He found all of it fascinating. There might just be a career for him in Hollywood after all.

"An audition!" Gabrielle raged. "You can't be serious!" She listened to her father on the phone. "Who the hell is running Trinity Pictures? You or Mark Bauer? Thanks, Daddy. Thanks for nothing!"

Grace walked into the dressing room carrying a long white box tied with a red ribbon as Gabrielle slammed down the phone.

"What the hell are those?" Gabrielle snarled.

Grace handed Gabrielle a small sealed envelope. "Take a guess. They just arrived."

Gabrielle ripped open the envelope, once again without a return address, reading aloud the small card:

Gabrielle, you're the only woman for me. The only woman I'll ever love. No other woman has captivated me the way you have. Your devoted fan.

She tossed the card to the floor, ripping away the red ribbon on the box and pushing away the tissue paper, unveiling a dozen red roses. "The usual." She shoved the box at Grace. "Get rid of them."

For the past three weeks, every day she was at the studio, Gabrielle had been receiving a dozen red roses from a mysterious fan. Before that there had been letters, praising her performances on the show. At first she had been flattered, but now it was getting eerie. Spooky. This unknown person seemed to be obsessed with her. But she didn't have the time to deal with it. The best thing to do was just ignore him. Eventually—hopefully—he would tire of her and leave her alone. She'd just have to be careful and more aware of what was going on around her. In the meantime she had more pressing matters to worry about.

"What do you want me to do with them?" Grace asked.

"I don't know! Just get them out of my sight!"

Grace, enjoying seeing Gabrielle so unnerved, didn't offer any words of consolation. "Right away."

When Grace left, Gabrielle rummaged through her Fendi shoulder bag for her *Long Journey Home* script. It was the first time she was looking at it. She'd been so sure the role of Olivia would be hers that she hadn't even bothered reading the script. All that mattered was for her father to get her the film career she wanted.

She'd been so confident that she'd be starring in *Long Journey Home* that she had asked her producer for time off. He had refused and so Gabrielle had quit the show. What did she need "The Yields of Passion" for? She was going to be a film star.

Now the writers were busy working on a way to get her off the show. In a month Serena Taylor would be gone. What would she do if she didn't get the role of Olivia?

Gabrielle started reading. She was going to have to give one hell of an audition.

Drew jogged along Malibu Beach, lost in his thoughts as he stared out at the Pacific Ocean. He always enjoyed the time he had between films. It gave him a chance to relax and unwind before spending weeks in front of a camera.

The sand beneath his feet felt moist and soft. The breeze blowing in was refreshing and he could taste a tangy saltiness in the air. The sun felt just right on his skin. Usually when Drew jogged he only wore a pair of shorts, leaving his chest bare. The less he wore the less constrained he felt.

Drew couldn't wait to get started on *Long Journey Home*. He had a feeling about this film. A very good feeling.

"Hey! Watch where you're going."

Before Drew could look up he crashed into the person, bringing the two of them down into the sand.

"I'm terribly sorry," he apologized, offering a hand.

The woman pushed away his hand, getting to her feet on her own. She was wearing white shorts and a lime green halter top. Her auburn hair was pulled back from her face and worn in a ponytail. Her face radiated a glowing tan and the scent of her was fresh and clean. She looked like she belonged on the beach.

She also looked uninterested in him. Could that be possible? Even if he was unrecognizable with the sunglasses and baseball cap he was wearing pulled low over his forehead, he'd like to think he had some appeal.

"I'm sorry," he apologized again, trying to make his words sound more sincere. He somehow wanted to snare her attention . . . prolong their meeting. "I should have watched where I was going."

"You've got that right, buddy." She brushed the sand off her shorts, attempting to make her way around him. "Excuse me."

Drew didn't want her to go. "Mind if I jog along with you?"

She held up a halting hand. "Nothing personal. You're cute but I'm not interested." She started jogging off. "See you around."

"See you around," Drew echoed. For a moment he was tempted to follow after her, but he didn't want her to think he was harassing her. Despite saying he was cute, she'd also said she was uninterested.

Drew picked up his pace, heading down the beach in the opposite direction.

Laura slowed her pace, wondering if the guy she had crashed into was following. He was more than cute. He was gorgeous! And he'd seemed interested in her.

But, as always, the defense mechanisms had sprung into action and she'd nearly bitten his head off. All she'd really wanted was for the conversation to continue.

Did she dare peek over her shoulder to see if he was following?

Laura turned around with an expectant smile. Then it disappeared. He wasn't there. He hadn't followed her. Her eyes scoured the beach. He wasn't anywhere in sight.

Laura kicked at the sand. Damn Nico Rossi for making her so afraid! Even after all these years he still had a stranglehold on her life. Because of him she was afraid of men.

She took one last look around the beach. Okay, he was gone. But if he was a jogger, chances were he'd be back. Maybe their paths would cross again. If they did, she'd definitely be less assertive and much nicer to him. She wouldn't scare him off.

Laura kicked at the sand again before continuing her jog. Nico Rossi would be forgotten once and for all. He was ancient history and belonged in the past.

Nico cradled the phone to his ear. He was allowed only one call per day and his fifteen minutes were nearly up.

"So her trail leads to New York? Start looking everywhere. I don't care how long it takes or how much it costs. As soon as you find something, give me a call." Nico stared at the creased photo of Laura he held in his hand before crumpling it into a ball. "Laura and I got unfinished business."

CHAPTER NINE

"Wʜᴀᴛ ᴛʜᴇ ʜᴇʟʟ is going on?" Daniel demanded coldly, shutting off the stereo. Paula Abdul's voice, singing "Cold Hearted," instantly died. Daniel stared around the living room filled with lounging male bodies. All were perfect creations with their gleaming white teeth, golden tans, shiny heads of hair, beautiful features and carefully delineated bulges. And all their eyes possessed a touch of arrogance . . . the same arrogance possessed by Jaime.

Jaime wove his way to Daniel, offering a champagne glass. He wore a blue silk shirt unbuttoned to the navel and tight white jeans. He pressed the glass into Daniel's hand. "Drink up, lover. You look like you could use it."

Daniel accepted the glass, gesturing with it toward the others. "It's after midnight. What are all these people doing here?"

"Only a little party," Jaime whispered into Daniel's ear. His tongue licked Daniel's earlobe. "The guys want to have some fun. I thought you'd be up to it." Jaime placed a hand on Daniel's crotch. "How 'bout it?"

Daniel squelched the desire rising within him, allowing his anger free reign. He drained the champagne, shoving the empty glass at Jaime. "I want everyone out!" he hissed. *"Now!"*

Jaime flicked his straight black hair off his forehead, a cocky grin on his face. The arrogance in his midnight blue eyes was raging. "Whatever you say, *boss.*"

Daniel turned his back on Jaime and headed for his bedroom, ignoring those in his path. Thirty minutes later there was a knock on his door.

When Jaime entered, Daniel's anger returned. "Are you crazy?"

Jaime gave Daniel a bored look and flung himself across the

king-sized bed, propping his stockinged feet up on the wall. "All I did was invite a few friends over."

"Who do you think you're kidding? Those 'friends' of yours were all hustlers and your party was out of control. I could hear the music blasting all the way down the canyon and nobody was hiding their drugs. Suppose someone had called the police? Then what?" Daniel grew angrier as he envisioned the scenario that could have taken place. He paced back and forth before Jaime, the bottom of his silk paisley dressing robe billowing out. "This is just the kind of stuff the *National Enquirer* feeds on."

"You used to like my parties. There was a time when you couldn't get enough of them. You used to love *indulging* yourself."

"Not anymore. My God, Jaime, I've got an image to protect."

"What image?" Jaime scoffed. "Everyone in Hollywood knows you're gay."

"I don't care what everyone in Hollywood knows! I care what my fans think! They're the ones who made me. I'm not going to wind up like Rock Hudson!"

"Of course you're not! You're in control of your life." Jaime jumped from the bed and slipped behind Daniel, massaging his shoulders. "Danny, you're so tense. Let me loosen you up."

Daniel tried to pull away but Jaime held his grip. Daniel didn't resist as Jaime steered him toward the massive king-sized bed, continuing to massage.

"What's bothering you? You've become so uptight lately. I only threw together the party because I thought you needed to unwind."

Daniel closed his eyes, rolling his head from side to side. "I'm up for a role in *Long Journey Home*. I really want it, but Mark Bauer has been taking his time. He's already spoken to Paul Newman and Robert Redford."

"Don't worry. If you want the role, it's yours." Jaime's lips descended upon Daniel's forcefully. "When have I ever known you not to get what you want?"

He pushed Daniel back down on the bed, spreading his arms out and opening his robe. Daniel was already erect. Jaime took Daniel's erection in his mouth, trailing his shaft with his tongue.

Daniel reached for Jaime's head, wanting to hold it in place, but Jaime pulled away his mouth, slapping away Daniel's hand.

"Naughty, naughty!" Jaime scolded. "You're not allowed to touch." He reached under the bed for two leather straps with studs and lashed Daniel's arms to the headboard. He took Daniel's face in one hand, taking a hard kiss for himself before checking the restraints. "That'll hold you. Now it's time for me to change."

Striding over to the stereo, Jaime turned it on. Madonna's voice blasted out, singing "Vogue." Jaime began dancing to the music, stripping away his clothes as Daniel's gaze followed his every move. When he was naked he danced before Daniel a few minutes longer. Then from a dresser drawer he took out a black leather mask, arm-length black leather gloves, and a black leather bikini thong. After changing into the outfit, Jaime ripped away Daniel's robe.

With one finger he traced a route along Daniel's body, stopping at the tip of his erection. Jaime's finger slowly circled the head of Daniel's erect penis. Daniel struggled against his bonds, hungry for satisfaction, trying to use his legs to pull Jaime to him.

Instantly, Jaime lashed Daniel's legs to the bottom footboard, wrapping a black silk scarf around Daniel's mouth. Eyes wide with excitement, Daniel awaited Jaime's next move.

Reaching for a bottle of baby oil, Jaime poured it over Daniel, massaging it into his skin.

"How does this feel?" he whispered.

Daniel's eyes closed in ecstasy and a soft moan escaped from behind his gag. Daniel's erection bucked upwards and Jaime poured some oil over the shaft, massaging it in. His first strokes were slow. Then they became faster and faster.

"You can't come, Danny," Jaime warned, shaking a stern finger, before massaging faster and faster. "If you do, you'll be sorry. Very sorry."

Daniel struggled for control, but the heat of his erection combined with the coolness of the oil and the smoothness of the leather made his body scream for release. He ejaculated with great spurts into Jaime's gloved hands.

"Bad boy, Daniel," Jaime scolded, removing the gloves. "*Very* bad boy."

Jaime pulled away the gag and meshed his lips with Daniel's. "You have to be taught a lesson."

"No," Daniel pleaded, his excitement growing.

"*Yes*," Jaime promised.

From beneath the bed he pulled out a leather whip, cracking it in the air. This was his favorite part of the game. Now he could take his frustrations out on Daniel. He hated being Daniel's kept boy. He hated not knowing when it would all end and when someone else would take his place.

He wanted to be an actor. He wanted to star in movies. Daniel had promised to help him, but so far Daniel had done nothing for him. *Nothing!*

Jaime uncoiled the whip, snapping it into the air with a flick of his wrist. It made an ugly crack. Jaime smiled down at Daniel.

Daniel wasn't going to get off easy. No way. Jaime was the one in control. Last year the old fag hadn't even been into S&M until he had shown him the way. Now Daniel couldn't get enough of it.

And Jaime couldn't get enough of Daniel's lifestyle. When the time came, he was going to be sure he had a nice hunk of Danny Boy's pie.

The tip of the whip touched Daniel's chest before snapping back. "Oh yes," Jaime whispered. A very nice hunk.

The phone was ringing. Kelly struggled to open her apartment door. Not bothering to turn on a light, she stumbled through a maze of unpacked boxes and cartons as she dashed for the phone.

"Hello?" she breathlessly asked, leaning against the counter separating the kitchen and dining area. She tossed down her keys and ran her fingers through her hair. "Hello?"

"Hey, did you lose my number?"

The voice was familiar but she couldn't place it. Whom did it belong to? "Who is this?"

"What!" the voice exclaimed. "Don't tell me you've already forgotten. I don't believe it! It's Graham . . . Graham Denning."

Graham Denning! He was calling her! Instantly, Kelly felt the same warm rush she had felt on the plane. "How could anyone forget you?"

"Apparently you have." He pretended to sound hurt. "I haven't heard from you since the day we met. Are you giving me the brush-off? Don't you like me? I kinda like you, pretty lady."

Kelly faltered. He liked her! Well, *kinda*. And he'd called her pretty lady! "I've been busy," she apologized. "Moving. Working. I lost your number and didn't have a chance to try and find it. Where are you calling from?"

"New York."

"New York?" Kelly quickly calculated the time difference. "It's three A.M. out there. Why are you calling me at three A.M.?"

"I could say your lovely face haunts my every moment, making it impossible for me to sleep, but I'd be lying."

Kelly giggled. "So why are you calling?"

"I was too wound up to sleep. My agent called tonight. Looks like I'll be coming back out to the coast in a month once this play wraps. There might be a part in a movie for me."

"How wonderful!"

"We'll see. I'm not holding my breath. Things have fallen through for me before. Theater, especially in New York, is what I love best."

"How'd you get my number? It's unlisted."

"Your agent owed my agent a favor. Listen, I've been taping your show."

"You have? Tell me what you think." Kelly didn't know why, but she was dying for his opinion.

"You're good, Kelly. *Really* good. You're getting better and better with each show. I can notice the difference. In the beginning you were nervous, but you're gaining more and more confidence. I'm not just saying that. You've got a lot of talent."

"Thanks," Kelly gushed, suddenly feeling happy. The exhaustion from her long day at the studio slipped away. Her acting was good! Someone was actually watching her performance on "The Yields of Passion." "Your opinion means a lot to me."

"Well, I'll still keep watching. I have to confess, the show has kind of hooked me and it's the only way I'll see you until I return."

Kelly grew excited at Graham's words. He wanted to see her when he got back!

"Is it okay if I call you again?" he asked.

Kelly grinned in the darkness, twirling the phone cord around herself. "I'd like that . . . I'd like that a lot."

Diana was drunk. A dinner party in Bel Air followed by one nightcap too many had released the bitch in her. Now she was in a mean mood and when she was in a mean mood she loved taking her frustrations out on only one person: Kelly.

Propped up in her bed, dressed in a jade negligee and surrounded by many frilled pillows, Diana aimed the remote control at the VCR, turning it on. Kelly's face then filled the screen as she declared her love for Frost Barclay. Then Frost took Kelly in his arms, lavishing her with kisses, declaring his eternal love and promising never to leave her.

"Hah!" Diana bellowed, taking a long sip from the bottle of scotch she cradled under one arm. "Ridiculous. No man would *ever* love Kelly!"

Diana never missed an episode of "The Yields of Passion." From the moment Kelly had debuted on the show, she had made sure Esmerelda taped it daily. Every night Diana settled down in bed with a bottle of scotch, watching Kelly's performance and tearing it to shreds.

"Is the network *insane?*" Diana screamed at the top of her lungs, staring with disbelief at Kelly's face on the television screen. "She can't act!"

Kelly thought she was Miss High and Mighty now that she was on TV. She never called or bothered to visit. The ungrateful little bitch!

Diana clicked off the VCR and struggled to her feet, heading for Kelly's old bedroom.

It was still a little girl's room. Diana had never allowed Kelly to change a thing. In the open doorway she stared at the pink-and-white striped walls, the plush pink carpeting, and white canopy bed covered in ruffles.

There were movie posters from Adam's films on the walls and the shelves were crammed with books, dolls, and toys.

The sight of Kelly's empty bed drove Diana wild. She felt *cheated*. Kelly didn't *need* her anymore. How she had loved tossing that in her face!

Diana ripped at the wallpaper, tearing it off in shreds. Adam's movie posters were crumpled and torn. Grabbing a pair of scissors off the white wicker desk, she hacked away at the bed. Porcelain dolls crashed to the floor, their beautiful faces cracking open before being stomped beneath Diana's feet.

Through her destruction Diana laughed and laughed. When she was finished she was breathing heavily. She surveyed her handiwork with pride, but it still wasn't enough.

She wanted to do *more*.

She still wanted to hurt Kelly.

Snatching up the pink princess phone, Diana collapsed on top of the shredded bed, dialing her daughter's number.

* * *

The ringing phone woke Kelly immediately. Blinking in the dark, she checked the time. One thirty. Surely it couldn't be Graham again?

Kelly turned on a light and picked up the phone. "Hello?"

Diana's voice, harsh and abrasive, blasted through. "Kelly, *darling*, it's your mother. I hope I'm not disturbing anything." There was an ugly laugh. "Hah! Listen to me. What am I saying? You're probably alone in bed wearing a flannel nightie. Like always!"

Kelly almost dropped the phone. It had been years since she'd been the victim of one of her mother's night rages. Often there had been times when Diana would come home drunk and vent her hostilities out on Kelly, shaking her awake from her sleep and making her do the most bizarre tasks.

There had been the time when she was ten and had to drain the pool at three o'clock in the morning, scrubbing every inch of it with Comet. Then when she was twelve she'd had to clean out all sixteen closets in their house. Another time she'd had to strip away the wallpaper in their dining room and whitewash the walls. And on one occasion she'd had to take out of the pantry every jar of preserves that their cook had spent a month making, empty the jars and then wash each and every jar by hand.

There had been one hundred jars.

Always she had been petrified by Diana's anger. This time was no exception.

"What man would ever want *you*, Kelly? Even though you've grown into a beautiful woman, you're still an ugly duckling. You're lacking what I've *always* had. Polish, style, sophistication and breeding! My parents were descended from English royalty, but *your* father was the son of a coal miner. I know which side of the family you took after. Those inbred genes wave off you like a scarlet flag. Why I ever married him, I don't know. He was never good enough for me."

"I'm not going to listen to this!" Kelly shouted. "I'm not going to listen to you slander Daddy. I'm hanging up."

Adam Stoddard was all Kelly had left. In her mind he was a valiant prince who would have made her life a fairytale if he hadn't died. Life with Diana wouldn't have been as ugly as it had been because Daddy would have protected her and Daddy wouldn't have let her down.

"Don't you *dare* hang up on me!" Diana screeched. "Always ready to come to his defense, aren't you? And just because you're an *actress*, you think you're something special. Well, you're not!

I'm still this town's queen. I'm still the best and if I wanted to I could destroy your *career* with the snap of my fingers."

"Try it, Mother. Just try it." Kelly was sick of playing the victim, sick of always being the object of her mother's fury. She was tired of making excuses for Diana's behavior. It was time she stood up for herself and fought back. Let's see how much her mother liked getting it. "Your power in this town is zero. It's all gone. No one respects you anymore. They pity you!"

"Don't you dare talk to me that way!" Diana raged. "Do you know how much you cost me? Do you? I lost *everything* because of you! *Everything!* My husband, my career, my Oscar. I was supposed to be the star of *Banquet. Me.* But when I found out I was pregnant I had to drop out of the picture. Filming couldn't wait and so they replaced me with Iris Larson. From day one that tramp was determined to seduce Adam.

"Because of my pregnancy we couldn't have sex. The doctor warned against it. Your father had a voracious sexual appetite. At first he was able to handle it, but by my fourth month he was climbing up the walls. He tried coaxing me into his bed, but I was adamant in my refusals. When it came to sex, your father was a weak man. When he arrived on location Iris was waiting and she didn't waste any time making her move. I heard all the stories about what went on during filming. Somehow all the stories made their way back to me. Iris made sure of that.

"*I lost everything because of you!*" Diana screamed. "You were the biggest mistake of my life and whenever I look at you I remember the misery and anguish I went through. I *hate* you!"

Kelly held the phone away from her ear. "I'm hanging up now, Mother," she stated quietly. "I don't have to listen to any more of this." Kelly had heard this story too many times over the years, always when Diana was drunk.

"Why not?" Diana spat out. "What else have you got to do? There's no man in your bed to satisfy you. Hell, you wouldn't even know how to satisfy a man. Take a good look in the mirror, honey. You've got new hair, new clothes, new makeup. So what? You're still alone. You don't have a man and you'll never have one. Never!"

Kelly held back her tears. "You're wrong, Mother."

"Who do you think you're kidding?" Diana sneered. "No man would go for a wallflower like you. Get real! You're not Melissa Duke, the character you play. You're Kelly Stoddard and no one will ever love you."

"Want to bet on that, Mother?" Kelly's voice was one of hardened steel.

"You're on."

"Prepare to lose, Mother." With that Kelly slammed down the phone, burying her head in her pillow as a stream of tears traveled down her cheeks. "Prepare to lose."

Laura awoke with a scream, kicking away her sheets and scrambling to turn on a light as Grace came running into the living room.

"Laura, what's wrong? Are you okay? That scream jerked me awake."

"It was just a nightmare. Only a nightmare," Laura assured with what she hoped was a brave smile. She looked around the now-lit living room, taking comfort in the warm light as the image of Nico, vivid only seconds before, now faded.

"Some nightmare. You're trembling. Want to talk about it?"

Laura rubbed her hands up and down her arms, pretending to warm herself. "I'm not trembling; I'm shivering. Can you turn down the air conditioning?"

"Sure," Grace said, stifling a yawn. "Want me to stay with you?"

Laura shook her head. "I'm fine, really. I think I'll watch some TV for a while." She reached for the remote control and turned on the set. Canned laughter from an old episode of "I Love Lucy" blasted forth. "Sorry if I woke you. I was just spooked. You know how dreams can be."

"Well, if you say everything is fine I'm going to head back to my bedroom. If you need me, give a holler, okay?"

After Grace left Laura clutched her pillow tightly to her chest as she allowed herself to tremble. Deep, long shudders racked her body and brought tears to her eyes as she remembered every last detail of her dream with Nico. There was no forgetting the look of sick violence that had gleamed in his eyes the entire time.

"No," Laura whispered with determination, wiping away her tears and pushing away the image of Nico. "No. You're never going to hurt me again. I won't let you. *I won't let you!*"

* * *

Gabrielle was a heavy sleeper. Next to sex there was nothing she loved more. It took twenty-five rings before the phone woke her up.

Opening her eyes, she saw the right side of the bed was empty. No Harrison. She fleetingly wondered where he was, then realized she really didn't care. She snatched up the phone.

"Yes?" she asked somewhat sleepily.

There came the sound of deep breathing. Inhale. Exhale. Inhale. Exhale. Perfectly paced. Nothing else.

"Who is this?" Gabrielle asked in the surliest tone she could muster, now fully awake and trying to ignore the wisp of fear swirling in her stomach. "I'm trying to sleep."

"It's *me*, Gabrielle, your biggest fan," a voice hissed. "I've waited *so* long for this moment. I've been waiting and waiting."

"Is this some sick joke?"

"Did you like the roses?"

"I don't want your roses. I don't want anything from you. Just leave me alone."

"But why? I love you, Gabrielle. In the weeks to come I'm going to show you just how much."

"What do you mean?" She turned on a bedside lamp to illuminate the dark bedroom.

"Can't spoil the surprise, but you'll *love* it."

Gabrielle's sleepy mind scrambled for something to say, something that would make this guy leave her alone. "Look, I'm flattered by all your attention, but I'm a married woman."

"Harrison is a small inconvenience. I can take care of him. By the way, I love your negligee. Red is definitely your color."

Gabrielle gasped. He knew her phone number! He knew the color of the negligee she was wearing! What else could he possibly know?

"Is it lonely being all alone in bed? I could come over if you want. Just say the word."

Gabrielle shrieked, dropping the phone and turning off the light. She ran to the windows, closing the drapes. Then she locked the bedroom door and ran back into bed, huddling beneath the covers.

From the fallen phone a soft and silky voice continued to hiss.

"Soon, Gabrielle. *Soon.* Soon we'll be together. *Forever.*"

CHAPTER TEN

HARRISON TRAILED an ice cube along Grace's naked body, leaving behind a shimmering wet path. He started at the middle of her forehead, moving down to the tip of her nose. Then he outlined her lips, top to bottom, before moving to her chin and down the curve of her neck. Between her breasts he allowed the ice cube to melt a bit. Then he removed it and circled the nipples of each breast. Next he allowed the ice cube to travel down her stomach, pressing down on her navel before ending at the moist center between her legs.

With his tongue, Harrison dried the path he had outlined. When he came to the center of her breasts, he allowed his tongue to suck heavily at the wet flesh. Then he focused on her erect nipples, rolling them around his tongue before continuing downward. Arriving at the center of her spread legs, Harrison pushed his tongue in as far as it would go.

Grace arched her lower body, twisting her fingers through Harrison's hair as she pushed his face downward, wanting his tongue to probe as far as possible, yet delaying his moment of entry.

Grace's hands impatiently tore at the thin straps of silk covering Harrison's erection. When he was freed she grasped his thick shaft in her hand, caressing the burning heat of his stretched flesh, guiding him toward her center.

When the tip of Harrison's erection inched forward, Grace sprang up, locking her legs around his waist.

"Go deep," she urged, rubbing against Harrison's body. "Go as deep as you can."

The sun beat down on them, adding to the sweat already beading on their bodies, generated by the burning desire within them and the steam bubbling from the water of Harrison's hot tub.

Harrison and Grace twisted and turned, their slick bodies becoming more and more frenzied as their passion mounted and peaked.

"No one satisfies me the way you do," Grace confessed, wiping away wet strands of hair from Harrison's forehead.

He gave her a kiss before jumping into the hot tub. "Aaah," he moaned, relishing the soothing jet spray. "This is almost as good as a session with you."

Grace propped herself on an elbow, an amused look on her face as she reached for a nearby platter of fruit, removing a plump, dark purple cherry. She bit into the moist piece of lush sweetness, squirting the cherry's rich liquid over her lips. "Almost?" she teased. Her tongue darted out of her mouth, licking at the juice.

"*Almost*," Harrison softly affirmed. "Come on in."

"Soon." Grace reached for another cherry, devouring it with tiny, sensuous bites. "How are things with Gabrielle?"

Harrison's eyes watched Grace's mouth. "The same. She's busy worrying about Mark Bauer's screen test."

"I can't believe she's quitting her soap," Grace scornfully remarked. "There's no way Mark Bauer would cast a hack like her."

"I love the way you have with words. Another reason why I think she's leaving the show is because of that fan. He's really thrown a scare into her."

"I never thought I'd see the day when Gabrielle would be hiding from attention. She's been maintaining a really low profile."

"Has she gotten any more gifts from him?"

"The roses have stopped coming and she told me there haven't been any more phone calls. It was probably some harmless nut. What did the police say?"

"Told her to remain alert at all times. Try not to go anywhere alone. The usual. If Paul hadn't returned to Las Vegas, she probably would have gone running to him. Whoever it was gets a vote of thanks from me. He knows how to put Gabrielle in her place. Living with her has been smooth as silk and she hasn't been bugging me about my writing." Harrison lounged in the water. "Leaving me time for the finer things."

Grace knelt at the edge of the hot tub. In one hand there were a handful of cherries. She crooked a finger at Harrison, urging him to come over.

Harrison looked at her slyly. "What do you plan on doing with those?"

Grace took Harrison's face in one hand. With the other she

started squeezing the cherries, dribbling the juice over his lips. She then placed her lips upon Harrison's, sucking them clean. "How *is* your writing coming? Tell me about your new screenplay."

"It's progressing. I've got about thirty pages." He reached for Grace but she pulled herself away.

"How soon can I see it?"

"Not yet. It's very rough." Harrison stretched an arm out to Grace, but she ignored it. Instead, she reached for another handful of cherries, squeezing them over her nipples before returning to Harrison. She allowed his tongue to lick at both. When the juice was all gone Grace pulled herself away from Harrison again, inching back out of his reach.

"Don't keep me waiting, Harrison. I don't like waiting. I'm a very impatient girl."

She walked around the rim of the hot tub, Harrison's hungry eyes following. Then she threw herself into his arms, wrapping her arms tightly around his neck as he entered her.

Grace gasped, mounting Harrison and meeting his thrusts. "Don't disappoint me, Harrison. I know you can do it. You just have to want it badly enough. I'll do whatever I can to help you. You do know that, don't you?"

"Don't worry. Pretty soon we're going to be on top," he vowed, a new tone of determination in his voice. "Trust me."

Mark watched Gabrielle's image on the movie screen, cupping his head in both hands. She was awful.

Mark was sitting in a private film theater on the Trinity Pictures lot. Unwinding before him was Gabrielle's screen test for *Long Journey Home*.

When it came to his films, Mark became an obsessed man. All the pieces had to fit. Precisely. There could be no substitutes. No compromises. Ever.

Mark relied a lot on his instincts. Drew Stern was going to be fantastic as Matt Thomas. Mark had long admired Drew's talent, and playing Matt would help Drew grow up, so to speak, in the eyes of the critics and make him accessible to a larger audience. Diana Halloway was going to be murder to work with—her fits and tantrums were notorious, as legendary as she was—but Mark thrived on challenge. What he'd needed for Ellen Thomas was a woman whose beauty had faded after a hard life. Ellen had to be bitter, left only with her memories of a time that was no more—a time when she had had it all—and Diana fit the bill perfectly.

If everything worked out, Daniel Ellis would be playing Eric Thomas. Eric was a broken man, a dreamer who had never achieved a dream, but thought there was still time—that he'd have a second chance through his sons.

The search for an actor to play Patrick Thomas, Matt's younger brother, was wrapping up. Mark had his eye on several up-and-coming actors.

That only left one major role to be cast: Olivia.

The character of Olivia Thomas was innocent, vulnerable, sensual, and determined. She evolved from an adoring wife married straight out of high school to her childhood sweetheart to a bewildered widow at the age of twenty-one, falling in love with her brother-in-law and later marrying him. Then, when her husband returns from Vietnam, not dead as presumed, she pits brother against brother with shattering results.

Mark turned off the projector, flicking on the lights. He rubbed at his tired eyes.

Gabrielle was all wrong for the part. She was too sexy—too alluring. True, her screen test had turned out better than he had expected. And maybe one day he'd be able to use her in something, just to keep Paul Fontana happy, but she was all wrong for *Long Journey Home*.

Heather slowly lowered her sunglasses down the bridge of her nose, her eyes widening with surprise. She couldn't believe what she was seeing. Peter Fontana was cruising!

Heather gripped the steering wheel of her parked Mercedes in excitement, slumping down so she wouldn't be seen. For most of the afternoon she had trailed Peter from one end of Hollywood to another, keeping a respectable distance between their cars. All she had wanted was a chance to talk with him again . . . to plead her case and gain an audience with Mark Bauer.

Yet she hadn't been able to talk to Peter. In each store he had visited he had been extremely impatient with the salespeople and Heather had kept her distance. Talking with him now wouldn't get her anywhere.

After the last of Peter's purchases were made at the Irvine Ranch Market, a gourmet grocery in the Beverly Center, Heather decided to follow him home. After finding out where he lived, she might just return in something slinky . . . with a bottle of champagne. Though this wasn't usually her style, she was getting desperate. And desperate times called for desperate measures.

Peter's apartment building in Westwood left Heather gasping. The place was too expensive for someone who was only an assistant. Could there be more to this? Maybe he was being kept by a Hollywood wife who was married to an older, less exciting guy. Maybe Peter would want that kept quiet.

Strumming her red nails along the dashboard, Heather decided to stick around for a while.

Fifteen minutes later Peter reemerged. His image shocked Heather. Gone was his entire preppy look—no khakis, tasseled loafers, or Ralph Lauren polo shirt. Instead he was wearing skin-tight black jeans, and a sky blue tank top showed off his well-proportioned chest and arms. A gold chain was around his neck and a gold stud earring was in his left ear. His straight ash blond hair had been moussed and spiked.

Peter looked *hot* . . . and ready for action. Could he be . . . ? The thought had never entered her mind and Peter had hardly advertised the fact. Did that mean he was just a private person or, if he *was* a homosexual, was he trying to hide that fact? But why?

Knowing she was on to *something*, Heather had started her car, following Peter right into the heart of West Hollywood's gay district, trailing behind him on foot after he parked his car.

There was no mistaking the eye contact Peter was making as he assessed the other males he passed. It was only a matter of time before he scored.

Deciding she had seen enough, Heather returned to her Mercedes and headed back for her condo in Hollywood Hills, wheels spinning in her head. Obviously she'd hit pay dirt and had only scratched the surface of things. There was more to the situation. *Much* more. She could feel it. Why else would Peter be leading a double life? But how could she find the answers? How could she use the information to her advantage and get Peter to help her to the chance she felt she deserved? She desperately wanted the role of Olivia Thomas. She *knew* she could do it. All she wanted was a chance to prove herself. But playing *nice* wasn't getting her anywhere.

Heather thought long and hard, not knowing what her next step should be. Then she picked up her car phone and dialed her agent's number.

"Jinxie, it's Heather. I need some advice, along with a little bit of help."

"I really appreciate you setting up this interview," Laura said.

Grace waved a hand. "No problem. I heard Kelly Stoddard was looking for an assistant and thought you might be interested." Grace knocked on Kelly's dressing room door. "Take it from me, there's nothing to it."

"Come in," a voice called.

Kelly smiled warmly as Laura and Grace entered. After making introductions, Grace excused herself, leaving Kelly and Laura alone.

"Would you care for a drink? Mineral water? Juice?"

Laura politely declined. "I'm fine."

Kelly gave Laura a warm smile. "Okay, then let's get started. Basically what I'm looking for is someone who's organized. I started on the show two months ago and already I'm swamped." Kelly gestured at the tons of fan mail. "All of this has to be answered. Then there are interviews to be set up, lunches, award shows to attend." Kelly rolled her eyes heavenward. "There's more to being on a soap than they tell you."

Grace had already told Laura the starting salary, which Laura thought was more than fair. And Kelly seemed nice. Working for her wouldn't be a hardship.

"Think you could handle it?" Kelly asked, prodding Laura from her thoughts.

"Sure!" Laura eagerly answered. "Does this mean the job is mine?"

"Only if you want it."

"Then you've got yourself an assistant!"

"Great! When can you start?"

"How about tomorrow?"

"Fabulous."

"What time should I show up?"

As Kelly was about to answer, her phone rang. "Excuse me for one moment." She picked up. "Kelly Stoddard speaking."

"Hey, beautiful, it's your one and only."

"Graham! Hold on a minute." Eyes sparkling and cheeks flushed, Kelly turned back to Laura. "How does nine sound?"

"Perfect." Laura started on her way out. "See you tomorrow."

Kelly's head bobbed enthusiastically. Daily phone calls had become a part of her and Graham's lives. They spoke to each other at least once a day, sometimes twice, giving each other updates on what was going on in their world.

Graham's phone calls were the highlight of Kelly's day, especially when he called at night. After being surrounded by people all day she hated returning to the emptiness of her apartment. It left her with a cold, lonely feeling.

Although she had been getting her fair share of invitations, Kelly really wasn't into the party scene. And she hadn't heard from Diana since her phone call. Kelly refused to make the first move. Her mother owed her an apology and this time she wasn't budging until she got one.

Graham was the only steady thing in her life besides her work. The sound of his voice always warmed her and she couldn't wait to see him again. With each passing day she was coming to depend on Graham more and more. She was making him a part of her world—a part of her life. She realized she was falling in love with him and it was the most wonderful feeling imaginable.

"I miss you," Kelly confessed. "I can't wait till you come back out here."

"I know how to fix that," Graham mysteriously alluded. "Interested in hearing how?"

"I'm listening."

"I don't have to work this weekend. How about flying out here? We'll have a blast."

Kelly was silent for a moment as her insides churned with excitement. A weekend in New York with Graham! How could she say no? Three whole days together—sharing time, learning about each other and becoming closer. And if she went to New York there was a strong possibility she and Graham would make love. To be able to share such an intimate act as lovemaking with Graham would bring her even closer to him. She couldn't deny that the thought was appealing and one which she'd been thinking a lot about lately. And she so wanted to see Graham . . . to have his arms around her . . . to have his lips brushing over hers . . . to be able to have him look into her eyes and see the growing love she had for him. Hopefully, when she looked into his eyes, she'd see that same love.

"A weekend in New York sounds fantastic!" Kelly agreed without hesitation.

CHAPTER ELEVEN

After meeting with Kelly, Laura decided to go down to Rodeo Drive. She was feeling wildly impulsive, so why not splurge on herself? Not only did she have a job and a place to live (through a friend of Grace's she was subletting a house in Coldwater Canyon from a female director who was spending the year in Europe), but it looked like the pieces of her new life in California were falling nicely into place.

Laura spent an hour going from shop to shop. The cold reality of the exorbitant prices quickly brought her back to her senses. So much for her wild impulsiveness.

Strolling down South Robertson Boulevard, Laura passed an outdoor cafe called Michel Richard. There were a number of pink clothed tables with fresh floral arrangements, shaded by striped umbrellas. The look of the place said money. Stopping to examine the menu posted, Laura saw she was right. The prices were just as outrageous here as they'd been in the stores she'd visited.

Looking up, Laura was surprised to find a man staring at her. Seated at a nearby table, his dark sunglasses fixated on her, he toasted her with a glass of white wine.

Suddenly Laura's heart started pounding. It was *him* . . . her hunk from the beach!

Laura sent him a smile, but didn't move, intrigued to see what would happen next.

He returned her smile, revealing a dazzling one of his own. He gestured for her to come over.

"Me?" she mouthed, pointing to herself while looking around, as though he meant someone else.

He laughed, nodding vigorously.

Laura was already weaving her way through the tables.

* * *

Drew couldn't believe it. She was coming over. His girl from the beach was coming over!

He took off his sunglasses and stood up, ready to draw out a chair for her.

It was then, as he stepped out from beneath the shade of the umbrella, that a fan from the street recognized him.

"Look!" she shrieked to her female companions. "It's Drew Stern!"

Suddenly there was a group of overexcited females forming, heading in his direction. Drew, not wanting to get caught in the middle of it, threw down a few bills and hurried off to his car.

He glanced over his shoulder with a look of regret as Laura reached his empty table.

Laura stood still with an open mouth at the abandoned table, unable to believe what she was seeing and hearing. That had been *Drew Stern. The* Drew Stern. Twice their paths had crossed and twice they hadn't been able to introduce themselves.

Laura traced a finger around the rim of his wine glass. What were the chances of their ever meeting again?

She released a sigh. Slim. Very slim.

Gabrielle, clad in a red leather double-breasted blazer with gold buttons and a red leather mini-skirt, made an imperial entrance into her agent's office. Tossing back her mane of raven curls, she gave Mitzi Carson a calculating look.

"Let me get this straight," Gabrielle repeated, after having rushed over from the studio. "They want me to stay on the show? I thought they couldn't wait to see me go."

"The Serena/Chet/Melissa triangle is hot. The show's ratings are going through the roof. The producers don't want to lose you."

"What are they offering?"

"What does it matter?" Mitzi gave Gabrielle a shrewd look. For twenty-five years she had been Hollywood's top agent and when it came to money for her clients, she was like a shark in blood-filled waters. "They want you, so they'll pay. I'll make sure of that."

"What did you ask for?"

Mitzi demurely patted her frosted coiffure. Putting on her Matsuda eyeglasses, she skimmed through her notes. "A thirty percent pay hike, three months vacation, plus time off to do at least two outside projects a year should they arise."

"Sounds good," Gabrielle affirmed. She might as well take the money and run. Who knew what was going to happen with Mark Bauer? "Keep me posted."

"Things should be wrapping up pretty quickly. They're anxious to keep you. So tell me, how are things going with Mark Bauer?"

"They're not," Gabrielle snapped, irritated at the mention of his name. "I read for him and did a screen test. That's it. I haven't heard from him since."

"Gabrielle," Mitzi scolded, "you sound like you've given up. I think Mark just needs a little time in reaching his decision."

"He's got Daddy in his corner," Gabrielle pouted. "There aren't any other strings I can pull."

"Oh, yes, there are," Mitzi confidently stated. "And this you can handle on your own." Mitzi flipped through her Rolodex. After finding the card she needed, she handed it over to Gabrielle. "Take this," she instructed, holding it out.

"What is it?"

"Mark Bauer's home address." Mitzi gave Gabrielle a pointed look. "I think you'll find some use for it. Wouldn't you agree that a *private* audition might be more beneficial? After all, Gabrielle, you are a girl of *considerable* talents."

Gabrielle, knowing Mitzi was a firm believer of the casting-couch system, took the hint. "Does he have any preferences?"

"Just do what you do best."

Gabrielle got to her feet, slipping the card into her lizard-skin clutch. "No problem."

Kelly wanted to look spectacular for Graham, which was why she was buying up a storm at Neiman-Marcus. Later in the day she'd head over to Sassoon to get her hair done and to Elizabeth Arden for a facial. She wanted to look stunning when she stepped off the plane.

Kelly had just stepped out of a dressing room with a gold silk organza dress by Donna Karan and a gathered red jersey by Isaac Mizrahi that she was intending to purchase when Diana emerged from another dressing room.

"Kelly, darling," Diana warmly greeted. "Where have you been keeping yourself? We haven't spoken in ages. That show must be running you ragged."

"Hello, Mother," Kelly stiffly answered. "You're looking marvelous, as always."

"What have I done *now?*" Diana huffed with exasperation as she admired herself in a full-length mirror, shooing away a hovering sales clerk. "Honestly, Kelly, you're always in a snit."

"You know what you've done," Kelly hissed under her breath, not wanting to cause a scene.

Diana gave Kelly a blank look. "I have no idea what you're talking about."

It looked as if Diana meant what she was saying, but Kelly wasn't going to let this slide. "Mother, I am not a child anymore. You cannot bully me. I won't allow it. Either we have a relationship or we don't. The decision is yours."

"My God, Kelly! You make it sound like I don't love you . . . like I don't give a damn about you." Diana gave a hollow laugh and Kelly squirmed under her mother's intense gaze. They were on thin ice, skirting the truth as they had for so many years.

And what was the truth? Kelly honestly didn't know. It seemed with each passing year her mother's love for her grew less and less. The most frustrating thing of all was that she didn't know why! What had she done that was so terrible? Why was her mother's heart closed to her? Hers wasn't. She loved her mother so much, but for some reason her mother didn't want her love. It was as though she were pushing her away. As if she didn't want to love her own daughter.

"Do you want me in your life, Mother?" Kelly asked point-blank. "If you don't I'll be happy to oblige."

"Kelly!" Diana was shocked. "Of course I want you in my life. Darling, whatever it is I've done, I'm sorry." She whirled before Kelly in a strapless chiffon gown with a two-tone bodice designed by Bob Mackie. "What do you think? I may buy it to wear to Mark Bauer's party."

"It's lovely."

Diana glanced at the pile of outfits draped over Kelly's arm. "What brings you shopping? I never thought you were a clothes horse."

Kelly decided to drop the issue of the phone call. Diana had apologized as though she had no recollection of the incident. She *had* been awfully drunk. "I'm going to New York this weekend."

"How nice." Diana fussed with her hair. "Visiting old friends? Your friend Jill?"

"No, Jill's in Europe. A new friend. Someone I've recently met," she revealed, eager to confide in her mother.

"Sounds like a man." Diana gave a vacant smile before holding up two gowns. One was a Geoffrey Beene black crepe with quilted silver spirals. The other was a Karl Lagerfeld red chiffon. "What do you think of these?"

Kelly ignored the question. "It *is* a man."

"Wonderful," Diana said absently. "Tell me, does the red make me look too old?"

Kelly bit her lip. It was obvious her mother was interested only in herself. As always. She stifled a sigh. When would she ever learn? Kelly decided she wasn't going to volunteer any more information about Graham. If her mother wanted to learn more, she'd have to ask on her own.

"Both gowns are stunning, Mother."

"You're right," Diana agreed. "I'll take them both." She handed the gowns to the sales clerk before heading in the direction of the dressing room. Then she whirled around at Kelly. "Don't let me keep you. I'm going to be here awhile." She blew her daughter a kiss. "Let's do lunch next week. I'll call. Promise."

Mark's head was throbbing. All he wanted was two aspirins, a cold shower, and a nice long sleep.

He'd had one hell of an afternoon. First there'd been a meeting with the budgeter he'd hired for *Long Journey Home*. The two had spent the last three hours going over above-the-line and below-the-line costs. It looked like it would be costing twenty-five million for the picture to be made, possibly reaching thirty in the event of delays and unforeseen circumstances. And then there'd be another five million for advertising and publicity once the picture was released. Looking over the figures, Mark had released a sigh of relief. The numbers gave him plenty of breathing space. Hell, he'd probably even bring the picture in under budget.

Then Jinxie Bishop had called. Diana Halloway wanted more stature given to her participation in the film. Not only did she want a box drawn around her name in the title credits, but she also wanted the phrase, "and starring Diana Halloway as Ellen Thomas" added. She also wanted a first-class Winnebago dressing room in Nebraska and approval over all publicity photographs distributed to the press.

Mark, in a moment of weakness, had agreed to the Winnebago and photograph approval but not the drawn box, cutting Jinxie off as he was preparing to announce an additional list of demands.

Walking through his beach house to the bedroom, he stripped, tossing pieces of his clothing left and right. When he opened his bedroom door, he was naked.

As naked as Gabrielle Fontana Moore, who was lounging on top of his bed.

"At last!" she purred in a seductive whisper, turning on her side as she stretched out. "I was beginning to wonder when you'd show up."

Mark's headache was forgotten as he drank in Gabrielle's lush figure. "What are you doing here?" he managed to ask in amazement.

Despite himself, Mark was becoming aroused. There wasn't much he could do to hide that fact except by cupping his hands over his crotch. It didn't help to hide his growing erection.

"Don't be shy!" she laughed. "I've been waiting for you. It's been so lonely and boring. For hours all I've been doing is thinking of you." She ran a hand along the back of her neck, fluffing her raven tresses out around her shoulders. She gave Mark a hungry look. "Aren't you going to join me?"

"No!" he stated angrily.

Mark's eyes searched the bedroom for Gabrielle's clothes so he could toss them to her but he didn't see them anywhere. Grabbing a terrycloth robe from behind the bedroom door, he shrugged into it.

"Party pooper," she pouted, pursing her lips. "I liked what I was seeing." She arched her body upwards, flaunting her breasts. She cupped one, holding it out to Mark. "Do *you* like what you're seeing?"

Mark tore away his eyes. "Gabrielle, I want you to go." He held open the bedroom door, refusing to look at her.

"But I don't want to. I've waited so-o-o long for you," she whispered forlornly.

"I know what you're up to and it isn't going to work."

Uncurling herself from the bed, Gabrielle got to her feet, stretching before Mark. She padded over to him, a seductive smile twitching on her lips. "What am I up to?"

"You want the role of Olivia and you think you'll get it by sleeping with me."

Gabrielle batted her lush eyelashes. "How can you say such a thing?" she innocently asked. "I think that's insulting. I'm attracted to you, Mark." She reached into the opening in the front of his robe, seizing his erection. "Aren't you attracted to me?" Her grip was one of both firmness and caressing softness as she led him back to the bed.

"I'm good," she whispered. "*Very* good."

She sat down on the bed, spreading her legs as she pulled Mark onto her lap and into her. Locking her legs around him, she started rocking.

Mark couldn't control himself. It had been so long since he'd had a woman and when he became involved in a new project sex was the farthest thing from his mind. Yet here was Gabrielle giving him what he had denied himself for too long.

But this was madness! Was he crazy? He had to be out of his mind! Paul Fontana had him under his thumb and there was no doubt in his mind that Gabrielle was using sex to manipulate him. Did he really need to be under her thumb, too?

The sight and smell of her drove him to a state of maddened indulgence. God, how he wanted her! She was a slab of forbidden richness oozing with primal desire. Had it ever been this good before? He rocked deeper into her, winding his fingers through her hair, pulling back her head and exposing her neck as he bit into it, sucking with his tongue. Mark hurried his thrusts, eager to reach the pinnacle of the rushing climax he was riding and reaching a decision. He wouldn't let her control him. Though he had succumbed to Gabrielle's advances this one time, he wouldn't let it happen again. He couldn't. The danger of the situation was too great. Any involvement with Gabrielle Fontana would be lethal.

Gabrielle relished her victory. Her mouth found Mark's and she took his lips with a consuming ferocity. Fueled not by passion but determination, Gabrielle drained Mark of all resistance. How he wanted her! There was no stopping him. She hardly had to do anything. Good. After tonight he'd be unable to resist her advances, and anything she wanted would be hers.

Anything.

CHAPTER TWELVE

KELLY SEARCHED the faces milling about, hunting for Graham. Then, through the crowd of travelers swarming in and out of JFK, she saw him and started waving. A smile easily spread across her face at the sight of him.

"Kelly!" he shouted, weaving through the people. He threw his arms around her, giving her a hug as he lifted her off her feet, whirling her around.

Kelly gasped, then laughed as she held onto him. "Such enthusiasm!"

"Can you blame me? For weeks you've only been a voice on the phone."

"Don't tell me your memory is going," Kelly teased, looking down at him with a smile.

"I've missed you." Graham brought his lips to Kelly's, placing a tentative kiss, as though unsure whether he should. But Kelly's lips responded to Graham's, easily yielding . . . hoping for more. Graham gave her another kiss, then put Kelly down, taking a step back and caressing a cheek. "I'd never forget a face as beautiful as yours."

Kelly blushed, unsure if it was because of the compliment or the way she'd responded to his kiss. "Why don't we get my luggage? We've only got seventy-two hours. Let's not waste them standing around here."

Graham grinned, snaking an arm around Kelly's waist and drawing her close. "Let's go," he said, leading the way.

Kelly, enjoying the feel of being nestled so close to Graham, kept up with his pace.

* * *

Graham wouldn't hear of Kelly staying at a hotel. Since he was apartment sitting a duplex on West-Seventy-fifth, he offered Kelly the use of a guest room.

"Of course, you could share the master bedroom with me," he ventured to say as he carried in Kelly's luggage. "If you wanted," he hastily amended.

Why had he said such a thing? Graham berated himself. He wanted everything to go perfectly this weekend. He didn't want to spoil anything. Kelly was so unlike Diana. She wasn't vain and self-centered. She was warm . . . generous . . . loving. Graham had never been one to believe in love at first sight, but Kelly was putting ideas in his head.

Kelly mustered a coy smile, determined to hide her pleasure and excitement. "We'll see. For now the guest room is fine. Maybe I'll change my mind later."

Kelly wanted some time alone with Graham first. She wasn't going to jump right into bed with him. She wanted to become comfortable being around him and gradually lead up to things.

Maybe she was a romantic, but Kelly couldn't help the way she felt. She wanted some sort of level of intimacy before taking such a giant step. After all, she and Graham were on the verge of building a relationship. Their phone calls had built a foundation, but this weekend would cement their efforts.

Remembering the way Graham had made her feel at the airport . . . anticipating . . . longing . . . desirable . . . made Kelly want to explore those feelings some more. To do so, they'd have to start their weekend.

"Why don't we see the sights?" she suggested brightly. "I can unpack later."

They spent the rest of the day traipsing from one end of Manhattan to the other. There was a carriage ride through Central Park; a trip down to the Village where they made a stop at the Actor's Playhouse where Graham was performing. The theater was darkened and deserted. Graham led Kelly to a front-row seat. Then he jumped up on the stage and started reciting some of his lines, as though performing in front of a full house. Kelly was enraptured and when he had finished, she jumped to her feet, clapping wildly. Their next stop was a trek through the Museum of Modern Art. That night they saw *Phantom of the Opera* and topped off their evening with dinner at Tavern on the Green.

During the entire day, Kelly and Graham were comfortable with each other, enjoying being together. They were constantly talking or pointing things out to one another, and as if by mutual consent, their hands remained locked together as veiled looks were exchanged, promising revelations when darkness arrived.

Graham and Kelly returned to the duplex at midnight. As Kelly stepped out of her satin pumps, Graham locked the duplex's door.

Kelly collapsed on the couch, wiggling her toes. "My feet are killing me from all that walking we did today."

Graham knelt before her, taking a black-stockinged foot in his hand, massaging it. "How does this feel?"

"Heavenly."

Graham's hand moved along Kelly's lower leg. "And this?"

"Wonderful."

Kelly's legs widened and provided space for Graham, allowing him access as he moved in closer. "Should I go higher?" he asked, a hand resting on her knee.

"Yes," Kelly whispered, her throat dry. "Yes."

"Are you sure?"

Kelly nodded. She wanted to feel Graham's touch move up her body . . . stroking her most sensitive areas . . . bringing her the satisfaction she so wanted.

Graham's hand moved to her thigh and rested at the catches of her garter belt. He undid the snaps on one leg, unrolling the thin wisp of black silk in one fluid motion before moving to the other leg. When they were removed he unzipped the back of her black organza evening gown.

Kelly knew she was on the brink of something she had never before experienced and she savored it. This would be her first time making love. She had always kept her distance from the opposite sex . . . staying aloof . . . pretending disinterest . . . ignoring the yearnings stirring inside her . . . not wanting to take a chance.

All because her mother said no man would ever desire her.

Verbal attacks from Diana had always been a part of Kelly's life. As far back as she could remember Diana was always snapping at her, finding fault with her appearance; restricting what she could and could not wear; criticizing her efforts in school; embarrassing her in front of guests until her cheeks burned red with humiliation and her eyes brimmed with tears.

"Kelly's an introvert," Diana would say whenever introducing her to guests. "She's even afraid of her own shadow. I don't know where she gets it from. Adam and I were always the life of any party. Say boo and she jumps five feet into the air. Isn't that right, Kelly?"

Kelly, always fearing she would say the wrong thing and later invoke Diana's wrath when they were alone, would keep her eyes glued to the floor, only nodding. Then, despite wanting to stay and introduce herself . . . to prove Diana was wrong about what she said, Kelly would leave. No one took the center of attention away from Diana Halloway.

Another familiar litany:

"Stand up straight! Must you always slouch? And do *something* with your hair! Why must it always look so limp and straggly? You're a poor reflection of me, but can't you *at least* try and look your best?" Diana would always then release a mocking laugh. "Let's face it. You're no beauty. The boys are hardly going to be beating down your door, but you could at least try to make an effort to look presentable."

Because of Diana's criticisms, Kelly avoided mirrors . . . not wanting to look at herself . . . hating what she was seeing . . . seeing only what Diana could see.

Then that all changed the night of her Sweet Sixteen party.

Her party was to be held at the Beverly Wilshire. Over a hundred guests had been invited and Diana had spared no expense. Kelly suspected this was because Diana was giving the party more for herself, than for her daughter.

At six o'clock Kelly was in her bedroom, staring in dismay at the party dress her mother had selected for her to wear. It was beige with a sweetheart neckline. Kelly hated it. Just once she'd like to wear something pretty. Why were all the clothes her mother bought for her shapeless and boring and *always* beige?

She was surveying her closet for a possible alternative when there was a knock on her bedroom door.

"Who is it?"

"Are you decent?"

"Uncle Daniel!" Kelly slipped into her robe before flinging open the bedroom door. "What are you doing here?"

Under his arm was a large white box. Behind him were two strangers. Daniel led them into the bedroom.

"You're getting the star treatment. Tonight's your night to shine, honey!" He pointed to the woman. "This is Monique. She'll be doing your makeup." He pointed to the man. "Bruce will be doing your hair." Daniel gave Kelly a hug and a kiss before pressing the box he carried out to her. "This is a new dress to replace that beige rag you showed me last week. It's pretty and sexy and bursting with color."

Kelly peeked into the box. "Uncle Daniel, it's gorgeous!"

"I can't wait to see you in it. I'd better run now. If the wicked witch catches me here, I'm dead." He looked to Monique and Bruce. "You have ninety minutes till Diana gets back from the Wilshire, so don't waste a second."

They didn't. After shampooing and conditioning Kelly's hair, Bruce cut it in layers. The result, after blow drying, was a bouncy, fluffy mane.

Monique gave Kelly's pale lips the color of sun-ripened fruit; her cheekbones were warmed with peach blush; mascara and eye shadow were sparingly applied in order to highlight Kelly's cobalt blue eyes.

Neither Bruce nor Monique would allow Kelly to look at herself in a mirror. They told her to wait until she was fully dressed. After they left she slipped into the strapless jade silk party dress Daniel had brought. It fit perfectly, hugging her body in all the right places.

Holding her breath, Kelly closed her eyes and peeked out at her image in her mirror. She gasped, her eyes springing open. The effect was dazzling. Mesmerizing. She couldn't believe what she was seeing. Was that really Kelly who was looking so beautiful? *Was it?*

Kelly approached the mirror tentatively, her image growing with each step taken forward; each gesture she made perfectly imitated. It *was* her. *It was!*

Kelly's elation was only momentary, for as she was twirling before her mirror her bedroom door crashed open. Standing in the doorway, honey-blonde hair swirled in a severe upsweep to dramatically display her cheekbones, dressed in a black silk Valentino, was Diana. Daniel's words came to mind: *the wicked witch.* Kelly swallowed nervously. How right he was.

"Aren't you—"

The words died in Diana's throat and her violet eyes widened with shock and surprise. "What have you done to yourself?"

It wasn't a scream. It wasn't a shout. It was a deadly whisper. Kelly's blood chilled.

"You can't seriously expect me to let you leave the house looking like that."

Kelly admired herself in the mirror again before gathering up her courage. Then she turned to face her mother. "Why not?

What's wrong with the way I look?" she dared to ask. "I think I look nice."

"Nice? You think you look *nice?*"

Diana was on Kelly in a flash. Grabbing her by the neck, she shoved her face into the mirror, pressing it against the glass. "Take a look . . . a *good* look. You're painted up like a whore!"

"I am not!" Kelly tried to twist free of her mother, but Diana held on tight, reaching for a jar of cold cream. Unscrewing the lid, she shoved it at Kelly. "Take that stuff off your face and then get out of that dress."

"No!"

"Do it. *Now!*"

"No!" Kelly stubbornly refused. She wasn't going to change the way she looked. *She wasn't.*

"If you don't take that makeup off right this minute and change out of that dress, your party is off."

"I don't care." Kelly gave her mother a hard stare, deciding to be rebellious. "It's your money you'll be wasting. If I'm not there you'll look like a fool."

Diana's face grew red with anger. "You ungrateful little wretch!" she exploded, releasing Kelly and throwing her in the direction of her bed. Kelly skidded across the bedspread. "After all I've done for you! After all I've given you!" She dug her fingers into the cold cream and pounced on top of Kelly, pinning her down. She smeared the cream over Kelly's struggling face. Globs of cream fell down the front of Kelly's silk gown and flew into her hair. Diana retrieved the jar and kept scooping out the cream, furiously rubbing it into Kelly's face, as if wanting to tear her skin off.

"Stop!" Kelly cried, wiping at her face and coughing, trying to push Diana off her. "Stop it!"

Diana shoved Kelly off the bed and onto the floor. Kelly landed with a thud as Diana began throwing handfuls of cold cream at her sobbing daughter.

"How awful. How simply awful," Diana cooed when the jar was empty, looking down at Kelly. "You're a mess. Well, don't worry. You can change." She dropped the empty jar of cold cream beside her daughter, neatly wiping her hands together. "I'll see you downstairs."

"No, you won't," Kelly adamantly shouted, refusing to release the tears she could feel brimming in her eyes. "I'm not going!"

"Yes, you are," Diana ordered in a steely whisper from the

doorway, "otherwise I'll cut every last inch of hair off your head while you're sleeping tonight."

Kelly blinked at her mother in disbelief, but could see she was serious.

"You have fifteen minutes to make up your mind."

Kelly attended her Sweet Sixteen. When Daniel saw the way she looked, not wearing the party dress he had purchased, her hair in a listless ponytail and not a touch of makeup on her face, he was puzzled. Monique and Bruce had told him that Kelly's transformation had been breathtaking.

"Kelly, what happened? Where's my Cinderella?"

"I'm sorry, Uncle Daniel," she explained as best as she could, trying not to cry before slipping away, afraid she'd break down and tell him the whole horrid story. "It just wasn't me."

But it was. Kelly's ruined Sweet Sixteen had given her a glimpse at the person she could be . . . the person she had always been. All she'd have to do was wait till she was eighteen and off to college. After that, she'd be free.

Once at NYU, Kelly made herself over. Boys started paying attention to her, asking her out. Although liking their interest, she stuck to her studies. She was just getting used to her newfound looks. Becoming a part of the social scene would take time.

Yet she was drawn into NYU's social whirl after becoming roommates with Jill Kramer, who quickly became her best friend. Jill was the center of almost every campus event. If a party was going on, Jill found out the details and was there. With a little bit of arm twisting, so was Kelly, who began to find it easier and easier to mingle with the opposite sex. Soon she was going out on dates, sometimes seeing the same fellow more than once. But always, when things started progressing toward sex, Kelly would pull back, hearing her mother's mocking taunts:

"No man will ever be satisfied with you. You're going to be alone, Kelly. Alone! Always! Because that's what you deserve!"

Kelly shut out Diana's voice, chasing away the horrid memories. She wasn't going to spoil this moment. She wasn't! Not like she had always done before. This time there would be no turning back.

"What's wrong?" Graham asked, concern in his eyes.

Kelly quivered under his gaze, seeing how much he cared. "Just love me," she whispered, drawing him close to her. "Just love me."

* * *

Gabrielle opened her eyes to Saturday morning sunshine. And the sight of Mark Bauer's bare bottom.

"Where do you think you're going?" she purred, snatching at his bottom.

Mark neatly sidestepped her grasp. "To the studio. I've got work to do."

"On a Saturday?" Gabrielle threw back the sheets, exposing her naked body in an alluring pose. "Work on *this*."

Mark groaned, his desire for Gabrielle returning in a rush. Since last week, when he'd found her in his bed, he hadn't been able to get enough of her. Whenever he least expected it she was there, offering herself. And he was constantly succumbing to her advances, much to his regret. All rational thinking fled his mind when it came to Gabrielle. Making love to her was the most sensuous indulgence imaginable.

"Come on, Mark. It's Saturday." She stirred restlessly, sucking on a finger. "We've got the entire weekend to ourselves."

Mark found himself weakening. But he really had to get to the studio. There was tons to do and already his dalliances with Gabrielle had put him behind schedule. He had to end this with her before he became too entrenched. Before it became too late.

He shook his head. "I can't."

Gabrielle extended a hand. "Yes, you can," she coaxed breathlessly. "If anyone knows that, it's me. Yes, you can."

Mark's resistance melted and he returned to bed.

"Breakfast in bed," Harrison announced, laying a tray across Grace's lap.

"Croissant, strawberry jam, coffee and juice. Very impressive," Grace complimented. She dipped a finger in the pot of jam, tasting it. "Mmm. Fresh."

"And," Harrison added, an arm hidden behind his back, "one other item."

"Don't keep me in suspense, darling," Grace murmured, biting into a croissant slathered with strawberry jam.

Harrison whipped out his arm with a flourish. "The first fifty pages of my screenplay."

"Harrison!" Grace squealed, reaching for the pages. "Can I read it?"

Harrison drew back his arm, shaking his head. "Not yet. It's rough and it's still not finished."

"But Harrison," Grace pouted. "I want to read it. Why'd you show me the pages you've already done if you won't let me read it?"

"I wanted to show you I'm on the ball." He dropped the pages to the floor, joining Grace in bed. "I'm doing this for you, Grace. You're my inspiration."

"I'm sure what you've done so far is marvelous." Grace dipped a finger in the pot of strawberry jam. "Since you won't let me read what you've done so far, let's make the most of this weekend. It isn't very often that Gabrielle goes away, leaving us to play."

"I wonder where the little alley cat has slinked off to."

"Who cares?" Grace undid the drawstring of Harrison's silk pajama bottoms. Taking her finger heavy with strawberry jam, she coated his growing erection, lowering her face.

"I just love fruit with breakfast, don't you?"

Kelly awoke to an exquisite sensation. A pair of warm, strong arms were holding her, drawing her close as a trail of kisses moved from her shoulders, up her neck and then to her lips.

"Graham," she murmured, twisting around to face him as she opened her eyes.

His smoldering gray eyes glowed with warmth. "Morning, pretty lady," he greeted, placing a gentle kiss on her lips. "Sleep well?"

Kelly swept her fingers across his bare, sculpted chest, grinning sheepishly. She brought her eyes to his as she ran her fingers through her tousled mane of hair. "Wonderfully. I had the most fabulous dreams."

"About a certain lover?" he coaxed, returning his lips to hers.

Kelly met Graham's lips with a yearning intensity, eager to re-create the magic from the evening before. "My *only* lover," she stressed.

Graham had been a wonderful lover, taking the utmost care in pleasuring her. When she'd whispered in his ear that this would be her first time, he had proceeded gently, telling her not to worry . . . that their lovemaking would be every bit as wonderful as she had imagined.

Kelly had known what to expect when Graham entered her . . . she expected the pain . . . yet she was totally unprepared for the way her body responded to his. Upon joining together she clutched at him with fevered desire, unable to get enough of his touch . . . his scent . . . his taste. Wanting to meld herself with Graham, she met his thrusts with equal fervor and unabashed demand, claiming the release of sexual satisfaction.

Now, as her carnal appetite reasserted itself with a consuming force, Kelly rolled on top of Graham, surprising him with her brazen move.

"I like a lady who goes after what she wants."

Kelly rubbed herself against Graham, her nipples instantly hardening. "Here's a suggestion. Why don't we spend the rest of the morning in bed?"

"Just the morning? How about the whole day?"

"Think you're up to it?"

With his teeth, Graham nipped at Kelly's breasts lovingly. Then he pulled her closer to him and with surprising swiftness flipped himself on top of her. Kelly gasped as his growing erection rubbed the inside of her thigh. Tingles of anticipation coursed through her in a rushing surge. She couldn't wait to have Graham inside her again.

"What's your answer?" she demanded breathlessly.

"Sounds good to me." Graham slid into Kelly with exceeding slowness. "What are we waiting for? Let's get started."

The scene was Malibu Beach. Although Peter hated to admit it to anyone, he was a slave to the sun. Whenever he had a chance he worked on his tan.

He'd already been on the beach for three hours, eyes closed, body oiled, basking in the Saturday sunshine when a shadow was suddenly cast over him.

Opening his eyes, Peter cupped a hand over them as he sat up, staring at a man he had never before seen.

He was handsome, with chiseled features and long sun-streaked hair. His well-proportioned chest and sculpted legs and arms were golden brown. Ice-blue eyes studied Peter intently, accompanied by a friendly smile.

"Hi," he greeted, extending a hand. "My name's Barry. I ran out of suntan oil and wondered if I could borrow some of yours."

"Sure." Peter tossed him his bottle.

"Thanks." He poured some of the oil into his hands, rubbing it over his chest and arms, then down his legs and across his shoulders. "Could I ask another favor?"

"Go ahead."

"Mind getting my back?"

"No problem."

Barry sat before Peter, handing him the suntan oil. Peter poured the oil over Barry's back, rubbing it in.

"Spread it all around," Barry said, moving his back under Peter's hands. "Harder. Massage it in as deep as you can." He pushed his back into Peter, closing the distance between them and causing Peter's legs to widen.

Barry trailed a hand down one of Peter's legs. "Looks like you need some more oil."

Peter pulled away from Barry, embarrassed by his erection straining against the front of his trunks.

"What's wrong?" Barry turned around, a knowing look in his eyes.

"Nothing," Peter stammered. "All done."

"Your back looks like it needs a touch up. Let me return the favor."

"I'm fine."

Barry locked a hand around Peter's wrist, removing the suntan oil. "I insist."

Barry turned himself around, cradling Peter between his legs, pouring the oil over his back. His hands dug in, massaging forcefully. "How does this feel?"

"Okay."

"Just okay?" Barry pressed himself closer to Peter, his own erection pressing into Peter's bottom. "What about this?"

Peter didn't know what to say. Usually he was the one who went looking for action. He was usually the one in control of the situation. His sexual activities were always separate from his everyday life. Yet here he was being seduced on the beach in front of everyone!

"You're hot," Barry husked into Peter's ear. "Why don't we go cool off? We can go into the water, or if you like, we can go to my place. I've got a house on the beach. We could shower off . . ."

The invitation was left dangling and it was up to Peter to decide what he wanted to do.

Barry's arm snaked around Peter's waist and he caressed the front of Peter's bathing suit. "Well?"

Peter placed his hand over Barry's, moving it up and down. His erection thrilled with an impatient demand for release.

"Let's go," Peter answered.

Daniel bounced on the diving board, jumped in the air, and neatly sliced into the shimmering blue water of his swimming pool.

Under the California sun he swam his usual ten laps, and then did another ten as a burst of adrenaline surged through him, fueled by the thoughts in his head.

Early this morning his agent had called. The role of Eric Thomas was *his*. He hadn't wanted a part so badly in years.

Daniel cut through the water with broad, powerful strokes, relishing the exhilaration. He felt so goddamn unbeatable. Like he could conquer the world.

Emerging from the pool, Daniel toweled himself off, then applied a protective layer of sunscreen. Although Daniel maintained a healthy tan, he was extremely careful not to overexpose himself. The last thing he wanted was leathery looking skin.

Daniel had just settled himself on a chaise lounge when, wearing only the briefest pair of Speedos imaginable, Jaime sauntered over, munching on the celery stick in his Bloody Mary.

"Look at you resting on your laurels," Jaime taunted. "Working on your tan for pretty boy Drew Stern?"

"Shut your mouth!" Daniel ordered sharply. He'd just about had it with Jaime's wisecracks. Every day it seemed Jaime's nastiness went farther and farther, his barbs getting uglier and uglier, almost wanting to see how far he could go before Daniel stopped him.

"Oooh!" Jaime squealed. "You're raising your voice. Getting forceful, Danny?"

Daniel closed his eyes, choosing to ignore Jaime.

"Don't waste your time, lover," Jaime stated. "Drew Stern is as straight as an arrow. You won't be getting him into your bed. Bet you'd like to though, wouldn't you, Danny? You'd love a taste of Drew Stern's tight ass, but you're not going to get it. Why should you? I'm the only one who finds an old fag like you attractive."

Daniel's eyes popped open. "Get out!" he raged, jumping to his feet. "Get out!"

Jaime shoved Daniel down onto the chaise lounge, quickly positioning himself on top of him, boxing him between his legs. "You don't mean that, Danny. If you threw me out you wouldn't be getting your ten inches daily and I'd hate for you to be deprived." Jaime drained the rest of his Bloody Mary, throwing the glass on the Italian tiled patio where it shattered. He grabbed Daniel between the legs, kneading through the material of his bathing suit. "Ready?"

"No! I don't want to!" Daniel said. "Get off me!" He tried freeing himself from beneath Jaime, but couldn't.

"I see that gleam in your eye," Jaime scolded. He lowered his head to Daniel's, planting a kiss on resisting lips. "Come on, Daniel. Admit it."

The touch of Jaime's lips inflamed Daniel's blood and he found himself responding.

"Good," Jaime cooed, feathering his fingers through Daniel's hair, moving down the back of his neck and caressing his shoulders. "Good."

"I want you, Jaime," Daniel stated feverishly.

"And you shall have me," Jaime promised.

Pleasuring Daniel was the last thing on Jaime's mind. His agent had just called, telling him once again he hadn't gotten a role he'd tested for. More than anything else in the world, Jaime wanted to be an actor. He envied all that Daniel had, wanting it for himself, wanting to be at that same pinnacle, yet unable to scale the heights.

Rather than blame the lost roles on lack of talent and training, relying solely on his looks to land him the parts he wanted and thought he deserved, Jaime blamed Daniel for his dead-in-the-water career. The old queer would neither pull strings nor call in favors, and that made Jaime's blood boil.

Flipping Daniel onto his stomach, Jaime tore away Daniel's trunks, spreading open his buttocks, getting ready to plunge forward without hesitation or warning. Without lubrication. A malicious smile twitched on his lips.

"Let's get started."

CHAPTER THIRTEEN

KELLY WAS HURRYING to pack her bags. Yesterday she and Graham had been out all day. Then last night they hadn't gotten in until 3 A.M. and this morning they'd decided to spend more time in bed since this was her last day in New York.

Kelly smiled as she remembered her lovemaking with Graham. How was she going to get through the next month without him? His lovemaking had spoiled her. Yet once he finished the play he'd be back in L.A. and then every day and every night would be as wonderful as the last three.

Kelly shut the suitcase, then popped into the bathroom, collecting her toiletries. She checked the time on her watch. Where was Graham? She had two hours before her flight. He'd disappeared an hour ago, refusing to tell her where he was going.

Just then she heard the door to the duplex open. Grabbing her suitcase and shoulder bag, Kelly rushed out into the living room.

"Where've you been? We're running late."

"I had to pick something up."

"What?" Kelly noticed Graham had a huge smile on his face, along with a large wicker basket hidden behind his back. "Is that for me?"

"Who else? Want to take a peek or are we running too late?" he teased, stepping away.

"Yes, I want to take a peek," Kelly stated excitedly, dropping her bags and reaching out.

Graham brought around the basket. "Here's someone to keep you company until I get back out there. I'll admit I'm jealous that she'll be snuggling with you for the next month."

Inside the basket was a white angora kitten, a red bow tied

around her tiny neck. Swatting at the end of the ribbon with a paw, she looked up at Kelly and meowed.

"Get it away!" Kelly whispered hoarsely, backing away from the basket, a look of frozen fear etched on her face. "Get it away."

Graham looked puzzled. "Kelly, what's wrong? Don't you like her?" He put down the basket, scooping up the kitten and cradling her against his chest. "She's very friendly." He held the kitten out. "Here, why don't you hold her?"

"No!" Kelly shouted, still backing away. "I don't want it! Get rid of it! Get it out of my sight!"

With tears in her eyes, Kelly raced back into the bedroom, slamming the door shut behind her.

"Sure you have to leave?" Barry asked, lighting a cigarette.

Peter sat on the edge of the bed, sliding into his shorts and buttoning his shirt. "I'm running late."

"Yesterday was great." Barry tossed back the sheets, crawling over to Peter. He wrapped an arm around his chest, nuzzling his neck. "How about a repeat performance?"

Peter removed Barry's arm, jumping to his feet.

"What's wrong?" Barry asked. "Yesterday you couldn't get enough of this scene. You were all over me last night. Now you're running back into the closet." He inhaled on his cigarette, releasing a smoke ring. "Is that what it is?"

Peter avoided Barry's gaze, grabbing his wallet and loose change.

"Looks like I've hit a sore spot," Barry taunted. "What's the matter, Peter, can't face the truth?"

Peter brushed a lock of hair off his forehead, locking gazes with Barry. "What can I say?" His tone was hard, flat and unflinching. "When you're right, you're right." He snatched up his watch, strapping it onto his wrist. "See you around."

After Peter left Barry finished his cigarette, puffing away at it leisurely. Then he walked over to the mirrored closet across the bedroom and opened the door. Inside there was a video camera, still recording.

Barry turned off the machine, rewinding the tape. After the tape was rewound, he ejected it, returning to the VCR at the foot of his bed. Popping in the tape, Barry lit another cigarette and flicked on the TV, making himself comfortable as he prepared to watch.

Peter and Barry's writhing bodies filled the screen. After watching for a few minutes, Barry stopped the tape and picked up the phone, dialing a number.

"It's me," he said when the line was answered. "It all went as planned. Everything you want is on the tape. Drop by anytime. You've got Peter Fontana by the balls."

On the first Sunday of every month, Heather had brunch with her agent at his Beverly Hills estate. The purpose of the monthly meeting was to discuss her career and the direction it should be moving in.

Today they were outside by his pool, sipping mimosas and having Spanish omelettes.

"Who was that?" she asked when Jinxie ended his phone conversation. Before the phone had rung she had been about to bring up *Long Journey Home*. She'd started to regret having told Jinxie about Peter Fontana's homosexuality. After all, what he did with his life was his own business. There had to be some other way to get an audition with Mark Bauer. "Good news? You look like you're ready to burst."

Jinxie Bishop gave Heather a benevolent smile as he sipped his orange juice and champagne. Behind his thick-lensed glasses his magnified eyes twinkled with excitement. It was always this way when he discovered something *forbidden*. It only made his position in Hollywood stronger. He was one of the most powerful agents in the entertainment industry, and the reason for his power was his ability to unearth and collect secrets, using them to the advantage of his clients as he propelled their careers.

He was now going to be able to propel Heather to the top. Barry, one of the many outside sources he used to conduct his dirty work, hadn't failed him. Peter Fontana had fallen quite easily into the trap that had been set for him.

"Heather, darling, listen to me very carefully," Jinxie instructed, "for if you do exactly what I tell you to do the role of Olivia Thomas in *Long Journey Home* will be yours."

Heather's mouth dropped open and she stared at Jinxie, speechless. Then she managed to find her voice. "I'm listening."

* * *

"Mark, are you awake?" Gabrielle rubbed her body against his, fingers lightly tracing his penis. "Mark, honey?"

Mark groaned in his sleep. "Gabrielle, I'm exhausted."

Gabrielle caressed his growing erection. "Looks to me like you've gotten your second wind."

She climbed on top of Mark, turning him on his back as she slipped his erection into her. "How's this feel?" she asked as she started bucking against him, faster and faster.

"Terrific," he gasped, opening his eyes as he began participating of his own accord. "You're the best."

"I'm good at everything I do," she purred. "Will you let me show you how good I am, Mark?"

"You're doing fine right now."

She brought a finger to his lips. "Not in bed. In front of a camera."

"What are you talking about?"

She had him hooked. Now was the time to start reeling him in. "I want to be Olivia, Mark. I want to star in your movie. You still haven't cast the role. Give it to me." She pressed her lips to his. "Just think! Every day will be like this." Sensing that he was approaching his climax, Gabrielle started pulling away, delivering her ultimatum, "But if you don't cast me, this will be the last time we're together."

Mark grabbed at Gabrielle, climaxing deep within her. "Don't play games with me, Gabrielle."

"I'm not playing games. What's your answer?"

Mark flopped among the pillows, wiping at his sweat-beaded brow. "We'll see," he answered vaguely, already sensing he was weakening. "We'll see."

"Kelly, honey?" Graham gently knocked on the closed bedroom door. "Can I come in?"

Kelly opened the door, wiping away her tears. "I'm sorry. You must think I'm a fool."

Graham wiped away the trail of tears streaming down her cheeks with his thumbs, cradling Kelly's face beneath his hands. "I don't think you're a fool," he admonished, bringing his face close to hers. "But do you want to tell me what just happened out there?"

Kelly waved her hands dismissively. "It's nothing," she sniffed.

"It had to be something. When you saw that kitten you went as white as a sheet. Won't you tell me? Please?" he pleaded.

So many things were bottled up inside her. She'd kept them all to herself for such a long time. Maybe talking would help . . . get rid of some of the poison that had been eating away at her for so long. Looking into Graham's concerned face, Kelly made her decision, taking a deep breath.

"When I was a little girl," she began, "I had a kitten like the one you bought me. My godfather gave it for me for my eighth birthday. I adored her and never let her out of my sight, carrying her around in a small wicker basket.

"My mother didn't feel the same way about my kitten. She hated her on sight. She said cats were too much work; that they would constantly scratch the furniture; that they'd smell up the house. Of course, these were all excuses. She hated the kitten for two reasons and two reasons alone. The first was because it was a gift from my godfather, whom she despised."

"And the second reason?"

"The second reason was because I loved the kitten so much. Having it made me happy," she stated simply, "and if there was one thing my mother hated to see, it was me being happy. Anyway, my mother always showed her displeasure when I had my kitten around. And she wouldn't let me keep her in my bedroom. There were very strict rules pertaining to my pet, and my mother enforced them. Certain areas of the house, such as the second floor, were definitely off limits. Well, one day when my mother was out shopping I broke her rule and brought my kitten to my bedroom. Later I went outside to play and left her inside. Somehow she managed to get out of my bedroom and into my mother's, where she clawed at the wallpaper and drapes.

"When my mother got back from shopping, she called me to her bedroom, showing me what my kitten had done. I burst into tears, knowing she was going to take away my pet and if she did I'd never see her again. I told her I was sorry, promising that such a thing would never happen again. I told her I would pay for the damages and I would be a good girl, doing anything she wanted, so long as I could keep my kitten.

"My mother didn't get mad and she didn't scold me. That was a surprise. At the time I should have suspected that she was up to something, but I didn't. I thought I had gotten lucky and that everything was going to be all right. She only told me that rules were made for a reason and when they were broken, consequences had to be paid. Glad to be let off so easily, I wiped away my tears and asked her where my kitten was. She said she didn't know, but she'd help me look for her."

Kelly's voice turned low. "We both started searching. After an hour my mother found my kitten. She was in the lily pond. Dead. She'd fallen in and drowned."

"You poor kid," Graham commiserated, hugging her. "That must have been awful."

Kelly nodded. "It was, but wait. There's more to the story. Much more. Mother insisted on showing me what my disobedience and selfishness had done. She held me by the neck and wouldn't let me turn my head away from the pond where my kitten's body floated. I begged her to let me look away. I told her I'd never break any of her rules again. That I would be a good girl." Tears began streaming down Kelly's cheeks again. "I promised. I promised her I would be a good girl."

"What happened next?" Graham asked softly.

"I had to stare at the drenched body of my kitten while the gardener dug a grave and buried her."

"Jesus!" Graham exclaimed. "How could she have done such a thing?"

"Easy." Kelly's voice became hollow and her eyes took a distant look. She wiped away her tears with absentminded strokes. "Mother wanted me to learn a lesson. You see, her hands around my neck were soaking wet and I could see there were bits of white fur clinging to them, along with long red gashes down her fingers. The gashes looked like bites or scratches."

Kelly focused her eyes on Graham, giving him a sad smile as he gasped and realized what she was saying. "I'd crossed Mother and no one crosses Mother without paying the price. She said accidents happened, but I didn't believe her. I didn't believe her at all."

He was *so* incredibly sexy!

Laura flipped through the pictorial of Drew Stern in the latest issue of *US* magazine. *This* man, this Hollywood *star*, was a man she had run into twice. *Twice!* And she hadn't even recognized him!

Her eyes moved from page to page as she replayed their two encounters in her mind. Although she hadn't known who he was, she had found him attractive. She studied a full-page photo of a brooding Drew. The camera definitely loved him, giving his features a smoldering intensity. You couldn't help but look . . . stare . . . or want to know who Drew Stern was.

His eyes, two clear chips of blue ice, were almost hypnotic, locking you into his gaze. There was also the tiniest tinge of danger, warning one not to push too far or come too close. Laura vividly remembered Drew's eyes from their meetings. She hadn't even seen what the camera had captured in his eyes in this photo, but she had seen something else. There had been traces, faint traces, of hesitation.

Could it be that Drew Stern, the sexiest man in Hollywood, was afraid to introduce himself to a woman?

Why was that so unbelievable? Laura chided herself. He *was* a person, not some unapproachable god. And he hadn't had the bravura or swagger of a Hollywood star. Maybe that was part of the reason he had been so unrecognizable. He'd come across as a nice, normal guy.

Laura stopped in mid-thought. A realization had suddenly dawned on her. She was attracted to Drew Stern. She was thinking about him, wondering what it would be like to get to know him. Maybe even have a relationship—both sexual (well, what woman in America *didn't* think about having sex with Drew Stern?) and emotional.

The unusual factor in this scenario wasn't Drew Stern. It was the scenario itself. Of her having a relationship. Of even possibly making love. She hadn't thought of *that* in a long time. She hadn't found herself attracted to a man in the longest time.

Not since Nico.

After Nico she had closed her mind and her heart to the possibility of a relationship with any man. It wasn't worth the risk. The betrayal. The pain.

She had vowed never to fall in love again.

Yet somehow Drew Stern had managed to sneak around her resolve and here she was daydreaming about him.

"You want the magazine?" the gum-chewing, frizzy-haired cashier asked.

Laura tore her eyes from the magazine, startled. There had been a long line of grocery shoppers ahead of her when she'd started flipping through the magazine, Drew's face jumping out at her from the newsstands. Now she was next in line.

Laura closed the magazine, studying the cover shot of Drew. She'd probably never meet him again. Yet in a small way she owed him a lot. He'd managed to help her take a step forward when she thought she never would again. Maybe, one day, when she found someone, there'd be a chance to love again. If she did, she would owe it all to Drew Stern.

She tossed the magazine down, along with her other items. "I'll take it."

CHAPTER FOURTEEN

"Aren't you up bright and early." Gabrielle stood in the doorway of Harrison's study. "Busy writing?"

Harrison typed away at his computer keyboard. "What does it look like?"

"It *looks* like you're writing, but that doesn't necessarily mean you are. For all I know you could be typing gibberish."

Harrison held up a sheaf of papers. "Want to take a look?"

Gabrielle yawned. "I don't have time to waste on your scribblings." She held up a bound copy of Long Journey Home. "I've got a *real* script to read."

Harrison looked unimpressed. "Big deal. You've got a copy of the script. Too bad Mark doesn't have a *real* actress to read his lines. I don't even think sleeping with him would help your cause. You're a lousy actress. Face it," he mocked, "you're stuck out in soap opera land."

"Screw you!" Gabrielle shouted, throwing the script at Harrison, who promptly ducked. "So what if I'm not the world's greatest actress? At least I'm practicing my craft. At least I'm earning a salary. I *can* call myself an actress."

"Playing a sex-crazed bitch? You're only playing yourself. That's hardly a stretch for your *talents*," Harrison commented dryly, "if such a word were ever truly applicable to you."

"I'm making money at what I do," Gabrielle shot back. "I'm in demand. I've got an agent. I've got fans. What have you got to show for yourself? Nothing except for a five-year-old Oscar nomination. This town's forgotten you, Harrison."

"Don't be too sure of that," he retorted. "The script I'm working on right now is dynamite."

Gabrielle rolled her eyes. "You always say that. Either you

never finish what you've started or if you do, it stinks. I don't give a damn what you do with yourself any more, Harrison."

"So what are you saying? Do you want a divorce?"

"I'd love one, but my father would have a coronary. No darling, it looks like we're stuck with each other for a while longer. You lead your life and I'll lead mine."

"Like we always have. Don't worry, *darling*, you don't need my permission to sleep around."

"How big of you. Now here's a word of advice. Don't let me catch *you* sleeping around. I'd hate to have to tell Daddy about my philandering husband. He's *so* old-fashioned." Gabrielle took a deep breath. "I don't know what he'd do to defend my honor. Well, I've got to run. When Grace gets in tell her I won't be needing her at the studio, but I've left her a list." She kissed Harrison on the cheek. "Have a nice day, *darling*."

Harrison pounded on his keyboard in frustration. Damn that bitch! Damn her for threatening him! Who the hell did she think she was? He couldn't keep track of the number of times she'd cheated on him while Grace was only one of a handful of women he'd slept with during their marriage.

Harrison forced himself to calm down, clearing his head. He wasn't going to let her get to him. He was going to concentrate on his script and write. He was going to produce the best damn screenplay ever. It was going to be made into an Oscar-winning picture and then he'd be the one calling the shots. He'd have it all, including money and power. And he'd be able to do what he'd always wanted.

Get rid of Gabrielle.

"You've got an interview at three with *Soap Opera Digest,* a telephone interview with *TV Guide* at four and someone from *US* magazine will be stopping by to take some photos for a layout they're doing. I think it's called Daytime's Most Beautiful Women," Laura recited from the pad in her hand.

Kelly gave an exhausted sigh and Laura held up a finger, returning to her list.

"Hold on. There's a pile of fan mail and photos that you need to sign and you've got the soap-opera award show to attend at seven," Laura wound down, closing her pad. "Okay, you can collapse now."

"If only I could!" Kelly shook her head. "There don't seem to be enough hours in the day."

"They *have* been running you ragged," Laura remarked. "What are you up to? Seventy-five pages of dialogue a night?"

"Try eighty."

"Your new script arrived while you were blocking. I highlighted your lines."

Kelly gave a smile of appreciation. "Laura, I don't know what I'd do without you."

The past month had flown by for both Kelly and Laura and neither had had a problem adjusting to the other. Kelly was hardly demanding, grateful to have someone who kept her professional life in order and on track. And Laura went out of her way to do more than what was required. She found the world of television fascinating and every day there was something new and interesting to learn.

"So what happens to Melissa next week?" Kelly asked.

Laura raised her eyebrows. "Incest. Or so she thinks. Serena is coming out of her coma and the first thing she does is fiddle with a blood test in her quest to break up Chet and Melissa."

"I guess I'd better start practicing my anguish."

A tiny meow came from the floor and Kelly scooped up her small white Angora kitten. "What's the matter? Is Kitty hungry?" After having poured her heart out to Graham, he'd told her that he would take back the kitten, but Kelly had stopped him. His gift had been a gift of love and a gift of love could conquer anything, even bad memories from the past.

Laura rubbed the kitten's back. "She's so adorable. When's Graham coming back?"

Kelly hugged the kitten. "Next week."

"You must be excited."

"Extremely. I can't wait to see him."

"He must be really special. I'm looking forward to meeting him."

"He is special," Kelly agreed. "Very special."

Gabrielle answered the knock on her dressing-room door, finding herself staring out at Frost Barclay. She gave him a bored look.

"Gabrielle, it's been a while since we've practiced lines." He stepped into the dressing room. "Why don't we make up for lost time?"

Gabrielle ignored his invitation for some sexual antics. Frost Barclay was of no use to her and she'd already sampled him. Why waste her time?

"My character has been in a coma for the past month," she snapped. "I haven't had any lines!"

Frost waved a script in front of her. "You do now. Serena's coming out of her coma."

Gabrielle snatched the script, flipping through the pages. "Thank God! If I had to tape another coma scene, trying to remain immobile, I was going to scream."

Mitzi had signed her to a new contract weeks ago, getting the money and perks she'd demanded. But the show's writer's had decided to be nasty and leave Gabrielle languishing in her coma longer than necessary.

"Serena's up to her usual tricks," Frost remarked smugly. "Looks like you'll be sticking around, then?"

"Looks that way."

"Whatever happened to your plans for a big film career?"

Gabrielle slammed Frost's script into his chest. "Don't worry about me, Frost." She started pushing him backwards, out of her dressing room. "My plans are right on schedule." She gave him a condescending look. "I've moved on to bigger and better things."

She slammed the dressing-room door in his face.

After slamming her dressing-room door in Frost's face, Gabrielle started pacing.

What was the deal with Mark? She knew she had him wrapped around her little finger or, rather, locked between her legs. He couldn't get enough of her. Yet for weeks he had failed to make good on his promises. All she got were elusive answers to her questions. She was tired of waiting.

Marching across her dressing room, she picked up the phone and dialed Mark's private number at Trinity Pictures.

Her voice was as sweet as honey when he answered. "Sweetie, it's Gabrielle. Listen, sugar, I've just gotten my new script and it looks like Serena is going to be in the thick of things again. I have to know your decision about *Long Journey Home* so I can let the writers know what's going on. I have the part of Olivia, right? I can tell the writers to work around me?"

"Not yet," Mark answered.

The honey disappeared, replaced by battery acid. *"When?"*

"I don't know."

Gabrielle lost her temper. First there had been Harrison's remarks this morning. Then Frost Barclay's innuendoes. And now this!

"Listen and listen good, Mark, because I'm only going to say this *once*. Understand? *Once*. I want an answer by the end of the day. Otherwise it's over between us. *Over*. You got that?"

Gabrielle slammed down the phone with satisfaction.

Mark winced, holding the receiver away from his ear. There was no longer any getting around it. He was going to have to make a decision.

For the past month he'd been putting Gabrielle off while searching for an actress to play Olivia. Julia Roberts and Meg Ryan had both been on the top of his list, yet neither actress was available. And Laura San Giancomo was tied up with Steven Soderbergh's next film.

Unknown actresses and minor film and television actresses were all tested in the hopes of putting off the inevitable: giving Gabrielle the part.

He still hadn't found anyone.

What was he going to do? He couldn't ruin his film just because sex with her was the best he'd ever had.

Could he?

Maybe he'd be able to help her. Teach her. Draw out a performance and help her grow as an actress. He knew he was grasping at straws, but he wanted some acceptable reason to justify casting her. He wanted some reason that made sense.

He picked up the phone, dialing Gabrielle's number, ready to give in.

But then he cut the connection.

He couldn't do it. He couldn't give in. *Long Journey Home* was still his baby. He'd overcome Paul Fontana and that had been the hard part. Surely he could ignore his erections.

He'd keep doing what he'd already been doing: putting it off. He'd appease Gabrielle by giving her another screen test, only this time it wouldn't be a blind reading. He'd give her time to prepare, get her in costume and makeup, use one of the sets, *AND* he'd have her test with Drew Stern. All of it would keep her happy. If only momentarily.

Meanwhile he'd use his reprieve to keep searching and pray he found someone soon.

He'd also keep himself out of Gabrielle's bed.

"Mark Bauer's office."

"Hello, Peter. This is Heather McCall."

He'd heard the name before but couldn't recall where he'd heard it. "Yes? How may I help you?"

"Don't tell me I'm going to have to give you a hint. I thought I was unforgettable!" she laughed. "I'm that perky, or as you probably think of me, that pushy actress who kept bugging you for an appointment to see Mark. I wanted to audition for the role of Olivia in *Long Journey Home*."

Now he remembered! "Yes, what can I do for you, Ms. McCall?" She'd been pushy, but he had admired her persistence.

"No need to be so formal. Call me Heather. And it's not what you can do for me, but what *I* can do for *you*. I'm extending an invitation. Drinks at my place, tonight at six. I live in the Hollywood Hills. Let me give you the address."

"Drinks?" Peter was confused. "Why? What for?"

"I'll explain it all when I see you."

"I don't know if I can come. I've got other plans."

"Cancel them. They'll keep. You can always go cruising after we meet. See you at six."

Heather ended the conversation with that little tidbit dangling, leaving Peter with a panic-stricken look on his face as he clutched the phone, a feeling of dread spreading throughout his body.

"Here it is!" Harrison proudly stated, waving a script in the air as he rushed out to the pool where Grace was. "I've finished my screenplay."

Grace abandoned the eight-by-ten glossies of Gabrielle that she had been autographing, giving Harrison an exuberant hug. "I knew you could do it! I'm so proud of you!"

"I want you to read it. Now! Right this second!" Harrison opened the script to page one, placing it in Grace's lap, hovering above her. "Go on," he urged. "Start."

"Harrison, I can't read with you peering over my shoulder. I need to be able to concentrate."

Harrison, a nervous mass of creative energy, paced before Grace, running his hands through his hair. "I don't want you to feel pressured. God, no! I'm just dying for you to read it. I want your opinion . . . some feedback.

"I can't believe I've finally finished it! It was bouncing around my head for so long and now it exists. It's down on paper. I feel really good about the story and writing. I haven't felt this way in ages!" he proclaimed. "I think it's the best thing I've ever done."

"Harrison, calm down!" Grace laughed. "You're making me dizzy with all your pacing."

"I can't help it," he honestly admitted. "I feel so good."

"Darling, you need to calm down. Why don't you go for a swim and I'll fix you a drink."

"While I'm swimming you'll start reading?"

Grace brought a finger to Harrison's lips. "Hush. I'll start it tonight and don't worry. You'll get my opinion." She retrieved the script from the patio table, hugging it possessively to her chest. She was so proud of Harrison! He'd done it! If the screenplay was as good as he said it was, they were one step closer to being together. "I'm going to savor every word on every page. Count on it. I've waited a long time for this."

"You're right on time."

Heather, wearing a black lambskin skirt and jacket, held open the door of her apartment. "Don't be shy. I won't bite." She opened the door wider. "Enter."

Peter followed Heather through her condo, noticing the movie posters on the walls. All were from the B movies she'd starred in.

"Some of your masterpieces?" he pointed out.

"Is that a tone of condescension I hear in your voice?" she scolded. "Peter, I'm surprised. You shouldn't be throwing stones. I thought you were the open-minded type. Willing to take chances. Acceptable to changes. Live and let live."

"What's *that* supposed to mean?"

Heather moved behind an open bar. "No need to sound so harsh." She displayed a bottle of scotch. "Care for a drink?"

"I'll pass."

"Well, sit down. Make yourself comfortable."

Peter grudgingly sat down in a white leather armchair. "Can we get down to the reason I'm here?" he snapped.

Heather emerged from behind the bar, flicking her bangs into place. She situated herself on a white leather sofa, seductively crossing her legs. "Can't we at least try to be civil? I like you, Peter. I really do."

"Pardon my skepticism, but I find that hard to believe."

"Why? It's true."

"If it were true it wouldn't stop you from trying to blackmail me. Now would it? Why don't we get down to business?"

Heather was aghast. "Peter! Blackmail is *such* an ugly word. All we're going to be doing is helping each other. What's so wrong with that?"

"Save the dramatics for when you're in front of a camera, Heather, and get to the point. I have a sneaking suspicion I know what this is all about."

"Do you?" She took a sip from her drink.

"You want the role of Olivia in *Long Journey Home* and you think you're going to strong-arm me into pressuring Mark to give you the role. Guess again."

"No, *you* guess again. You see, Peter, there's the matter of your little secret, which, if you choose not to play by my rules, will become public knowledge."

"Prove it," he smugly countered.

Peter's anxiety from Heather's early call had evaporated. What could she prove? And who would believe her? She'd just be coming across as a vindictive actress out for revenge after failing to get a part she'd wanted. That wouldn't do her career any good.

Heather gave a sigh of resignation. "I wish I didn't have to do this, but I guess it's time we got down to the nitty-gritty." The lights clicked off and the wide-screen TV turned on. She aimed her remote at the VCR. "Take a look. Here's a home video I think you may be interested in."

Watching the screen as images of himself and Barry together in bed unrolled, Peter suddenly felt sick as his mouth turned dry and then filled with bitterness.

"Where did you get that?" he barely managed to whisper.

Heather turned off the TV, flicking on the lights. "Does it matter? The tape is in my possession, and if I so choose I can show it to anyone I desire."

She headed for the bar and fixed another scotch, which she

promptly handed to Peter. "Drink this. You look like you could use it."

Peter sipped the scotch. "What do you want?" he croaked, though he knew what her answer would be.

"Peter, you laid the cards down on the table earlier."

Peter closed his eyes. "Olivia," he moaned.

"Yes," Heather mused, "that *would* be very nice but I'm not that obnoxious. Peter, I'm willing to play fair. All I want is what I've wanted all along. Simply a chance to audition for Mark Bauer."

Peter, draining his scotch, looked at her in disbelief. "That's it?"

"That's it!" Heather readily agreed. "I want you to pitch me to Mark. Fire up his enthusiasm. Pull out all the stops. I've made a video of my best stuff for you to show him. After you get me the audition, I'll handle the rest."

"What if I can't?"

"We can't have that kind of attitude," Heather admonished. "You *will*. You better. Otherwise your father's going to learn that the family name ends with you." Heather toasted Peter with her glass. *"Capisce?"*

Cameras clicked, bright lights shone and microphones were thrust forward as Drew Stern tried to weave his way through reporters and photographers, making a beeline for the entrance to Spago's.

A reporter from "Entertainment Tonight" boldly thrust herself in his path, hurling a question. "Drew, is there anyone new in your life?"

Drew neatly sidestepped her, continuing onward. *New?* he wondered. *When is there ever* anyone *in my life?*

"Drew, are you seeing anyone?"

I wish I were. A face floated through his memory as he remembered an encounter on a beach and another at an outdoor cafe. *Who was she? And why couldn't he seem to forget her?*

Once inside the restaurant Drew made a point of mingling, moving from one group to another. The greetings were warm but tentative. Confused. Drew Stern was an oddity at a Hollywood party. And he always came alone.

Drew could care less about the murmurs his appearance was causing. He didn't plan on staying long. Hollywood parties were not his style. Pretense and falseness were traits he was not interested in cultivating. All Drew wanted to do was make good films. He could care less about Hollywood frills and fanfare.

The private party at Spago was to promote an action adventure film being released by Paramount the following month. The sweet smell of box office was definitely in the air. The producer, Chuck Marsden, had invited Drew personally. Affection for Chuck, as well as their working relationship, made Drew attend the party.

Snagging a glass of champagne from a passing tray, Drew's eyes roamed. Quite a turnout.

Goldie Hawn and Kurt Russell were deep in conversation with Mel Gibson and Cher. Off in a private corner, Donna Mills was sipping a glass of champagne while Joan Collins nibbled at some caviar. Faye Dunaway was busy captivating the attention of Jack Nicholson and Alec Baldwin.

About to take a sip of his champagne, Drew's hand froze in mid-air as a figure passed him by.

It was her!

Abandoning the champagne, Drew followed after the woman across the restaurant, trying to keep her within his sights and close the gap between them. She was wearing a short red silk dress and her hair was piled on top of her head in a topknot. She looked so sexy from behind that all Drew could suddenly think of was making love to her.

She had just reached the front door when he closed the distance and tapped her on the shoulder, ready to meet her at last and learn her name.

"Yes?" she asked, a note of indifference in her voice, turning around.

Drew's smile fell as they came face to face. It *wasn't* her.

"My mistake," he apologized, preparing to turn away. "I thought you were someone else."

"Glad you made the mistake." Now that she knew who he was, the indifference was gone from her voice. She placed a restraining hand on his arm. "Hold on! Don't go, sugar." He noticed her voice had a light, southern lilt. "Don't hurry off." She extended a hand. "My name's Mona." She raised an eyebrow. "You're Drew Stern."

Her excitement was evident. "Yes, I am," he admitted.

"Honey, you look so disappointed. Am I that displeasing to the eye?"

Drew admired her well-proportioned physique. "Hardly. It's just what I said. I thought you were someone else."

"Well then," she whispered, nestling herself closer as she entwined an arm through his, "why don't we have our own private party?"

Drew wanted to say yes as she moved suggestively against him. To lose himself in the comfort of a woman's arms would be bliss. Yet if he were to do that his coupling with Mona would be nothing more than an act of selfish pleasure. There would be no love in their lovemaking—no deepfelt emotions or stirrings of the heart—only a desire to satisfy a physical yearning.

Though many women had tried to gain entrance to his heart over the years, none had ever succeeded. Drew wouldn't let them. He was afraid of what would happen if he allowed someone to get too close. If he allowed himself to care about someone. The thought was frightening. What would happen if he allowed himself to love—to cherish someone and then lose that someone?

He didn't know the answer to that question. He'd never had to find out. The last thing Drew wanted was more pain. He'd already had a lifetime of it.

"What do you say?" Mona urged, giving him a wicked smile as she jiggled her breasts. "I'll be whoever you want me to be."

Drew stared into Mona's face, searching for something he couldn't define or find. What he knew for sure was that this wasn't the woman he wanted to be with. This wasn't the woman whose face was consuming him, returning with more and more frequency as each day went by. The woman he wanted was the woman on the beach. If she had been the one standing before him, he would have been willing to take a chance.

"That's the problem," Drew sighed, extracting him arm and losing himself back in the party crowd. "You can't."

"Excellent performance," Jinxie enthused, emerging from Heather's bedroom after Peter had left. "You really are a remarkable actress. Even better than when I was listening to you on the phone this morning. You remembered your lines and you delivered them with conviction. Nice bit of improvisation, too." Jinxie fiddled at the bar, making himself a drink and toasting Heather. "Bravo, my dear."

Heather sat down on the sofa, brushing her bangs off her forehead and draining the drink she had been nursing with one long swallow. "I hated doing that."

"You *hated* doing that?" Jinxie's words dripped with scorn. "Haven't you been hounding me for weeks to get you an audition with Mark Bauer? And didn't I try, though not with much success? Don't you want a chance at this part? That's all you've been crying about for weeks! Hell, I wanted you to demand the part from Fontana but you didn't want to handle things that way. You said you wanted a chance to prove yourself; that all you wanted was an audition. Well, honey, you're getting your chance!"

Heather squirmed uncomfortably, unable to refute what Jinxie was saying. "Yes, but . . ."

"No buts!" Jinxie commanded. "How badly do you want this part, Heather?"

"Badly," she confessed, remembering the promise she had made to her mother. Yet she had also promised her mother that she would make her proud. What would she think if she knew what she was doing? She could still recall the panic and alarm in Peter's eyes when she'd threatened to reveal his secret. *Nothing* gave her the right to invade his privacy and turn his world upside down, no matter what her reasons. Not even a promise. What she had done was unforgivable. Yet it wasn't like she really *was* going to reveal his secret. She'd *never* do that.

"Good. I'm glad that's settled." Jinxie left his empty glass on the bar top and prepared to leave. "Here's a bit of advice, Heather. Lose your conscience. No one needs one in Hollywood."

CHAPTER FIFTEEN

Grace turned the last page of Harrison's screenplay.

"Shit!" she screeched, throwing the script across her bedroom.

Harrison's screenplay *sucked!* How could he say this was the best thing he'd ever written? No studio in their right mind would seriously consider making *Dangerous Parties* into a film, not in the condition the screenplay was in.

Dangerous Parties was supposed to be a thriller, yet neither the characters nor their actions were intriguing. Set in a small Southern town, *Dangerous Parties* focused on dirt-poor Melanie Dalton, a conniver and schemer who'd do anything, even commit murder, to marry into the town's richest family. Hutch Nelson, her lover, is just as ruthless and devious. Working together throughout the story, they suddenly both decide to turn the tables on each other and it's only a matter of time before one sticks their knife in the other's back.

Grace snatched up a pen and pad. Harrison had had enough time to do things solo. Now it was time for her to intervene. She was going to have to help him fix *Dangerous Parties,* making a list of the screenplay's good and bad points.

Almost everything was wrong. Melanie had to come across as a bitch from page one and remain that way throughout the story. As written, Harrison had her constantly being indecisive. The only person she should be thinking about was herself. It had to be clear to the audience that Melanie had no conscience and no morals. She'd use anyone and do anything to get what she wanted. Sheer ruthlessness had to come across.

Hutch, on the other hand, needed a weakness and that weakness was Melanie. He had to be a dupe, vulnerable to her charms and willing to take risks—risks that would cost him his life.

The sex scenes were flat and had to be punched up. They needed to be dangerous and erotic. Couldn't Harrison have used their times together for reference? Or at least rented *Body Heat?*

Grace began scribbling furiously as the ideas poured forth. She'd show Harrison what to do to whip *Dangerous Parties* into shape. She had to. Otherwise Harrison was going to remain married to Gabrielle and that was the last thing she wanted. She'd waited long enough for this screenplay.

"Going to lounge in bed all day?" Gabrielle asked contemptuously.

"Why not?" Harrison cradled his head behind folded arms. "I deserve it. My screenplay's finished."

"Whoopee." Gabrielle twirled a finger in the air. "Is it gathering dust as we speak?"

"My agent will be getting it shortly."

Gabrielle looked surprised. "You still have one?"

"I could ask you the same thing."

"I'd love to continue this chat, but I'm running late."

"Where are you off to so early?"

"Trinity Pictures. I'm doing a screen test with Drew Stern."

"So?" This time it was Harrison's turn to look unimpressed. "You expect your *talent* to land you this part?"

Gabrielle ran a hairbrush through her hair. "Who said anything about talent?" she scornfully asked. "I've got Mark Bauer in my bed and he can't get enough of me. By tonight the role of Olivia will be mine."

"Fat chance. After your screen test with Drew Stern I wouldn't be surprised if Mark castrated himself to save his picture."

"You've got me in stitches," Gabrielle murmured dryly, fastening on a pair of earrings. "But today's my day, Harrison. Nothing is going to spoil things for me. Not even you."

Nico gave the warden a belligerent sneer, taking the seat before his desk. "What's this about?"

The warden shuffled a pile of papers on his desk, then looked Nico in the eye. "Much as I dislike the subject, it's about your parole."

Nico leaned forward eagerly, struggling to maintain his elation. The warden wouldn't look so displeased if things weren't in his favor. All right! He was on his way out sooner than he'd expected. "Yeah?"

"The parole board has reached a decision. You'll be free in one month, Rossi. Make sure this is the last time we see you."

Nico smugly leaned back into his seat. He'd been right! In one month he was going to be a free man again and back on the outside. Able to roam wherever he wanted.

And track down whoever he wanted.

In one month's time he'd be free and hot on Laura's trail. Then he'd be back in her life.

It was payback time!

"You don't like my screenplay," Harrison stated.

"Darling, of course I do," Grace easily lied. She'd have to tread carefully. Harrison had an ego. "It's just that I think there's room for improvement. Only some polishing up—you know, to smooth out the rough edges."

Harrison paced Grace's bedroom. He'd come over expecting to make love and instead she wanted to discuss changes in *his* screenplay. "It's fine the way it is," he stated flatly.

"But Harrison, you haven't even looked at my suggestions." She pressed her handwritten notes into his hands. "Don't be so close-minded. I'm only trying to help."

Harrison tossed the pages to the floor without even looking at them. First Gabrielle attacked his writing and now Grace. "What makes you such a know-it-all? I'm the writer, Grace. *Me!* Not you. I'm the one who created the characters. I'm the one who toiled in front of my computer. *Dangerous Parties* is razor-sharp and in perfect shape. If you don't like it, too bad. Go write your own screenplay. Let's see how easy you think it is. Writing is hard work, Grace. Do you know how agonizing it is to transform images into words? It's torture. Only when you write your last sentence do you feel satisfaction because it's finally over. It's all done—finished and out of your system. I won't let you take that feeling away from me!"

Grace had never before seen Harrison so angry. She didn't know what to make of it. "Sweetie, don't get so defensive," she soothed, trying to wrap an arm around him. "I know how hard you've worked."

He pushed her away. "No, you don't. Otherwise you wouldn't be so quick to criticize." He angrily snapped his fingers in her face. "I can't write a screenplay like that. *Dangerous Parties* was in my head for months before I was able to sit down and start writing. Months!"

"Your story is a bit off, but nothing that can't be fixed," she tried to explain before Harrison cut her off.

"No!" he shouted. "*Dangerous Parties* is perfect as is, Grace. You'll see. You'll all see."

He stormed out of Grace's bedroom and the next thing she heard was the apartment door opening and then slamming shut.

Grace stared at her copy of Harrison's screenplay. He was wrong. *Dangerous Parties* wasn't perfect and right now Harrison was too hot-headed to listen. His pride had been sorely injured, but had she been the sole cause?

No. It had to be Gabrielle. When Harrison had shown up, she could see that he was in a foul mood. Her criticism hadn't helped. And somehow Gabrielle had demeaned Harrison's writing and he had taken it out on her, refusing to listen to what she had to say. How she despised that spoiled, selfish bitch! She'd love to put her in her place. One of these days . . .

She'd have to help him. She'd be able to. After all, she had been an English major and had taken a few creative writing classes. She certainly didn't have a *passion* for writing, but she had tried her hand at it once or twice and knew she could do it.

If Harrison was too stubborn to do a rewrite, then she'd just have to do it for him.

"Mark Bauer's office."

"Hello, Peter," Heather purred silkily. "I'm just checking in. Have you spoken to him yet?"

"Not yet," Peter bit out tersely. He was getting sick of these daily calls. She was hounding him both at home and at the studio. "I haven't had a chance."

"You've had a week," she reminded.

"Mark flew out to Nebraska to check on the locations with the line producer," he explained. "I told you that already."

"Tell me something I *don't* know. Something I want to hear. I'm losing patience, Peter."

"Well, I'm sorry."

"No, you're not. Not yet. But you will be if you try and double-cross me."

"I told you I would talk to him and I will!"

"When, Peter? When? I'm sure he's called while he's been out in Nebraska. You could have brought the subject up then, but you didn't, did you?"

"The timing wasn't right."

"Save your excuses. Look, you told me he was due back in today. Where is he?"

"He is in but I don't know where he is at the moment."

"Find him!" Heather exploded. "I've run out of patience. I'm tired of waiting. I want everything finalized by the end of today."

"Today?" Peter sputtered. "You can't be serious."

"I'm *very* serious when it comes to my career. You should know that," she reminded. "Start making things happen, Peter, or I will."

"What do you mean?"

Heather sighed. "You know what I mean, but it looks like I'm going to have to spell it out. Please remember, Peter, I'm not trying to play the heavy. I'm only doing what I have to do. For my career. If my audition isn't set up by the end of the day, then Daddy Fontana is going to be invited to a very special screening, in which he will be the viewer and I will be the projectionist. He'll get to see your film debut. *Ciao*, Peter."

Peter slammed down the phone, breaking out into a cold sweat. He glanced at his wristwatch. Eleven o'clock. He had seven hours to track down Mark, pitch Heather, show him her videotape, and fire up Mark's enthusiasm.

Peter's fist bounced off the top of his desk. He hated being in the position he was in. He felt so helpless—yet feeling helpless wasn't a strange feeling. After all, he had no control over his life—he didn't live it the way he wanted. He chose to remain in the closet, pretending to be something he wasn't, ashamed to reveal his true desires and feelings except during the safety of darkness when anonymity was guaranteed.

Yet strangely enough, his after-dark interludes lowered his self-worth. In a way he was settling for second best because he was dividing his life into different sectors, rather than living it as a fulfilling whole. And now he was a victim of the secret he was too ashamed to reveal.

Would it be so horrible if he admitted to his homosexuality? If he did, there would be no turning back. No more pretending. In a way he'd be branded . . . labelled . . . separated from everyone else and unable to put back on the mask he'd been hiding behind.

Then there was Paul. His father would never, *ever*, understand. Without a second's hesitation, he'd be cut out of his father's life. No one, not even family, was allowed to displease Paul Fontana.

There was no predicting the repercussions if Paul Fontana was displeased.

How would Gabrielle react? Would she still love and support him? Would she still be there for him?

He couldn't do it! The risks . . . the costs . . . they were all too great.

Peter left his desk and went off in search of Mark.

"Very good, Heather," Jinxie lauded, settling back in his black leather swivel chair as he peered down at her from behind his desk. "Very good."

Heather tossed the cordless phone she had just finished using at her agent. Suddenly unable to stand the smug look on his face, she began pacing his office.

That morning she had come to a realization. Jinxie was enjoying this sick game he had orchestrated. He liked pulling strings and she was no different from Peter Fontana; Jinxie was pulling her strings as well. She was doing what he wanted her to do because he knew how much she wanted to be a part of *Long Journey Home*.

When she had first come to Hollywood she had vowed never to let herself become sucked up by Hollywood's dark side . . . and yet here she was becoming a part of it. She felt like a vampire, sucking away at Peter's vulnerability. She couldn't stand what she was doing to him and the rationalizations she made to herself to ease her guilty conscience were worthless. The misery she was putting him through was unconscionable and with each passing day she was finding it harder and harder to live with herself. She wasn't eating. She wasn't getting enough sleep. All she could think about was Peter. And herself. What would happen the next time she didn't get a part she wanted? What would she do then? How far would she go? How much of herself would she be willing to sacrifice?

Those thoughts scared Heather and she didn't want to find the answers.

There was only one way to prevent that.

"Do stop pacing," Jinxie complained. "You'll leave track marks in my carpet."

Heather stopped pacing, staring at her diminutive agent.

"Well, haven't you got anything to say?" he demanded.

Heather looked him straight in the eye, raising her head proudly, knowing her decision was the right one and looking forward to fixing things with Peter Fontana.

"Jinxie, you're fired," Heather announced slowly, deliberately, taking the utmost care to deliver her words with importance before walking out on her sputtering ex-agent.

"Let's try it again," Mark patiently directed, "only this time with more hesitancy. Olivia hasn't seen Matt in three years. Feelings are still there, still familiar, but the feelings are also new . . . different . . . she doesn't know how to handle them. She's confused."

Gabrielle gave Mark a scathing look. "That's the third time you've told me that. I'm not an imbecile."

"Then get the scene right," he gritted from between his teeth. "Olivia's not a cat in heat."

Mark, Drew, and Gabrielle were on soundstage seven on the Trinity Pictures lot. Gabrielle, devoid of makeup, her thick hair plaited into a braid and wearing a worn cotton dress, had just walked into her bedroom, surprising Drew after he'd come out from the shower wearing only a towel. The day was supposed to be hot and Gabrielle had just returned from the fields . . . her body smudged from the toil of hard labor and glistening with sweat.

"The sight of Matt awakens feelings in her," Mark explained. "This is her first love . . . the man she married . . . the man she gave her virginity to. She doesn't know how to handle the emergence of her old feelings. Part of her wants to throw her arms around him and feel his embrace, but she's afraid he'll reject her, thinking that he'll feel she's abandoned his memory by marrying his brother."

"I've read the script," Gabrielle hissed. "I know what makes Olivia tick."

"Then show me," Mark ordered before focusing his attention on Drew. "Great job," he complimented. "Keep it up." Mark retreated behind his camera. "Let's try it again. From the top."

Mark started filming and from the moment Gabrielle opened her mouth, despair filled him. This wasn't working. This wasn't working at all. Despite the clothes, the set, and Drew's presence, Gabrielle wasn't Olivia. He wouldn't even have to bother viewing the rushes. It was all before him.

Mark continued filming despite his revelation. He was going to keep up this charade and then figure out how to untangle himself from Gabrielle.

Today.

"Peter, can I talk to you?"

Peter looked up from his desk, glowering at the sight of Heather. "What are you doing here?" he viciously snarled as the pressures of the last few days came crashing down on him. Once again Heather was getting ready to play her game . . . to make her demands . . . to threaten him unless he did her bidding. He was sick of it. He was so fucking sick of it!

Heather jumped back in shock. Never before had she seen such anger and hatred. Peter's handsome face had contorted into an ugly mask of aggression.

And she was the cause of it.

Jumping from behind his desk, Peter shoved his wristwatch in Heather's face. "Check the time. I've still got a few hours. Or have you decided to lower the boom earlier?"

"Peter, you have every right to be angry—"

"Angry? You think I'm *angry?*" he shouted, cutting off her words. "I'm *livid!* You've got me in a corner with my back pressed against the wall."

"Peter, I'm sorry," she whispered, her voice faltering.

"Sorry? What good does sorry do? Nothing you ever do will make things up to me."

"I hope this will." Heather reached into her shoulder bag, handing Peter the tape Jinxie had made. She'd made sure she had held onto it after Barry had brought it over to Jinxie's estate that Sunday afternoon.

Peter looked at the tape with skepticism. "What's this?"

"The tape."

Peter crossed his arms over his chest, looking at Heather warily. "Why are you giving it to me? Why *now?* I haven't gotten you to see Mark yet."

"Forget Mark. Forget all about the audition." Heather pressed the tape on Peter until he accepted it. "What I did was terribly wrong. I just hope one day you'll be able to forgive me. Maybe by that time I'll have forgiven myself."

"You're serious," Peter said softly.

Heather nodded her head wearily. "Believe it or not, Peter, I didn't like what I was doing to you."

"Then why did you do it?"

"I suppose you could say I became blinded by my ambition and lost sight of what's right and wrong and of who I really am." Heather shrugged. "Or you could call me stupid for listening to my ex-agent. In any event, the important thing is you've got the tape and I can start living with myself again." Having finished what she'd come to say, Heather turned her back on Peter and started walking away.

"Heather?" Peter called.

She stopped at the door and turned. "Yes?"

"Thank you," he said.

"You're welcome, Peter." Heather's voice was choked with emotion. "You're very welcome."

Gabrielle was fuming as she drove to the studio in Burbank where "The Yields of Passion" was taped. Her screen test with Drew Stern had been disastrous. Of course it wasn't *her* fault. Mark had done his utmost to make her nervous and self-conscious in front of the camera as he criticized her over and over.

It was as though he'd *resented* her and hadn't wanted her to give a good performance.

Had he? Gabrielle smirked as she pulled into her parking space. She'd just have to be a bit *persuasive* with him this evening.

As she was striding through the studio on her way to her dressing room, Grace hurried toward her, bearing a two-pound box of Godiva chocolates.

"For you," Grace said. "They were just delivered."

Gabrielle propped her sunglasses on top of her head, taking the box and ripping open the card, which said:

THE WAITING IS ALMOST OVER.

The card was unsigned.

Gabrielle lifted the lid off the box, inhaling the rich scent of chocolate. She ran her fingers over the selection. *Mark*, she decided. This had to be his way of apologizing. Well, he had another thing coming if he thought a fifty-dollar box of chocolates was going to smooth things over and get him off the hook.

She popped a dark chocolate into her mouth, savoring the melting richness. She popped another into her mouth, and then another before offering the box to Grace. "Have one."

Grace politely declined. "I'm watching myself."

Gabrielle popped another two chocolates into her mouth, then covered the box, shoving it at Grace. "Get rid of these before I gorge on them," she ordered before stomping off in the direction of her dressing room.

"You're due in makeup," Grace called. "You have to be on the set in twenty minutes."

"Let them wait," Gabrielle snarled. "I've got a phone call to make. A certain someone is going to get a piece of my mind."

Mark had just settled himself behind his desk, swallowing two aspirins with a cup of black coffee, when his private line started ringing.

Gabrielle.

He ignored the ringing. This was the first step in cutting himself free. However, despite his resolve, an image of Gabrielle, *ripe, sensuous Gabrielle,* suddenly filled his mind, as he saw her offering herself to him, promising untold delights. Mark groaned, closing his eyes, reliving the ecstasy. How he wanted her! Maybe one last time before he broke the news to her.

He was reaching for the phone when Peter came into his office.

"Found you at last," Peter exclaimed.

"In the flesh." Mark withdrew his hand from the phone quickly, relieved that Peter had shown up in the nick of time. He pointed to his ringing phone. "Answer that, would you? Tell whoever it is that I'm not here."

Peter gave Mark a quizzical look. He'd never answered Mark's private line and had been told he didn't need to. As he was about to pick up the receiver, the ringing stopped.

"They'll probably call back," Peter commented.

"Count on it," Mark muttered morosely before focusing his attention on Peter. "What did you need me for?"

Peter knew he didn't owe Heather McCall any favors, especially after the hell she'd put him through. But she had also ended that hell when she had given him the tape and not demanded anything. And she had also helped him realize that he had to make a decision regarding the way he lived his life. He couldn't hide in the shadows forever. She'd made him face up to that and for that he owed her.

As hard as it might seem to someone else, he had also felt sorry for Heather. He'd gotten the sense that Heather was basically a good person (though she had been misguided by her agent, and like she'd said, been blinded by her ambition). If he spoke to Mark and arranged an audition, it would show he didn't hold a grudge and it might help Heather forgive herself.

"I know you've been looking for an actress to play Olivia," he began, "and I know your search hasn't been going well."

Mark gulped his black coffee. "Tell me about it."

Peter placed Heather's eight-by-ten glossy and resumé, along with her videotape, on Mark's desk. "I think I've found the actress you've been looking for."

"Really?" Mark carefully studied Heather's photo. "Who is she? What's she done?"

"Her name is Heather McCall and she's done a number of B movies. Most of it is horror and exploitation stuff, but she's got screen presence. More importantly, she's got talent. Her resumé came in a while ago, but you didn't bother taking a look at the material her agent sent along. I did."

Mark tossed Heather's photo to one side. "So she's more than tits and ass?"

Peter nodded, pointing to the videotape. "If you need convincing, play the tape. Heather's put together a number of dramatic pieces, even something from *Long Journey Home*. She's good, Mark. Really. All you have to do is take a look for yourself."

"It sounds like she's sold you. She's certainly attractive and I'm having no trouble visualizing her as Olivia." Mark closed his eyes, pairing Heather off with Drew Stern. They'd definitely look good together on screen, but would there be any chemistry? More importantly, could she act?

Mark opened his eyes, flicking his head to the videotape. "Play it."

Thirty minutes later when the tape ended, Peter turned to Mark expectantly.

"Well?"

"Get her in here. Today. Tonight. As soon as possible." Mark's excitement was mounting. "Get Drew Stern on the line and get him back here. I need him to run some lines." Mark released a howl of delight. "It looks like we've found our Olivia!"

* * *

"You've got an audition," Peter said, deciding not to reveal too much to Heather. "How soon can you get here?"

"Peter, I told you to forget about it. I don't want an audition. I don't deserve it."

"Mark Bauer says you do. So how soon can you get here?"

"Peter, why are you doing this?"

"Hey, all I've done is arrange an audition. You have to do the rest. I know how much this meant to you. It made you do things you ordinarily wouldn't do. Now, are you on your way out the door or do I have to come and drag you down here?"

"I'm on my way out the door! Thank you, Peter." Heather's voice bubbled with excitement and gratitude. "You don't know how much this means to me."

This time it was Peter's turn to say, "You're welcome."

Gabrielle was seething, her thoughts focused on Mark as a hairdresser worked on her hair. Where was he? He hadn't answered at the studio or at his place. She'd have still been on the phone, calling all over town, if the director hadn't come storming into her dressing room, disconnecting the line she was on, and demanding she report to the set.

"Don't pull," she snapped, venting her fury at the hairdresser as a hairbrush moved through her curls.

"Sorry, Ms. Moore," he apologized.

Gabrielle ignored the apology, placing a hand to her stomach. For the last ten minutes tiny pains had flashed through her abdomen. Now the pains were getting stronger, becoming sharper and lasting longer.

"Watch that hairspray," she said irritably as the hairdresser hovered over her. "You're getting it in my eyes."

The hairdresser gave a final spray before removing the tunic covering the evening gown Gabrielle was wearing for her next scene. "All finished."

"At last!" Gabrielle stated exasperatedly. Admiring herself in the mirror, she gave her hair a few final pats. "It certainly took you long enough."

Rising from the chair, a searing pain ripped through Gabrielle's stomach. She clutched at her middle and gasped, doubling over.

Gabrielle opened her mouth and struggled for air as she tried to straighten up. She couldn't—it hurt too much. Another pain ripped into her and she slumped against the counter into an array of hairspray cans, blow dryers, curlers, and brushes.

All fell to the floor, clattering loudly, followed by an unconscious Gabrielle.

CHAPTER SIXTEEN

Grace was pacing the emergency room of Los Angeles Hospital. Looking up, she caught sight of a harried-looking Harrison and rushed to his side.

"Harrison, thank God you're here!"

"What happened? What's going on?" he asked, taking her into his arms, forgetting their argument of that morning and trying to be as affectionate as possible without giving anything of their affair away. "The studio called and said Gabrielle had been rushed over after collapsing."

"They think she's been poisoned. Her stomach is being pumped right now."

"Poisoned?" Harrison stepped back, disbelief etched on his face. "How could that have happened?"

"A box of Godiva chocolates was delivered to Gabrielle at the studio this afternoon."

"But who would want to poison Gabrielle?"

"It has to be that fan of hers. The one who's been sending her letters and flowers. Who else could it be?" Grace's eyes brimmed with tears. "This is all my fault! I feel so guilty. I should have warned her. I should have said something."

"What are you talking about? Why would any of this be your fault?"

"This creep has been harassing Gabrielle, and when those chocolates arrived I should have made the connection."

"You're not to blame, Grace. After all, he's been lying low for a while. We all thought he'd gone back into the woodwork. Let's leave this to the police to figure out." Harrison put a reassuring arm around Grace's shoulders, kissing her forehead. "You okay?"

"I am now that you're here," she sniffed, looking up at him.

This was the perfect opportunity to mend fences and she wasn't going to pass it up. She forced a fresh onslaught of tears. "I'm sorry about this morning. I guess this is my day to screw things up."

"Hey, forget it," Harrison soothed. "I have. Let's just get through this. Have Paul and Peter been called?"

"I only told the studio to call you. Your name was the first that popped into my head."

"Why don't I go look for a pay phone?" He gave Grace another kiss. "Can you handle being alone?"

Grace kissed Harrison. "I'm fine now that you're here."

"I'll be back as soon as I can."

As Harrison headed off, Grace dabbed away her tears, priding herself on her performance. A little sympathy never hurt. Turning, she saw the doctor who had hurried after Gabrielle when she'd been rushed in. Grace instantly applied a look of concern and worry on her face.

"Doctor, how is she?" she asked in a compassionate rush of words. For added effect she nervously wrung her hands.

"She'll be fine, Ms. Warren. We're getting ready to move her to a private room."

"Thank goodness! When I think what might have happened . . ." Grace shuddered.

The doctor nodded his head in agreement. "She's a very lucky lady. If she had eaten any more of those arsenic-laced chocolates we might not have been able to save her."

"Can I see her?"

"Only for a few minutes."

Gabrielle, still unconscious, was hooked up to a number of tubes and monitors. The silence of the room was punctuated by the intermittent beeping of the machines. Although Gabrielle was deathly pale, the rise and fall of her chest indicated she was very much alive. Grace stood above Gabrielle, watching her breathe, a look of pure hatred on her face.

"Damn you, bitch!" she hissed under her breath. "Why didn't you die?"

After Gabrielle's collapse, taping for "The Yields of Passion" was cancelled for the day. With some suddenly unexpected free time on her hands, Kelly decided to do something brave.

She was going to pay her mother a visit.

The first thing she did after driving from the studio was buy a bottle of champagne at Jurgenson's on North Beverly Drive, topping off the bottle with a bright, festive bow. Then she bought a dozen balloons inscribed with "Congratulations" and a dozen red roses.

Last week Diana had signed the contracts for her role in *Long Journey Home* and although Kelly had phoned to congratulate her, she thought a visit would be a much nicer touch.

Yet when Kelly arrived at Diana's, she found her mother wasn't in.

"Ms. Halloway will be out all day," Esmerelda explained. "She won't be home till very, very late. I have her call you?"

"That's not necessary." Kelly pressed her gifts on the Mexican woman. "If you'll just mention that I stopped by and see that she gets these."

"*Si.* I will do so."

Kelly gave a gracious smile. "Thank you, Esmerelda."

Later that night at eleven the phone rang. Kelly glanced up from the novel she was reading, staring at the ringing object in terror. *Diana.* She'd come home and found her gifts.

Was she angered by the gifts? Had they somehow offended her when they were meant only to please? Was she now about to be subjected to one of Diana's night calls, filled with ugly criticisms and harsh words? There hadn't been a night call since that one time so many weeks ago. Would this be the first of more to come?

The phone kept ringing. With a shaking hand, Kelly answered, barely bringing the phone to her ear.

"Hello?" she whispered, trying to keep her voice steady.

"Kelly, darling," Diana sang out gaily. "You're *such* a sweetheart. As we speak I'm sipping the marvelous champagne you brought and staring at your lovely balloons and roses."

"I'm glad you like everything."

"Why wouldn't I? It's all wonderful! There really was no need for all this, but thank you, Kelly. It means a lot."

Kelly was stunned. *Profuse* thanks, let alone thanks, were rare from her mother. "You're welcome. I wanted to let you know how proud I am."

"You're *so* thoughtful. Darling, we must get together soon. When is that boyfriend of yours going to be back in L.A.?"

"Next week."

"Well, we're going to have to have dinner together. The three of us. I'm dying to meet him. Let me check my appointment book." The sound of flipping pages traveled over the line. "How does next Thursday sound?"

"Perfect," Kelly answered, not wasting any time in accepting. She really did want her mother to meet Graham. Maybe, just maybe, things would start being right between them. Smoother. If this phone call was any indication, they were on the right track. "I can't wait."

"Wonderful. It's a date. We'll go to La Scala. Let me let you go since I know you've got to get up early. I'm looking forward to next week, Kelly. I can't wait to meet your boyfriend."

Diana slowly relished the rest of her champagne, popping the balloons Kelly had brought one by one with a straight pin, contemplating what she would wear for next Thursday's dinner.

She'd have to look her best. After all, she was meeting the man in Kelly's life and she *so* wanted to make a good first impression.

Kelly. What a fool! She'd gobbled up her few words of sweetness like a thirsty man dying for water. Now she probably thought they were on their way to a real mother/daughter relationship.

Never.

Kelly had cost her so much and she'd *never*, ever, forgive her.

She refilled her empty champagne glass as she walked to her wardrobe. Opening the door she stepped into a deep walk-in closet. At her selection were a number of elegant outfits designed by some of the world's foremost designers. Any would be perfect for a dinner date.

But Diana didn't want to wear something tasteful and elegant. She wanted something sleek, tight and sexy. Something that would make her look ravishing, outshining any attempt of Kelly's to look beautiful.

Yes, Diana mused thoughtfully, going through her hangers, she needed something stunning, an outfit that would stop a man in his tracks and put certain ideas in his head.

Diana was positive she'd find something. She had to. It wasn't every day that one seduced her daughter's boyfriend.

CHAPTER SEVENTEEN

"What the hell *is* this?" Gabrielle screeched at the top of her lungs, furiously shaking her copy of the *Hollywood Reporter*.

A nurse came running into Gabrielle's hospital room. "Ms. Moore, please calm down."

"Don't tell *me* to calm down," Gabrielle raged. She threw the paper at the nurse, angrily tossing back her sheets. "That *bastard* gave *my* part to some unknown bitch."

The nurse picked up the fallen paper, looking at it in confusion. "Who? What are you talking about?"

Gabrielle pulled out the tubes in her arm, seizing her folded clothes from a nearby chair. "Can't you read? Mark Bauer has given Heather McCall, some shlocky B-movie actress, the plum role of Olivia in *Long Journey Home*."

Gabrielle disappeared into the bathroom, emerging dressed within seconds. She waved her hairbrush furiously. "He's not getting away with this. He's not!"

The nurse, realizing Gabrielle was serious about her intention to leave, tried to exert some authority. "Ms. Moore," she commanded, stepping in front of Gabrielle, "I'm going to have to insist you step back into bed this minute."

"Forget it!" Gabrielle shoved the gray-haired nurse to one side, depositing her on her abandoned bed. "I've been cooped up in this place for four days. I'm checking out!"

"Did you miss me?"

What a question! The sound of Graham's voice was a wonderful way to greet each new morning. And the nights! Kelly couldn't think of ending her day any other way than in Graham's arms. "You bet I did. I'm so glad you're here to stay."

"Me too." Graham's arms wove around Kelly, spanning her waist. "I've got an idea. Want to hear it?"

Kelly twirled the hairs on Graham's strong forearms, brushing her fingers up and down as his hold drew her closer. The intimate touch of his flesh ignited shivers of pleasure and desire. "I think I'm going to like this," she murmured.

"Let's try something daring."

Kelly looked up at Graham over her shoulder. "Such as?" she asked mischievously.

He leaned over her, whispering into her ear as he nibbled on her earlobe. When he finished, Kelly turned over on her side, looking at him with wide-eyed surprise.

"Are you serious?"

"Never more. So what do you say? Want to give it a whirl?"

"Let's!" she enthusiastically agreed.

"Where is he?" Gabrielle demanded, storming past Peter into Mark's office. "Where the hell is he?"

Peter rushed in after his sister. "Gabrielle, what are you doing here? Why aren't you at the hospital?"

Gabrielle, standing behind Mark's desk, was tossing papers left and right. "Where is he, Peter? Where's that worm? I want to see him and I want to see him *now*."

"He's not here. He's in Nebraska checking on a few last-minute things before shooting starts." Peter came around the desk, snatching the rest of Mark's papers out of his sister's grasp. "Mind telling me what's going on?"

"He *screwed* me," Gabrielle growled, "and I've got nothing to show for it! He screwed me over, in and out of bed. He told me I had the part of Olivia and then he gave it to that nobody."

"He did not," Peter snapped, gathering up the papers Gabrielle had scattered around the office, "so stop acting like a spoiled brat. Mark has been trying to cast the part for weeks and although I know you auditioned twice, you were not Mark's first choice."

Gabrielle's eyes narrowed. "Oh, I wasn't?"

Peter realized he'd let something slip . . . something that was going to get Mark in hot water. Of course, he'd be on Gabrielle's shit list too if she knew how he'd helped Heather win the role. But as much as he loved his sister, she *wasn't* ready yet to tackle a role like that of Olivia. "He needed someone with more experience."

"And that tart's got it? You're supposed to be on *my* side."

"Would you stop dumping on Heather? You know nothing about her. Obviously Mark thought she was the best candidate." Peter threw a pile of papers on top of his boss's desk, preparing to sort them out. "Save the theatrics. You're not dealing with Dad."

"What are you talking about?" Gabrielle huffed.

"Let's cut to the chase, okay? We both know the truth. First you tried to get Dad to put the squeeze on Mark. When that didn't work you started sleeping with him."

"How can you say such things to me?"

"Let's not get into a fight. I'm not judging you, Gabrielle. I know you have your own certain style of doing things . . . and if it works for you, all the better. One of the things I admire about you is that you know how to go after what you want."

"Only this time I didn't get what I wanted," Gabrielle grudgingly admitted.

"Only this time you didn't get what you wanted," Peter agreed. "Have you calmed down?"

"Somewhat."

"How'd you find out about Heather?"

Gabrielle waved her copy of the *Hollywood Reporter*. "So when is he coming back?"

"He'll be back by the end of the week. In time for the party."

"Party?" Gabrielle pounced on Peter's second slip. "What party?"

"Gabrielle . . ." Peter warned.

"Peter, I've thrown in the towel concerning *Long Journey Home*," she glibly said. "That doesn't mean I don't like knowing about a good party. Are you going to tell me?"

Peter gave in. "Mark's giving a party for the cast and crew before everyone goes on location."

"Where's the party going to be?"

"What does it matter? You're not invited."

Gabrielle gave her brother a patient look. "Of course I am. Daddy's probably been invited and I'll just tag along with him. I want to see Mark before he leaves Hollywood. Don't worry, Peter." Gabrielle raised two fingers and crossed her heart. "I promise to be on my very best behavior."

* * *

"Breakfast at the Beverly Hills Hotel. How unlike you!" Diana exclaimed, sliding into the seat offered by Paul Fontana. "What's the occasion?"

"Why, we're celebrating! I'm so pleased you're going to be a part of *Long Journey Home*."

Diana sipped at her mimosa. "I had to make a living somehow," she stated dryly.

"Still upset over your new contract with the casino?"

"Don't you mean *old* contact? The same one you signed me to in 1965?" She took another sip of her mimosa. "Let's not open old wounds, shall we? Tell me, how's Gabrielle?"

"She's going to be fine. Thank God." Paul pounded an angry fist on the table. "When I think that I came close to losing her, it makes my blood boil."

Diana's eyes became dreamy and faraway. "Yes, I know how you feel." For a few seconds she'd taken a trip back to her past, but as quickly as the trip had begun, it was over and she returned to the present, focusing on Paul. "So do the police have any leads?"

"None. They're up against a brick wall. The only angle they've got is that fan who's obsessed with her."

"Has she heard from him since the chocolates were delivered?"

"Not a word and I'm going to make sure she doesn't. I'm taking special steps to insure her safety."

"With you taking charge, she doesn't have a thing to worry about. You always did know how to take care of a problem."

"No one knows that better than you, Diana."

"Are you going to tell me why you wanted to see me?"

"I've already told you. To celebrate."

Diana shook her head. "I don't buy it. You want something from me, so let's get to it."

"Why would you say that?"

"Because it's always been this way between us, right from the beginning. And it always will be. One of us always wants something from the other."

"There *is* a favor I'd like," Paul admitted.

"A *favor*." Diana looked at Paul skeptically, then shrugged. "Sure. Why not?"

"Diana, why don't you believe me?"

"No one does favors for Paul Fontana. If they did he would have to do something in return."

"How quickly she forgets! I did a favor for you a long time ago, Diana."

"Twenty-five years ago, to be exact. And I'm still paying for it." Diana gave Paul a sour smile. "Not that I'm bitter about it." She patted Paul on the hand. "Let's not dredge up the past. What do you want?"

"It's really very simple. I'd like the honor of escorting you to Mark Bauer's party."

"Is that all?" Diana still looked skeptical. "Why?"

"You know the answer to that, my dear," Paul supplied smoothly. "You're the essence of Hollywood. You have star quality while I'm the new kid on the block. My acceptance by the people who matter depends on the company I keep."

"We'd make quite a pair."

"All eyes would be on us. And of course, we'd be the topic of conversation."

"I suppose it would be worth my while to be connected to you," Diana mused. "And I could use the press coverage. The tabloids will eat this up." She dwelled in her thoughts for a few seconds, then toasted Paul with her champagne glass. "What time will you be picking me up?"

"Well, isn't this cozy?"

Harrison and Grace, entwined in each other's arms, opened startled eyes, staring in shock at Gabrielle.

"What are you doing here?" Harrison managed to croak out.

Gabrielle angrily pointed to Grace in her bed. "What's *she* doing *there?*" Gabrielle stalked around the bed. "My, my Harrison, I'm shocked. I didn't know you were capable of making love with *such* enthusiasm."

"It's not what it looks like," he tried to explain, throwing back the sheets as Grace clutched them to herself.

"Am I hallucinating?" Gabrielle asked coldly.

"This is the first time it's happened."

Gabrielle gave Harrison a scornful look. "Do you take me for a fool?"

"I'd better go," Grace said quietly, stepping out of bed with the sheet wrapped around herself.

"Good idea," Gabrielle agreed, "but drop the covering. No way I'm letting you walk out of here with one of my Porthault sheets."

Grace dropped the sheet, giving Gabrielle a frigid look. "Anything else?"

"Yes." Gabrielle gave a wide smile. "You're fired."

"Fine," Grace spat. With a defiant look she turned to Harrison. "I'll call you later."

"No need to call," Gabrielle informed sweetly. "Stick around. This shouldn't take too long." Stepping to the closet, she removed two suitcases, sliding them over to Harrison. "Start packing."

Harrison looked even more shocked than when he'd opened his eyes and found Gabrielle towering above himself and Grace. "What? Gabrielle, we need to talk."

"I warned you, Harrison. I told you what would happen if I caught you cheating on me."

"You can't be serious! You can't divorce me."

"But I can and I will. For infidelity. I hope the two of you will be very happy together. I know I'll be very happy with the two of you out of my life. If you'll excuse me, I'm going to take a shower. You have until the end of the day to pack all your stuff."

After Gabrielle exited, Grace lost all control, throwing a crystal decanter across the bedroom. "That promiscuous bitch! How dare she divorce *you* for infidelity." She couldn't stand the way Gabrielle treated Harrison. All these years she'd stripped him of his dignity with her blatant affairs and now she was going to publicly humiliate him, making him look like the one at fault. After all he'd been through he'd be leaving this marriage with nothing! She couldn't allow that to happen. Harrison deserved better. He deserved it all!

"I could kill that bitch," she whispered, giving Harrison a deliberate look as they locked eyes.

"Step in line," he growled, "because I'm one step ahead of you. I'd like nothing more than to strangle her with my bare hands."

"Esmerelda!" Diana impatiently called upon entering her mansion. "Esmerelda, answer the phone!"

The phone continued ringing and Diana cursed the Mexican maid aloud. "That woman is never around when I need her!" Removing an emerald-studded earring, she snatched up the phone.

"This is Diana Halloway."

"Mother, it's Kelly."

Diana injected a tone of warmth into her voice. "Darling, it's good to hear from you. Is dinner still set for tomorrow night?"

"I'm sorry, Mother. We're out of town and have to cancel."

Diana debated on how she should answer. She loved keeping Kelly off balance. She could rant and rave about Kelly's inconsiderateness. Or she could keep spreading sweetness and warmth. Since she hadn't met Kelly's boyfriend yet, it would be better to continue with the sweetness.

"Naturally I'm disappointed, but we'll have to reschedule. Call me when you're back in town and we'll pick a night."

"Mother, you're so understanding. Gotta run. Bye."

Diana hung up, refastening her earring and giving herself a pat on the back for her performance while replaying the brief conversation she'd had. Kelly had sounded happy. *Too* happy. There had been an unexpected tone of lightness and merriment in her voice. Diana *hadn't* liked it. What could possibly be the reason for Kelly's happiness? Her boyfriend? Well, she'd make it a point to find out. And then she'd do something about it. Something nasty.

Didn't they always say most happiness was shortlived?

"What'd she say?" Graham asked, sticking his head around the shower door. He wasn't sure what he thought about Kelly's mother. After a few of the stories she'd told him, his opinion of the woman wasn't very high.

"I didn't tell her."

"You didn't tell her? How come?"

Kelly shrugged. "I don't know. I guess I still wanted to keep it between us."

"Tell me some more about your mother." Kelly was extremely tight-lipped when it came to her mother, though Graham was curious. Whenever he tried asking questions, Kelly always managed to avoid the topic. "What's she like? What's she do?"

"Not today." She slipped out of her camisole, joining Graham in the shower. She started soaping his back as the warm water cascaded over their bodies. "Today belongs to us."

"What do you think your mother's going to say when you tell her she's got a son-in-law who swept the woman he loves to Las Vegas for a quickie wedding?"

Kelly proudly rubbed the gold band worn on her left hand. "Congratulations, of course. What else would she say?"

* * *

"When they told me I had a visitor I didn't think it would be you," Nico said, a touch of awe in his words.

Paul Fontana gestured to the chair across from him. "Have a seat, Nico. You're looking good. How've they been treating you?"

"As well as can be expected."

Paul reached into his jacket pocket, handing Nico a Cuban cigar. "Thought you might like one of these."

"Thanks." Nico pocketed the cigar.

"I hear you're getting out soon."

"Three weeks."

"Any plans?"

"Not at the moment. Unless something happens to come along." Nico was quick to pick up on Paul's vibes. "You looking for someone to work for you?"

"Nico, I'm a man who believes in rewarding loyalty. You kept your mouth shut about the Fontana family during the hijacking trial. When the prosecution wanted to bargain and cut you a sweet deal, you didn't say a word. You didn't have to do that. I don't forget things like that."

"The family was always good to me."

"I have a proposition for you, Nico. A temporary assignment and a very easy one. I'm coming to you because you're the best. My daughter Gabrielle is my most prized possession. She's an actress. Maybe you've seen her on TV. Anyway, in the last few weeks she's been bothered by a persistent fan and it's come to a point where her life is in danger. Nico, I want my daughter kept safe. I want someone with her twenty-four hours a day until this nut is caught. I'm offering the job to you. There'll be your own car, an apartment, and lots of money. What do you say?"

"I say yes, Mr. Fontana." Nico's sources had tracked Laura down to L.A. It was time for him to head the hunt himself and move in for the kill. "Definitely yes!"

CHAPTER EIGHTEEN

"What do you mean I can't come along?" Jaime whined. "This is going to be a hot party!"

"You know why you can't come along," Daniel answered, slipping into his tuxedo jacket. "We can't be seen together in public."

"Why not?"

"I can't take the chance. The press is going to be there early in the evening."

"So what? Your homosexuality is no big secret. The press has kept its lips shut all these years. One more night won't matter."

"I'm not going to flaunt my private life!" Daniel snapped. "I've always conducted myself with discretion! Case closed. Let's not get into the usual argument." Daniel picked up a bottle of Polo, preparing to spray himself, but Jaime slapped the bottle of cologne out of his hand.

"Case *not* closed. I won't miss this party! It would be a great way for me to make connections. You're supposed to be helping me with my acting career, Daniel, but I'm going nowhere!"

"That's your own fault! I can't give you an acting career, Jaime. You have to work for one and work hard. I've offered to pay for acting lessons, but you've turned me down. All you want to do is take the easy way. Life isn't easy, Jaime. It's time you realized that and grew up. Show me you're making an effort and I'll do the same. I'll try to do whatever I can to help you. I believe in helping talent grow."

Jaime grabbed the front of his crotch, thrusting it obscenely at Daniel. "This is the only *talent* you like watching grow!" he leered.

"You're making a fool of yourself."

"Am I? And you're not? Tell me, Danny boy, who's your date for tonight? Is it that fag hag, Vanessa Vought?"

"Shut your mouth, Jaime," Daniel warned. "Bitterness doesn't suit you. It makes you very ugly and I don't like ugly things . . . ugly things can very easily be replaced."

Diana was putting the finishing touches on her appearance.

If there was one thing she loved, it was a good party, especially one where she got to be the center of attention. Mark Bauer's party at the L.A. country club promised both.

Diana had spared no expense in preparing herself. After all, the paparazzi would be out in full force and she wanted to look dazzling.

Her gown was a Nolan Miller original of blue satin sprinkled with sequins. Sapphires and diamonds adorned her ears and throat. A hair weaving at Vidal Sassoon that afternoon, costing seven hundred dollars, had given her honey-blonde head extra bounce and fluff.

She looked at least ten years younger than her forty-nine years. Maybe she'd catch someone's eye tonight. Someone young and gorgeous who'd pleasure her nonstop. Ending the evening in bed with Paul Fontana was not high on her list.

For a moment she thought of Graham. Unquestionably he'd been one of her best lovers. He'd had such energy and passion! She supposed part of her had been waiting for him to come crawling back. But she hadn't seen or heard from him since that day when he'd found her in bed with Paul.

Graham's problem was that he'd had too much brains, unlike most of her past studs. The silly boy had actually expected her to treat him as an equal. Totally unacceptable! No one was her equal! No one came before her! No one was more important than she!

Diana slipped a white mink stole around her shoulders, taking one last inspectory look in her mirror. Tonight she'd find a replacement for Graham.

She might as well forget all about him. After all, he was old news. He'd probably decided to return to New York and stayed there. She'd probably never even see him again.

"Honey, are you ready?"

Kelly came bustling out of the bathroom in a strapless gown of lilac silk with embroidered beads. "Almost." She bared her back to Graham. "Just zip me up."

"Not so fast." Graham's lips traveled up the smoothness of Kelly's back, his hands slipping around the front of her gown, cupping her breasts.

"Nice," she murmured, "but aren't we running late?"

Graham zipped up Kelly's gown. "Right you are, Mrs. Denning."

Mrs. Denning. Kelly thrilled at being called that. Her eyes fell upon her wedding band. She never tired of looking at it. Or at the man she had married. The man who had been her husband for a week now.

Graham had moved in with her and at long last she had what she'd wanted her entire life: *a home.* Now when she returned to the apartment at the end of a long day, she didn't come home to darkness . . . loneliness. She came home to Graham . . . her husband.

For the first time in her life, Kelly felt loved, wanted and secure.

She still hadn't told her mother she was married. Part of her was afraid, fearing Diana would somehow find a way to spoil what was so wonderful between herself and Graham. But that was silly. How could her mother spoil things? Even if she disapproved of the marriage, there was nothing she could do. Besides, in the event of Diana's wrath, Kelly had Graham to support her. Graham was all that mattered.

Kelly planned on telling her mother the news tonight. At Mark's party. It was unavoidable since they'd both be there. Yet somehow she felt more comfortable . . . safer . . . doing it in front of others. But she hadn't told Graham her mother would be at the party . . . that her mother was the famous Diana Halloway. That could wait until the last possible moment. Until it could no longer be avoided.

"You look beautiful," Graham whispered lovingly, kissing her on the cheek.

"You look pretty dapper yourself," she complimented. "I still can't believe we're going to a party given by Mark Bauer. I didn't even know you two were friends."

"Not friends, exactly. Good acquaintances. I've tested for Mark a few times. Even though I haven't gotten the roles I've gone up for, he's been encouraging."

"Why wouldn't he be? You're a wonderful actor. One day you'll work with him. I know it."

Graham gave Kelly a secretive smile. "You may be right, love. You may be right."

Drew adjusted his cufflinks, straightened his tuxedo tie, and ran a brush through his hair.

As usual, Drew looked perfect. And, as usual, he didn't have a date for this party. Travis had offered to set something up, but Drew had refused his agent's offer. He wouldn't have felt comfortable with a stranger and tonight was too special a night to spoil.

Drew couldn't wait for tonight to unfold. After tonight, they would be one step closer to making *Long Journey Home*. Tonight the magic started! He'd get to meet his co-stars, fellow professionals who were driven by the same force as he. Later he'd get to meet the crew, who wouldn't think working with him was at all unusual. Both groups would treat him like a regular guy. Just someone doing his job. He'd have the best of both worlds while he was doing what he loved best.

He knew showing up dateless would make him fair game, but he didn't care. Tonight was going to be different. He didn't know why. It was just a feeling he had.

Laura couldn't believe it. She had a date!

Last week at the studio one of the assistant directors had asked if she wanted to go to a party being given by Mark Bauer. Instantly intending to say no, she'd surprised herself when she'd opened her mouth and said yes instead.

Laura honestly couldn't say she'd been upset by her answer. Jack was a nice enough guy and she'd had a whole week to change her mind. Yet with each passing day she'd found herself getting more and more excited. It wasn't excitement over Jack. She was simply looking forward to a night of fun—the preparation, dancing, mingling, meeting other people. She needed to get out some more. It would be good for her.

She spoiled herself with a steaming thirty-minute bubble bath and facial. Afterward she smoothed Giorgio-scented powder and lotion into her skin, followed by a light spritzing of the famous scent.

She applied little makeup to her face—a subtle touch of blush, a light coat of mascara. Her hair was pinned up in a loose but elegant upsweep.

When it came time to unzip the garment bag delivered that afternoon from Kelly, Laura shivered with excitement. When she'd mentioned having a party to go to and not knowing what to wear, Kelly had instantly offered one of her own gowns.

"I insist," Kelly had said. "My closets are brimming. One less gown won't make a difference. We're about the same size so there shouldn't be a problem."

Pushing away the tissue paper cushioning the gown, Laura revealed a very expensive-looking strapless black silk creation. She immediately fell in love with it and, crossing her fingers, slipped into the gown, praying it would fit.

It did. Perfectly. She gave a sigh of relief, admiring her image in the mirror.

She'd done it. She looked picture-perfect. She didn't know why, tonight of all nights, this was so important to her.

Laura gazed at herself critically. She *did* know why. If she were honest, she'd admit it had to do with Nico. Nothing she'd ever done had ever been good enough for him. And he'd let her know his displeasure. How he'd let her know!

She touched her cheek, remembering a time when the skin hadn't been so perfect. Instead it had been bruised; battered; swollen.

No! She *wouldn't* think of Nico. Tonight she answered to no one but herself. Only herself.

She took one last look in the mirror, satisfied with her appearance, before leaving to meet Jack.

"The sight of you makes me sick."

"Likewise, but get used to having me around, babe. I'm not moving out."

Harrison settled back comfortably on the couch. As Grace had told him, he didn't have to move out. Half the house was in his name and he'd invested five years in this marriage. He wasn't leaving till he got his fair share.

Gabrielle, clad in a red Valencia gown with a plunging neckline and chalk bugle beads, stomped a high-heeled foot. "This is *my* house."

"*Our* house," Harrison corrected.

"I want you out!"

"I'm not going anywhere."

Gabrielle gave Harrison a crafty smile. "Want to bet? Guess who I'm going to be seeing tonight?"

Harrison couldn't care in the least. "Who?" he asked disinterestedly.

"*Daddy.*"

Gabrielle uttered the word heavily and with importance . . . like a magic word. She needed to say no more, noting with pleasure the way Harrison's body tensed, though he tried to hide it. He shrugged his shoulders nonchalantly. "So?"

"So tonight the dirty linen gets aired. How do you think Daddy's going to react when I tell him you've cheated on me? Of course, I'll mention finding you and Grace in our bed. That'll *really* infuriate him."

"You wouldn't."

"But of course I would! I'm his little girl and *no one* hurts Daddy's little girl." Gabrielle pondered for a moment. "I'll be sure to sound distraught . . . the devoted wife betrayed. There'll be tears, and naturally my voice will quiver. It'll be some performance, Harrison. And you said I couldn't act!"

"You spoiled, self-centered, obnoxious bitch!" Harrison shouted, jumping to his feet. "You think you can scare me by running to that Mafia goon you call a father? You're not so innocent yourself. How do you think your father will like hearing about *your* extracurricular activities?"

"Lies," Gabrielle sang. "Daddy won't believe you. Daddy only believes what he wants to believe. What *I* tell him will be the truth . . . accepted without question. Honey, you're still up shit's creek."

"Ever hear of California community property law?" Harrison trumped. "What's yours is mine. At least fifty percent."

"And fifty percent of what you have is zero. You're not laying a finger on *my* money."

"*Our* money," Harrison corrected.

"Keep dreaming," Gabrielle scoffed. "Daddy will personally persuade you to leave this marriage the way you arrived: empty-handed. To think I once thought you had talent. I thought you were a genius with words. Instead you were a flash in the pan."

Harrison grabbed Gabrielle by the arm, squeezing tightly. "You destroyed my talent, hovering over me like a vulture, pouncing on my screenplays and disregarding them without a second thought because you thought they weren't good enough. You! You! You! All you've ever thought about in this marriage is yourself! You never loved me and you never cared about my writing, except when you thought it might do your career some good."

"Let go of my arm," Gabrielle demanded through gritted teeth.

"You smothered my talent. You strangled my creative spark." Harrison shook Gabrielle. "You kept hounding me and hounding me for the perfect role!"

Gabrielle tried to pull free of Harrison but his grip only grew tighter. His shaking increased. His eyes gleamed with hatred and a hint of lost control.

"Over and over I kept rewriting and rewriting . . . doubting myself . . . questioning myself . . . dreading what I had once loved so much. You've destroyed me." Harrison let go of Gabrielle, pushing her to the floor with a forceful shove. "I'm not going to let you get away with that."

"I'd rather be dead than see you get one red cent of mine," she spat out.

"That can be easily arranged."

Gabrielle gave Harrison a dark look as she got to her feet, straightening her gown. "Are you threatening me?"

"Why would I do that?"

"Because you're desperate." Gabrielle released a rich, throaty laugh, waving at everything around them. "You've gotten accustomed to having the finer things. You can't bear to give this all up."

"I'm not going to."

"Guess again," she stated with deadly intent. "Tonight's your last night under this roof. I'd advise you to pack your bags. Daddy will be returning home with me tonight and I'd hate to think what would happen if he found you here."

"If you think you're getting away with this, you're crazy," Harrison screamed as Gabrielle made her way out. "I'm not going to let you! You're going to pay, Gabrielle! Pay! Tonight you're going to pay!"

"Darling, I'm back!" Vanessa Vought exclaimed as Daniel stepped into the interior of her black stretch limousine.

"And looking just as gorgeous as ever."

"Flatterer!" Vanessa promptly kissed Daniel on both cheeks. "I've missed you so much."

"Same here. So are you going to clear up the mystery? You've been gone for eight months with neither a letter nor call. Where'd you disappear to? And why?"

"We'll get to that in a minute, darling," Vanessa promised, blue eyes shining bright with mystery, reaching for a bottle of chilled champagne. "First we have to have a toast."

The cork flew from the bottle of champagne with a hearty pop. A thin wisp of vapor spiraled upward, followed by a gurgle of white frothy foam. Vanessa quickly filled two glasses, handing one to Daniel.

"Here's to *Long Journey Home*. May the project bring you only good things despite having to share the screen with Diana Halloway."

"I'm glad to see things haven't changed."

Vanessa lightly clinked her glass against Daniel's before taking a sip. "You know how I despise that woman."

"I'm hardly her biggest fan."

Vanessa tossed back her sleek cap of ebony hair, fussing with the wave that covered one eye. "Dear Diana. I'm sure she's going to be quite pissed seeing me this evening. After all, it is her night."

"Stealing the spotlight from her has always been one of your favorite things."

"How it has!" Vanessa enthusiastically agreed. "Tonight won't be an exception. I've got one hell of a bombshell to lay on her."

"Does this have anything to do with your extended absence?" Daniel asked wisely.

"You're so quick to make the connection."

"Enough with the suspense. Where were you?"

"In a villa in Algiers."

"Algiers? What were you doing there?"

"Writing," Vanessa answered simply, though her eyes sparkled with excitement.

"I didn't know you had any inclinations to write a novel."

"Darling, who said anything about writing a *novel*?" Vanessa gave Daniel a cheshire grin.

His eyes grew wide behind his champagne glass. "You don't mean—"

"But I do!" Vanessa purred. "Isn't it delicious? I've penned my autobiography!"

"Vanessa, have you flung any mud?" Daniel asked, giving her a naughty look.

"I love that hopeful tone in your voice." Vanessa trilled. "But of course! I've included *only* the juiciest tidbits."

"Might I ask who figures most prominently in this exposé of your life?"

"You know the answer to that as well as I do," Vanessa scolded, giving Daniel a playful slap. "The one and only Diana Halloway."

"She's not going to be pleased."

"Who cares? It's about time someone exposed the real Diana. That bitch has fooled everyone for years. I took off the kid gloves and went after her with both barrels."

"How so?"

"Remember Iris Larson?"

"Angel, who *doesn't* know who Iris Larson was!"

"Well, she was one of my closest friends. Did you know she was pregnant with Adam Stoddard's child?"

Daniel's eyes widened with shock. "What? Are you sure about that?"

"Absolutely, though nobody knew Iris was pregnant. When she found out she was pregnant she went into hiding to protect Adam. If you'll recall, everybody knew about their affair. When I managed to find her, hiding in Palm Springs, I saw she was pregnant. When I asked her who the father was, she told me it was Adam. She also told me that despite Diana's own pregnancy, Adam was going to leave Diana for her."

"Whatever happened to the baby?"

"The baby was born dead and Iris went into a deep depression. Diana didn't help matters. She sent Iris a black baby's bonnet and booties, along with baby pictures of Kelly. At night she would call Iris and play a tape recording of a crying baby."

"Are you absolutely sure about all this?"

"Daniel, why would I make up something like this? Diana tortured poor Iris and she's going to pay!"

"Something's not right," Daniel murmured to himself. "The facts just aren't adding up."

"What do you mean?"

"You know Adam was my best friend. He'd have mentioned something like this to me, and yet . . ."

"Yet what?"

"Let's drop it for now. Tell me, have you got a publisher?"

"Swifty is holding the auction next week. He expects plenty of bidders."

Daniel gave Vanessa a shrewd look. "Plan on announcing your literary endeavor this evening?"

"Naturally!" Vanessa enthused. "I *have* to ruin Diana's evening before she ruins mine."

CHAPTER NINETEEN

Catching sight of a waving Kelly, Laura made her way through the party crowd, eager to leave behind her date.

"You're a lifesaver," she breathed upon reaching Kelly's side.

"Why's that?"

"In spite of my protests, Jack has had his hands all over me."

"Forget Jack and mingle. You'll meet someone else."

"Sounds like good advice. Maybe if I ditch that creep I can have a good time."

"That's the spirit," Kelly encouraged. "Why don't you join Graham and me at our table?"

"Great. I'm dying to meet him. Where is he?"

"He's off getting us drinks."

"I guess there must really be a few good guys still left out there."

"There are," Kelly affirmed. "There definitely are."

"Graham, what a lovely surprise!"

Graham turned around with two drinks in his hand, facing Diana. "Your voice is dripping with sincerity."

"And yours with sarcasm." Diana stuck a finger in Graham's scotch, stirring it, then sucking her finger dry. "Tell me, have you abandoned your *acting* career for bartending? If so, I'll have a martini, extra dry."

Graham discarded the scotch Diana had stuck her finger into, ordering another. "I'm not the bartender, Diana. I'm a guest."

"How'd you swing that? Did someone pay you to escort her? Times hard? I thought you were above that kind of thing."

"I'm here with my wife."

"Your *wife?*" Diana exclaimed incredulously. "I don't believe it!"

"Why not? What's so funny?"

"I thought you were married to your career. That nothing else came before it. Don't you want to be a star, Graham?"

"Being a star never mattered to me. That was *your* bag, not mine."

"With a little wifey tying you down you don't have anything to worry about." Diana shook her head regretfully. "You could have had it all, Graham. I would have seen to it."

"Your promises were empty, Diana. The only important person in your life was you. Want to know why? Because you can't love. You don't know how. I do. And I also know there are more important things in life than fame and fortune."

"Such noble words!" Diana said scornfully. "So tell me, when do I get to meet the little woman?"

"I'm sure your paths will cross this evening. When they do, I'll make an introduction."

"Did you tell her about us?"

"No," Graham answered coldly. "I saw no need to."

"Don't worry. I won't tell her we were *intimate*," Diana leered suggestively. "Besides, why would I want to tell your wife about us? What could I possibly gain from telling her what we shared?"

"I find it hard to believe that we ever shared anything," Graham stated dryly.

Diana sighed dramatically. "You're not going to forgive me for sleeping with Paul Fontana, are you darling? Well, here's a confession." She leaned forward to whisper in Graham's ear. "You're much better at bed sports than he is." She stepped back and closed her eyes, shuddering. "How I loathe that man's touch!"

"Yet you still sleep with him."

"Yes, I do," Diana agreed. "Paul Fontana is a powerful man. He can do anything . . . anything I ask."

"That must be nice," Graham observed.

"It is . . . until you have to pay the consequences." Diana broke free of her thoughts. "Run along, Graham. I'll be waiting with bated breath until Mrs. Denning and I have a chance to meet."

* * *

"White wine please," Laura requested.

Smiling her thanks to the bartender, Laura made her way back to Kelly, noticing the faces around her. She couldn't believe it! She was standing elbow to elbow with some of Hollywood's more memorable stars. There were Mickey Rourke, Kevin Costner, and Tom Hanks; Dennis Quaid and Meg Ryan gazed at each other while Warren Beatty whispered into the ear of a new lovely.

Laura stopped in her tracks, craning her neck at an incoming couple. Was that Daniel Ellis with an arm around Vanessa Vought? She began walking again, though her eyes remained focused on the moving couple. Yes! Yes, it was they!

Just then she slammed into a immovable slab of masculinity, her white wine sloshing over the side of her glass.

"I'm terribly sorry," she apologized, shaking her dripping hand. "I don't know—"

The rest of her words trailed off as she looked into those ice blue eyes she had been unable to forget.

It was *him*.

It was *her*. Drew couldn't believe it. Their paths had crossed again.

This time he wasn't going to let her get away. He held out a hand. "Drew Stern. And your name?"

Laura blinked disbelieving eyes, expecting him to disappear each time she opened them. It was Drew Stern. He was standing in front of her. Introducing himself! "Laura Danby," she managed. She dabbed at the sleeve of his jacket with her napkin. "Forgive my clumsiness."

"Don't worry about the tuxedo. It's rented." He gave her a full smile of reassurance.

Laura felt weak in the knees. *This* was being star struck. Or was it more than that?

"Are you with someone?" he asked.

"I was, but now I'm alone."

"Would you like to spend the rest of the evening with me?" *Please let her say yes,* Drew prayed. *Let her say yes.*

Laura gave Drew her most dazzling smile. "I'd love to."

This was the *real* Hollywood, Heather realized in awe, taking note of the powerful producers, directors, agents and stars around her.

Soon she would be a permanent part of this world.

Eyes were cast her way and Heather met the stares. She could see the questions: *Who is she? What's she doing here? Why did Mark Bauer cast her—was he crazy?*

No one went out of their way to greet her—to make an introduction and include her in a group. The ranks had closed and would not open until she had proven herself.

Fine. Heather squared her shoulders, cutting through the room, dazzling in a beaded leopard black lace gown by Bob Mackie. Apparently tonight was to be the first step.

She would show them all.

"*Who* is that hunky specimen in the corner?" Vanessa whispered to Daniel.

"Where?"

Vanessa pointed a finger. "Over there."

Daniel followed Vanessa's finger. "I don't know."

"Well, love, he's been keeping a *close* eye on you. There's more than curiosity in those eyes."

"Really?" Daniel's interest perked and his gaze returned to the young man Vanessa had pointed out. "He *is* lovely to look at."

"Go for it," Vanessa urged. "Make an introduction. Obviously the poor boy is too shy to make the first move. It's about time you traded in Jaime. I'm going to circulate. I'm hoping to run into Diana."

"Don't start any fireworks unless I'm there to watch," he called over his shoulder as he and Vanessa parted.

He's coming over, Peter realized. *He's coming over!*

A web of excitement spread throughout Peter's body as Daniel Ellis drew closer.

Peter had heard the rumors about Daniel, but hadn't known if they were true. But he wanted to find out. He wanted to find out first hand.

"Impressive crowd," Daniel commented, drawing up next to Peter.

"Very impressive," Peter agreed, glancing at Daniel from the corner of his eye. Daniel's profile was rugged and chiseled; his lips slightly moistened.

"My name's Peter Fontana," he introduced, turning to Daniel and offering a hand.

Daniel took Peter's hand in his, covering it with the other as they shook. He didn't let go. Instead, his hand held onto Peter's, thumb rubbing his palm. "Nice meeting you, Peter."

Peter didn't let go of Daniel's hand. "Nice meeting you, Daniel."

***

Paul Fontana felt like a god. Surrounding him were Hollywood's most important movers and shakers, lauding him with praise and good wishes. Trinity Pictures was *the* studio on everyone's lips. Mark Bauer's five-year contract would do for Trinity what Eddie Murphy's had done for Paramount. No one knew how Paul had done it. Yet it was unanimous that *Long Journey Home* would be the first of many successes.

Paul returned the greetings, smiled, and shook hands as he memorized faces and names, filing away the information until the day it would do him the most good.

"Having a good time?" he asked Diana, a comfortable arm draped around her shoulders as they veered through the party crowd.

"Fabulous," Diana drawled, wishing Paul's hands were off her. From the moment he'd picked her up he'd been much too feely. He'd ruined her makeup on the drive over with his insistent kisses and she'd had to fix her hair. On the dance floor his hands had squeezed her bottom once too often and at one point he'd even suggested they slip away for ten minutes. The nerve! Diana Halloway *did not* engage in quickie sex!

When she made love the sessions were long, slow, and intense—greedy kisses and frenzied pawing weren't tolerated. Graham had known how to make love. Why hadn't she slept with him one last time? He'd been *so* good! Seeing him again had put ideas in her mind . . . had reminded her how good it was to make love with a younger man.

The idea stuck in her mind as she envisioned Graham naked, approaching her. So what if he was married? She loved a challenge, and forbidden fruit was always so much more tantalizing.

She slipped free of Paul's arm, giving him a sweet smile. "Darling, I'm going to go look for Kelly. Manage without me?"

"I'll try, but hurry back."

"As soon as I can," she lied. How Paul wanted to end this

evening was perfectly clear, but not if she had anything to say about it.

She went off in search of Graham.

Laura and Drew were in a world of their own, oblivious to the party around them, concentrating only on each other.

They were sitting outside on the terrace, talking over sips of champagne and nibbles of Petrossian caviar on toast points.

"I can't believe you're sitting across from me," he said.

"*You* can't believe it?" Laura exclaimed. "*I* can't believe it! I'm sitting across from the biggest box-office draw in America!"

"Does that impress you?" Drew asked quietly, hoping she said it didn't.

"Well, sure!"

"Why?" Drew didn't want to believe that Laura was interested in him as Drew Stern—Movie Star. If so, his impression of her was wrong and he didn't want that to be. He was enchanted by Laura Danby. She was beautiful and witty, easy to talk to, and he could spend hours alone with her. Tonight could lead to so much more . . . to what he had always wanted . . . if only he was right about her.

"There's something special about you that separates you from everyone else," Laura answered honestly. "I don't know what it is and I can't put my finger on it, but it's there and it draws you. It's what comes across when you're on a movie screen. You're one of a kind, Drew. You're in a class by yourself."

"Maybe I don't want to be," he said. Her perception of him was flattering, but it also held a painful truth. He *was* in a class by himself . . . an empty class of his own making. "Maybe I want to be like everyone else."

"In what way?"

"Why don't I tell you a little about myself first? It'll help you understand."

For the next hour Drew spoke about himself and his ascent to stardom. He included everything, leaving out nothing. It was the first time he had ever relived his past with someone else. Although the retelling was unpleasant, he wanted to tell it all to Laura. It was important that she know who he was. Why he was the way he was.

"You've lived quite a life," Laura said quietly after Drew had finished.

"Have I? I suppose." Drew ran a finger over the rim of his champagne glass, staring down at the golden liquid as he swirled it around. "I'd trade it all in a minute if I could have what everyone else has always had."

"What's that?"

"A family. A sense of belonging. Knowing I mattered in someone's life."

"But Drew, you have millions of fans worldwide. Of course, you matter."

"It's not the same thing."

"I know it isn't." Laura placed a reassuring hand on Drew's arm. "Don't be so hard on yourself. Someday you'll have what you really want. If you want it badly enough you can't give up hope."

"Someday?" Drew looked up at Laura, placing his hand over hers. "Maybe I've already found what I've been looking for. I've been a loner, Laura. For years I've been on my own, shutting out the world, although that really wasn't what I wanted."

"Then why have you?" Laura asked softly.

"Because I was afraid. Because I wasn't willing to take a chance. All this time I've wanted to let someone in. And now I think I've found that someone." Drew put down his champagne glass and swept Laura into his arms. Holding her felt good. So very, very good. "I'm willing now. Will you help me, Laura?"

Laura's throat had gone dry. She gazed into Drew's eyes. How could she say no to this man? He had bared his soul to her and in doing so had already taken the first step. She wanted to help him. She did. And she wanted to become a part of his life. She couldn't ignore how she was starting to feel about him. It felt wonderful!

But would it be fair to become involved with Drew without telling him all about herself? Didn't she owe that to him? Didn't he need to know what becoming involved with her would mean?

"Laura?"

Drew looked at her doubtfully, as though fearing what her answer would be. She couldn't let him down. She couldn't! And if she was honest with herself, she couldn't let herself down. Here was a chance to start over. All she had to do was take that chance. And she wanted to. How she wanted to!

She chased away her thoughts of the past. It was all over and done with. Only the present mattered. Only Drew mattered.

"I'll do whatever you want," she told him. "I promise."

"Show me how to love, Laura," he implored. "Teach me how to trust. I don't want to be alone anymore."

Laura wrapped her arms around Drew, nestling close to him. "I don't want to be alone anymore either. We'll do this together, Drew. For ourselves and for each other."

Drew's lips then came down upon Laura's and they sealed their vow with a kiss.

Mark watched the party in progress, his eyes moving from one star to the next. Once again he'd brought Hollywood's most famous faces together. And naturally, his name was on all their lips.

They all knew how good he was. They all knew how good *Long Journey Home* would be. And they all knew there would be future Mark Bauer projects needing to be cast.

Mark enjoyed the evening's homage to him. After tonight there would be three months of hard work ahead of him. He wouldn't be the center of attention again until *Long Journey Home* was released.

"Hello, Mark. You're looking pretty happy with yourself," Gabrielle purred, sliding up next to him.

"Gabrielle!" Mark choked out, his champagne sliding down his throat the wrong way at the sight of her. "What are you doing here?"

"I never miss a good party." She ran a finger down the lapel of his tuxedo. "I must say I was disappointed that I didn't get a personal invitation."

Mark laughed. "You know how these things can get overlooked."

"How I do," she murmured. "You seem to have overlooked our arrangement concerning *Long Journey Home*. The role of Olivia was to have been given to me. You promised."

"What are you talking about? I never promised you anything."

"Well, you certainly dangled a silver plum before my eyes. Was that just to entice me into bed? If it was, I don't think my father will like hearing about it."

"Wait a minute! You were the one who came after me!" Mark hotly reminded, not liking the way past events were being twisted and distorted. "If you recall, I found you in my bed."

Gabrielle angrily jabbed a perfectly manicured nail into Mark's chest. "You owe me, Mark, and you owe me big! No one fucks Gabrielle Fontana without paying a price."

"Yeah? Well, I got news for you, babe," he taunted, fed up with having to put up with her antics. "This time I got the honey for free! There's not one thing you can do to change that. It's about time you learned you can't always get what you want. Welcome to the real world."

"No, Mark," Gabrielle disagreed. "Welcome to *my* world, where every wish comes true."

"Just what the hell do you want?" Mark was at the point of exasperation. "You want a part in a future film? Fine. You've got it. Now get off my fucking case."

"I don't want a part in a future film. I want the role of Olivia," Gabrielle quietly stated.

Mark stared at Gabrielle ludicrously. "You're crazy. There's no way I'm dumping Heather."

"Don't push me, Mark," Gabrielle warned in a steely whisper. "Otherwise I'm going to go to Daddy. You wouldn't like that. I'd have to tell him how you screwed me. How you promised and promised me the role of Olivia if only I'd sleep with you. And then I'd have to tell him how you didn't give me the role after I did what you wanted. He *won't* be pleased."

Mark grabbed Gabrielle by the arm, squeezing with all his might. "Keep your filthy lies to yourself."

"Let go," she warned, twisting herself free. "I'm going to go mingle. You think over what I said. Think of the damage I can do." She blew him a kiss. "Catch you later."

"I saw you huddling in a corner with Mark Bauer before." Kelly gave Graham an inquisitive look. "Keeping a secret?"

"My, you do have an eagle eye."

Kelly teased Graham with a kiss. "You didn't answer my question. There'll be no secrets in this marriage."

Graham gave Kelly an eager look, bursting to tell her his news. "Well, there was something I did want to tell you. Actually, I've known since we've gotten back from Las Vegas, but I wanted to wait until tonight to tell you."

"What is it?" she urged. "Don't keep me in suspense." She held up a halting hand. "No. Wait. Let me guess. Mark wants to use you in a future film."

"Better than that. He's given me a role in *Long Journey Home*. He's going to announce it tonight."

"Graham, that's wonderful," Kelly gasped in delight, throwing her arms around him. "I'm so proud of you."

Graham swung Kelly around. "Do you know what this means? It's a step up. People are going to start noticing me. The only drawback is in being separated from you for three months."

Kelly drew back from Graham, a look of panic on her face. "You're going to be gone for three months?"

"Hey, I'll be back."

"Where will you be going?"

"We'll be doing location shooting in Nebraska. Why do you look so surprised?"

"I guess I thought you'd be filming here in L.A."

"Sure, the interiors. But the farm is the backdrop of this story and Mark is a fanatic when it comes to his films. Every last detail has to be authentic." Graham noticed Kelly was silent and lifted her chin, looking into her eyes. "What's the matter? Why the frown? Aren't you happy for me?"

Kelly didn't want to spoil the moment for Graham—she didn't. But they were married only a week and he was getting ready to leave her for three months. When she'd married Graham she hadn't thought she would ever be alone again. She didn't want to be alone. Not again. Not so soon.

She loved Graham with all her heart—he made her feel special, something she had never before felt. She didn't want to lose that feeling. Was she being selfish for feeling a bit cheated? She knew about Graham's career—knew how important it was to him—but she had thought they'd have more time together.

"Well, Kelly?"

"Of course I'm happy for you!" Embarrassed by her prolonged silence, the words came out in a breathless rush. "It's just that I'm going to miss you."

"I'm going to miss you, too. But there'll be phone calls and you can fly out on weekends when it fits your schedule."

"But I don't want just phone calls and weekends." Kelly decided she couldn't hide the way she felt. Graham had to know her feelings. For any marriage to work there had to be openness and honesty. "I want *you*. Graham, why couldn't we have discussed this?"

He gave her a hurt look. "I wanted to surprise you. I wanted you to be proud of me. Kelly, this is an enormous boost for my career. I can't pass up a chance to work with Mark Bauer. Sometimes sacrifices have to be made."

"I know. It's just that this was all so unexpected."

"I'm sorry."

"Don't be sorry. Just make me a promise."

"Anything."

"Promise me you'll give the finest performance of your career."

Graham's eyes sparkled. "Done! Anything else?"

"One other thing," Kelly continued, looping her arm through Graham's as she led him in search of two glasses of champagne to celebrate with. "No more surprises." She gave him a serious look. "I hate surprises."

Heather was busy heaping her plate with a selection of delicacies from the buffet. Keeping with a seafood theme, she had selected mussels and clams in a delicious black bean sauce, Norwegian salmon, and baby lobster. She was spooning a bit of Beluga caviar onto her plate when suddenly she was shoved from behind. She lurched forward, the contents of her dish scattering across the buffet.

"So sorry," a voice behind her drawled. Then, as she turned, "Aren't you that awful B-movie star?"

Heather came face to face with Gabrielle Fontana Moore. Though they'd never before met, she knew the score with this one. Gabrielle had wanted the role of Olivia. That little shove had been no accident.

"Aren't *you* that horrible soap actress?" she snapped back.

"*Actress* is the applicable word," Gabrielle decreed haughtily.

"That's a matter of opinion."

"Well, here's an opinion shared by almost everyone in this room. Mark Bauer is a fool for casting a no-talent like you in a multi-million-dollar production."

"Sour grapes? Rumor has it you were *panting* for my part. Was that true when you weren't in bed with him?"

Heather's remark hit the bullseye.

"You little bitch!" Gabrielle raged, raising a hand that promptly connected with Heather's cheek.

Heather's eyes narrowed. Not caring what anyone would think or say, she reached for the spoon nestled in a mountain of sour cream, scooping up a large blob. Then she aimed directly between Gabrielle's breasts, where the sour cream landed with a loud plop.

Gabrielle's smirk disappeared as she looked down in horror. The sour cream was oozing down the front of her Valencia gown.

"Why you—" she gasped.

No one got the better of Heather McCall. Nor did they ever mess with her twice. Not after she finished with them. Picking up the silver tureen of sour cream, Heather charged forward, burying Gabrielle's face in it.

Gabrielle shrieked, wiping the sour cream from her eyes and face as she stormed away from the sounds of laughter echoing throughout the room, leaving a dripping white trail behind.

"I guess slapstick's not her cup of tea," Heather commented to no one in particular, licking away a trickle of sour cream from a finger.

It had been such a long time for both of them.

In the darkness of his bedroom, Drew caressed Laura with the softest of embraces, knowing something special was about to happen and that something this special didn't happen often.

"You're so beautiful," he whispered. "Has anyone ever told you how beautiful you are?"

Laura shook her head. "No one but you."

Drew traced a finger along a cheekbone and down her neck to between her breasts. "You are," he affirmed. "Laura—"

His voice quivered with an unspoken hesitation, as if unsure that what he wanted was what she wanted.

"Yes," she urged, her lips daring to join his with undisguised passion. "Yes."

Tonight she was going to slip through the barriers she had created and escape the chains of her past. She was going to embrace passion . . . embrace desire . . . and embrace the man who was making her feel so vibrantly alive.

"Love me," she fervently whispered.

Drew's fingers found the zipper of her gown, pulling downward. The gown fell to the floor in a luxurious mound of silk and Laura stepped out of it as Drew's fingers eased sensuously down her bare back.

She gasped, suddenly breathless. Shivers of pleasure from such unrestricted contact traveled down her spine. Laura trembled with excitement, knowing that this pleasure was only a sampling of a greater ecstasy to come.

"Your skin is so soft," Drew said, giving her a lingering kiss, his lips hovering above hers before moving to her neck, kissing one side and then the other as his hands spanned around her waist before lifting her to him.

Laura's arms wrapped their way around Drew's neck. She was aware of nothing but him as his lips moved first from one breast and then the other, his tongue luxuriously rolling around each of her nipples . . . hardening them with each taste he took . . . teasing them with his tongue until the tiny mounds of sensitive flesh were stretched as far as they could go.

Laura felt as though she were spinning uncontrollably through a universe of sweet sensation she had never before experienced . . . powerless to do anything except relish her visit to this exquisite new world she had ventured into . . . had never even known existed . . . but was thoroughly enjoying because of Drew.

Somehow they made their way to the bed, as though seeking an oasis for their mounting passion before succumbing to the ultimate satisfaction.

Laura sank down upon the bed, gazing up into Drew's ice-blue eyes with unabashed wanting.

"Your turn," she told him, reaching to unbutton his shirt with trembling fingers, impatient to feel herself pressed against him.

The satiny smoothness of his bare chest thrilled her. Rising to her knees, she traced the sculpted contours with her tongue, moving lower and lower until she reached his belt and removed it in two quick moves.

Next she undid his trousers, unable to resist slipping a hand inside. Hot pulsing flesh throbbed with demand at her touch. Drew groaned, eyes half-closing.

He didn't know how much longer he could last. The jolts of delight ripping through his system were becoming stronger and stronger. He didn't know how much more he could take. But he wanted to find out.

He managed to shed the rest of his clothes and then he and Laura were both naked, their eyes drinking in each other as they realized what was to come next.

He descended upon her slowly . . . wanting to take his time . . . wanting to savor every last detail no matter how small, so that later, when he was alone, he could re-create the experience. A long time ago he had learned the importance of memories. Of creating them. Of remembering to keep them because sometimes they were all you had.

Overwhelmed by a raging hunger for release, Drew plunged

deeper into Laura, his thrusts becoming more and more frenzied as she bucked against him.

Laura felt the waves building as she tossed her auburn head back. As the first arrived she opened herself to a blanket of surging delight. After that it was nonstop and Laura simply basked in a sea of contentment. Never before had lovemaking been this good.

Drew surrendered to his climax, abandoning his self-control, no longer able to deny himself and shuddering with intense relief.

After that they slipped beneath the sheets, arms cradled around the other's waist, heads resting together.

"That was nice," Laura whispered, snuggling closer.

Drew kissed her again. What Laura had given to him was priceless. And for that he would always love her. "It was," he softly agreed.

Diana arched an eyebrow, blinking disbelieving eyes at the sight of Kelly and Graham together, heads nestled intimately. This was definitely an interesting duo and one that merited instant investigation.

Excitement coursed through Diana. This was going to be such fun! Not only would she have the pleasure of flirting with Graham, but she'd also be diverting his attention from Kelly. Whatever could he be discussing with her?

With a glass of champagne raised in one hand, Diana swooped down on the couple.

"What have we here? I didn't even know you two knew each other."

Graham shot Diana a dark look. There was no mistaking the mocking tone in her voice—the disbelief. She was getting ready to play a game but he wanted no part of it.

"We more than know each other, Diana."

"Really? Do fill me in." Diana drained her champagne glass, handing the empty glass out to Kelly. "Be a love and get me a refill. Graham and I have some catching up to do."

"Get your own refill," he snapped, snatching the glass from Kelly and shoving it back to Diana. "She's not your servant."

Kelly looked from Graham to Diana in confusion. Something was going on here—something she didn't like. There was a current of hostility between the two.

Kelly looked at her mother, noticing the glint in her eye. It was a predatory glint. She was after something. There was no mistaking that look of hunger—of wanting. Her mother wanted Graham.

Kelly edged closer to her husband, comforted when he wrapped an arm around her. Diana's eyes widened at the gesture.

"How cozy," she purred. "Getting a thrill, Kelly?" She laughed hysterically.

Kelly burned under the intense assault of her mother's mockery. She wasn't going to be spoken to like this in front of her husband. Just as she was about to open her mouth, Graham spoke.

"Don't you *ever* talk to my wife that way again," he ordered.

Diana's laughter died. "Wife? Did you say *wife?*"

"Losing your hearing as the years go by, Diana? You heard me. *Wife*," he repeated. "Kelly is my wife."

"You've got to be kidding! You can't be serious!" Diana looked from Kelly to Graham. Both their faces were blank. They didn't know. They honestly didn't know!

"I assure you he is," Kelly stated coolly, staring down her mother. Now was the time to make it clear that Graham was off limits. "We were married last week."

"This is too much!" Diana screeched, bursting into fresh peals of laughter, clutching her sides.

"What's so funny, Mother?" Kelly demanded evenly. "You can't believe someone as wonderful as Graham could love me? Is that it? Well, let me tell you—"

"Mother?" Graham gasped in horror, cutting Kelly off. "Did you just call her *mother?*"

"Graham, what's wrong?" Kelly asked, panicking as she watched her husband turn ashen.

"I can't believe it!" Diana bellowed, thoroughly enjoying herself, tears streaming down her cheeks. The cat was out of the bag! "This is simply *too* delicious!" She continued laughing while onlookers watched.

"Stop it, Mother!" Kelly's patience snapped. Something was going on—something she didn't want to know. Why was Graham reacting the way he was?

"She's your mother?" he whispered, closing his eyes in resignation.

"Yes, she's my mother. Graham, why is that so upsetting? Is it because I didn't tell you? Darling, I'm sorry."

"*Au contraire*," Diana gushed, holding up a finger, so willing to provide Kelly with the missing pieces. "It's not what you didn't tell him, but what *he* didn't tell *you*."

"What are you talking about?" Kelly asked, even though she didn't want to know. If it involved her mother, it wouldn't be good.

"Let me enlighten you. I simply *must*. I can't pass this up! But where to begin?" Diana mused. "*Where* to begin?"

Kelly was in no mood for her mother's games. "Get to the point!"

"My, you're anxious! Well, here it is. Kelly, *dearest,* my darling, *darling* daughter, you're married to my *ex-lover!*"

Diana relished the look of horror spreading across Kelly's face as her news sunk in.

"No," she whispered. "You're lying. It's a lie."

"But it isn't. Ask Graham. He'll tell you the truth, won't you, Graham?"

Kelly's voice quivered. "Graham?"

He opened his eyes, revealing a look of utter bleakness and hopelessness. "It's true," he confirmed. "What she's said is true."

Kelly couldn't make sense of it all. This couldn't be happening to her. Her mother couldn't be destroying her happiness. She thought she had finally escaped from Diana's destructive grip. She'd thought she was finally free. But she wasn't. She was right back where she started. At Diana's mercy.

She couldn't stand the sight of her mother's gloating face. Nor the sight of her sickened-looking husband, who had kept such a secret from her. Without a word to either of them, Kelly turned and fled, ignoring Graham's cries as he followed after her. Behind her she could hear Diana's mocking laughter.

"What's wrong with her? After all, it's all in the family."

"Don't you look like the cat who's swallowed the canary."

Diana whirled at the sound of her archrival's voice. "Vanessa! I see you're looking just as haggard as ever."

"While you're looking just as cheap as always," Vanessa countered. "Really angel, strapless gowns are a no-no when one's breasts are starting to sag."

"I'm so glad to see you're following your own advice," Diana stated sweetly. "Tell me, where've you been hiding all these months? Your face looks tighter. More plastic surgery? You should have had more extensive work done, darling."

"How you go on!"

"Seriously, darling, when are you going back into hiding?"

"You'd love that, wouldn't you? Then all my parts would come to you first."

"They always did."

"Who are you kidding? When they want talent they come to me. When they need to scrape the bottom of the barrel, they come to you."

"What delusions you weave," Diana snorted.

"Are you doubting me, Diana? When I have the perfect example? Mark Bauer offered me your role in *Long Journey Home* first. Much as I hated to turn down the role, I just couldn't fit it into my busy schedule."

"Well the part's *mine* now and will be immortalized by *me*. And what are you so busy with? Your life is so empty. No husband. Your children don't talk to you. No lovers. Nothing."

"Except my awards, especially my Oscar. By the way, did I ever thank you for turning down *Manipulations*? If I hadn't been for you I wouldn't have gotten my statuette," Vanessa reminded, knowing the Oscar was a particularly sore point with Diana. "You almost had one, didn't you Diana? At least that's what you claim, but honey, your performance in *Banquet* would never have matched Iris's."

"Don't mention that slut's name to me," Diana growled.

"You were always so jealous of Iris. Could it be because she was so much better than you? As an actress. As a lover."

"She never got Adam," Diana hissed. "He stayed with me."

"It was only a matter of time before he left you for her. I knew it. Iris knew it. And *you* knew it."

Diana yawned. "This conversation is starting to bore me."

"Then let me get to the point. You wanted to know what I've been so busy with. I'll tell you. I've been writing."

"Writing?"

"Yes," Vanessa answered. "Pages and pages. I've been writing my memoirs."

"What could you possibly have to say?" Diana sneered.

"Plenty. But the book's not just about *me*, love. It's also about the people who have been in my life. Their influence. My feelings about them. People like Daniel, Adam, Iris. And, of course, *you*."

Diana's head snapped to attention. Her eyes became twin lasers, shooting venomous daggers at Vanessa. "What are you planning to say about me?"

"Wouldn't you love to know! You'll just have to be patient and wait for it to hit the bookstores."

"Over my dead body," Diana snarled, knowing that whatever Vanessa had to say wouldn't be complimentary. "My attorney will be in touch with yours."

With that Diana stormed away.

"Did you enjoy your little session?" Daniel asked, sliding up to Vanessa.

"Immensely." Vanessa accepted the glass of champagne offered. "But darling, I think Kelly needs you."

"What happened?" he asked, his concern evident.

"Diana dropped some sort of bombshell on her. The poor girl looked devastated." Vanessa took a sip of her champagne. "Honestly, when it comes to mothering, Diana Halloway makes Joan Crawford look like Donna Reed."

Gabrielle was in the ladies' room, scrubbing at her evening gown furiously, a scowl on her face.

Damn that little bitch! Not only was her gown ruined, but she had been made a laughingstock in front of everyone. No one did that to Gabrielle Fontana. No one. That little bitch was going to be sorry she'd messed with her.

Gabrielle tossed the paper towels she had used into the sink. This was hopeless. She was going to have to go home and change.

At that moment the door to the ladies' room opened. She turned around. When she saw who had entered, a sneer washed over her face.

"*You*," she spat out. "I thought we said everything we needed to say to each other. What are you doing here?"

As Gabrielle's anger consumed her, lashing out and striking with a slew of ugly words, she failed to notice the anger brewing in the person standing across from her. She also failed to notice that the person's hands were rising, clenching and unclenching, heading straight for her throat.

"Kelly, wait! Kelly! We have to talk!" Graham implored as he chased after her. "Please."

Kelly stopped running, stopping in her tracks as she brushed away the tears she had been unable to hold back. She hadn't wanted to cry. She didn't want to cry, but everything had turned so horrible.

Graham and her mother had been lovers. There would never be any escaping that.

"Kelly? Sweetheart?"

"Don't call me that," she said, keeping her back to him. "How could you do this to me? How?"

"Do what?"

"Not tell me you and my mother had been lovers."

"But Kelly, I didn't know she was your mother. All the time Diana and I were involved, she never once mentioned you. You never came to visit. As far as I knew she didn't even have children."

"Come on, Graham." Kelly didn't hide the disbelief in her voice. "Diana Halloway is a public figure. She's been in the media for years."

"You haven't," he pointed out. "I knew nothing of Diana's past. This is as much a shock to me as it is to you. There were no photos of you around the house. There were never any phone calls between the two of you, and as I said, Diana never *once* mentioned you. It was almost as if you didn't exist."

He's right, she thought. There was no escaping what he'd just said. For as long as she could remember, she hadn't existed for her mother—she hadn't been a part of her life. He was right. "What about when we became involved?"

"How was I supposed to make a connection when we met? The two of you don't have the same last name. You never told me who you were." Graham stepped in front of Kelly so that he could face her. "It was all a coincidence. A horrible coincidence."

A tear trickled down Kelly's cheek. "What are we supposed to do now?"

Graham lifted away the tear with a finger. "Get on with our lives. Kelly, I love you. That hasn't changed. Diana means nothing to me. There was never anything good between us, and what we once had is over. Diana is selfish and self-centered. She's never thought of anyone but herself. She doesn't know what the word love means."

"What *does* the word love mean? To us?" she whispered, wearily resting her head upon his chest, drained by the ugly surprise that had been sprung on her. "Tell me. Please."

Graham cupped Kelly's face between his hands, caressing her

cheeks. "It means not wanting to lose the person who means everything to you. It means hurting when the person you love is hurting. It means being unable to imagine a day going by without that person in your life."

Graham's words touched Kelly's heart, melting away the bitterness that had begun to take root. She collapsed in his arms, hugging him fiercely. "Oh Graham, I love you so much. I don't want to lose you, but I'm so afraid I will."

"Never," he vowed, kissing her passionately. "Never. Do you believe me?"

"I want to, Graham. I really want to, but my mother hates me so much," she confessed.

It was the first time Kelly had ever publicly stated what she felt were her mother's true feelings toward her. Diana *hated* her—for whatever warped, twisted reasons she had.

"I don't know why, but she does. She'll do anything to destroy my happiness." Kelly clutched at Graham. "*Anything.* What's going to happen when you go off filming with her? What then?"

"Nothing. Kelly, I love *you*," he reassured her. "Do you understand what I'm saying? *You.* We'll get through this. I won't let Diana destroy us. After this film she's out of our lives forever."

"I can almost believe you," Kelly said wistfully.

"Believe me," Graham vowed, kissing her again.

"Now this is a sight I'd like to see more of," Daniel exclaimed as he neared the two. "Are you okay, Kelly? I heard you had a run-in with your mother."

"I'm fine, Uncle Daniel," she sniffed, giving him a brave smile. "I've learned to handle my mother."

Daniel gave Kelly an encouraging wink. "That's my girl. Why don't you fix your face? There's a party still going on."

"We'll be waiting," Graham said, eyes shining with love.

Stepping into the ladies' room, Kelly was puzzled by the darkness. Running a hand along the wall, she found the wall switch and flipped it on.

Soon the bathroom was filled with light, revealing the patterned wallpaper, ornate mirrors edged with scroll, marble counters and sinks with brass fixtures, the lounging couches in a pink-and-white striped pattern and the dusty rose carpeting.

It also revealed the lifeless body of Gabrielle Fontana Moore.

At the sight of Gabrielle's body, Kelly stopped in her tracks, her evening bag falling to the floor and snapping open, contents spilling out.

Kelly's mouth dropped open next, releasing a scream.

PART TWO

AUGUST TO OCTOBER 1990

CHAPTER TWENTY

Nico Rossi was standing guard. Per Paul Fontana's orders no one except doctors or nurses were allowed in his daughter's hospital room.

Gabrielle Fontana Moore was in a coma, connected to a respirator to help her breathe. She hadn't opened her eyes since the night she had been strangled ten weeks earlier. No one knew when or if Gabrielle would ever open her eyes again.

Nico had arrived in Hollywood a week after the attempt on Gabrielle's life. As soon as he arrived Paul had him guarding Gabrielle twelve hours a day, with a second guard taking over when it was time for Nico to be relieved. Until Nico had arrived, Paul had remained by Gabrielle's side twenty-four hours a day.

The Paul Fontana whom Nico met in Gabrielle's hospital room wasn't the dapper don Nico remembered. Instead, he was unshaven, red eyed, and disheveled. He was also enraged and his reddened eyes burned with murderous intensity.

"I want you to find the person who did this to my daughter. I'll handle the rest!"

Nico searched for answers when he wasn't guarding Gabrielle. The police were useless. Days had been spent questioning the guests at Mark Bauer's party but no one had seen or heard anything unusual. There had been a minor brawl between Gabrielle and Heather McCall, an actress, but their brawl had been only a catfight, not something that would escalate into murder.

Gabrielle's husband, Harrison, who stood to gain the most by her death, had also been cleared as a suspect. He had an alibi for the time of Gabrielle's strangling.

The only angle the police had that made any sense was the one concerning Gabrielle's obsessed fan. Who else could have done it? Nico tended to agree and thus he was pursuing that angle.

When he wasn't busy reconstructing Gabrielle's last days, he spent the rest of his time doing something he enjoyed: tracking down Laura. To his surprise, her name had been on Mark Bauer's party list and when he had shown her photograph to those who had been at the party, they had recognized her instantly. But no one knew where she was or who she had come to the party with. All Laura Danby had been to them was a face.

Nico was a patient man. Already he had gone through half the guest list. He was getting close. He could feel it. Someone on the list knew who Laura Danby was. When he found that person he'd know where to find Laura.

Kelly didn't know how much more she could take.

In her hands was the latest issue of *Inside Access*, a hot selling tabloid paper. On the cover, arranged in a triangle, were three photos: one of her, one of Graham and one of Diana. The headline read: SHARE AND SHARE ALIKE—STUD ACTOR PLEASURES BOTH MOTHER AND DAUGHTER.

She wasn't even going to bother reading the story. She knew how it would read, word for word. For the past ten weeks every tabloid in the country had offered their own version of the Kelly Stoddard/Graham Denning/Diana Halloway love triangle. Theory after theory was formulated and aired. The latest claimed that Diana and Graham had rekindled their affair during filming of *Long Journey Home*.

Kelly refused to believe it. Whenever she and Graham spoke he told her not to believe what was being printed. Nothing was going on between him and Diana. It was all lies—vicious, ugly lies.

Kelly wanted to believe Graham. But it was so hard smothering that tiny twinge of doubt within herself that demanded escape— threatening to compromise her love for Graham and filling her mind with images of him and her mother making love day after day. If she gave in to her doubt it would be like tossing oil onto a fire—it would soon be raging and out of control, ready to consume her.

Diana's silence wasn't helping. Her mother hadn't picked up the phone to call and refute the rumors. But there had been her phone call the night after Mark Bauer's party.

"Darling, you know how I am when I can't have something. It

only makes me want it more! I find the forbidden *irresistible*. But I want you to know I'll try to control myself . . . as best as I can. For you. And if I lose control, try to understand . . ."

Kelly managed to forget the call when it first came. She was too busy answering questions for the officials investigating Gabrielle's strangling. Afterwards, all she could think about was her mother's call.

Had she been giving her a warning? A promise? Had Diana been trying to put her on her guard? Had she only been toying with her, hoping her imagination would run wild? The delay in shooting didn't help as her mother's call kept eating at her. She wanted to tell Graham to stay in Hollywood and forget about *Long Journey Home*. There would be other films—other opportunities.

Yet how could she make such demands of the man she loved? How could she say she didn't trust him to remain faithful to her? It wasn't Graham she didn't trust—it was her mother.

In the end she had kept her silence, making love with total abandon her final night with Graham.

Since then she had ignored the stories; ignored her doubts; fought the urge to take a plane to Nebraska to see for herself if what was being printed was true.

There were only two more weeks of filming in Nebraska left. Then everyone would be back in Hollywood. This would all be over.

Kelly dropped the tabloid into the garbage as she headed to take her morning shower. Once *Long Journey Home* wrapped, the tabloids would have nothing else to write. They'd have to look elsewhere to fill their pages.

Kelly removed her headband, shaking her hair free as she turned on the water. Why were they so consumed with focusing on her and Graham?

Kelly stripped, jumping under the spray. She just couldn't understand why.

"Of course, you can believe what I'm saying," Diana purred into the phone. "When Graham Denning gets back to Hollywood he's going to ask his wife for a divorce. Yes, he has proposed to Diana Halloway, but she hasn't given him an answer. When will she? I don't know but I can try to find out for your next issue. Of course what I'm telling you is true. I'm Ms. Halloway's personal assistant. Now this *is* going to be *Inside Access*'s cover story? Excellent. I'll call when I have more news."

Diana hung up the phone in her trailer with satisfaction. Not only was she destroying Graham and Kelly's marriage, but she was giving herself tons of national coverage. Nebraska was *so* boring. Left and right there was nothing but acres and acres of farmland and cattle. She had to do *something* to amuse herself. And this little something was paying off. Naturally the situation would be much sweeter if she really were sleeping with Graham again, but she wasn't. Unless they were filming, Graham kept his distance from her. But there were still two weeks of filming left. More than enough time to stage a seduction. After everything she'd told the tabloids, she'd hate to be made a liar.

Mark viewed the rushes from yesterday's filming with glowing pride. Fabulous! *Long Journey Home* had the look of a winner. That feeling was reinforced day after day as he viewed the masterful performances of his stars. They were all delivering one hundred percent, even Diana, who was well known for her prima donna antics during filming. Yet even she was on her best behavior, showing up on time and on top of her lines. It was as if they all knew this was the film for which they'd be remembered.

Mark turned off the projector, stretching in his seat. There had been problems—what film didn't have its fair share? The first week of filming there had been torrential rains. Afterwards they'd had to wait for everything to dry, since the land was left so muddy. Then Daniel came down with the flu and they had to shoot around him. And then there had been the initial delay in filming because of Gabrielle's strangling. Only after the police had questioned everyone at his party were they allowed to get on with their lives.

Mark didn't spend much time thinking about Gabrielle. He needed to concentrate fully on *Long Journey Home*. What had happened to her was certainly awful, and if it were possible for him to change things, he would, but knowing the type of person Gabrielle was, she had gotten what was coming to her. Of that there was no doubt in his mind.

Peter knocked on the door of Daniel's trailer.

"Come on in."

Peter entered Daniel's trailer, a load of scripts tucked under one arm. "Mark's rewritten a scene for this afternoon's shooting."

"He loves keeping us on our toes. Toss it over." Daniel caught the script, paging through it as he lounged on the couch. "Take a seat. How's it going?"

"As well as can be expected."

"How's your sister?"

Peter's throat tightened. "No change."

"Don't give up hope."

Peter shook his head defiantly. "I won't. Gabrielle's going to pull through this. I know she will. She's a fighter." Peter didn't dare believe anything else. The thought of losing his sister was impossible to comprehend.

"Want to talk?" Daniel asked.

Peter nodded, abandoning the scripts as tears came to his eyes. Daniel came over to him, holding him close as he wrapped an arm around him, rocking him gently.

"It's all right," Daniel comforted. "It's all right."

"No, it isn't," Peter sobbed.

Mark had told him he didn't have to come to Nebraska; that he'd find someone else to work for him while Peter remained in Hollywood, but Peter had refused Mark's generous offer. There was nothing more he could do for his sister and the thought of seeing her in the state she was in was too much to handle.

"I don't know what I'll do if I lose Gabrielle. She's always been there for me. She's always taken care of me. She's the one person I can depend on. I love her so much. She's all I have left."

"There's still your father."

Peter laughed through his tears. "He doesn't love me. He never has. I'm a major disappointment. I'm too much like my mother. We both refused to live up to his expectations. When he looks at me he sees her and he'll never forgive her for what she did to him."

Daniel didn't know what to say. Marina Fontana's suicide was common knowledge in Las Vegas and Hollywood circles. But many said that Paul Fontana's neglect of his wife as he created his illegal empire was the main factor for her suicide.

"It's his fault that Gabrielle is in this coma, just like it's his fault that my mother is dead."

"What are you talking about?"

"I love Gabrielle with all my heart, but she's spoiled. That's my father's fault. All her life he's given her everything she's wanted and she's come to believe that whatever she wants she should get. At times it's made her bitchy and manipulative. I chose to ignore that side of Gabrielle, but it was there, created by my father. My sister, determined to have her own way, probably pushed someone too far and that's why she's in that coma, courtesy of Paul Fontana."

"Peter, you can't say such a thing!" Daniel admonished. "The police think it was a fan of your sister's. Look, can I give you some advice?"

"Sure."

"Try to mend things with your father. I know it won't be easy, but make an effort. If Gabrielle doesn't pull through this, he's all you have left."

Peter shook his head. "You're wrong." His lips touched Daniel's. "I also have you."

"Just think! When we get back to California every day will be like this," Drew said.

"I hope so," Laura murmured contentedly, snuggling closer to Drew's naked body, enjoying the afterglow of their lovemaking.

"Do you really?" Drew asked.

"I do."

"Then will you marry me?"

Laura bit her lower lip. This wasn't the first time Drew had proposed to her. The second time she had come to Nebraska he had proposed. As much as she had wanted to say yes that first time, as well as the second and now this third time, she couldn't. How could she explain to Drew that she wasn't ready to make such a permanent commitment? Her life was just beginning to fall into place. She wanted to enjoy what she and Drew had started and not rush into anything. She was scared of losing the love they had discovered if they moved too quickly.

"Drew, I'd love to marry you—"

"All right!" Drew enthusiastically howled, flinging out his arms. "The lady has come to her senses." He scrambled from beneath the sheets, bouncing on his knees. "We'll have the biggest wedding Hollywood has ever seen."

"Drew, you didn't let me finish. You're hearing what you want to hear," Laura gently chided. "I'd love to marry you, but I can't. Not yet. I think we're moving too fast. We need some more time."

"No, we don't," he stubbornly insisted. "Laura, we were meant for each other. It's right between us. It always will be. Can't you see that?"

She did. And it scared her. Drew loved her with his heart and soul. If she ever did anything to betray that love, she'd never forgive herself. But they needed some more time. She couldn't explain it, but it was a feeling she had. She didn't feel safe. She knew it was because of Nico and she knew she had to forget him, but nightmares were hard to forget. They never died and haunted you when least expected. Until she shook this feeling, until she felt secure about her life, she couldn't jeopardize what she and Drew had.

"Drew, please be patient."

Drew sprang off the bed, angrily pacing. "I'm tired of being patient, Laura. Every time I propose, you turn me down. I'm beginning to wonder if you love me."

"How can you say such a thing? I do love you. Don't you believe me?"

Drew did believe her. But he was so afraid of losing her. It had taken him a lifetime to find Laura and now that he had found her, he wanted her in his life forever.

The way she made him feel was indescribable. When they were together time had no meaning and everything they did together was experienced as though for the first time. Nebraska was a place filled with simple pleasures: skimming pebbles off the top of a pond; walking in the sunset; picking a bouquet of wildflowers in a field meant for making love.

Remembering the way he and Laura had acted on those occasions made Drew smile.

"Of course I believe you." Drew returned to the bed, crawling across the sheets to Laura, planting a kiss on her nose. "How about a compromise?"

"What?"

"Move in with me?"

Laura could see the hope glistening in Drew's eyes. She couldn't ignore it. Maybe moving in together would make things easier. "I like that idea. A lot." She wrapped her arms around Drew, kissing him. "Kelly was nice enough to let me spend a week with you. Let's enjoy ourselves."

Grace removed her glasses, massaging the bridge of her nose. She'd been up ten straight hours working on the final draft of

Dangerous Parties between sips of black coffee and puffs of unfiltered cigarettes. But at last the screenplay was finished. And it was damn good.

The screenplay Harrison had written no longer existed. Instead, thanks to her efforts, *Dangerous Parties* now had motive, direction, and conflict. Grace ran her fingers over the pages of the finished screenplay, satisfaction ripping through her. *This* screenplay was going to sell and it was going to make *lots* of money for her and Harrison.

Soon she and Harrison would have it all. There was just one small fly in the ointment: Gabrielle. If only she'd died that night she'd been strangled! But leave it to Harrison to screw things up!

Grace chided herself for being so harsh with him. After all, the intent had been there.

Grace would always remember that night. She'd been here in her apartment, working at her computer, when suddenly there was a tremendous pounding on her apartment door.

"Grace, let me in!" Harrison pleaded. "Let me in!"

Opening the door, she'd let in a wild-eyed Harrison, who instantly grabbed her by the arms.

"I've been here all night. Understand? If anyone asks I've been here all night."

"Harrison, what's going on?"

"Don't ask any questions," he said, slamming shut the door. Crossing the room, he closed the drapes over the windows and sliding door leading out to the balcony. Tearing off his clothes, he settled himself on the couch. "Just do what I tell you. We've been here all night working on *Dangerous Parties*. It got late and I decided to spend the night on your couch."

"Whatever you say," she agreed, holding off on her questions, deciding to wait for a more opportune moment.

The next morning Gabrielle's strangling was the cover story in all the newspapers. Grace didn't beat around the bush.

"You strangled her, didn't you?" she said, waving the morning paper in his face.

They were in the kitchen. Harrison swatted away the newspaper, giving her a bleary-eyed look while pouring a cup of coffee. "No, I didn't. I'm telling you the truth."

"Then why were you in such a panic last night? My God, Harrison, this is attempted murder! You're asking me to give you an alibi and still you're keeping me in the dark. If you want my help you're going to have to level with me."

"I went to Mark's party last night," he admitted wearily. "I slipped in unnoticed. Gabrielle and I had had some words before she'd left for the party and I wasn't about to let her spin a bunch of lies to her father. I was hoping I could talk some sense into her. I wanted to talk to her alone so I followed her to the ladies' room. Big mistake. She freaked out at the sight of me. It looked like she'd lost some kind of fight and she was taking all her anger out on me. It didn't take long for my own anger to ignite. She kept belittling me and laughing at me, promising that she was going to destroy me and leave me with nothing. She told me she was going to tell her father whatever lies she wanted.

"I saw red then and the next thing I knew my hands were wrapped around her throat. I probably would have killed her, but she kneed me in the balls and I lost my grip. She broke free and swore I'd regret what I had done. I tried reasoning with her, apologizing, but she wouldn't listen. Finally, I left.

"I was outside the country club when the commotion started. One of the valets asked what was going on. Someone said a woman had been strangled and it looked like she might be dead. In that moment my blood chilled. I couldn't believe what I was hearing. It was impossible! Grace, I swear to you, Gabrielle was still alive when I left her. She was coughing and massaging her neck, giving me murderous looks. You have to believe me. You have to help me."

In the end Grace chose to give Harrison an alibi. How could she not? She loved him. And though she found it hard to believe Harrison would attempt murder, stranger things had happened. Whether or not he had strangled Gabrielle was no concern of hers —the bitch had gotten what she deserved, especially after all she had done to Harrison. And now Grace intended on getting what she deserved.

She dialed Harrison's number, impatiently waiting for him to answer. They had decided to keep some distance between each other to keep up appearances. Grace had used the time to finish polishing the screenplay, though Harrison had been skeptical of her efforts when she told him she'd be doing a rewrite. Now that it was finished it was time to indulge herself.

"Harrison, darling," she husked sexily into the phone. "It's Grace. Guess what? I've finished the rewrite."

"Does this mean we can see each other again?" Harrison's eagerness was unmistakable.

"It certainly does. How about if I come over?"

"I'll warm up the hot tub."

"Wonderful. I'm ready to make up for lost time."

"Don't forget the screenplay," he reminded. "I can't wait to play critic."

"Very funny," Grace said. "Don't worry, I won't forget it. In fact, be prepared to have your socks knocked off. Mark my words, Harrison. This screenplay is going to change our lives."

CHAPTER TWENTY-ONE

KELLY WANTED NOTHING more than a hot bubble bath and some soothing music. Her body was knotted with tension and it wasn't solely because of the exhausting fifteen-hour day she was putting in.

The latest issue of *Inside Access* claimed Graham was going to divorce her and marry Diana. More lies, of course. But lies that were hitting too close to home.

How many times had she imagined the scenario? Whenever she closed her eyes the scene replayed itself. Upon his return Graham would leave her, claiming he'd never loved her and was returning to Diana. Seeing the bold headline had made her fears seem all too real.

Kelly couldn't wait for the day's taping to end. They were doing a party sequence and all she had to do was stand around in a cocktail dress, pretending to make polite conversation when she didn't have to deliver her lines. The bright lights were giving her a headache and when the director called for a break, she gratefully dashed into the shadows.

"Ms. Stoddard?"

The voice came from a looming figure. His muscles were tight and constrained, packed into an expensive Italian suit. A white silk shirt was open at the collar with a gold herringbone chain nestled in a mat of dark hair. His face was covered with the lightest trace of five o'clock shadow, highlighting his flashy grin and piercing eyes. A gold Rolex watch, chunky link bracelet, and diamond-studded pinky ring were the finishing touches. In the air there was the overwhelming scent of his cologne.

Normally Kelly wasn't one to make snap judgments, but the man standing before her was bad news. She disliked him instantly. He was a predator—he reeked of determination and stark brutality, along with male arrogance and dominance. And she could sense he wanted something. From her.

"Yes?" she asked somewhat frostily.

"Allow me to introduce myself." He extended a hand. "Nico Rossi."

Kelly, not wanting to appear too bitchy, took his hand. "What can I do for you, Mr. Rossi?"

"Call me Nico." He gave her a smile, which she did not return. "I've come to see you on a matter of business. Paul Fontana has asked me to look into his daughter's strangling. I understand you were the one who found her."

"Yes, I was. But I've already told the police everything I know. I'm sorry to say it isn't much."

"Could you repeat it for me?"

Kelly did as he asked, though she wasn't pleased with the way Nico was blatantly ogling her.

"Is that all?" she asked after concluding things. "If so, I'm due back on the set."

"One more thing before you go." Nico placed a restraining hand on Kelly. He showed her a photograph. "Recognize her?"

The photo was of Laura. Kelly looked from the photo to Nico's face, noticing the way his eyes had narrowed, his mouth tightened. Had he noticed that she recognized Laura? What possible connection could Laura have to this hood?

"I have to go," she said.

"You didn't answer my question, but that isn't necessary." Nico's grip tightened. "You recognize her."

"What if I do?" Kelly asked, stalling for time, her mind scrambling to give a plausible answer.

"Tell me what you know."

"She was my assistant. I fired her last week," she lied.

"Where is she now?"

"I don't know."

Nico's grip grew tighter. "Don't play games with me, bitch," he hissed. *"Where is she?"*

"Ouch! You're hurting me!" Kelly clawed at the iron fist wrapped around her arm. "She said she was leaving town. I don't know where she's gone, so kindly take your hands off me before I call security."

"Kelly, everything okay?" one of the assistants asked.

Nico's iron grip melted away. Kelly massaged her arm, which

she could tell was going to be bruised the next day. "Fine. Mr. Rossi was on his way out."

Nico tipped his head to Kelly, a content smile on his face. "Thank you, Ms. Stoddard. You've been most helpful."

Kelly's stomach lurched at the malicious delight etched on Nico Rossi's face. As soon as she got a chance she was heading for a phone. Laura had to be warned.

Graham crumpled the latest issue of *Inside Access,* tossing it in the trash. He was sick of all the slander and lies. When was it going to end?

When he had spoken to Kelly earlier that morning, she'd tried to sound like everything was fine, but he could tell from her voice it wasn't. Her cheeriness and laughter had had a false ring. Most painful of all was when she'd told him she loved him—the unwavering certainty that had always been in her voice wasn't.

There was a knock on his trailer door, distracting him from his troubling thoughts. "Who is it?"

It was the last person he wanted to see, least of all be alone with. Already the crew had started looking at them strangely. Diana, wearing only a black silk kimono, came in carrying a copy of the rag he'd just discarded.

"I was getting my hair fixed when I saw this," she exclaimed.

"I've already seen it, Diana."

"It's shocking! We really ought to do something about it."

For once Graham was surprised he and Diana were on the same side. "Like what? You can't win with these people. If you go after them you only give them more to print."

"Silly boy! That's not what I meant." In a flash Diana dropped her kimono, standing naked except for a pair of black silk stockings, red garter belt and spiked heels. She pulled away the ribbon holding her hair back, shaking it free. "Let's *really* give them something to write about."

Without giving Graham a chance to react, Diana moved in on him, pushing him down on his bed. She climbed on top of him, entangling him between her legs as she locked him in an embrace, tearing open his shirt and assaulting him with hungry kisses.

"I've missed you, Graham. God, how I've missed you making love to me."

"Get off!" Graham protested, attempting to break free of his position beneath Diana, though it was hard maneuvering in the narrow bed.

In that moment the door to Graham's trailer burst open, followed by the unmistakable snap after snap of a photographer's camera.

This final assault launched Graham into action. He shoved Diana to the floor as he lunged after the photographer, who made a hasty escape. Meanwhile, an unperturbed Diana retrieved the kimono she had discarded and slipped back into it, awaiting Graham's return.

When he came back, he held a roll of exposed film up in the air. "The little shit thought he was free and clear, but I taught him a few things about invasion of privacy."

"Care to pick up where we left off or is the mood gone?"

"Get out," Graham ordered with disgust. "You make me sick. I'd never cheat on Kelly . . . let alone cheat on her with you."

"My, my. A white knight." Diana was amused. "I thought they'd all disappeared."

"The only thing that's disappearing is your sex appeal."

Diana's face hardened, her hand whipping across Graham's face. "You'll pay for that remark, Graham. Oh, how you'll pay!"

When Diana returned to her trailer, she wasn't surprised to find she had a visitor.

"Do you have the film?" she asked harshly.

The photographer Diana had hired, his face black and blue and swelling from Graham's beating, gave a crooked grin. "Yeah, I made the switch before he caught up with me. It went just like we discussed."

Diana reached into a pocket of her kimono, holding out a check. "Here's the amount we agreed to."

The roll of film and check exchanged hands.

"What are you going to do with those photos?" he asked, folding the check in half.

Diana formed a tight fist around the roll of film, giving the photographer a look of sheer pleasure. "When the timing is right I'm going to arrange a little pictorial with lots and lots of national coverage."

* * *

Grace was where she most wanted to be: in Gabrielle's bedroom, wearing Gabrielle's sexiest negligee, while in bed with Gabrielle's husband.

She leaned her head upon Harrison's chest, listening to his heartbeat, toying with his chest hairs. "If Gabrielle were to die, who inherits everything?"

Harrison's fingers played with Grace's short hair. "I would, naturally."

"Have you given it much thought?"

"Given what much thought?"

Grace shifted into a sitting position, the floral linen sheets covering her nakedness. "The possibility of Gabrielle dying."

Harrison gave Grace an uncomfortable look. "What kind of a question is that?"

"A logical one. Admit it. You'd love to be the grieving widower."

"Why all the questions?" he asked suspiciously. "I don't want to discuss Gabrielle."

"Relax, lover. You'd think I was trying to get you to incriminate yourself. Don't worry. Your secret is safe with me." Grace's hand ducked under the sheets, nestling between Harrison's legs. "I only want to know what you want so I can give it to you."

"I want you," he rasped, flinging away the sheets as he impaled Grace with urgency.

"And I want you," she moaned as she welcomed her fast approaching climax, surrendering herself to its shivering ripples of pleasure.

Afterwards, when she and Harrison lay relaxed in each other's arms, Grace decided to ask Harrison what he had thought of her rewritten version of *Dangerous Parties*. He'd had the screenplay for over a week now and she was dying to hear his opinion.

"Have you had a chance to look at the screenplay yet?" she asked.

"Yes, I have."

"And?" Grace asked expectantly, waiting for Harrison's answer as though it were a doctor's diagnosis.

"It's wonderful. You really surprised me."

Grace was elated. She gave Harrison a beaming smile. "Do you mean that?"

"Except for one small change which I can handle myself," he added, "it's perfect."

"What didn't you like?" She looked at Harrison worriedly.

"Was the final scene too long? Or was it the murder by the pool?" She held up a hand. "Wait, don't tell me. You make the change. I trust you."

"You've done a marvelous job, Grace." Harrison kissed her possessively . . . almost savagely. "I'm proud to have my name on this screenplay. You don't know how much all your hard work means to me."

An hour after Grace left, Harrison headed to his study and decided to make the one small change he had mentioned. When he'd told Grace he was proud to have his name on the screenplay for *Dangerous Parties,* he'd meant it.

But only his name belonged.

Ripping away the title page that listed both he and Grace as the screenwriters, Harrison replaced it with a clean, new page bearing his name alone. He then picked up the phone and called his agent, ready to discuss his hot new screenplay.

Was she doing the right thing?

Laura listened to Drew in the shower, her packed suitcase in one hand. The last week with Drew had been sheer bliss. She'd never before loved anyone the way she had come to love him. If anyone had told her she'd one day be walking out on the man she loved, she wouldn't have believed them. Yet here she was doing just that.

As much as it hurt her . . . would hurt Drew . . . she had no choice. She had to do this. Before it was too late.

Kelly's call had come an hour ago, while Drew was filming. Kelly's words still rang in her ears, *"A man named Nico Rossi is looking for you."*

After finding out what Kelly knew, Laura assured her she'd be able to handle things, declining Kelly's generous offer of assistance. The fewer people in her life involved with Nico Rossi, the better. No one could help her. Not when it came to Nico.

She then packed her things immediately and waited for Drew's return. She had been unable to leave without seeing him one last time.

When he'd gotten back from filming, she had thrown her arms around him.

"Hey, you act like you haven't seen me in ages."

"I missed you." She hugged him tightly. "Make love to me," she whispered fervently into his ear. "Show me how much you care. I need that, Drew. Please. I need that so much."

"Laura, is something wrong?"

"Wrong?" She laughed nervously. "Why would you think anything is wrong?"

"Because you're acting strangely. Did something happen while I was gone?"

"Nothing happened. Honest. I just want to be close to you. Am I wrong to want that?"

"No, you're not," he answered.

Slowly he peeled away her clothes, taking the utmost care in pleasuring her, not thinking of himself but only of her, as if he knew how much this time together would mean to her.

Laura hugged Drew tightly once again, not wanting to let go, not wanting to relinquish what he had given her all these weeks. For once she left, she would never feel this way again.

His lips found hers and they kissed, mouths open, tongues entwining as they drank from each other. Laura's hands found their way under Drew's workshirt, caressing his back before slipping down the front of his stomach, snapping open his jeans.

She pushed away the worn denim, releasing his throbbing erection. And then she received him . . . slowly . . . achingly . . . relishing the pleasure this act of intimacy was creating.

"Drew," she moaned breathlessly, meeting his thrusts and riding him with a fevered intensity, rubbing her hardened nipples against his. She nipped at his neck . . . devoured his lips . . . writhed in sweet torment as she fast approached the peak of their passion.

Her insides were yearning for release. But she didn't want it. She didn't. Because after she reached that pinnacle . . . once she was satisfied . . . her lovemaking with Drew would be over. And once it was over she would never feel this way again.

She fought back the pleasure. She fought back the heightened sensations. Yet with every touch of Drew's her body became more and more maddened, screaming for release until finally she was unable to deny herself any longer.

"Yes," she gasped, allowing herself to become engulfed by the searing desire Drew had ignited within her. The ecstasy was indescribable, but Laura welcomed it, savoring the delicious rapture she was experiencing as she gazed into Drew's eyes.

"I love you," she whispered, kissing him deeply one last time. "Always remember I love you."

Laura looked wistfully at the closed bathroom door. Becoming involved with Drew had been a mistake. She had known this was coming but had refused to accept the inevitable.

Like Drew, she hadn't wanted to be alone anymore. The fact that someone as wonderful and loving as Drew had wanted her in his life made the idea of a relationship all the more appealing. She had started dreaming, imagining a future with Drew, forgetting why she had been alone so long.

Nico. He had sworn to one day find her and exact his revenge. He had sworn to destroy her happiness and those who mattered in her life.

Like he had done with her baby.

If he learned about Drew, he would kill him.

Laura didn't know where she would go, only that she had to start over.

"What's with the suitcase? Where are you going?"

Lost in her thoughts, she hadn't heard the shower stop running. Now Drew, dripping wet, clad only in a towel, looked at her with bewilderment.

"Laura, are you leaving?"

The disbelief in his voice, layered with unmistakable hurt, cut achingly into her heart. "Yes, I am," she whispered, the words barely escaping.

"Without saying goodbye?" Somehow he knew she was leaving him for good. That she wouldn't be coming back. "Why, Laura? Why are you leaving? What have I done?"

Once again Drew felt like a little boy being shuffled from one foster home to another. Back then he'd learned to stop caring . . . stop trusting . . . stop loving because those emotions had had no value in his world. But now that he had learned how to use those emotions again, to fully enjoy them, he didn't want to lose them. He didn't want to discover they still had no value.

Laura wanted to make something up—place the blame on Drew for pressuring her to marry him—anything to sever the bond they had formed. But she couldn't do that. She wanted Drew one day to find someone else to love. "You've done nothing," she weakly supplied.

"Then why are you leaving?"

"I have to. Don't ask me to explain, Drew," she begged. "I can't."

"You can't. *You can't!*" he shouted, punching a fist into the trailer wall. Laura jumped back in fright. "You damn well better!"

"Drew, I have to leave." Laura grabbed her suitcase, backing away. "I have to catch a plane out of Omaha."

"You're not going anywhere!" He grabbed for her arm, pulling her to him. "Tell me what's going on. *Tell me!*"

"Let go of me!" she screeched.

Laura's shriek cut through Drew's anger like a hot knife and when he looked into her cowering face, he saw raw, undisguised fear there. The effect was cold-sobering and Drew released her immediately.

"Laura, you can't think for a minute I was going to hurt you. I love you. I'm upset. I can't bear the thought of losing you."

"I'm sorry, Drew. I'm so sorry," she sobbed, unable to hold back her tears. "I hope one day you'll be able to forgive me."

"Forgive you? Laura, I love you!" he implored, taking a step forward. "Doesn't that mean anything to you?"

"It means everything to me." This time she sobbed uncontrollably. "But I can't love you. I can't!"

With that Laura bolted from the trailer, leaving Drew and her suitcase behind.

CHAPTER TWENTY-TWO

RIDING IN THE ELEVATOR up to their apartment, all Graham could think about was Kelly. He'd missed her so much. He couldn't wait to wrap his arms around her again, holding her close and never letting go.

He didn't know how he had survived their time apart. As wonderful as the filming of *Long Journey Home* had been, it hadn't compared with being a permanent part of Kelly's life.

Opening their apartment door, Graham discarded his suitcases. Kicking off his shoes, he padded softly into the bedroom.

His breath caught at the sight of Kelly. Lying on top of the satin-encased bed, wearing a white silk negligee, she was bathed in an incoming shaft of moonlight. Graham knelt by her side, bringing her hand to his lips as he roused her to wakefulness.

"Darling, I'm back," he murmured.

Kelly stirred, opening her eyes. At first she blinked away sleep, but then her eyes widened with surprised delight.

"Graham! What are you doing here?"

"Location shooting ended ahead of schedule. I didn't let you know because I wanted to surprise you. We have three days together before I'm due at the studio."

"I missed you so much."

"And I missed you," he said, lowering his lips to hers.

"I didn't think we'd ever be this way again," she confessed as he gently pulled away the straps of her negligee.

"Why?" he asked, bringing his lips to her breasts. "Because of those rumors and tabloid stories? Ignore them. It's all a bunch of lies." Soulful gray eyes gazed at Kelly. "I love you and only you. Remember that always."

"I will," Kelly gasped as her dormant passion came alive under

Graham's touch. Her lips met his again, hungry for his taste and yearning for the intimacy she had been denied by his absence.

She allowed her hands to explore the smooth contours of Graham's body as she drew him nearer. Having him so close again after having been alone for so many weeks was pure heaven. The touch of him . . . the taste of him . . . the scent of him made her almost giddy. And made her want him with an all-consuming desire.

"Graham, I love you," she whispered softly. "I love you so much."

Graham gazed tenderly at Kelly, a look of promise in his eyes. Then he started to make love to her.

Kelly gasped with unimaginable pleasure and delight as Graham slid into her, enjoying the feel of having him inside her once again. She met his thrusts eagerly, riding the turbulent whirlwind of desire he was stirring within her.

"I'm so glad you're back, Graham. Now everything is going to be just the way it was before."

"Jinxie, darling! I'm back!"

"Diana, do you have any idea what time it is? It's after midnight."

"Darling, you're my agent," she reminded, switching her cordless phone from one ear to the other as she sank deeper into her bubble-filled tub. "You work for me twenty-four hours a day."

Jinxie's sigh was clearly audible. "So what do you want?"

"What's next for me after *Long Journey Home*?"

"If you want to do a TV movie, I can get you that. Would you want to do a few guest spots? One or two variety specials are being planned and your usual spot with Bob Hope is open. Take your pick."

"They're all the same. I've done it all before. I want something different," she moaned. "Something challenging."

"Like what? Any ideas? You've done practically everything."

"Not quite," Diana corrected. "I haven't done daytime and there's a marvelous soap I'd *love* to be a part of."

"Are you serious? A daytime soap? For you? Why kill yourself?"

"Jinxie, don't be so closed-minded. I told you I wanted a challenge."

"What's the name of this show?"

" 'The Yields of Passion,' " Diana breathlessly revealed.

"The show sounds familiar," Jinxie mused. "Why is that?" A second of silence. "Hey! Isn't that the soap your daughter stars on?"

"It is. You're so perceptive, Jinxie. You know, if you approached the producers, I'm sure they'd love to have me."

"Why's that?"

"Publicity. They can create tons of it."

"Just because you're Kelly's mother? I don't think so. Besides, what would they do with you?"

"I've come up with a delicious plot twist that I'm sure the writers are going to just gobble up. Ready?"

"My ear is glued to the phone."

"I want to be written onto the show as the mother of Kelly's character and I want my character to have an affair with Kelly's character's husband."

There was a slow intake of breath on Jinxie's end. "Hot stuff!"

"The hottest! Now Jinxie, it's up to you to get me on this show. You pitch the idea, the publicity angle, everything. Got it?"

"Do I ever! Diana, it's sheer genius!" Jinxie was practically palpitating. "We're going to have the network eating out of our hand."

"Just get me on the show, Jinxie," Diana ordered somewhat testily.

"You'll have a contract by the end of the week," he promised.

"Wonderful!" she purred contentedly. "I can't wait to start working with Kelly."

Drew Stern was getting drunk. Sequestered in the darkness of his beach house, he sat in the living room, a bottle of tequila in his hand.

After Laura had left him in Nebraska, he'd managed to hold himself together. He'd still had a film to do. No one had known anything was wrong and he'd given a brilliant performance, both on and off camera, carrying on with his life as though nothing were wrong.

Yet once he had gotten back to Malibu, alone in his beach house, he'd allowed the mask he'd been wearing to fall away, streaking his face with bitter tears.

All he wanted to do was forget the pain . . . forget the memories . . . forget the image of Laura's face.

He brought the bottle of tequila to his lips, grimacing at the taste of the liquid. Yet he swallowed. His heart was in a million pieces and his life was in a shambles. For three days he'd allow himself the luxury of total oblivion and of feeling sorry for himself. After that the mask would go back on and he would work on putting his life back together. The way it had been before Laura. The way it would always be. For he was sure of one thing. He'd never love again.

The figure moved slowly, stealthily, down the hospital corridor. At one A.M. the corridor was darkened and deserted, the only glow of light coming from the nurses' station.

Unhurried footsteps stopped, having reached their destination. An eye was pressed to the vertical sliver of glass in the doorway and fingers brushed over the name plate of the patient within.

Room 514 belonged to Gabrielle Fontana Moore. Poor Gabrielle. Languishing in a coma and attached to a respirator to help with her breathing. What would happen if the respirator was turned off? There was only one way to find out.

The door was opened a crack and the figure slipped inside, eyes moving first to Gabrielle and then to her bodyguard, who was asleep in his chair. A satisfied smile played along the figure's lips as step by careful step was taken further into the room.

The figure reached the respirator, fingers dancing with glee along the buttons and switches until they found the one they were searching for. One flick was all it would take and Gabrielle Fontana Moore's days would be over. If not, there would be other opportunities.

Beads of sweat popped out over the figure's forehead as it gave a quick glance to the bodyguard. At any moment he could awaken. But then again, he might not. A longer glance at the comatose Gabrielle, looking deceptively innocent, replaced the nervousness and ignited seething anger.

The risk was worth it. Fuck the consequences. Gabrielle deserved to die. She was only going to be getting what she deserved.

The switch to turn off the respirator was flicked and the figure fled just as the machine's alarm alerted the nurses' station.

CHAPTER TWENTY-THREE

GRACE WAS RE-READING the front story in the *Hollywood Reporter*. What she was reading was impossible. Utterly impossible. There had to be some sort of explanation.

Yet there wasn't. The cover story was plain and simple. Trinity Pictures had just optioned the film rights to Harrison Moore's latest screenplay, *Dangerous Parties*, for a staggering six-figure sum. Both Mel Gibson and Julia Roberts claimed to be expressing interest, with Mark Bauer possibly directing. Sole credit for writing *Dangerous Parties* was given to Harrison Moore. *Nowhere* in the article was any mention of her name. The same was true in the other trade papers.

Grace's anger grew and grew with each story she read. Storming out of her apartment, clutching the *Hollywood Reporter* in a tight fist, she headed straight for her car with one destination in mind. She was no fool. She knew a double cross when she saw one.

The signs had been there. Oh, how the signs had been there! Yet she had chosen to ignore them and now look where she was.

After starting her car she slammed down on the gas, roaring into traffic on Olympic Boulevard as she recalled her last conversation with Harrison.

"Harrison, it's Grace. Where have you been hiding yourself lately?" She stretched across her empty bed with the phone. "I've been lonely."

"I've been busy."

"That doesn't tell me much," she said, miffed by his evasive answer. "Surely you can find an hour for me. It's been two weeks since we've made love."

"I'll find time for you soon. I promise. Maybe this weekend."

She was slightly mollified. "All right. I don't mean to nag. I know you've been playing devoted husband at the hospital. Listen, what's going on with *Dangerous Parties*?"

"What do you mean?"

"Have you given it to your agent?"

"Not yet. I'm working on those changes."

"Hurry up, darling. I want to get rich."

"Who doesn't, Grace? Who doesn't?"

There had been no weekend together. Harrison had managed to cancel and she, of course, had forgiven him. But there would be no forgiving *this*. If Harrison thought she was going to let him get away with peddling *her* screenplay as his own, he was crazy. She had too much on him. Way too much. No way was she winding up with the short end of the stick. Not after all she had done.

She swerved from lane to lane, ignoring the other drivers as she broke the speed limit. All she could think of was Harrison. He'd made a mistake. A big mistake.

And she *never* forgave mistakes.

Grace found Harrison lounging by the pool, his body glistening with suntan oil. She slapped him hard with her copy of the *Hollywood Reporter*.

"You bastard!"

"Something wrong, Grace?" he asked, continuing with his sunning.

"You know exactly what's wrong, you fucking rat! You stole the screenplay I helped you work on and peddled it as your own."

"Don't flatter yourself, Grace. It's not as if you wrote the thing from scratch. I did that. You just played around with a few words and flipped a few scenes."

"Like hell I did! I tore apart *Dangerous Parties* and rewrote it word for word, scene by scene. You haven't had an original thought in years, Harrison. *Dangerous Parties* was a piece of shit until I got my hands on it. I did something you were too fucking lazy to do. I *wrote!*"

Harrison removed his sunglasses, glaring at Grace coldly. "So? What's your point?"

"I want what's mine, Harrison. I want my fair share from the deal you made."

Harrison laughed. "Dream on. You've wasted enough of my time with your ravings."

"You're not going to get away with this."

"Why not? You can't prove a thing. I've got all my drafts of the screenplay and my notes. I even have your notes, which you so generously gave to me. Where's your case, Grace?"

Grace fumed. He was right, but that didn't mean she was going to give up without a fight. "I swear to God you're going to pay!"

Harrison got to his feet, perching his sunglasses on top of his head. Taking hold of Grace's arm, he started leading her to the front gates.

"What are you doing? Get your hands off me!"

"Unless you've guessed otherwise, our affair is over. I'd advise you to slink away quietly. If not, I promise to make things very difficult for you."

Grace angrily snatched her arm free. "So you think you're on top of the world . . . the one calling the shots. Guess again, buddy," she sneered. "You're about to be knocked down. Let me tell you about the *new* screenplay I've started working on. The story is fascinating. A talentless screenwriter tries to strangle his wife. He doesn't succeed and he needs his mistress to give him an alibi. She does so and then he double-crosses her. She then goes to the police and tells them she lied when she gave her lover his alibi."

"You've got nothing on me. Nothing!" Harrison crowed. "You can't touch me. Go ahead. Spill your guts. It's your word against mine. Anything you say I'll use against you. I'll twist every one of your accusations, because if I go down, Grace, you're coming with me. Now get off my estate before I have you thrown off."

"This isn't over, Harrison," she vowed before stalking off. "Not by a long shot."

Grace drove furiously, her mind busy plotting. If Harrison thought she was going to let him have it all, he was sadly mistaken.

She'd been stupid in trusting him. Loving him. Yet she had never suspected Harrison had it in him to be so manipulative and cunning. Well, if he wanted to play those types of games, he'd better get ready to expect the same from her. She was going to bring him down and leave him with nothing.

Grace pounded the steering wheel in frustration, fighting back her tears. She wouldn't cry. She wouldn't! Yet it hurt so much. She'd loved Harrison with all her heart. She'd wanted to spend the rest of her life with him. She'd thought Harrison had felt the same way, but obviously he hadn't. He'd used her . . . used her love for his own selfish purposes.

She'd been such a fool! She would have waited forever for him to leave Gabrielle. And look at the risks she had taken. Like turning off Gabrielle's respirator last night. Thank God she hadn't told Harrison what she had planned on doing. If she had she'd probably be rotting in a jail cell right this minute. Thanks to her, he was now a rich man.

The decision to turn off Gabrielle's respirator had been an easy one. Her philosophy had always been that when you have a problem, just eliminate it. Gabrielle had been the only thing keeping her from having it all—from becoming Mrs. Harrison Moore. Now Gabrielle no longer mattered. Grace didn't even know if she was dead. Before getting ready to call the hospital, she'd seen the story of Harrison's sold screenplay.

Destroying Harrison was all that mattered now. She wouldn't go to the police about Gabrielle's strangling—she didn't want the police to start formulating any sort of theories. There were still a few tricks left up her sleeve. All she had to do was figure out which one to use against Harrison.

After Grace's departure, Harrison returned to his chaise lounge, applying a fresh coat of suntan oil. He slid his sunglasses back into place and spritzed some lightener into his hair to streak it. Had to have that golden California look.

Harrison was thoroughly enjoying his newfound freedom. With Gabrielle languishing in her coma and Grace now out of the picture, his life had never been sweeter. If he wanted, it could always be this way.

His confrontation with Grace was the farthest thing on his mind. When the timing was right, he'd deal with her. He wasn't worried. He had plans. Big plans. He was on the verge of having it all: fame, fortune, prestige. His plans most certainly didn't include Grace Warren.

Which was why, after she'd given him her screenplay, he'd had no qualms about the prospect of murdering her.

It had to be done. Grace was a threat he couldn't allow to exist.

The phone by the pool started ringing. After taking a sip of his gin and tonic, he answered. Peter Fontana's exuberant voice was at the other end.

"Harrison, great news. Gabrielle has come out of her coma!"

The phone slipped from Harrison's suddenly lifeless fingers.

Heather smiled for the camera, undulating to the rhythm of Janet Jackson.

This was her fourth photo session since coming back from Nebraska. Already she had been mentioned in *Vanity Fair*, *Entertainment Weekly* and *American Film*. *People* was going to be doing an issue on stars of the nineties. Not only had she been profiled but her photo was even being included on the cover with three other rising stars.

Her first cover! *People* magazine! She'd be everywhere! Heather was ecstatic. Her star was definitely on the rise.

"What's next, Heather?" the reporter from *Premiere* asked. Unlike a few other reporters she'd dealt with, he wasn't treating her like a brainless bimbo. He definitely seemed interested in what she had to say. He reminded her of Peter.

"I don't know yet. I've gotten some offers, but I don't know what I want to do next."

Heather's thoughts returned to Peter as the reporter smiled at her. She didn't know how it had happened, but she and Peter had become close friends. They were now part of each other's lives. They met for lunch and dinner, went shopping, to the movies and sometimes the beach. They confided their problems and offered advice. Totally unexpected results, considering the circumstances of their meeting.

Their friendship had grown in Nebraska. One day she found him sitting on the steps of the white clapboard farmhouse being used in the film. Filming had ended for the day and from where Peter sat you could see the sun setting, a great, huge orange ball.

"Mind if I join you?" she asked. She hoped he didn't send her away. Though everything was going well, and she had no problems with the crew or her co-stars, there wasn't really anyone she could talk to.

Peter looked startled to see her. "I didn't hear you."

"Something bothering you? Is it your sister?"

He shook his head. "She's always on my mind, but that's not what's bothering me."

"Does it have to do with Daniel Ellis?" she ventured.

He looked at her in panic. "Is it that obvious? Does everyone know?"

"Peter, calm down. All I've noticed is that there's an attraction between the two of you."

"I slept with him yesterday," Peter stated matter-of-factly, focusing his gaze on her.

"So? What you do is your own business."

Peter laughed sarcastically. "How I wish that were true, but it isn't. What I do is everyone's business, because homosexuality isn't the norm. You don't know what it's like, Heather. You don't know what it's like wanting to be like everyone else, but being different. Having different feelings that feel *so* right, but aren't because society says it isn't right. It makes it hard to be yourself. You learn to make compromises . . . to try and fit in while keeping a part of yourself, that secret self, alive."

"Is that why you've been leading a double life?"

"Why else? I'm ashamed of what I am," he told her sadly. "That's why you were able to get the upper hand."

"Peter, I'm really sorry about what I did with Jinxie," she stated emphatically. She felt so low! "I had no right to manipulate you the way I did."

"Don't apologize. Like I told you that day, you taught me a valuable lesson. You taught me that I can't hide. That I have to make a decision. I can't lead two lives. Only one."

"If you ever need anyone to listen, I'm here. Really." She clasped Peter's hand. Why hadn't she noticed it before? Had she been too wrapped up in herself? There was such pain in his eyes. If she could ever do anything to lessen it, she would in a second.

"Thanks, Heather. That means a lot."

The cameras continued clicking, bringing Heather back. "Let's see that smile," the ponytailed photographer called.

Heather flashed a brilliant smile, though her mind was still on Peter.

CHAPTER TWENTY-FOUR

THE IMPOSSIBLE HAD happened. Gabrielle Fontana Moore was alive and well.

Two weeks of the finest private care speeded the road to recovery. Surrounded by tons of floral arrangements, balloons, and get-well cards, having her every whim catered to, Gabrielle basked in the attention she was receiving, eager to get back into circulation.

After her respirator had been turned off, and the nurses rushed to her side, Gabrielle had continued breathing on her own. Then, six hours later, her eyelids fluttered and miraculously opened, returning Gabrielle to the land of the living.

The doctors couldn't explain it. There had always been the possibility that Gabrielle could come out of her coma at any time. Perhaps it would have occurred sooner if the respirator had been disconnected earlier. That had been suggested at one point, but Paul had been adamantly against it.

The disconnected respirator was an unsolved mystery. Someone had meant to kill Gabrielle again. Could it have been the person who strangled her?

When questioned by the police, Gabrielle claimed she was unable to provide answers. She told the police her attacker had come from behind and she hadn't seen anything. Of course, she was lying. She knew who had strangled her.

Per her request, she received no visitors at the hospital except Peter and her father. Her time spent recuperating wasn't wasted when she was alone. She was busy planning her revenge.

She had scores to settle.

Picking up the phone, Gabrielle dialed a number. When the line was answered, her voice was cold, harsh and unflinching.

"I want to see you. *Now*. We have plenty to discuss. If you're not here within the hour, the police will have a warrant for your arrest for attempted murder."

Gabrielle disconnected the line.

"Something smells good," Peter said, a towel wrapped around his waist, bare-chested as he padded into the kitchen.

"Pancakes," Daniel said. "With blueberries. Hot off the griddle."

"You've sure learned your way around my kitchen."

"Your bedroom is my favorite room."

Peter hugged Daniel from behind before sitting down. He still couldn't believe how happy he was. Becoming involved with Daniel was the best thing that had ever happened to him. Never in his life had he felt so loved and wanted. So whole. He finally felt as though he belonged.

Daniel introduced him to a world he had previously looked at through a window . . . longing to be a part of but never daring to take a step inside. Until now.

He got to know men who were just like him. There was no more hiding in dark bars. Rather, there were friendships and a sense of pride in who he was.

Daniel placed a plate of pancakes in front of him. "Eat up."

"These look great," Peter said as he started digging in. "I'd like to wake up to these every morning."

"Just the pancakes?"

"No." Peter put down his fork, looking at Daniel. "How much longer are you going to allow Jaime to stay in your life?"

"Is that a note of jealousy I hear?" Daniel asked with a smile.

Peter shrugged. "Maybe it is. I don't know. I only know that I don't like him. The sooner he's out of your life, the better."

"That seems to be the general consensus," Daniel stated, sipping his coffee. "I guess everyone saw what I didn't. Don't worry. I'll handle Jaime."

Buffy Stanton, a sleek looking blonde and host of "Morning Talk," a successful TV show originating daily from Hollywood, smiled into the camera.

"Good morning and welcome to another edition of 'Morning Talk.' I'm Buffy Stanton. Have we got an exciting show for you today! Our first guest is someone we all know very well. She's done it all. Movies, television, Las Vegas and Broadway. Now she's making her mark on daytime TV. Will you please give a warm welcome to the one and only Diana Halloway!"

The applause was thunderous as Diana, clad in a white silk shantung bustier, with a matching slender skirt, her hair in an upsweep, made her entrance. The audience gave her a standing ovation, to which she waved, blew kisses, and took a bow before joining Buffy on the couch where she conducted her interviews. Cheeks were brushed and Diana took a sip of water from a coffee mug as the audience continued clapping. Finally the excitement died down.

"Some greeting," Buffy enthused.

"But the best because it's from my fans."

More applause before Buffy was able to speak again.

"You've been *so* busy! Let's catch up. First, you recently finished *Long Journey Home* with Mark Bauer and a stellar cast. Now you're on 'The Yields of Passion,' one of daytime's highest rated soaps, and the ratings are sure to go higher. But why daytime, Diana? You're a star!"

Diana rolled her eyes theatrically. "Buffy, I've lost count of the number of times people have asked me that question. 'The Yields of Passion' is a quality show with tons of talented people working on it. When the producers approached me, I couldn't turn them down."

"Your daughter Kelly stars on the show. Did that have any bearing on your decision?"

"Naturally. The opportunity to work with my daughter was irresistible." Diana gave the camera a dazzling smile.

"Did you know your storyline ahead of time?"

"That I would be having an affair with my daughter's husband?" Diana gave a trilling laugh. "Yes, I did. But Kelly and I discussed it before I signed on. We both knew we'd be able to handle things. You must remember, Buffy, it's only a story!"

Buffy gave the audience a knowing look. "Is it, Diana?"

"Now, Buffy, curb your imagination," Diana scolded, playfully swatting at her.

"Let's get serious. Is the storyline causing problems in light of the rumors circulating?"

"That I *really am* having an affair with my daughter's husband? Buffy, darling, life doesn't come to a halt because tabloids print tawdry stories."

"But these stories are hitting *so* close to home!" Buffy proclaimed. "Graham Denning *was* your . . . good friend. Hasn't that put a strain on things?"

"Of course. But we're all adults. We've learned to accept the situation."

"Did anything happen between you and Graham during filming?" Buffy asked slyly.

"You're in such a sneaky mood, Buffy!" Diana chided. "I'm not going to deny or affirm anything. Graham and I were once close. We had an intense, passionate relationship."

"Was the sex good?"

"Darling, have you taken a look at Graham Denning? What do you think? Yes! It was delicious!" she raved. "Naturally when you're in such a confined area with the person who once drove you wild in bed, old feelings do arise."

"Are you talking about yourself or Graham?"

"Buffy, I've always prided myself on my self-control," Diana confessed. "Graham, on the other hand . . ."

"Did Graham lose his?" Buffy pounced.

"If he did, could you blame him? He's a passionate man. My daughter is a charming young woman, but she's still got some growing up to do." Diana arched an eyebrow at Buffy. "When you've had cream it takes some getting used to milk."

"Unless you nip at the cream now and again," Buffy countered.

"Yes," Diana agreed, smiling into the camera again.

"You're the last person I expected to have as a visitor," Gabrielle commented.

"Thanks for seeing me," Grace said.

"You've got five minutes, so make it fast. I'm expecting someone."

"Now that you're out of your coma, I'm sure you'll be eager to resume your acting career."

"What does it matter to you?"

"I've found the *perfect* screenplay. It's a thriller that will make the actress who gets the leading role a star. It's got everything. Murder, sex, suspense. In the right hands, it could be a runaway hit . . . and launch a film career."

"What's it called?"

"*Dangerous Parties.*" Grace handed Gabrielle the screenplay she held under her arm. "It's a *Body Heat* for the nineties. Gabrielle, this role is perfect for you. I knew it from the moment I started reading it. You'll become the new Kathleen Turner."

"I'll take a look at it." Gabrielle tossed the screenplay to one side. "Why are you so hot on this script? Why'd you bring it to me?"

"I owe you one."

"Because you were sleeping with my husband?" Gabrielle snorted. "If you want Harrison, he's yours. I should have gotten rid of him ages ago. Here's some advice, though. He's a loser."

"Tell me something I don't already know," Grace proclaimed knowingly.

"Sounds like the affair is over."

"It is. I can't believe how much time I wasted on him. He's a nothing!"

"Too bad I didn't catch the two of you sooner."

"Harrison is going to get his just desserts," Grace vowed. "Wait and see. In the meantime, read that screenplay and then give me a call. You won't be making a mistake, Gabrielle. Trust me."

"Jaime, I want to have a word with you."

Jaime, loaded down with bags and boxes from some of the poshest men's stores on Rodeo Drive, peered at Daniel over the top of his sunglasses. "Let me get this stuff upstairs first."

"Don't bother. It's all going back."

Jaime dropped his packages to the marbled floor, where they thumped loudly. He removed his sunglasses, hooking them down the front of his tennis sweater. He gave Daniel a sour smile. "I don't think so."

Daniel angrily waved a handful of bills. "I think so. I'm the one who pays the bills around here, not you. You've been charging up a storm." Daniel inspected Jaime's white linen slacks, tennis sweater, Gucci loafers, gold watch and bracelet. "From the looks of it, you're not lacking a thing."

"Call them perks. I'm entitled."

"You're entitled to nothing," Daniel raged. "Not when it comes to my money."

"Tightening the purse strings, are we, Danny? Well, listen and listen good. I put up with plenty of your shit. I don't get to go to your fancy parties or be seen out with you in public because you're afraid of what people might say. I can't have any friends over here. The only time you come sniffing around me is when you want to get fucked." Jaime savagely kicked his packages at Daniel. "Well, this is the price you're going to have to pay for services rendered."

"Not anymore. If you want your freedom so badly, there's the door."

Jaime's eyes narrowed and an ugly smile played over his lips. "Thinking of replacing me, Danny? Perhaps with that Italian stud you got close with in Nebraska?" He relished the startled look of guilt edging over Daniel's face. "Don't look so shocked. I have my spies." Jaime crossed his arms over his chest. "If you want to get rid of me, Danny, that's fine. But I'm not going to make it easy for you. I've gotten accustomed to a certain standard of living. I think I'm entitled to a little severance pay."

"How much?"

"Let's see," Jaime calculated, gathering his scattered packages. "Why don't we go with a nice even number? A hundred thousand should do. Plus, I get to keep my Jaguar and you pay for an apartment for the rest of the year." He started up the stairs. "You go write my check. I'll start packing. I'll be out of here by the end of the day and you'll never have to see me again." He gave Daniel a wide smile. "Promise."

In his study Daniel wrote out the check for a hundred thousand dollars with a trembling hand. Jaime had taken things better than he had expected. But that meant nothing. Jaime couldn't be trusted. This was blackmail, pure and simple, but he didn't care. He just wanted Jaime out of his house . . . out of his life. Then he and Peter could start their future together. Having Peter in his life was worth more than a hundred thousand dollars.

Jaime was packing as he told Daniel he would. There was no reason not to. He knew Daniel would give in to his demands.

Yet Daniel thought he wouldn't be seeing him after today. Wrong. He would. As long as Daniel's well was filled, he was going to keep coming back and back. Until the well was dry.

And then Jaime planned on having his revenge.

"Wondering why I asked to see you?" Gabrielle asked, glaring coldly at the man who had tried to kill her. "Well, let me put you out of your misery. Lucky for you I'm the forgive-and-forget type. My demands are simple. Give me what I want and we should have no problems. Otherwise, you'll find yourself behind bars."

Mark Bauer broke out into a cold sweat, the look of dread on his face growing with each word Gabrielle uttered as his mind replayed the night he had tried to strangle her.

Mark had had enough. He was sick of the Fontanas and catering to their demands. Paul Fontana had him by the balls and now Gabrielle was squeezing. No more. He was sick of jumping at the snap of their fingers.

When he was able to break away from the party he stormed into the ladies' room where he had watched Gabrielle disappear after her confrontation with Heather. He found her coughing and massaging her neck. At the sight of him she shot him a dark scowl.

"This must be my night to deal with losers! What do you want?"

"What did you tell Heather?" He had heard the two exchange heated words and could only imagine what Gabrielle had told Heather to make her so angry. "If you've done anything to jeopardize my picture . . ."

"Don't you mean *our* picture?"

"You never give up, do you?" he shouted, reaching the point of exasperation. "Get it through your thick skull. You're not going to be a part of Long Journey Home."

"Then neither are you. After I fill my father's head with my version of the events that went on between us, not only will you be taken off *Long Journey Home*, but you'll never work in this town again."

"You wouldn't dare!"

"Want to bet?"

Mark knew Gabrielle was serious. There was no mistaking the intent of her words. "Maybe I was wrong before," he hastily interceded. "Maybe I can find a small role for you."

"I want the role of Olivia."

"Gabrielle, trust me on this," he pleaded. "Olivia isn't the right role for you just yet. You need—"

"I want the role of *Olivia*," she demanded.

"Gabrielle, please." He ran a frantic hand through his hair. "Be reasonable."

"I want the role—"

"You can't have it!" he shouted, his patience snapping. *"There's no way I'd let a no-talent like you ruin my picture!"*

"Then you just kissed your film career goodbye," she hissed, a twinkle of sadistic glee in her eye. "Tonight is your last night in Tinseltown. If I were you I'd get back out there and enjoy it while you can."

Mark grabbed for her as she prepared to leave. "You can't do this to me!" All his years of hard work were at stake. Once Gabrielle stepped outside this room it was over. He knew she'd deliver on her promise. He couldn't imagine never making another film again. He lived for the entire process, from beginning to end.

"Get your hands off me," she ordered.

"No. Gabrielle, you have to listen to me."

"You had your chance and you blew it." She pulled herself free.

"No! I won't let you do this to me! I won't!" he shouted, lunging at her from behind as his hands wrapped around her throat and squeezed with all their might.

Mark's lips twitched nervously. "Gabrielle, you have to believe me. I didn't mean to strangle you. You just pushed me too far."

"Next you'll be telling me you've been racked with guilt."

"I have," he honestly admitted. He knew his words sounded inane, but they were true. He wasn't a man of violence. He hadn't intended on strangling Gabrielle, and the sight of her lying unconscious at his feet had plagued him for weeks. His conscience wouldn't let him forget what he'd done. Nights had been sleepless. Only the filming of *Long Journey Home* had been able to help him temporarily forget, pushing Gabrielle to the back of his mind.

"Save the speech and let's get down to business."

Mark clenched his fists, smothering a growing spark of anger. She was doing it again! The only other thing that had helped with his guilt was knowing he wasn't completely at fault. Gabrielle had brought the violence on herself. It looked as if they were getting into a replay. He couldn't lose control. Too much was at stake. "What's it going to cost me for you to *forget?*"

"Don't sound so dubious," she berated. "All I want is what I've always wanted. A film career."

"You've got the starring role in my next picture. It's yours," he said without hesitation. Actually, he couldn't wait for her to do her first movie. The reviews would be scathing. Maybe that would take her down a few pegs. "Anything else?"

"That was understood," she purred. "But I also need your help in settling an old score."

"With whom?"

"Heather McCall," she pronounced, her dark eyes filling with anger. "And you're going to do *exactly* what I tell you to do."

CHAPTER TWENTY-FIVE

SHE HAD TO BE CRAZY.

Laura couldn't believe she had given up Drew because of Nico.

When was it going to end? When was she going to have her life back?

For a while, for such a sweet while, she had almost had it back. *Almost.* And then she had thrown it all away, thinking it would be easy to start over again. But it wasn't.

From the moment she had returned to New York she had been unable to forget Drew. Her heart still ached over the look on his face when she had left him. And she still remembered the way he had made her feel. Special. Safe. Loved.

So many times she wanted to pick up the phone and call him. Just to hear the sound of his voice. Just to hear that he was okay and getting on with his life.

But a call wouldn't be enough. She'd want to talk to him. Then she'd want to see him. Touch him. Make love with him again, creating another memory she could cherish always.

It had gotten to the point where she was constantly thinking of him.

That had to mean something. It did, she kept telling herself. It meant there was only one thing left to do. The *right* thing.

Her mind told her she shouldn't, trying to warn her. Prevent her from what she was about to do, telling her she had already done the right thing. Her heart disagreed, telling her she *should* be doing this. Encouraging her. Building hope. Telling her she should trust in her love for Drew. If she did, they'd both make it.

There was no way around it for her. She had tried getting on with her life . . . starting over without Drew. But she had been unable to. She couldn't live without him.

She only hoped it wasn't too late.

Laura stepped up to the airline counter, dropping her suitcases. "I'd like a one-way ticket to Los Angeles, please."

Nico kicked open the door of Laura's New York City apartment, storming his way inside.

Eyes searching everywhere, he hunted for Laura as he went from room to room, hoping for the slightest indication of movement. He'd love to find her hiding in a closet or huddled in a corner, trying her best not to be seen. He wanted to find her and watch her tremble with fear before dispensing the punishment she deserved. Like he had in the old days.

Yet all was quiet. All was still.

She wasn't here. From the looks of things she wouldn't be back. There were no clothes in the closets or drawers. No toiletries in the bathroom or bedroom.

Nico let out a guttural scream. Where the fuck was she? She was always one step ahead of him. One fucking step! Well, he'd find her. He had all the time in the world. After coming out of her coma, Gabrielle Fontana had told her father she didn't need a bodyguard and Nico had gone his way after dispensing, per Paul's orders, with the bodyguard who'd been sleeping the night Gabrielle's respirator had been turned off. Nico had taken care of the job neatly and efficiently with some piano wire, hiding in the backseat of the cocky young guy's car.

Spying a note pad by the telephone, he snatched it up. Grabbing a pencil, he shaded in the indentations on the clean sheet. It was worth a shot.

A smile spread across his face. Bingo! He knew where she was headed.

It was time he returned to Tinseltown.

Kelly was in her dressing room, forcing herself to concentrate on her script. Lately she'd been having trouble remembering her lines. Missing cues. Having to do retakes. What had once come so easily was now exceedingly difficult. She was doing more than making mistakes. She was causing delays in taping, much to the displeasure of the producers and director.

Kelly knew why she was having such problems. The answer was obvious: Diana.

From day one her mother had done everything in her power to fixate herself as the star of "The Yields of Passion." And everyone involved with the show fell over themselves to please her! All Kelly could do was watch helplessly as she had so many times before. No longer was she an actress in her own right. Once again she had fallen under her mother's shadow, losing whatever attention was coming her way.

Right from the start she had known this would happen, but tried not to let it bother her. After all, she had lived in her mother's shadow her entire life. Though she hadn't been exactly thrilled when she heard her mother would be joining the show, there really wasn't much she could do except quit. And she wouldn't do that. At the time she had loved her job and thought she'd be able to withstand Diana's six months on the show.

But then the storyline was announced.

Whatever calm had been attained after *Long Journey Home* had wrapped was lost. The tabloids once again started churning out their stories. Every week there was a new headline featuring herself, Graham, and her mother. Naturally, parallels were drawn to the show.

The result was increased tension between Kelly and Graham, higher ratings for the show, and an indefinite stay on the soap for Diana.

Kelly abandoned her script, deciding to distract herself with some television. Flipping it on, she was surprised to see her mother's face on an afternoon talk show.

Surprise turned to anger as she turned up the volume.

Kelly bolted from her dressing room, storming to Diana's. Without even knocking, she barged in, startling the hairdresser who was working on Diana's hair.

"Mother, I want to talk to you," she demanded.

"I'm listening." Diana's eyes remained glued to the copy of *Vogue* she was reading.

"In private."

The hairdresser quickly disappeared while Diana continued reading. "Do make this fast, Kelly. We're due on the set in twenty minutes."

"Look at me, Mother."

"Darling, I'm capable of doing two things at the same time."

"Look at me!" Kelly screamed.

Diana slowly closed her magazine, turning to Kelly with a sly smile. "Is something wrong?"

"You know there's something wrong, Mother, and I want an end to it. I'm sick of it, Mother. Sick of it! I know you thrive on notoriety, but I don't! I want you to put an end to these games!"

"What are you talking about?" Diana innocently asked.

"I just saw you on another talk show, Mother. As usual, you managed to bring up your affair with Graham."

"Is that what's got you in an uproar?"

"Don't play games with me, Mother!" Kelly snapped. "Graham and I want an end to it. We're fed up with the innuendos. The tongue-in-cheek remarks. We want you to stop it."

"I'm only playing with the media."

"You're destroying our lives!"

"Don't get so melodramatic, angel. We're not taping."

"Stop it, Mother! Just stop it!"

"Don't tell me what to do, Kelly," Diana ordered, her voice hardening, no longer in the mood to toy with Kelly. "If you and Graham don't like the rumors circulating you're certainly invited to express your own point of view."

"You know we can't. It wouldn't matter what we said. The media is in a frenzy over this."

"Then my advice to you is to wait for this to all die down."

"You know it won't. Mother, *you've* got to do something."

"What would you like me to do, Kelly?" Diana asked harshly. "Put my career on hold because you can't tolerate some outside pressure? It's part of the business, honey, so you better get used to it. Or can't you hack it? I can. I'm an actress. Part of my job is to keep myself in the public's eye so they don't forget me. Let me remind you, Kelly, I *did* have an affair with your husband."

"And let me remind *you* that your affair with *my* husband is over and done with," she flared.

"Yes, but the public is so fascinated over the fact that we shared the same man. They want to know everything. Do you know one talk show host actually asked me which one of us Graham preferred in bed? Tell me love, has he told you?"

Kelly blocked out her mother's words, unable to listen to any more of her garbage. "No more, Mother," she warned. "No more."

"When the topic comes up, I can hardly avoid it." Diana rose from her chair, fluffing her hair as she stared in the mirror. "Anyway, enough of this. I've got a scene to tape. Your husband and I are in bed today." Diana's eyes, glistening maliciously, locked with Kelly's. "I'm having so much fun. Isn't it amazing the way art imitates real life?"

Until deciding what her next move would be, Gabrielle had sequestered herself at the Beverly Hills Hotel in a two-bedroom suite. She'd dismissed the bodyguard her father had wanted her to have at all times. She was a big girl. She'd be able to take care of herself. It wasn't as if her life *really* were in danger, though it was nice having her father think so, constantly doting on her. Besides, she didn't need someone bringing stories back to her father.

Wearing a one-piece red bathing suit, her dark hair in a topknot, she was working on her tan out by the pool while sipping a piña colada.

She was also finishing the screenplay Grace had given her to read.

After turning the last page, she did nothing. Except tightly clutch the screenplay. Then the excitement built. This was *it*. This was the screenplay that would make her a star.

Gabrielle immediately called Grace.

Grace arrived promptly an hour later.

"This screenplay is fabulous!" Gabrielle announced.

A satisfied smile played along Grace's lips. "I thought you might like it."

"Like it? I *love* it."

Grace settled herself in a chair opposite Gabrielle's chaise lounge. "You're going to love it even more after I tell you who wrote it."

"Who?"

"Harrison."

Gabrielle blinked. "You're kidding, right?"

"I'm not. In Hollywood, Harrison Moore is considered the sole creator of *Dangerous Parties*."

"That note of bitterness in your voice is intriguing. Go on," Gabrielle urged.

"I'm not going to bore you with a long story. All I want is to see Harrison screwed. The bastard thinks he's on top of the world. I want to see him on his knees. I thought you might be interested."

"Am I ever! Grace, I like the way you think. Even more, I like the idea of screwing Harrison over. How'd you like your old job back? The first thing you can do is tell me everything you know about *Dangerous Parties*. As you're well aware, I've been a bit out of touch. But now I'm ready to get back into action." Gabrielle held up the screenplay. "This is my stone and I'm going to kill a lot of birds with it."

"Peter, help!" Heather wailed, breezing into Nicky Blair's.

"What's wrong now?" he sighed.

"I'm so confused and I don't know what to do." Heather sipped the chablis Peter had ordered for her. "I just got off the phone with Travis Sawyer, my new agent. This is crisis city. *Playboy* wants me to do a centerfold and they're offering five hundred thousand dollars."

"Nice piece of change," Peter whistled.

"Don't I know it! Peter, what should I do? Tell me."

"What do *you* want to do? This is your decision. How do you feel?"

"I want to do it!" Heather declared in a rush. "God, all that money! Five hundred thousand dollars. I'd ask for it in singles and roll around naked in it."

"Then there's your answer. Interesting concept for your layout."

"But what about my career? Am I going to be sabotaging my career?"

"Kim Basinger didn't."

"Good answer, Peter," Heather enthused. "Very good answer. But I'm still unsure."

"Look, anything Playboy does is going to be tasteful. And you'll be in great company. Joan Collins, Sherilyn Fenn, and Joan Severance have all posed. Why don't you hold them off for a while? Tell them you haven't ruled out the possibility, but you just aren't sure. What's guaranteed is the offer will remain open. They could even jack up their price."

"You're right. I'll stall. Now enough of my babbling. You wanted to discuss something with me."

Peter took a deep breath. "Daniel wants me to move in with him."

"What did you tell him?"

"I told him I needed some time."

"Here's the same question you shot me: what do *you* want to do?"

"I want to move in with him. Our story would be that I'm his new assistant. Heather, I care about him and want to be with him."

"Then there's your answer."

"You don't know how much I want to do this, but I'm scared."

"Don't be. The best things in life are worth the risk."

"Are they? I feel like I'm sacrificing one world for another. I don't know if I'm ready to do that yet."

"You're not sacrificing anything," Heather stated firmly. "Remember, there's the cover story. You can always fall back on that. And I'll always be here for you, Peter. I don't know what I'd do without you. You've become my best friend."

Peter kissed Heather's cheek. "And you've become mine. Thanks for listening."

CHAPTER TWENTY-SIX

Laura was exhausted. She'd gone from the airport straight to Drew's Malibu beach house, where she'd waited six hours for him. When it looked like he wouldn't be coming home that night, she'd left a note in his mailbox and caught a taxi back to the house she'd been subletting in Coldwater Canyon.

After the taxi dropped her off, she struggled with her suitcases as she searched for her keys. All she wanted was to drop off to sleep so that when she opened her eyes it would be tomorrow. She couldn't wait to see Drew again.

Dropping her suitcases, Laura inserted her key and opened the front door. With her suitcases in tow, she kicked the door shut, berating herself for not turning on a light. Groping through the darkness, she found her way to the bedroom. There she turned on the lights and got the shock of her life.

Nico Rossi, shirt sleeves unrolled, muscles flexed, brass knuckles gleaming on one fist, rose from the bed, a smile of cruel anticipation etched on his face.

"Laura, baby," he greeted. "Why are you just standing there? Is that any way to greet your loving husband?"

"Esmerelda!" Diana shouted. "Esmerelda, get up here this second."

The Mexican maid clambered up the stairs to answer her mistress's call. "Yes, Ms. Halloway?"

Diana pointed to the dusty boxes cluttering her immaculate bedroom. "What are those doing in here?"

"The exterminator sprayed the storage room and had to move the boxes. I forgot to put them into one of the spare rooms."

"Well, it's too late now!" Diana snapped. "Make up one of the guestrooms for me. I can't sleep in here with all this dust. See that the bedroom is restored to its usual state in the morning."

"Yes, Ms. Halloway," the maid dutifully replied, relieved that she'd gotten off so easily.

As Diana followed after Esmerelda, she accidentally knocked over one of the dusty boxes. The brittle Scotch tape holding the box closed broke and the contents of the box spilled to the carpet.

"Damn!" Diana cursed, bending to her knees. Esmerelda joined her, but when Diana's eyes fell on the items revealed, she shooed away the woman.

"I can handle this, Esmerelda," she instructed in a choked voice. "You fix the guestroom."

After Esmerelda left Diana's fingers brushed over the items she hadn't seen in years. Forgotten. Pushed to the farthest corners of her mind.

She lovingly fingered the tiny dresses edged in ruffles and lace; the soft blankets and pillows trimmed with ribbon; the booties and rattle and silver comb and hairbrush she had purchased after learning she was pregnant.

Tears welled in Diana's eyes as she touched each item and held it before returning it to the box. Beneath the blanket there was a framed photograph of Adam holding an infant Kelly. Diana picked up the frame, gazing into the face of the man she had loved with all her heart. Until he had betrayed her.

Why, Adam? Why did it all have to go so wrong?

Diana found her answer in the newspaper clippings scattered on the floor. All detailed Iris Larson's accidental drowning in her pool. Diana's pain turned to bitter anger at the sight of them.

"You bitch! You thought you had it all, but you didn't! You tried to take away what was rightfully mine, but I wouldn't let you. I took it all back! I made you pay. Just like I made Adam pay." Diana stared with hatred at the framed photograph in her hand before smashing it into the wall, where the glass shattered into pieces. "Just like I'm going to make Kelly pay."

"What's the matter, Laura? Speechless?"

"What are you doing here?" she whispered, paralyzed with fright.

"What kind of question is that? I came to see you."

Laura hadn't experienced this kind of fear in years. Not since the last time she had been with Nico. Her legs wouldn't move. She couldn't breathe. She couldn't think. All she could do was remember the pain as her eyes focused on Nico's brass knuckles as he drew closer.

Nico stepped in front of her. He brought a hand to her cheek. She flinched, her eyes squeezing shut.

"Don't hurt me," she whimpered. "Please don't hurt me."

"But Laura, you've been such a bad girl," he reprimanded. He brought the brass knuckles against her cheek, gliding them up and down slowly. "Refusing to give me an alibi when those cops questioned you about where I was the night of that hijacking and then filing for divorce the way you did when I was locked away was very bad. You still belong to me."

"I don't belong to you!" she said in a surprising burst of defiance.

"No?" Nico grabbed Laura by the front of her blouse. "Who do you belong to?" He shook her viciously. "That movie star you've been fucking?"

Laura's eyes widened and Nico laughed. "I know all about him, sweetheart. I learned plenty tracking you down."

"I don't belong to you, Nico," she repeated. "I don't belong to anybody." She took a deep breath. "And I don't love you anymore," she stated in a rush.

"But you once did, didn't you, Laura?" His lips traveled along the nape of her neck. "Didn't you? You promised to love, honor, and obey me."

She was repelled by his touch, but she tried not to show it. The last thing she wanted to do was make him angry. "Once," she truthfully replied, remembering a time when she *had* loved Nico Rossi. Loved him so much that she had married him after only six months of dating.

How could she not? Nico had once been the perfect man. He lavished her with gifts, showered her with attention, and made love to her like no other man ever had.

Their wedding was like a page from a fairy tale; their honeymoon an exotic tour of the world. After the honeymoon they settled down in Las Vegas where Nico, involved in hotel management, got a job at the Fountain.

After starting his job Nico was transformed. No longer was he the man Laura had fallen in love with. Instead he became involved with a fast crowd, staying out all night, drinking and gambling, driven by an insatiable thirst to lead the good life. Flashy clothes and purchases too expensive for their budget followed. As did the bills. Laura started working as a blackjack dealer in one of the casinos. Nico didn't like it, but he always took her paychecks and tips. The last thing he wanted to do was give up his new lifestyle.

At first she tried to be understanding. She knew Nico was working long hours . . . trying to make an impression on his way to the top, although she wasn't too pleased by the shady types he associated with. Their ties to the Mafia were obvious, and as she watched Nico become closer to these men she became uneasy.

Then there was their marriage. With Nico working nights and herself working days, they hardly ever saw each other. When they did, Nico was always eyeing her suspiciously, questioning her movements, inspecting her appearance. His jealousy amused her at first, but then unnerved her as it became more and more obsessive. He accused her of cheating on him; of sleeping with other men. She told him she wasn't—that she loved only him—though she was starting to doubt her feelings for the man she had married.

They hardly ever made love and when they did Nico was no longer the same gentle lover. Instead, his motions were fast and furious . . . hard . . . sometimes even brutal, as though he were taking his frustrations out on her. Wanting to punish her. Blaming her for his lack of success. Laura missed the intimacy they had once shared, but she decided to be patient. To give Nico some more time.

When she tried talking to him, he ignored her. One morning when she insisted he listen, playfully refusing to hand over his pants as he was getting dressed, she received a black eye.

Laura was stunned when her husband's fist smashed into her face; Nico was instantly contrite, apologizing profusely, tears streaming down his cheeks, overwhelmed by his guilt.

The first time Laura didn't know how to respond. She gave Nico the benefit of the doubt, forgiving him, allowing him to make tender love to her. The restored intimacy between them allowed her to dismiss this one instance of domestic violence though it rested uneasily in her mind.

Not surprisingly, other beatings followed. Each time Nico was contrite. He never *meant* to hurt her, he said, but Laura knew he did as his violence grew more and more brutal: a broken arm, another black eye, bruises, a cracked rib. He enjoyed using her as his punching bag, venting his frustrations, blaming her for his failures. Laura became more and more scared. Soon she was sleeping behind a locked bedroom door, saving whatever money she could. Escape was the only thing on her mind. If she could have gone sooner, she would have, but she had no family—she had nowhere else to go. She had only herself and needed to be able to take care of herself when she fled.

And then she learned she was pregnant.

Laura didn't plan on telling Nico the news. He wouldn't believe he was the father. Already he had accused her of sleeping around. What she would have to do is leave sooner than she'd expected. It couldn't be helped. She was three months pregnant and could start showing at any time. If Nico found out she was pregnant, there was no telling what he would do.

Unfortunately Laura did find out.

It was a week after she'd learned she was pregnant. Still suffering from morning sickness, she'd returned home early, finding Nico waiting with a baseball bat in one hand. With the other he was replaying the message on their answering machine.

It was her doctor, calling with the name of an obstetrician he'd promised to recommend.

"You cheated on me," Nico softly stated, advancing with the baseball bat.

Laura held up her hands in defense, backing away. "No, Nico! No! I swear I didn't."

"Then why didn't you tell me I was going to be a daddy, Laura?" The bat swished past her head. "Why didn't you share your news?"

"I was scared," she sobbed, tripping and falling to the floor. "I was scared of how you'd react."

"Scared of your *loving* husband?" The bat crashed onto the floor, next to her head. Laura cringed, screaming. "Or scared that you'd be caught before you had time to cover up?"

"No!" she screamed as the raised bat descended again. "No!"

The baseball bat slammed into Laura's abdomen. Over and over. Her feeble pleas for mercy and her cries of denial to Nico's allegations brought no stop to his violence. It only brought a miscarriage.

After Laura was released from the hospital Nico was arrested. When the police asked her to verify Nico's statement that they had been in bed together at the time of the hijacking, Laura told the police officers that her husband was lying. He hadn't been sleeping with her—he hadn't been home. She didn't know where he had been. With Nico temporarily behind bars, Laura seized her chance for escape, flying to Santa Domingo for a divorce and then starting her life over, though she'd never forget the words Nico had uttered while beating her senseless.

"You belong to me, Laura. *Me!* No one else. You ever try to leave me for another man, I'll kill you both."

Nico's words had lived in Laura's heart for years, forgotten only when she'd fallen in love with Drew. Now, looking into Nico's face, contorted with anger and violence, Laura realized he had meant every word.

"You could love me again, Laura," he crooned, unbuttoning her blouse and seizing a breast. He squeezed it painfully, biting a nipple.

Laura remained motionless, allowing him to paw at her, wanting to pull away but fearful of his reaction. "No, I couldn't. It's been too long. We've changed. We're not the same people we once were."

"Absence makes the heart grow fonder." He grabbed her by the hair, twisting hard until he brought his face close to hers. "Say you love me."

"No! Let go of me!"

"Say it! Say you love me!" he insisted, twisting tighter. "I don't like your attitude, Laura," he responded to her silence, shoving her across the bed. "I think you need some time alone to think. If you don't start being nice to me, your pretty boyfriend isn't going to be so pretty anymore." Nico displayed his brass knuckles.

"Don't you dare hurt Drew!"

Nico shrugged. "You know me, Laura. I'm the jealous type. I'm liable to jump right out of the bushes and pound in his face. Break those beautiful pearly whites and that perfect nose. Now, if I had a little proof of your undying devotion . . ."

"What do you want from me?" she sobbed. "Do you want me to say I love you? Fine!" she spat out. "I love you, Nico."

"Better. Much better. But we'll have to work on the tone though. Put more meaning into it. We'll try again in the morning."

The bedroom door was closed and locked. Laura scurried from the bed to the phone across the room, only to discover it had been torn out of the wall. Laura smothered a wail of desperation. She was trapped. A virtual prisoner at Nico's mercy. No one knew she was back in Hollywood.

Then she remembered the note she had left for Drew. A spark of hope returned. When she didn't show up at the beach house tomorrow, he'd figure out something was wrong. He would save her. She knew he would.

By tomorrow night this nightmare would be over.

"Air France Flight 208 now landing in Paris."

Drew unbuckled his seatbelt as the plane landed, adding a fedora to his head and a pair of dark sunglasses to his eyes. With his luck a flood of fans would be waiting. Drew wasn't in the mood to sign autographs or pose for pictures. All he wanted to do was get to his hotel, have something to eat and then study his lines. Tomorrow he began working in a new David Wolper mini-series.

Though Drew didn't usually do television, the part he had been offered in this French Revolution mini-series had been too good to turn down. Besides, he had some extra time before his next screen project and he'd do anything to forget Laura.

Laura. The thought of her brought an ache to his heart. First he had tried forgetting her through liquor. Now work. Yet her face still haunted him. He couldn't forget her, but he had to. She'd broken his heart. She had told him she didn't want him in her life. It had to get easier. It had to.

He didn't know what the next step would be when he returned to Hollywood, but he'd have plenty of time to figure it out.

He would be in Paris for the next six weeks.

Graham crept up behind Kelly where she lay on the couch, immersed in a script. His hands moved to her shoulders, intending to massage gently. Yet at his touch Kelly jumped, whirling around and confronting him with anger.

"What do you think you're doing?"

"Kelly, calm down. I didn't mean to startle you. It's after midnight. You've been reading for hours. Don't you think it's time you came to bed?" He reached for the sash of her dressing gown, drawing her closer as he leaned forward for a kiss. "I'm lonely."

Kelly snapped the sash out of his hand, pulling away from his kiss. "Sorry, but I've still got to learn my lines." She reached for Kitty, thrusting the cat out at him. "Here. She'll keep you company."

Graham accepted the cat, placing her down on the floor, where she promptly scooted away. "I kind of wanted someone else in my bed. I want you. Your lines can wait till morning. Come to bed."

"I can't," she adamantly refused. "Now, if you'd just leave."

"Don't use that dismissive tone with me, Kelly. I don't like it."

"Sorry," she coolly answered, returning to her script.

"We have to talk."

Kelly closed her script, giving Graham an annoyed look. "About what?"

"Us. It's been three weeks since we last made love."

"Is that my fault?" Kelly's words were tinged with frostiness.

"You're contributing to the problem somewhat."

"How? I didn't even know a problem existed. I'm busy, Graham. That's all there is to it, plain and simple. I don't have time to coddle you, so I guess the honeymoon's over."

"I'm not asking you to coddle me, Kelly. I only want a little attention."

"I'm sorry if you're feeling neglected, but there's not much I can do. My storyline has been accelerated ever since Diana was written onto the show. I've got more lines—"

"So now we're getting to the bottom line," he interrupted, jumping on Kelly's words. "This has to do with Diana. With our affair. Kelly, I thought this was over and done with. I thought we were going to put this behind us."

"How can we put it behind us when it's being shoved in our faces every day?" Kelly's voice became hysterical. "I'm sick of it, Graham! So sick of all of it! The press, the show, Diana."

"What do you want from me?" he demanded somewhat testily. "Do you think I'm enjoying this? I'm not! What do you expect me to do?"

"I don't know!" she wailed. "All I know is that it's getting harder and harder for me not to picture the two of you together."

"That's no reason for you to feel threatened or jealous."

"I don't feel threatened or jealous! I'm just sick of being reminded that you slept with my mother."

"This will all blow over." Graham tried to wrap an arm around her. "In time."

Kelly shoved away Graham's arm. "That's everybody's answer," she laughed mockingly. "But will it? For how long? How long until it all starts up again?"

"We'll get through this. I know we will."

"I wish I had your confidence."

Graham panicked at the hopelessness in her voice. "What are you saying?"

"We need some time apart, Graham."

"Kelly, don't push me away," he begged.

"I have to sort out my feelings."

"Don't you love me anymore?"

Kelly looked at Graham sadly. "I do. But until I can accept what you and my mother had, until I can stop feeling so *angry* at you, I don't want to see you."

"This isn't my fault!" he flared with bitterness, frustrated at being pushed away.

"I didn't say it was. Try to understand. I can be honest about my feelings with you. I can't discuss this with my mother. Give me some time, Graham. *Please.*"

Graham threw his hands up in resignation. "If time is what you want, then I'll give you some time, Kelly. But I won't wait forever," he decreed. "Sooner or later you're going to have to learn to accept what's happened or make a decision you can live with."

"Thank you, Graham," she whispered.

He turned his back on her, returning to their bedroom. "I'll be out of here in the morning."

After he had gone, Kelly tried to go back to her lines. She didn't want to think about the words she and Graham had exchanged, but a wave of loneliness engulfed her and she abandoned her script. She felt so alone. More than she ever had before.

"I love you, Graham," she whispered, wishing she had told him the words, blinking back tears, wishing she had the strength to run after him and ask him to stay. "And I don't want to lose you. Not for a minute. I don't know what I'd do without you."

"This is the last one," Peter announced, dropping the box he was carrying with the others he'd already brought in.

"You're moved in at last!" Daniel exclaimed happily. "This calls for a celebration." He disappeared down into the kitchen, returning with a chilled bottle of champagne and two fluted glasses. Daniel pressed one glass into Peter's hand, then popped open the champagne, pouring a rich white froth into both their glasses. When the bubbles turned to golden liquid, Daniel clinked his glass against Peter's. "To us."

"To us," Peter repeated, sipping from his glass.

"Let's go into the study," Daniel suggested. "There's a nice fire waiting."

"I'd rather get settled in first."

"Sure." Daniel drained his glass empty in one gulp. "I'll show you our bedroom." He gave Peter a wink, tucking the bottle of champagne under one arm. "Why don't we just stay up there awhile?"

"*Our* bedroom?"

Daniel gave Peter a perplexed look. "What's wrong?"

"I thought we'd be having separate rooms. We're telling everyone I'm your assistant. Shouldn't it look that way?"

"What goes on behind these walls is our business and nobody else's."

Peter shifted uncomfortably. He could see Daniel wasn't pleased by his request, but he needed to be honest about his feelings. "You're right, but I'd prefer, for now, if we each had our own room."

"Why?"

"This is all a big step for me, Daniel. I've never been in a relationship before."

Daniel's brow furrowed. "You are now."

"Don't you see?" Peter patiently explained. "If I were to move into your bedroom I'd be more than your lover. Our lives would become intertwined and we'd grow dependent on each other. We'd rely on each other and be like any other couple."

"Is that so bad?" Daniel asked softly.

"No. And it's something that I really want. But I'm not ready to stop pretending," Peter confessed. "The wall I've built to hide behind is slowly breaking away, but it's still there. I want to be more than your lover, but I can't. Not yet. Not until I'm able to accept who I am. Then we'll have it all. Can you understand?"

Daniel took Peter's hand in his and led him to a door at the end of the hallway. "This is your bedroom," he stated. He pointed to the bedroom door at the opposite end of the hallway. "That's mine."

"Thank you, Daniel," Peter said, his voice choked with emotion.

CHAPTER TWENTY-SEVEN

"BREAKFAST MEETINGS are my favorite."
Gabrielle buttered a croissant, taking a bite while surveying the other diners breakfasting in the Polo Lounge.

"Mark, don't look so glum," she chided. "What I'm asking you to do is hardly difficult."

"You're not asking, Gabrielle, you're demanding. As you always are," he hissed. "I like Heather. She's a good actress and doesn't deserve this. She has a future ahead of her. Why do you want to sabotage her career this way?"

"Because I can," she crowed. "Tell me again what you're going to do. As we discussed."

Mark sighed. He had no choice. His back was to the wall and survival came first. "I'm going to offer Heather a five-picture deal with Trinity. Part of the deal is that she can't make any films for any other studio in town until she's fulfilled her obligation to us."

"And she never will," Gabrielle gleefully exclaimed. "Continue."

"Halfway through filming of the first film, she'll be dropped from the project and replaced. Everyone will be told she was impossible to work with." Mark gritted his teeth as he unpoured the lies Gabrielle had drilled into him. "We'll state that she was a prima donna whose ego blew out of control after *Long Journey Home*. She tried to upstage her fellow actors and refused to take direction or criticism."

"Heather will be told she's more suited to your next project, but of course, that will never happen," Gabrielle interjected. "Rumors will be spread, the tabloids will crucify her, and I'll do a little whispering in a few gossip columnists' ears. By the time Trinity dumps her, *Long Journey Home* will be a memory and whatever strides she's made will be forgotten."

"But why, Gabrielle?" Mark had lost count of the number of times he had asked this question. "Why?"

"Why not? You said it yourself. I'm a spoiled bitch. Plus, I'm also a sore loser. It's a lethal combination. Heather got the part I wanted in *Long Journey Home*. She also humiliated me at your party." Gabrielle looked at Mark slyly. "I'll never forget that, although I have been able to forget other incidents from that night."

"You win," Mark said in defeat. "I'll call her later."

"You make sure you do that," Gabrielle reminded. "Now let's move onto other matters. I hear you've acquired film rights to *Dangerous Parties*."

Mark looked at Gabrielle shrewdly. "Naturally you want the lead."

"I've read the screenplay and *love* it. Did you think I wouldn't expect the lead?"

Mark had no problems with Gabrielle playing the lead in *Dangerous Parties*. She'd do an adequate job and the screenplay had blockbuster written all over it. It wasn't Oscar material, but Mark liked taking a break every now and then. Films like *Long Journey Home* were near and dear to his heart—that was when he became involved in real filmmaking. *Dangerous Parties* was popcorn fluff, but it would sell tickets for Trinity and that would keep Paul Fontana happy.

Mark decided to put up a small fight. He didn't want Gabrielle to think he was giving in too easily.

"Gabrielle, I really think you should start with something smaller."

"Let's *not* go through our usual routine. I'm the one calling the shots. I expect contracts delivered to my agent by the end of the week. Since I've been written off 'The Yields of Passion' I'm ready to start when you're ready."

"But Gabrielle, if you gave me some time I could find the perfect vehicle for you."

"*This* is the perfect vehicle for me."

Mark threw down his napkin. "You win. But answer one question. When is this going to end? When are you going to stop pulling my strings?"

"When you're no longer of any use to me." She shooed him away. "You can leave, Mark. I have another score to settle."

"Anyone I know?"

"My husband." Gabrielle's eyes glittered maliciously. "I'm sure he'll be delighted to meet the star of your film, don't you?"

"Kelly, have you been working too hard?"

Daniel fretted over Kelly's tired appearance as she approached his corner table. She gave a wan smile before kissing his cheek and sitting down. "I've been putting in long hours."

"It's more than work," he astutely observed. "What's your mother done?"

"How did you know?"

"It's written all over your face. Your father used to sometimes have that same look after tangling with her. So what's she done?"

"What *hasn't* she done? She's done nothing to make things easier for Graham and me. I actually think she's enjoying all of this."

"Why wouldn't she? She's a selfish, cold-hearted bitch," he stated dryly. "Let's not mince words, Kelly. Or mask feelings. You know the way I feel about your mother and vice versa. We go out of our way to avoid each other, but we're tied together because of you. I love you, Kelly, and I don't like seeing you hurt. I won't stand by and let your mother make your life miserable. I think it's time she and I had a little talk."

Kelly sighed. "I don't know how much good that will do. Sometimes I just don't understand the way she acts." Kelly shook her head ruefully, reaching for her orange juice. "We're always at odds."

"Darlings, sorry I'm late!"

Vanessa, resplendent in white leather, swooped down on Daniel and Kelly, enveloping them in the scent of White Linen while planting kisses. In her arms were a dozen pink roses sprinkled with baby's breath and tied with a red bow. She promptly presented the roses to Kelly. "Happy birthday."

"Vanessa, these are lovely," Kelly said, though there was a look of confusion on her face, "but you've gotten your dates mixed up. My birthday isn't for another three months."

"It isn't? But I thought you were born in October. I'm usually good with dates and I could have sworn . . ." Vanessa reached into her handbag for a Virginia Slim, lighting it and puffing away. "Well, enjoy them. You look like you need some cheering up. What's that mother of yours done now?"

"Diana has already been discussed and discarded," Daniel said.

"Without me?" Vanessa pouted. "But I have to get my two cents in! She's threatening to sue Simon & Schuster, my publisher, over my memoirs. Kelly, it's a good thing I screwed up on your birthday. I'll have to fix the date in my book. Anyway, Diana's lawyers want a copy of the manuscript. No way! Let her sweat it out." Vanessa smiled at Kelly and Daniel. "Okay, Diana has been trashed. Let's talk about that wonderful man of yours, Kelly. Is he wearing you out?"

"Graham and I have separated," Kelly said quietly.

"Kelly, why didn't you tell me?" Daniel asked.

"It's only temporary. We need to sort some things out. We'll be back together soon."

"Watch out for that mother of yours," Vanessa warned. "If she thinks Graham is fair game, she'll go after him. Nothing has ever stopped Diana from going after any man she's wanted."

"It's good to be back in Hollywood," Paul Fontana exclaimed.

Diana gave a perfunctory nod as she writhed beneath Paul, feigning a state of ecstasy. In actuality, she was visualizing Frost Barclay in her bed and finding herself becoming quite aroused. Frost was a possible replacement for Graham. He was so young and virile. She could just imagine a session between the sheets with him.

Diana found herself responding to Paul as she visualized Frost as her lover. Yet before she could satisfy herself, Paul finished and rolled off her.

"I spoke to Mark Bauer yesterday. He tells me *Long Journey Home* is ready to be released. Mark disagrees, but I'm thinking of moving up the release date to November. Maybe around Thanksgiving weekend. What do you think?"

"Keep the film in December. Listen to Mark. This is an Oscar contender. We don't want to be forgotten when a slew of other films are released in December. Academy members have very short memories."

"Ready to start your Las Vegas gig?"

"Is it that time already?" Diana groaned. "It would be nice if I benefitted from my talents."

"You've been paid, Diana. In blood. You've got no reason to complain."

"Don't I?" she hissed. "You've been blackmailing me for the

past twenty-five years. I've never been paid a cent for performing at your casino."

"We wouldn't want Kelly learning the truth, now would we?" Paul asked, relying on the ace he always used.

"I don't know," Diana murmured, delighted at the look of surprise that flashed across Paul's face. "It might be interesting to see what kind of a shock the truth would have on her."

"Strangle anyone recently, Harrison?"

Gabrielle laughed with delight at the discomfort on her husband's face. "Relax. I'm only teasing."

"I wasn't responsible for your coma," he angrily said.

"If I hadn't kneed you in the balls, you would have killed me."

"But I didn't. Besides, you pushed me too far."

"Harrison, let's not bicker. Please sit down. After all, I did invite you to breakfast."

Harrison grudgingly sat across from his wife. What was she up to? He had to admit she looked good, the picture of perfect health, while he was sure he looked a mess. Ever since Gabrielle had come out of her coma, he had been unable to eat, sleep, or write, waiting for her to lower the boom. Especially if Grace decided to tell what she knew. Gabrielle couldn't prove he had tried to strangle her, but if Grace stepped forward . . .

He hadn't heard a peep from Grace since he'd dumped her and Gabrielle hadn't wanted to see him. Until today.

Harrison's dreams of having it all had turned topsy-turvy from the moment he had heard Gabrielle was out of her coma, envisioning a life behind bars. He couldn't let that happen. He couldn't. That was why he had decided to take certain preventive measures if the situation called for such action.

"Why did you want to see me?"

"Aren't you hungry?" Gabrielle pressed a menu forward. "Try the eggs benedict. They're divine."

Harrison refused the menu. "I'm not hungry. Let's just get to the bottom line."

"If you insist," she said. "As you know, Harrison, I'd planned on divorcing you."

"And you still are," Harrison provided. "Look, Gabrielle, if you want out of our marriage, fine. I won't fight you. In fact, I don't want a thing." Why go through the hassle? Soon he was going to be a very rich and very famous screenwriter. He didn't need

Gabrielle Fontana's dirty money. The sooner he cut loose from her, the better.

"I imagine you wouldn't," Gabrielle shrewdly countered. "Considering what a success you've become."

"What are you talking about?"

"Don't be so modest. I know all about *Dangerous Parties*."

There was no putting one past her! Damn! "You do?" He feigned disinterest, choosing to browse through his menu. Anything to avoid that smug look he saw creeping over her face.

"It's a wonderful screenplay. I loved every page of it."

"You did?" He didn't look up. He wouldn't. He knew what was coming. He knew it, knew it, knew it! He concentrated on the menu, locking down his growing anger.

"I couldn't put it down. It's going to make such a wonderful film."

Harrison dared to look up from his menu, retaining a neutral expression. "How did you happen to get a copy of the screenplay?"

"Grace sent me a copy. She'd already read it and urged me to take a look. Wasn't that thoughtful of her? After I read it we had a delightful chat. Did you hear I've hired her back?"

He should have known! That bitch! "What did you two discuss?" he managed to ask politely. He started curling the inside pages of his menu. He could only imagine what had gone on between the two of them.

"Lots of things," she alluded. "But mainly the screenplay. Grace thought I would be fabulous playing the lead and I couldn't agree more."

Harrison lost it. He slammed down his menu. *"Well, I disagree!"* he raged. "The role of Melanie was meant to be played by an actress, not an incompetent like you!"

"Harrison, you wound me," Gabrielle cooed, "but you have such a special way of doing that. This role is my big break and I'm taking it."

"If you think Mark Bauer will agree to this, you're crazy."

"He already has."

Harrison stared at Gabrielle in horror, knowing she was telling him the truth. "You're not going to get away with this! I won't let you. I've worked too hard and too long to let you destroy my screenplay."

"Your screenplay?" Gabrielle scorned. "Don't you mean Grace's?" She took pleasure in watching her husband turn pale.

"She's a *wonderful* writer. She let me read some of her stuff. Her style is *so* similar to that of *Dangerous Parties*, it's amazing! Can you imagine what would happen if a rumor got started?"

"Don't you dare!" Harrison hissed.

"Calm down, darling. We don't want bad press." Gabrielle sipped at her coffee. "That's one of the reasons why I'm not divorcing you."

Harrison's blood boiled; his eyes bulged; he gripped the sides of his chair to avoid wrapping his hands around Gabrielle's throat. "You're *not* divorcing me?"

"Why should I? Your star is finally on the rise again. You didn't think I'd miss out on the ride? I should be moving back onto the estate in the next week or two."

"You're crazy. Absolutely crazy."

Gabrielle blew Harrison a kiss. "Crazy like a fox."

Harrison bolted from his seat. "I'll stop you, Gabrielle. I swear to God I will."

He stormed out of the restaurant.

Outside the Polo Lounge Daniel whirled on Vanessa as soon as Kelly was out of sight.

"Why did you think today was Kelly's birthday? Why did this date stick out in your mind?"

"That's easy. Don't you remember? The same time Diana was pregnant with Kelly, I was knocked up by Neil Baxter, my second husband. Until I had my miscarriage, Diana and I shared the same obstetrician."

"But what about the date?" Daniel persisted.

"Give me a chance to tell the story! One day we were both in the waiting room, shooting daggers at each other, mind you, when the doctor's nurse tried to break the ice. She asked both of us when we were due to deliver and that's why I thought today was Kelly's birthday. Though I had expected to maybe be off on the date, I didn't expect to be wrong about the month. Not by three months." Vanessa gave Daniel an inquisitive look. "Why's this all so important?"

"It makes sense," he murmured under his breath. "I didn't believe him at the time. I thought he was drunk, that he didn't know what he was saying, but it all makes such perfect sense! How could I have been so stupid?"

"Didn't believe who?"

"Adam," Daniel answered absently.

"Adam Stoddard?" Vanessa didn't know what was going on. "What does he have to do with any of this?"

"Do you remember the name of the obstetrician you and Diana shared?"

"I think his name was Manning. Daniel, you didn't answer my question. What does Adam Stoddard have to do with all of this?"

Daniel once again ignored Vanessa's question. "Was he young? Old?"

"Who?"

"The obstetrician."

"*Ancient.* Daniel, *what's* going on?"

"It's a hunch," he admitted. "Nothing more. I'll probably need your help. Later."

"Aren't you going to tell me anything?" Vanessa wailed. "Is this something juicy?"

"Explosive. If I'm right it'll finally put an end to Diana's reign in this town."

Harrison jammed his key into the ignition of his silver Porsche. They were going to pay. Both of them were going to pay. He wouldn't let them get away with this. He wouldn't. Both Gabrielle and Grace were pure poison. He couldn't allow them to toy with him . . . to control his life. At any moment they could decide to destroy him.

Unless he destroyed them first.

Nothing was going to stop him from doing that. He'd go to any lengths to stop them. *Any* lengths.

Even murder.

The last person Daniel expected to see was waiting on his doorstep.

"What are you doing here?" he coldly demanded, slamming shut the door of his Corvette.

"Danny, is that any way to greet an old friend?" Jaime scolded, rising to his feet. "I came to see how you were doing without me."

"You know the answer to that."

"You don't even miss me? I'm disappointed."

"What do you want, Jaime? I don't have time for your games."

Jaime gave Daniel a wicked grin, reaching for his groin. "You used to," he husked, pulling down Daniel's zipper. "Why don't we have a go at it? For old time's sake?"

Daniel removed Jaime's hand before it could snake inside his pants. "I want you to leave."

"The Italian Stallion must be keeping you happy. You never passed up a chance to get fucked."

"I've changed."

Jaime raised an eyebrow, laughing. "I haven't. The little perks you've thrown my way have been fine, Danny, but if you'll pardon the expression, this dog wants a bigger bone."

Daniel started seething. When would he see the last of this leech? "What do you want now?"

"Only a favor. Don't look so nervous. Billy Cotter, a friend of yours, is head of casting at Trinity. I hear Mark Bauer is putting together a new project. I want to be a part of it."

"Good luck."

Jaime sighed. "I don't need good luck. I'm from the school that believes in making your own luck. Since Billy Cotter has a thing for boy toys, I want you to give the darling old queen a call. Tell him the tightest piece of ass he'll ever set his eyes on is available for a private audition. I'll handle the rest."

"I'm not doing it," Daniel answered immediately. "I *won't* do it."

"Yes, you will, Danny, otherwise your dark little closet is going to be flung open and exposed to a most unpleasant glare. The term is called outing and I'm sure you're familiar with it."

"You bastard!"

"I think I'll call Michelangelo Signorile. Remember him? He used to be editor of *Outweek* magazine. He'll make sure this tidbit gets around. Then I'll be in touch with the tabloids and talk shows. Geraldo will *love* this! After that the ball will roll on its own. Comedians will have a field day with you."

"You're despicable!"

Jaime gave a smug smile. "I am, aren't I? Now, are you going to call Billy Cotter?"

"Does it look like I have much of a choice?" Daniel knew he didn't. After all these years it was too late for the truth to come out. He'd grown accustomed to a lavish lifestyle and didn't want to give it up.

"Danny, no one's backing you into a corner." Jaime grinned wickedly. "Except yourself."

Daniel was unable to deny the truth of Jaime's words. That galled him most of all.

CHAPTER TWENTY-EIGHT

"Wake up, my sweet."

Laura bolted awake at the sound of Nico's voice in her ear. Clutching the sheets closely, she gave him a fearful look as he leaned over her.

"Don't I get a morning kiss?"

Laura brought her lips to Nico's. She didn't dare refuse his request. If she did, she would be punished. Over the past two weeks she had been reacquainted with Nico's methods, subjected to angry slaps, twisted arms, and towering rages when she didn't respond fast enough to a demand or answer a question the way he wanted.

"Open up," he ordered, thrusting his tongue into her mouth, his hands painfully gripping her head in place.

Laura accepted his tongue, resisting the urge to bite down hard on it, emitting false moans of pleasure while holding back the tears, desperately searching her mind for some idea of escape. Since the night she had found Nico in her house she had been a virtual prisoner. There was no way for her to escape. At first she had been allowed access to the entire house (though there was nothing she could use to defend herself and all the phone lines were cut). That was because Nico had gotten a guard dog, a vicious Doberman pinscher he called Satan, to roam throughout the house in his absence. Whenever and wherever she moved the dog followed, glaring at her, growling softly, watching her every step. If she moved too close to a door or window, he was in her path, jaws open, fangs bared and drooling.

She remembered when Nico had introduced her to the dog on her second day of captivity.

"I want you to meet someone, Laura," he had said, bringing the dog in on a leash. "This is Satan. He's a very special doggy. He watches people. Their every move. He knows what they can and can't do. Satan knows you're not allowed to leave this house, Laura. Let me show you what will happen if you try to escape."

Nico tossed the Doberman a raw steak. The dog quickly jumped on it, savagely tearing it to shreds, his muzzle dripping with blood.

"Satan likes meat, Laura. *All* kinds."

One day she had managed to trap the Doberman in the kitchen. Immediately he began frantically scratching at the door. Unable to get out of the house through the front door because Nico had installed a deadbolt that could only be opened with a key, Laura rushed to open a window, sticking her head out. As she was about to scream, Satan burst through the thin plywood door, charging at her. Laura screamed as his jaw clamped down on her ankle, pulling her away. She was dragged to the floor and hit her head on the corner of a coffee table. When she awoke she found herself back in her bedroom, her ankle chained to the bed.

"I really wanted to trust you, Laura," Nico had said, pocketing the key he had used to chain her to the bed. "But you let me down." He'd then slapped her across the face. "You're never going to escape from me. Get used to it."

After that she was kept locked away in her bedroom, chained to her bed with Satan standing guard at all times. Bars were installed over all the windows and doors leading to the outside. She was a prisoner.

She had to figure out a way to escape this madman. Time was running out. Nico said he was planning a surprise for her. She didn't dare imagine what it would be. She didn't want to.

"You're going to love it, Laura," he had promised. "After that I'll make love to you as my wife and not as some cheap whore who fucked a Hollywood pretty boy."

As she did every morning . . . every afternoon . . . every night, Laura wondered where Drew was. He was her only hope. No one else knew she was back in Hollywood. Why hadn't he come after reading her note? He had to come! If he didn't there was no one else to help her and already two weeks had gone by.

Please Drew, she prayed. *Please come.*

Nico brought Laura the breakfast tray he had prepared. "All your favorites. Only the best for the woman I love. Go ahead," he urged while patting Satan on the head. "Start eating."

The plate of scrambled eggs, bacon, and toast turned Laura's stomach. Retching, she ran to the bathroom, the long chain attached to her ankle trailing behind her, knocking over the plate as a wave of nausea overwhelmed her.

"You stupid bitch!" he raged. "Look at what you did."

Laura bent over the toilet with the dry heaves, while Satan began devouring the overturned breakfast. Nico kicked at the dog, who whimpered and ran away.

"Does the sight of me make you sick, Laura?" he demanded from the doorway. "Does it? Well, you better start getting used to it, especially seeing it above yours in bed. I'm here to stay."

Laura slumped to the tiled floor, resting her head against the cool porcelain bowl, a protective hand resting on her stomach. This was the fifth morning in a row that she'd been sick to her stomach. And she'd missed last month's period.

Drew, please come, she fervently prayed. *Please!*

Time was definitely running out. She didn't know what she was going to do. God help her if Nico found out she was pregnant with another man's baby.

Nico stood outside the locked bedroom door, trying to control his mounting rage as he listened to Laura's sobs. He couldn't afford to lose control. If he did, it would ruin everything. He still had the rest of his plan to carry out. There were still more surprises in store for Laura. Shocking surprises.

Nico smiled with sadistic glee as he visualized the days to come. He'd waited a long time for this, and once he wrapped things up here he'd be free of Laura and able to get on with the rest of his life.

Kelly twisted against the satin sheets, staring longingly at the unwrinkled side of her king-sized bed. It was a sight she had looked at for far too long. It was a sight she was tired of. Kelly knew if she wanted she wouldn't have to look at it any longer.

She didn't want to.

She'd had enough time to think. Enough time to make a decision. She loved her husband and wanted him back. The last few weeks had been harder on her than when Graham had been away filming. That was because she had pushed him out of her life—he hadn't had to leave.

A sigh quivered on Kelly's lips. What a fool she had been! She didn't care what the world thought. She didn't care what was printed. All that mattered was Graham. Having him hold her in his arms. Having him say he loved her. Having him make love to her.

Never again would she repeat her mistake. Never again would she make the wrong sacrifice. How quick she had been to take out her frustrations on Graham instead of confronting the true source of her problems: Diana. As always she had allowed herself to become a victim of her mother's machinations.

No more. Kelly threw back the sheets, eager to dress and get through this day. Then she would go see Graham.

Tonight was the last night she would sleep alone.

Graham bench-pressed another one hundred pounds, releasing ragged breaths as he lifted the weights up and down, tightening his muscles with each repetition.

The exercise was orchestrated by rote. All Graham could think about was Kelly. How much he missed her. How much he loved her. As promised he'd kept his distance, giving her the space she needed. But how long was he supposed to stay out of her life? He missed her. He wanted her back.

Graham abandoned the weights after completing his set, wiping away the glistening sheen of sweat covering his rock-hard muscles. He started on leg lifts, adjusting the weights to seventy-five pounds.

Gritting his teeth, he began pushing. This was all Diana's fault. She was doing all she could to destroy his marriage because he'd broken up with her. Well, she was in for a surprise. He wasn't a quitter. He wasn't giving up on Kelly or their marriage. He'd give Kelly all the time she needed to sort through her feelings, but he'd also present her with a possible solution.

Graham strained his body, pushing himself to the max, veins standing out rigidly against his slick skin. He'd thought long and hard about what to do about Diana. If Kelly was willing to listen, the solution he offered would give them another chance.

"Peter! Peter! Peter!" Heather exclaimed breathlessly as he held open his front door. "You're not going to believe this!"

"Whoa! Calm down! Take a deep breath and then *slowly* tell me what's going on."

Heather took a deep breath, then released it in a shriek, throwing her arms around him. "I just came from seeing Mark Bauer. He wants to sign me to a five-picture deal. Isn't that great?"

Peter's arms wrapped around Heather, whirling her in a hug. "Fantastic! Let's have a drink to celebrate. Mark must be really excited about your talent."

Heather followed Peter out to the pool. "I'll say. He wants me to work *only* for him."

"What do you mean, *only* for him?"

"If I sign this contract I can't work for any other studio in town except Trinity," Heather said as Peter gathered glasses and ice cubes.

"Are you sure you want to do that?" he asked while tossing strawberries and ice cubes into a blender. "I thought contracts like that didn't exist anymore."

"Sure they do," Heather shouted over the whir of the blender. "Look at Jessica Lange. When she did *King Kong* for Dino DeLaurentis he signed her to a seven-year contract."

"I'm not sure about this, Heather. Take some time and think it over. It sounds too restrictive. Are you sure you want to paint yourself into a corner?" He handed her a daiquiri.

"Paint myself into a corner!?" Heather exclaimed, taking a sip of her drink. "Mark Bauer is the best producer and director in Hollywood. He'll make my career."

"Suppose Mark somehow gets out of *his* five-year contract with Trinity? Like before your five films get made? Suppose you get stuck with some bozo or it takes ten years for your five films to be made?" Peter snapped his fingers. "There goes your career."

"You're giving me doubts, Peter," Heather confessed. "I hate it when I get doubts."

"Just don't rush into anything, okay?" Peter gave her a mischievous smile. "I know how hard you've worked to get where you are."

Heather swatted Peter playfully. "You rat! Okay, you have my solemn promise. Before I do anything I'll discuss it with you."

Diana awoke before her alarm clock went off. She'd been unable to sleep a wink the previous evening—she was in *such* a state of excitement. Today was the day Kelly received a shot of reality.

Or what Diana wanted her to believe was reality.

Her plan was perfection. Timing had been the most important

factor, which was why she had held off on releasing the photos of herself and Graham, patiently waiting for just the right moment to spring them on Kelly.

Today that moment arrived.

Last week Diana had received her script for today's taping. What had delighted her was that Kelly's character finally learned of her husband's affair with Diana's character. The two women would then have a confrontation.

Little did Kelly know that this performance was going to be impromptu.

The writers had done a good job with the dialogue, but Diana knew she could do better. Taking a pencil to her script she deleted lines and added a few choice words and phrases, envisioning the shock and speechlessness she would evoke from Kelly. How delicious! Kelly was going to look like a fool.

Then came the photos. She had made sure the photos of herself and Graham were delivered to every major tabloid in the country for their next issue.

The new issues would be out on the stands today.

By tonight, if all went according to plan, Kelly would lose it all: husband, job, self-esteem.

Diana couldn't wait to get to the studio and get things rolling.

There was also another reason for her excitement. Today was the twenty-fifth anniversary of "The Yields of Passion." In honor of the occasion, this afternoon's episode would be broadcast live.

Everyone involved with the show, from cast to crew, was a nervous wreck.

Except for Diana.

She was looking forward to today's live performance.

With a vengeance.

Daniel drove from Palm Springs back to Hollywood, mission accomplished. In the manila envelope on his dashboard were two pieces of paper. One was a birth certificate; the other was a death certificate. Both certificates had the same name.

Daniel had been able to track down Dr. John Manning in Palm Springs. Although the retired obstetrician was ninety-five, he still had a mind like a steel trap. That trap had opened to each of Daniel's questions.

The doctor also had his old records, allowing Daniel to make copies of what he needed. Two patients had interested him: Diana Halloway and Iris Larson.

Daniel still couldn't believe what had taken place. Adam *hadn't* been lying. He *hadn't* been drunk. It was all true. But why? Why had it all been allowed to happen?

Only one person knew the answers. Until today Diana had been the only person who knew the truth.

Not anymore. Now the truth was going to be used against her and Daniel would find the rest of the answers. Otherwise, he'd use the truth to destroy her. For Kelly's sake.

Diana and Kelly were in the midst of their confrontation scene on the set of "The Yields of Passion."

"How could you do this to me, Mother? How? You knew he was my husband. All along you knew. Why would you want to hurt me this way?"

Kelly, dressed as usual in muted peach and elegant pearls, her hair in a French braid, projecting a sophisticated look, gave Diana an anguished look.

The camera cut to Diana. As always, she was dressed in wild decadence: red silk, diamonds, mink coat, black leather gloves. "I couldn't stop myself."

"You should have tried."

Diana whirled on Kelly, throwing back her shoulders and moving in for the kill, a brazen look on her face.

Kelly looked at her mother in confusion. As she remembered Diana's next line, her character, Tanya, was supposed to ask for Melissa's forgiveness; she was supposed to be on the verge of tears. Where were the tears? What was going on?

Diana savored the look on Kelly's face. It looked like her daughter wanted some answers. Well, she was going to get them . . .

"Why should I have tried? You want to know why I slept with your husband? I'll tell you why. *Because I wanted to!* I knew he loved you and I wanted to destroy that love. Did you honestly believe I was going to allow you to be happy? After all the years of suffering you caused me? *I despise you!*"

Diana could see chaos was reigning behind the cameras and sets. No one knew what was going on. Or how to stop it. The show was being broadcast live. There were still ten minutes of airtime left before the next commercial. They couldn't stop broadcasting.

The show was her captive.

"It wasn't all that difficult to lure your husband back into my bed. After all, I was the better lover." Diana watched Kelly's face lose its color. "I was the one who was able to satisfy him. *Me.* You were never able to satisfy him—you were never able to measure up to me. And you never will.

"Did you know we laughed at you? All the time. Hours upon hours as we rested in the sheets where we'd enjoyed our passion." Diana moved closer to Kelly, spitting her words into her face. "You'll never be able to keep a man, *never,* because there'll always be someone like me waiting to take your man away."

Kelly shook her head in protest. This was wrong. All wrong! Diana wasn't supposed to be saying these things! These words weren't in the script. They hadn't been written!

She wanted to find the words to refute Diana's claims—to take away her sadistic glee. But she couldn't. Because she was no longer Melissa and Diana was no longer Tanya. This all had to do with Graham.

"The rumors were all true," Diana whispered. "Every last one."

"No," Kelly managed to answer from behind immovable lips.

"Yesss," Diana hissed, deciding to add more fuel to the fires she had already enflamed. She didn't care if she was fired. What she was about to do would be worth it. "No matter how vehemently *Graham* denies it, you know I'm telling the truth. Pictures don't lie, do they?"

"Cut to the commercial," the director screamed as the scene came to an end. He stormed onto the set, confronting Diana. "What the fuck did you just do? Melissa and Tanya were supposed to make up. This throws off all the episodes we've already taped!"

Diana wasn't listening. She was breezing off the set, humming merrily to herself, heading for her dressing room without so much as a backward glance at her trembling daughter.

Kelly fought back the tears. She wasn't going to cry. She wasn't!

What her mother had just done to her was deplorable. She'd intentionally, purposely, *maliciously* humiliated her in front of her co-workers and the millions of viewers who watched the show by blatantly claiming to be having an affair with Kelly's real-life husband.

It wasn't true. It wasn't! Diana wanted her to doubt Graham, but she wouldn't. She wouldn't!

The tears started escaping. Kelly brushed them away with the back of her hand. Looking around the set she could see faces etched in sympathy. Pity. But she also saw more. Sly looks. Smirks. Those who believed Diana.

Could it be? Could her husband be cheating on her?

Kelly ran to her dressing room.

The tabloids were waiting in Diana's dressing room. She delved into them, eagerly devouring the headlines, admiring the photos of herself and Graham in bed. Every photo taken had been used.

Diana squealed with pleasure. She'd done it. God, the exhilaration rushing through her was better than good sex. After this the marriage of Graham and Kelly Denning would be destroyed. There was no way Kelly would be able to deny what she saw with her own eyes. Which was why she had made sure a stack of all the tabloids she'd just received were also found waiting in Kelly's dressing room.

No one could say she wasn't a thoughtful mother.

How could this be? Kelly flipped through the tabloids she'd found in her dressing room.

How could this be?

Graham and her mother were in bed together. Were these old photos? Recent photos? She skimmed a few captions . . . *taken during filming of* Long Journey Home.

Recent.

During her marriage.

Recent.

Adultery.

Recent.

During filming of Long Journey Home.

Recent.

Pictures don't lie, do they?

Recent.

Everything Diana said was true . . .

"No!" Kelly wailed, wanting to escape from the truths wreaking havoc in her mind. *"No!"*

At that moment there came a knock on her dressing-room door.

* * *

Graham shifted the bouquet of roses he carried in one arm with the two-pound box of Godiva chocolates he carried in the other. Raising his free hand, he tapped his knuckles on Kelly's dressing room door.

"Kelly? Sweetie? Is my pretty lady in there?"

Graham was feeling like a total romantic, but how else did one feel when he was in love? He couldn't wait to make up to Kelly. He'd missed her so much! He wanted to see her face again, smiling and laughing. He wanted to hear her say she loved him and feel her arms around him as they made love nonstop.

The dressing-room door was flung open. Graham, preparing to step forward, found his path blocked when Kelly, cheeks streaked with tears, came from behind the door.

The look on her face was one he had never seen before: pure hatred.

"Kelly, what's wrong?"

Newspaper pages were flung at him. "You lied to me!" she screamed in anguish. "All this time you said you loved me you were lying! You played me for a fool! I thought you cared! I thought you loved me! But you never did! *You never did!*"

Breaking into sobs, Kelly tore past Graham, running for the nearest exit.

"Kelly, wait!" Graham called, dropping the gifts he'd brought and kneeling to pick up the fallen newspaper pages. "What's going on?"

"I'd say you're about to become a bachelor again," Diana called across from her dressing room.

"You! I should have known!" Graham sent Diana a contemptuous look. Then his eyes focused on the pages he held. "What have you done?" he gasped in horror. *"What have you done?"*

"Only what needed to be done."

Graham tore up the pages like a madman. "It'll take more than trash like this to break up Kelly and me."

"I saw the way she was throwing her arms around you," Diana gloated.

"She loves me!"

"*Loved*," Diana spat. "Now she *hates* you."

"Kelly will never hate me. She'll listen to me. I'll make her listen. You'll see," Graham vowed, realizing he'd wasted enough time on Diana. "She loves me."

"Good luck," Diana scoffed. "You'll need it."

Graham glared at Diana with hatred. "You're pathetic. One of these days you're going to get exactly what you deserve, you bitch! I only hope I'm there to see it."

Kelly's car wouldn't start. She jammed the key back into the ignition and turned it again. The engine sputtered once, then twice, before dying.

"Damn!" she shouted, pounding the steering wheel in frustration, then cupping her face in her hands. All she wanted to do was sob her heart out. She hurt so badly. How could Graham have done this to her? How could he have taken her love and so thoughtlessly discarded it? She thought he had loved her. But he hadn't. He'd *never* loved her.

"Kelly!" Graham shouted from across the parking lot. "Kelly!"

At the sound of Graham's voice she looked up in panic. He was headed for her car. She wiped away her tears with hurried strokes as she turned the ignition key again. She didn't want to see him again. She didn't want to hear any more of the lies that came off his lips so easily. "Start," she begged the engine. "Please start."

The engine refused her request. Looking through the windshield she caught sight of Graham as he grew closer. With nowhere to escape to Kelly immediately locked the doors and rolled up the windows while cursing her car's unreliability.

Graham reached the driver's side and crouched on his knees so that his face was level with Kelly's. "Honey, you have to listen to me," he implored.

"I don't want to listen to you. I don't want to listen to *anything* you have to say. *Ever!*" she shouted, a fresh veil of tears trailing down her cheeks. "You lied to me and I'll never forgive you for what you've done."

"Kelly, you can't believe what you saw—"

"Go away, Graham! Just go away and leave me alone. I never want to see you again." Kelly tried to start her engine again but she still had no luck. She pressed down on the car horn, hoping one of the guards at the main gate would hear it and come to investigate. She wasn't getting out of her car. She wasn't going to let Graham anywhere near her. Not until they were in a divorce court.

"No, I won't go away!" he refused. "Not again! Not until you let me explain."

"*Explain?*" she professed, a ludicrous expression washing over her tear-stained face. "Let you explain? What's there to explain? You and Diana have painted a *very clear* picture." Kelly gave a hysterical laugh. "Why should I let you explain? So you can ease your guilty conscience?" She leaned down on the car horn again, this time with all her might, letting the horn blare long and hard.

Graham pounded on the closed window separating him from his wife, his frustration mounting. "Open the door!"

"Not on your life! It's over between us, Graham. *Over!* My mother wanted you back and she's more than welcome to have you. I'm not going to fight for you."

"How can you say that?" he asked in numb disbelief. "How can you give up so easily? Don't you love me?"

"No!" Kelly spat with as much hatred and venom that she could muster from deep inside herself, wanting to hurt Graham as deeply as he had hurt her. "I don't love you. I don't want to love you. Not ever again. It hurts too much and I'm tired of being hurt. I don't love you anymore, Graham, not after what you did with her."

"I didn't do anything! I didn't sleep with her!"

"Ms. Stoddard," a deep voice asked, "is there a problem?"

Kelly rolled down her window at the sight of the two security guards. Both were stocky, muscular men, easily outweighing Graham.

"Yes, there is a problem. I'm sorry to have bothered you, but my car won't start. I would have called for a mechanic myself but as you can see, this gentleman won't leave me alone."

Both guards warily eyed a wild-looking Graham, who was breathing heavily.

"Let's move it along, buddy," one of the guards ordered, hand positioned on the nightstick fastened at his waist.

"No," Graham refused, making eye contact and not allowing himself to be intimidated. He turned his back on the guard and returned his gaze to Kelly. "I'm not leaving. Not until she listens to what I have to say."

"You'd better do as they say and leave," Kelly advised. "I'd hate to see you get hurt."

"You wouldn't let that happen to me."

Kelly looked past Graham, nodding at one of the guards. "Why wouldn't I?"

A beefy hand clamped down on Graham's shoulder. Graham

pushed it away savagely, whirling on the guard. "Keep your paws to yourself. I'm not going to hurt her. I'm her husband."

The guard looked at Graham skeptically before looking over to Kelly. "Is this true, Ms. Stoddard?"

"No, it isn't," Kelly answered evenly, finally in control of her emotions. "This man is *not* my husband. I don't have a husband. He's a complete stranger."

The guard gave Graham a forceful nudge in the ribs with his nightstick. "You heard the lady. Let's move it."

Graham swatted the powerful stick. "I'm moving. I get the message." He turned back to Kelly and gave her a sad, final look. "I get the message."

Kelly watched as Graham stormed off the parking lot, followed by one of the guards. The other remained by her car.

"Got to be careful of those fans," he said. "These days they're liable to try anything."

"Yes, they will," Kelly agreed, wiping away the last of the tears trailing down her cheeks, suddenly drained and exhausted. "That's what makes them so dangerous. They'll say anything to make you listen to them. Do anything to win your trust and confidence."

She tried the key in her ignition one last time. All she wanted to do now was get away. As far away from this nightmare as she could possibly go. When she turned the key in the ignition she wasn't surprised as the engine roared to life.

CHAPTER TWENTY-NINE

Jaime was pissed. He hadn't gotten the role he wanted in the new Mark Bauer picture, even after being balled by that aging queen who was Trinity's head of casting.

His words still burned in Jaime's ears. Billy Cotter had swivelled in his black leather chair, wiping away a light sheen of perspiration off his roly-poly features as Jaime tucked in his shirt and buckled his pants.

"Shall I read for you now?" he asked, reaching for the script on Billy's mica desk. "The part of Charlie is my favorite although I can see myself playing Hank." Both parts had equal screen time so Jaime didn't care which he was given.

"No need to read for me," Billy decreed.

"You know which part you want me to play?" This was it! He was on his way to the top. Once his face made it to movie theaters he was destined to become a star. He would have it all. More than Daniel Ellis, whom he'd leave far, far behind.

"Neither."

"What?"

"You're too old, Jaime."

"What do you mean I'm too old? I'm only twenty-five!"

"You've got that hard edge that all working boys acquire," Billy simpered. "It would translate onto the screen. You've been peddling your goods for too long, my dear boy." He scribbled out a check and tossed it out. "Buy yourself something tight. Maybe in leather. Got a number? I'd be happy to throw some business your way."

Leaving behind the check, Jaime had stormed out of Billy Cotter's office, stopping in the first restroom he could find. He made a beeline for the mirror and stared at his face, pushing back his dark hair, studying his features, looking for what Billy Cotter saw.

"He can't be right!" Jaime shouted, suddenly afraid, seeing a vision of himself ten years down the line, peddling his body down Hollywood Boulevard.

"No!" Jaime hissed. "No!" He stepped back from the mirror, pointing a defiant finger at his image. That would never happen to him. Never! He had Daniel and Daniel was going to keep paying and paying until Jaime had a nice little nest egg for his future.

He decided to battle his blues by going shopping. He'd go to Neiman-Marcus, Bonwit Teller, and Saks, buying whatever he wanted, whether he needed it or not, no matter what the cost. Why not? He wasn't paying the bills. Daniel was.

The nightmare started at Saks. He had decided to purchase four cashmere sweaters, two Perry Ellis suits, a Ralph Lauren blazer and a pair of Cole-Haan moccasins. When his Saks credit card number was punched in, the sales clerk frowned.

"What's wrong?" Jaime asked.

"There seems to be a problem," the clerk mused, dialing a number on the in-house phone. "Let me just double-check."

Five minutes later Jaime had his answer.

"I'm sorry, sir, but this account has been closed. Would you prefer using another credit card?"

Jaime numbly handed over his American Express. Then his Visa and Mastercard. Each time it was the same thing.

"I'm sorry, sir." The clerk's smile was no longer friendly and a possessive hand was on the piled merchandise. "But these accounts have all been closed."

At Bonwit Teller and Neiman-Marcus the same thing happened when he used his store cards.

"How unusual," the clerk at Neiman-Marcus commented.

"What?" Jaime practically barked, feeling completely powerless. He was getting sick of this. What the fuck was going on?

"Only your account has been closed. The other card member still has an active account. Perhaps you should talk to him."

"I intend to," Jaime growled before heading straight for Daniel's estate.

"I've been expecting you," Peter announced as he opened the front door.

Jaime was taken aback. He hadn't expected to be standing face to face with his replacement. His usual arrogance quickly sprang into play.

"Have you? Well, I'm here to see Daniel. Is he around?"

"Daniel's not due back until later tonight."

"I'll just wait," Jaime said as he tried to wedge his way past Peter.

Peter blocked his way. "No, you won't. You're not stepping foot inside this house. Anything you have to say can be said to me. I'm the one you really want to see anyway."

"Why's that?" Jaime sneered. "Want me to tell you how the old man likes it up his ass?"

Peter's fist connected with Jaime's jaw, sending him sprawling backwards. He stumbled out of the doorway, falling back outside and into a bed of daisies.

"Your days of being a parasite are over. I'm the one who closed out all your accounts."

Jaime glared at Peter, massaging his stinging jaw. "If you know what's smart you'll have them reopened. Daniel and I have an arrangement."

Peter shook his head defiantly. The sight of Jaime disgusted him. He should have figured out sooner what was going on. He should have known getting rid of Jaime wasn't going to be easy. But he hadn't. He hadn't suspected a thing until last week when he had answered the front door, staring with surprise at a messenger with overloaded arms. "Yes? Can I help you?" he had asked.

"Are you Jaime Barton?"

"No, I'm not," Peter bristled. Mention of Jaime always gave him a bad feeling. "Why?"

"He asked that his packages be delivered to his home." The messenger deposited the packages before removing his notepad from his jacket. "Your address is the one I have."

"Jaime Barton doesn't live here anymore."

"But this is the address the store gave me," the messenger insisted.

"If you want you can use the phone to make a call, but make it quick." Peter held open the front door. "I'm running late."

Five minutes later the messenger returned. "The purchases were all charged to Daniel Ellis's account. Does Daniel Ellis live here?"

"Yes, but Jaime Barton *doesn't*," Peter impatiently repeated. And then he realized what the messenger had said. "What do you mean the purchases were charged to Daniel Ellis's account?"

The messenger gathered up his packages. "It means Ellis is footing the bills for this stuff. Barton is able to sign off on purchases and we send the bill to Ellis. I guess Barton never gave the store his new address. Look, I'm going to take this stuff back to the store. Sooner or later Barton will come looking for it."

"No doubt about that," Peter quietly stated, the messenger's words sinking in.

Forgetting his appointment, Peter headed for Daniel's study, acting on a hunch. Rummaging through Daniel's oak desk, he found the box where Daniel kept his cancelled checks. He flipped open the box, shuffling through the old checks until he discovered what he was looking for.

There were checks made out to Jaime Barton. Checks made out to department stores, men's stores and restaurants, all attached to charge slips signed by Jaime Barton. All were for astronomical amounts.

Peter crumpled the checks he held in his hand. He was angry. Angry at Daniel for keeping this secret. Angry at Jaime for having the audacity to do this to Daniel. And angry at himself for being too blind to see it. He stared at the crumpled checks in his fist.

This was going to end. *His* way.

Peter focused his attention back on Jaime, unleashing his wrath. "You're out of Daniel's life, *for good*. It all ends today. The credit cards, the allowance, the rent. All of it. From now on you're on your own. If I ever see your face around here again, I'll make sure you're sorry."

"You're not going to get away with this!" Jaime screamed, picking himself up, his face turning red. "I won't let you!"

"I've got news for you, Jaime. I already have." Peter then slammed the front door in his face.

Grace clicked off her hair dryer, hurrying to answer her ringing phone.

"Hello?" she asked breathlessly.

"You still sound sexy."

Grace's voice instantly cooled and turned flat. "Harrison. What do you want?"

"I wanted to offer my congratulations. That was a pretty slick move getting Gabrielle a copy of *Dangerous Parties*. You knew exactly how to get back at me."

"I *was* proud of myself," Grace smirked.

"Yes, revenge *is* sweet, but Grace, as co-author of *Dangerous Parties*, doesn't it bother you that Gabrielle will be ruining our screenplay?"

"*Our* screenplay?" She gave a hollow laugh. "Shall I remind you that you've taken sole credit for *our* endeavor?"

"Grace, that's why I'm calling." Harrison's voice was cajoling. "I've been having second thoughts. I want to make things right between us. I've missed you."

"Yeah, right," she snorted in disbelief. "What's the matter, Harrison? Got writer's block?"

"Grace, it's true. I want you back. No other woman was able to satisfy me the way you did."

"You had your chance."

"How about giving me another?" he pleaded.

"No way."

"Grace, I'm sorry. Why don't we meet for a drink? Just to talk about old times."

"I'm busy," she lied.

"Not for this. I've got a proposition. What would you say if I told you I was willing to give you half the profits from *Dangerous Parties?*"

"I'd say I was dreaming."

"There's more."

"What else?"

"Something you've always wanted. How'd you like to become the next Mrs. Harrison Moore?"

"If you think I'm getting back on that merry-go-round, waiting for you to break free of Gabrielle, you've got another thing coming," she hotly stated.

"You won't have to wait," he promised. "In a matter of days I'm going to be a single man."

"Gabrielle has no intention of divorcing you," she reminded.

"Who said anything about a divorce?"

Grace's attention was captured. "What are you saying?"

"You know exactly what I'm saying. We're on the same wave length, Grace. I did it once and I'm willing to do it again. For you. Only this time I'll be sure to get the job done right. What do you say?"

"Sounds interesting. *Very* interesting. Can you be here in an hour?"

"I'm on my way."

* * *

What was Harrison up to now? Grace wondered.

She hadn't believed a word he'd said. She'd be a fool if she did. Biting her lower lip, she dropped the fluffy white towel covering her and padded to her closet. He was up to *something*, that was for sure, and she was intrigued enough by his proposition and what it might offer.

Surveying her wardrobe, she decided to wear her sexiest outfit. It wouldn't hurt. And she did want Harrison at his most vulnerable.

This time she was going to be the user. She was going to call the shots and get what she wanted: money, power, prestige. She wasn't going to allow him to hurt her again. But most importantly, valued above all else, was the one thing that mattered most of all.

Grace smiled a wicked smile.

Revenge.

It was genius. Sheer genius.

Harrison splashed on his cologne, reviewing his plan one last time, checking to make sure all his bases were covered.

Grace had been easy enough to handle. Her greed for the good things in life was like a neon light. It made her so easy to manipulate. All he had to do was string her along with false promises until he no longer needed her.

If all went according to plan, both Grace and Gabrielle would soon be dead and he'd be a free man.

Vanessa gulped down her martini, staring at Daniel in shocked silence. "Are you sure it's true?"

"Absolutely," he answered. "What you've told me only confirms it."

Vanessa poured herself a second martini. "Whoa! Heavy-duty stuff! I need another." She sipped her drink slowly, studying Daniel over raised brows. "What you've just told me is incredible."

"But possible. *Very* possible."

"If what Adam told you was true, then yes," Vanessa conceded.

Daniel began furiously pacing Vanessa's study, his hands running through his hair. "He *was* telling me the truth! The only thing

I don't understand is *why*. Why would Iris agree to such an arrangement?"

Vanessa settled herself among the cushions of her settee. "Only one person has that answer," she murmured.

"Diana," Daniel grimly stated.

"Think she'll talk?"

"She has no choice. I hold too many cards."

"You have to tell me what she says!" Vanessa implored. "This is so deliciously, deviously, *dementedly* Diana! It'll make such a juicy chapter for my autobiography."

"You can't use this for your book." Daniel's tone was insistent.

"Why not?" Vanessa's face was crestfallen.

"*Kelly*," he stressed. "We can't do anything that will hurt her. She's at the center of all of this, Vanessa. We have to protect her. Who knows what would happen if she learned the truth?"

"So what do you think of my plan?"

"It's good. Very good," Grace admitted, handing Harrison a bourbon. She remained standing above him, forcing him to look up at her, pleased with the way he was eyeing her.

She wore spiked heels and a clinging black floral tankdress—no bra, no underwear, no stockings. Her air conditioner was purposely turned off and as a result, her apartment was quite warm and her dress was glued to her body with a light sheen of perspiration.

"Why are you telling *me* all this?" she asked, fluffing her short cap of blonde hair. "You double-crossed me, Harrison. Suppose I wanted to get even? You've just given me your head on a silver platter."

He took a sip of his bourbon, craning his neck up at her. "I've kept my tracks pretty well covered. And do you really think anyone would believe that *I* was Gabrielle's obsessed fan?"

Grace looked at him admiringly. "I have to admit, you had me fooled."

Harrison looked quite pleased with himself. "I did manage to fool everyone, didn't I?"

"How'd you come up with the idea?"

"From a magazine article. It was about celebrities who had been stalked by their fans. Wouldn't it be nice, I thought after finishing the article, if Gabrielle had a fan who was obsessed with her? That would solve all my problems. And then I realized she could. She *would*. Me.

"I decided to start things slowly. First came the letters. After the letters there were the roses. Then I moved up to the phone call. That night she was alone I made the call from a hotel. I wanted to do things slowly, gradually. My goal was to create another person. I had to make everyone believe that someone else existed . . . someone who was obsessed with Gabrielle.

"After the phone call I decided it was time to make my move. That's when I sent her the chocolates."

"Those chocolates were a stroke of genius."

"They were a nice touch," Harrison admitted proudly. "Too bad she didn't eat a couple more. After the poisoned chocolates didn't work, I decided to lie low until her 'fan' decided to strike again. Of course, I had almost finished off Gabrielle myself when someone else had a stab at her. But now I think it's time that Gabrielle's fan make one last reappearance. Because with this final step he's going to accomplish his goal. This time she's going to die."

Grace leaned forward, prying Harrison's glass from his fingers. She dabbed the chilled glass over her chest and along her forehead. "And I didn't think you were creative. But you still haven't answered my question. *Why*, Harrison? Why are you telling me all this?"

Harrison's face flushed with the heat of desire. "Isn't it obvious? I want to make things up to you."

Grace walked over to the sliding doors leading out to the balcony. She stood in the moonlight, allowing Harrison to see her naked outline beneath the flimsy dress. Turning, she cocked her head, eyeing him coolly. "You're taking a lot for granted."

The humid air and sexual electricity in the closed apartment caused the sweat to pour from Harrison's body. Removing his shirt, he walked over to Grace, leaving a few scant inches between them. Both eyed one another with naked hunger, but neither made a move. Then Grace started to turn her back on Harrison and he grabbed her by the arm. Whirling her around, he pressed his mouth to hers, prying her lips open as his tongue plunged deep inside.

Harrison lifted Grace into the air, pressing her to the wall as her legs wrapped around him.

"Things were once good between us, Grace," he rasped. "Let me make them better."

Grace licked her lips. "How?"

Harrison bit into her neck, his excitement growing as she moaned with pleasure, begging him not to stop. His eyes blazed with triumph. "How?" he repeated. "By letting me give you exactly what you deserve."

"No wonder you've hated Kelly all these years."

Diana gave Daniel a look of contempt. "Do you blame me?"

"Yes! Yes, I do! Kelly's the innocent in all of this. She had nothing to do—"

"*She had everything to do with it! She was the cause of this whole ugly, sordid mess!*" Diana raged, lunging from the couch she was sitting on, her silk dressing gown billowing out. "*Everything!* She's the cause of it all!"

Daniel shook his head in disbelief. "And all these years you've been making her pay."

Diana's answer was short and succinct. "Revenge is sweet."

Daniel couldn't believe what he was hearing as he stared at the woman before him. In fact, none of what he'd heard over the past hour was believable. Yet it was all true. It *had* all happened, as Diana was so very ready to admit with an almost boasting tone to her words.

"The game's not over, Diana. It all ends today. From now on you're going to leave Kelly alone. I've seen what you've done to her over the years." He shook his head ruefully. "Now it all makes sense! But it's going to stop! I couldn't stop you before, but I can now."

Diana looked at Daniel with scorn. "What makes you so sure?"

"I'll tell Kelly the truth."

Diana released a hearty laugh. "You're bluffing."

Daniel looked at Diana coldly. "Call my bluff. I dare you. If you do, not only will Kelly learn the truth, but so will the rest of the world."

"Don't push me, Daniel," Diana hissed. "I'm warning you."

"Just think," he goaded, ignoring Diana's murderous glare as he paced her drawing room. "After Vanessa's autobiography comes out, with what we've just discussed included in the book, of course, and a chapter sympathetic to Iris, Kelly can then write a Mommie Dearest exposé of you. You always did give Joan a run for her money. All the tabloids will be after you and you'll get tons of bad publicity as the Iris/Adam/Diana love triangle is hashed and rehashed."

"You try it," Diana warned, gritting her teeth, "and I'll tell the entire world that you lusted after my husband and that on the night he died you professed your love and made a pass at him just before he went careening off Laurel Canyon. All the blame will be laid on you and *your* career will die overnight."

"You lying bitch! You *would* do something like that. Adam was like a brother to me. Your problem was that you didn't want to share him with anyone, which is why *you* drove him right into Iris's arms!"

Out for blood, Diana raked her nails across Daniel's face, slashing a cheek. "Get out of my house before I gouge your eyes out!"

Daniel dabbed at his bleeding cheek with a handkerchief. "So you want to play games? Fine. I have proof, Diana."

"Of course," she sneered.

Daniel grabbed Diana by the arm, delivering his words viciously. "Yes, I do. Unless you stop tormenting Kelly I'm going to show her the two certificates. You know the ones I mean. And then there's the medical records." He let go of her. "All I'm asking is that you leave Kelly alone and let her be happy. Haven't you held onto your bitterness long enough?"

Diana's eyes were pure venom and Daniel involuntarily took a step back.

"You're pathetic! Do you actually think that I'd be able to forget what was done to me? And by whom? Do you actually think you can call the shots? Iris tried. Adam tried. They're both *dead*."

"What are you saying?"

"What do you *think* I'm saying?" she asked derisively. "I have power, Daniel. I have connections . . . friends in high places. All it takes is a phone call. Just one call to have a request fulfilled. You've just tried to cross me. That was a mistake. A *big* mistake. Now you're going to be *very, very* sorry."

Daniel was becoming extremely uncomfortable with the turn the conversation was taking, although he was sure Diana was only trying to scare him. That's all it was. She was bluffing. "We've both said what we wanted. Think of what will happen if Kelly learns the truth, Diana. I'll give you some time to make a decision."

"You'll give *me* some time?" Diana yelled at Daniel's retreating back. "Nobody gives Diana Halloway an ultimatum. *Nobody!* I'm the one calling the shots!" She stormed after Daniel, high heels clicking furiously down the marbled hallway. "How's this for an answer?" she screamed as he walked out the front door. *"Go to hell!* Because that's where you're headed if you think I'm going to let you get away with this!"

Peter was sitting at the kitchen table, his throbbing fist soaking in a bowl of ice water when Daniel walked in.

"What happened to you?" Daniel asked.

"I could ask the same question." Peter took a closer look at Daniel's cheek. "Nasty. Sit down and let me take care of it."

"I'm fine."

"Sit," Peter insisted.

Daniel sat as Peter went for fresh water, antiseptic, and bandages. First he cleaned away the dried blood with water, then applied the antiseptic as Daniel flinched.

"Almost done," Peter soothed. "Mind telling me who you tangled with?"

Daniel rubbed Peter's red knuckles. "Only if you tell me."

Peter shook his head ruefully. "My fist connected with Jaime's chin."

Daniel's chair skittered back. "Jaime was here today? Why?"

"He was looking for you. When he couldn't find you he insisted on waiting but I have this thing about trash in the house." Peter bandaged Daniel's cheek. "All done." He began gathering up the supplies.

"What did he want?"

Peter turned around from the sink. "Why didn't you tell me you were still paying all his bills?"

"He told you that?" Daniel whispered.

"No," Peter stated angrily. "A fucking messenger from a department store told me. Last week some of his packages were accidentally delivered here. Then I went through your bills and cancelled checks. Daniel, he's been blackmailing you!"

"No, he hasn't."

"No?" Peter asked skeptically. "Then what do you call it?"

"Jaime just needs a little support until he gets on his feet."

"That's bullshit and you know it."

Daniel looked at Peter fearfully. "What did you do?"

"I closed all his accounts. That's why he was over here. He wasn't happy when I told him the gravy train had ended."

"Why did you do that?" Daniel moaned, cradling his head in

his hands. Now besides Diana's wrath, he also had Jaime's to contend with. "Why? Jaime has a short fuse. He's unpredictable. Who knows what he's liable to do?"

"I don't care," Peter announced, "and neither should you." Peter led the way out of the kitchen, shutting off the lights. "Come on. Let's go upstairs. There's something I want to show you."

They went to Peter's bedroom, where Peter held the door open. "Take a look inside."

Daniel did. "All your things are gone."

"That's right. I'm moving out."

"Because of Jaime? Because I didn't tell you I was still paying his bills? Peter, I'm sorry. Don't leave."

Peter's face broke into a grin. "Who said anything about leaving?"

He led Daniel further down the hallway to the master bedroom, flinging open the door. Inside Peter's belongings were mixed in with Daniel's. "I've still got to find room for a few things, but what do you think of our bedroom?"

"When did you decide to do this?"

"After my run-in with Jaime. That bastard pissed me off, Daniel. I can't explain it, but when he was threatening you, he was threatening me . . . *us*. A wave of protectiveness came over me; no way was I going to let that little shit pull that stunt. After he left I realized there was no reason why we shouldn't share the same bedroom. After all, I love you and I'll do anything for you, Daniel. Always."

Daniel took another look around the bedroom. Then he kissed Peter. "Thank you. This means a lot."

Peter fingered Daniel's bandage. "Want to tell me about it?"

"Can it wait till later?" His eyes glistened with anticipation. "I'm eager to break in our new bed."

Peter didn't need any coaxing.

CHAPTER THIRTY

"It's not often that you come to Las Vegas, unless it's to perform," Paul observed. "You must want something."

"You're so perceptive," Diana purred, her high heels digging into the plush carpeting as she made her way across the penthouse. She planted her moist, red lips on Paul's.

Paul ran a hand over Diana's buttocks. "No underwear. You must be planning on seducing me. What do you want this time?"

Diana threw back her head, releasing a throaty laugh. "You have such a suspicious mind."

Paul's eyes bored into Diana's. "But I'm right, aren't I?" He was no fool. He knew Diana had endured their relationship over the years only because he held the upper hand. If he so chose, he could destroy her at any moment. But he wouldn't. Still, for her to come to him, to make the first move, she had to have a motive.

She loosened his tie, unbuttoning the collar. "You once took care of a problem for me. I need for you to do that again."

Paul didn't mince words. "Are we talking murder?"

"Yes," she answered fiercely. "The sooner the better."

"Who is it this time?"

"Daniel Ellis."

Paul jerked free of Diana's embrace. "Daniel Ellis? Are you crazy?"

"He has to be eliminated, Paul."

"Why?"

"He knows too much. He found out the truth about Kelly and he's threatening to tell her."

"So? I thought you'd want that. If he told Kelly the truth you'd be out from under my thumb. I wouldn't be able to blackmail you any longer."

"I wouldn't think you'd want that to happen."

"It looks like I don't have any choice in the matter if Daniel decides to tell what he knows."

"You do have a choice. You can kill him."

"Don't you think it's time Kelly learned the truth?"

"No!" Diana vehemently cried. "She can't find out! Not yet! Not until *I'm* ready to tell her."

"You're going to get a perverse joy out of that, I can tell," Paul stated dryly.

"That's right," Diana swore. "I am. Now, are you going to do it?"

"Murdering Daniel Ellis is too risky."

"I have faith in you, Paul. You're very good at what you do." Malicious glee iced Diana's remaining words. "After all, Iris Larson's death never looked like murder."

Paul stared at the woman standing before him. Her beautiful features were a hardened mask and he could feel the waves of hatred radiating off her as they had almost twenty-five years ago in a scene almost identical to this one.

"I want you to do something for me."

Paul stared with open lust at Diana Halloway's lush figure. For months he had pursued the beautiful actress, courting her with flowers, jewelry, furs, dinner invitations. All of his attempts had been rebuffed; all his calls unreturned. And now here she was before him, asking for a favor.

"Since when do *you* tell *me* what to do?" His tone was slightly harsh. He wasn't going to make this easy for her. He wanted to see a little begging and groveling.

Diana lowered her eyes. "You're angry and you have a right to be after the way I've treated you. But you have to understand. I'm a widow. How would it look if I started seeing another man so soon after my husband's death? And you are a married man. I have to think of my reputation."

Her apology softened him a bit. "What did you want?"

"I know you're a successful businessman, Paul, but I've heard certain stories."

"What kind of stories?"

Diana shrugged, eyes still downcast. "They say you'll go to *any* lengths to get what you want. *Do* anything. Is that true?"

"When I want something I go after it, no matter what the cost or consequence," he boasted.

"We're alike," she murmured. "I feel the exact same way. Which is why I'm here."

"What is it you want?" he asked again.

Diana raised her head, a look of determination etched on her face. "I want you to kill someone for me."

Paul gazed at her with open scorn. "Is that all?"

"Why are you angry? You *have* killed before, haven't you?"

"Whether I have or haven't is *my* business, not yours. But tell me. Why should I do this for you, even if I were to consider it? What's in it for me?"

"What would you like?"

Paul cupped Diana's breast, fingering the nipple through the emerald green silk she wore. "You know what I'd like."

"Then you shall have it." She unzipped the dress, letting it fall to the floor, stepping out of it naked. "Let's get started."

Making love to Diana was everything Paul had expected. It was savage, demanding, and totally satisfying. Diana's sexual appetite was just as raging as his. Day after day, week after week, they met. It came to a point where he started neglecting his business. His family—wife Marina and two small children, Gabrielle and Peter—was completely forgotten. Diana was all he could think about.

Then came the day when Diana voiced her request again and Paul, totally bewitched, promised to do what she wanted.

"I think I've shown good faith," she began one afternoon after they'd finished making love in one of the suites at his hotel, three weeks after starting their affair. "It's only fair that you carry out your end."

"Suppose I don't?" he challenged.

She circled one of his nipples with her lips. "Then you'll never make love to me again. You see, Paul, I'm willing to become your mistress if you do this for me."

Having Diana as his mistress was irresistible, although Paul did have plans of his own. Plans that included Diana.

"Who do you want killed?"

"Iris Larson."

"You can't be serious!" he exclaimed.

"My husband is dead because of her. He was driving her car when the brakeline snapped. She's going to pay."

"Sounds like there's more to this story," he prodded. "For instance, what was Adam doing driving her car?"

"She was fucking my husband!" she spat out. "Are you satisfied? Is that what you wanted to hear? My husband preferred sleeping with her instead of me!"

"He was a damn fool," he whispered, lips brushing along Diana's neck and cheeks as he became aroused.

"Will you do this for me?" she begged. "All you have to do is make sure it looks like an accident."

"Yes," he fervently whispered as he felt his excitement grow, wanting always to experience this exquisite rush he had only with Diana. "Yes, I'll do it."

Paul made an appointment to see Iris when he was back in Hollywood, telling her he wanted to discuss the possibility of having her perform at his casino. In his mind he already had a plan for eliminating her.

Their meeting took place on her estate in Laurel Canyon, just the two of them, shortly after seven. Iris had looked her most seductive, dressed in clingy black silk, her blonde hair artfully styled in cascading layers, her piercing blue eyes dramatically lined in black and her full lips painted a rich, moist red.

She was a beautiful woman and Paul found himself attracted to her.

Until she opened her mouth.

Iris Larson was a bitch with a capital B, despite the Doris Day image she presented to the press and her fans. Her attitude to Paul was barely condescending. She made it clear that she didn't have time for him. She told him she was a *star* and she'd *never* degrade her star status by performing for a cheap hoodlum like him. Especially one involved with Diana Halloway.

Paul kept a smile on his face the entire time. When Iris's back was turned he spiked her drink with secobarbital. After she passed out he changed her into a swimsuit and brought her out to the pool. He threw her in, making sure she slammed her forehead on the edge so it looked as if she had banged her head before falling in.

After watching Iris sink to the bottom of her tiled pool, air bubbles disappearing, before her body returned to the surface, Paul decided to check her house for an appointment book that might refer to their meeting. It wouldn't be good to put ideas in people's heads, though if he was somehow questioned by the police he'd tell them his meeting with Iris had been an hour earlier.

There were no traces of his presence. He didn't find an appointment book or anything else relating to their meeting.

But he did find Iris's diary.

And it was jam-packed with explosive secrets.

Reading the pages, Paul's jaw dropped. What a tangled web!

Suddenly he knew why Diana had wanted Iris dead. The *real* reason.

He decided to return to his estate in Beverly Hills. He would leave the diary there, attend a dinner engagement, and then later see Diana.

But his plans changed when he got home and was confronted by his angry wife.

He hadn't planned on her anger, never before seeing her in such a state.

Then again, he hadn't planned on killing her.

Marina was a quiet, passive woman, who remained in the background and did as she was told. When he saw her transformed and realized that if she wanted, she *could* leave him, taking his children with her, he saw red. No one jeopardized his plans. He was the one who made all the decisions. No one told him what to do. And if they did, it was because he let them—because he wanted something from them.

Like he was doing with Diana. He was doing her bidding only because there was a prize to be claimed—Diana herself.

Paul had planned on leaving Marina eventually. He loved Diana. He wanted to marry her.

But now Marina was threatening to leave *him*.

He wouldn't allow her to do that.

He had never truly loved Marina. As he became successful, transforming himself from a street kid who ran numbers for the neighborhood bookie to a man of means, he realized he needed a wife to add the finishing touch. She'd have to be beautiful, educated, respectful. And she'd have to be able to provide him with children.

He met Marina at a church social in Brooklyn, properly chaperoned by her two spinster aunts. She was beautiful and innocent, newly arrived from Italy, where her parents had died in a hotel fire, and as sheltered from the world as a convent girl—everything Paul was looking for. She worshipped him at first sight. He married her after three months and relocated to Las Vegas.

To keep his new wife busy as his empire grew, Paul quickly made her pregnant, first with Gabrielle and then Peter. But two infants didn't stop Marina from becoming Americanized, much to Paul's regret. Nor did it stop her from questioning her husband's absences. When she discovered his first affair (this after four years of marriage and *many* affairs), he was properly chastised. But soon he began to suspect Marina was watching his every move and he hated it.

It made him angry, although he never acted upon his anger.

Until the night of Iris's murder.

When he got to the house in Beverly Hills, Marina flew at him, demanding answers, wanting to know where he had been. She had already questioned him about his relationship with Diana and this was the first thing she threw in his face before taunting him with her appearance, claiming to have slept with other men.

And then she threatened to leave him.

And that pushed him over the edge.

With Iris Larson's death all of Diana's problems had been solved. Why not solve one of his own?

With that thought he'd wrapped his hands around Marina's throat, squeezing with all his might while visualizing Diana as his next wife.

But he was in for a rude awakening.

After having his most trusted men dispose of Marina's body, arranging to make her death look like a suicide, he called Diana and asked her to come over.

He was waiting with an emerald-and-diamond necklace that had belonged to Marina. When they were making love he draped it around her neck as she asked him if he'd done as he promised.

"Of course. Don't worry. It won't even look like murder."

Diana moaned in ecstasy, clutching the necklace. "God, I love you."

That was all Paul needed to hear. He made his move. "Diana, I want you to marry me."

"You want me to marry you? Marry *you?*" She concentrated on fastening her newly acquired bauble around her neck. "Are you out of your mind?"

"I love you, Diana."

Diana preened at herself in the mirror across the room, pawing at the jewels around her neck. "Well, I don't love you."

"But you just said—"

"I didn't mean I *loved* you!" she snapped. "I love what you did for me. Look, we had some fun together and we both got what we wanted. But marriage? It wouldn't work. I'd say our business is finished." She started to get out of bed, preparing to leave.

He grabbed Diana by the neck, slamming her against the headboard of his bed. "Our business is *not* finished. Not until *I* say it is."

"Hey, let go! Quit it!" Diana twisted to break free. "You're hurting me," she whimpered as Paul squeezed the emerald-and-diamond necklace into her neck.

"I'll repeat my proposal. I want you to marry me, Diana."

"And I'll repeat my answer," she brazenly spat in his face. "No way! How stupid do you think I am? Marriage to a cheap hoodlum like you will get me nowhere, even if it doesn't ruin my career. I wouldn't even perform in your casino if you paid me."

It was the second time that evening he had been called a hoodlum. And he didn't like it. At all. "You're making a mistake," he warned.

"Of course," she scoffed, still squirming to escape. "A pair of cement heels are waiting for me, right?"

"No," he admonished in a deadly hiss. "More like the contents of Iris Larson's diary, detailing her affair with Adam and what happened afterwards."

The blood drained from Diana's face and the fight went out of her. "She kept a diary?"

"All the details are there. The little things you forgot to mention to me when you commissioned me for this job. A pretty twisted mess."

"What are you going to do with the diary?" she whispered.

"Why, nothing. It'll stay in my safekeeping. After all, as of next month you start performing at my casino. Six months out of the year will be fine. How does that sound?"

"Fine," Diana grudgingly agreed, mistakenly believing she had defused the situation and cooled Paul's simmering anger. "What will my pay be?"

"Pay? *Pay?*" he mocked. "Diana, don't you remember your earlier words?" he admonished, snatching the emerald-and-diamond necklace off her neck as he plunged into her, catching her unprepared. *"Nothing."*

* * *

Diana waited expectantly for Paul's answer.

She knew he was purposely making her wait, taking his sweet time before he told her his decision.

Diana balled her hands into fists, smothering her seething rage —a rage she had been carrying since her meeting with Daniel Ellis last week.

No one, but *no one*, told her what to do. And Daniel was going to learn that lesson. Just like Iris had.

Diana allowed herself a smug smile. Iris had thought she was the one in control—that she could call the shots after Adam's death. She almost had. But Diana had showed her. She had come to Paul and Paul had handled things neatly and efficiently. Though in the end, she had paid dearly for his assistance— twenty-five years of blackmail. Yet if she had to do it over again, she would.

Now she was going to show Daniel. With his death her secret would remain safe and her revenge would be complete.

"You're looking very pleased with yourself," Paul commented.

"I was thinking of Iris. How I had the last laugh."

"So you did. You really despised her, didn't you?"

A deep corrosive hatred, still alive after all these years, spewed forth. *"Despised* her? I *hated* her! I will *never* forget what she took from me! You know that. You have the diary. You've read the pages. And you know why the contents of that diary have to remain secret."

"Yes," he murmured. "If Kelly knew the truth, your little vendetta against Iris would come to an end."

"Precisely. And I'm having *too* much fun to let Daniel Ellis spoil it. So are you going to do what I want? Are you going to kill him?"

"You mean arrange another accident?" Paul looked into Diana's expectant face, thinking long and hard before giving his answer. "No."

"No?" she repeated in disbelief, slamming her fist down on his desk. "Why not?"

"Why should I involve myself in another mess you've created? Have you forgotten that I'm trying to clean up my image?"

"How can you do this to me?" she shrieked. "After everything I've done for you?"

"You've done nothing but pay back a debt." Paul gave her a sly look. "Now, if you were to make this worth my while, I *might* give your request a little more thought and be able to arrange something."

"How?" she suspiciously asked.

Paul shrugged. "I don't know. Give it some thought. Other than yourself . . . what could you possibly offer me?"

It was then that Diana *knew*. In his crude way Paul was telling her what he wanted—he still wanted *her*. As his wife. But after the way she had shunned his proposal the first time, he wasn't about to propose again. He wanted her to come to him . . . crawling . . . begging . . . pleading as she offered herself to him in return for Daniel's death.

Diana didn't want to do it. She *wouldn't* do it. If she married Paul she would become trapped. She would lose all her freedom. She would become his possession and *nobody* owned Diana Halloway.

"Sorry," she coolly drawled. "I'm drawing a blank."

"Guess you don't want Daniel dead badly enough."

She could see the cold fury in his eyes. Her answer had been like a slap. Once again she was spurning him. Despite the momentary satisfaction, she decided to make amends.

"But I do," she implored. "Why don't I give it some more thought?" She *did* want Daniel dead. Badly. But how badly depended on how much she was willing to sacrifice. "Give me some more time."

"Take all the time you need," Paul answered with a grin, accepting her compromise, "because unless you come up with the answer I'm looking for, Daniel Ellis is going to remain very much alive."

From her window seat Kelly stared out at the pedestrians walking along Fifth Avenue, wondering if their lives ran smoothly or if they were just as complicated as hers.

"Aren't you dressed yet?" Jill Kramer, Kelly's roommate from college, came into the guest bedroom Kelly had been given at the Kramer apartment. "I thought we'd do a little shopping this morning and then have lunch at Le Cirque."

Kelly shook her head wearily, resting her forehead against the window, eyes still glued to the street outside, not bothering to turn her head and look at Jill. "I'm not in the mood."

"*Kelly*," Jill intoned sharply, wanting her best friend to pay attention to what she was about to say, "it's been three weeks since you left Graham and in that time you haven't been in the mood to do anything! You won't eat. You won't talk. You won't go out. You don't care how you look. All you do is keep yourself cooped inside. When are you going to get on with your life?"

After fleeing from Diana and Graham at the studio, Kelly had packed a bag and headed back to New York. She'd needed to escape from Hollywood and leave her problems behind. All she had wanted to do was return to New York. In New York she had always had control of her life—a sense of security—something she hadn't had since returning home.

After checking into the Waldorf she'd called Jill in London and told her what had happened. Despite Kelly's protests, Jill was instantly on the next plane out and insisting that Kelly move into the guest room in her parent's duplex off Central Park.

"How much longer are you going to hide?" Jill asked.

"I'm not hiding," Kelly said, resting her head on her knees, her once luxuriant mane of caramel hair, now dull and unkempt, falling over one shoulder as she continued looking outside.

"Bullshit!" Jill snapped, dark eyes blazing. "You're hiding and you know it. Your life's at a standstill."

"Wrong. My life's in pieces and I don't know how to put the pieces back together. I don't know what my next move should be."

Jill was incredulous. "You don't know what your next move should be? Well, if that's your only problem I'll give you a clue!" The petite brunette marched herself over to Kelly and gripped her friend by the shoulders, forcing her to turn and face her. "Get yourself on the next plane back to Los Angeles. Then find your husband and work out your differences once and for all."

"There are no differences to work out." Kelly's voice was emotionless. "It's over between us."

"It's not over!" Jill refused to let Kelly give up so easily. She had to talk some sense into her. She had to get her to do something. "You love Graham. You told me so yourself. Over and over. I could hear it in your voice every time we spoke. He means everything to you, Kelly. You don't give up a love like that without a fight. How can it be over?" she asked.

"Because it is! He slept with my mother!"

"*Before* he married you!" Jill reminded.

"And after!" Kelly hotly retorted, suddenly angry and trying to pull away from Jill. "You saw those headlines."

Jill wouldn't release her hold. She forced Kelly to continue looking at her. "Don't run away, Kelly. Please," she implored. "Haven't you done enough running?"

Kelly slumped back down on the window seat. "What else can I do?" she asked in resignation.

Jill repeated her earlier words. "You can fight for your husband."

"I'm tired of fighting," Kelly said softly.

"Get untired!" Jill demanded. "I'm not going to get off your case until you give Graham another chance. You haven't even heard his side of the story. Don't you at least owe him that?"

"I don't owe him anything!" Kelly snapped.

"What about yourself? Don't you owe it to yourself to settle things with Graham once and for all? This is unfinished business, Kelly. You have to get it out of the way. And what about your career?"

"What about it?" Kelly could care less about her career. She was never going to go back to "The Yields of Passion." Let the producers sue her for breach of contract. She didn't care.

"This is what she wants—you do realize that, don't you?" Jill commented. "You're playing right into Diana's hands. You've allowed her to win. She's destroyed your marriage. She's destroying your career. Fight back, Kelly. Fight back! I know you can do it! You can't give up. You've worked too hard and too long to let it all slip away. Everything you always wanted is yours—someone to love, the career you've always wanted. Are you going to let her take it all away from you? Are you going to let her win? If you want to give up your career, fine. I'm not going to give you any argument. I'm not going to try to stop you. There are hundreds of other things you could do with the rest of your life besides acting. But I'm not going to stand by and let you give up Graham so easily. A special love comes along only once in a lifetime, Kelly. If you still love Graham, then fight for him."

Kelly didn't respond to Jill's words. Instead she continued staring out the window. Then she spoke quietly. "I'd like to be alone, please, if you don't mind."

"I'm going," Jill said in a resigned voice, "but Kelly, *please* think about what I've said. It isn't over. Not yet. Not unless you want it to be. You've still got a chance. Go to Graham. Talk to him. Tell him how you feel and then listen to what he has to say. Make your decision after that. Otherwise, for the rest of your life, you'll wonder what could have been."

* * *

"Hey, this is a surprise," Peter said as Heather joined him on the terrace where he was having breakfast. "Pull up a chair. Daniel is doing laps. Have you eaten?"

Heather waved away the servant hovering with a silver coffee pot. "I'm not hungry."

"Heather, what's wrong?" Peter asked, instantly zeroing in on her mood. "Is it bad?"

"Very bad. Oh Peter, I don't know where to begin except to show you."

"Show me what?"

"This." She placed the folded newspaper she carried under her arm down on the table, opening it to the morning's headline. "I guess you haven't seen it yet."

At first Peter thought it was a trick. That Heather was playing a practical joke with one of those dummy newspapers where you can have anything you want printed up. But when he looked into her drawn and panicked face, he knew it wasn't. What he was reading was true. For all the world to see.

And now the entire world, his father and sister included, knew he was gay.

Jaime Barton had decided to launch a palimony suit against Daniel. He was suing for five million dollars. The details of Jaime and Daniel's relationship were all there, including mention of Peter as the "other man" who had supposedly broken them up. There were also photos of the three of them with the story.

"Peter, I'm so sorry," Heather whispered, tears glistening in her eyes, wishing she could do more.

Peter was suddenly nauseous. He pushed away the plate of French toast he had been ravenously digging into only moments before. "What am I going to do?"

"What can you do except talk to your father and sister?"

"I'm not talking about myself!" Peter exclaimed. "I'm talking about *Daniel*. This is going to destroy him."

Peter wasn't referring to Daniel's career. He was referring to Daniel himself. For the last thirty-five years Daniel had pretended to be something he wasn't. Now the mask had been stripped away, exposing the man he really was, leaving him vulnerable as he tried to deal with the ugliness of the press and those who would attack him. They wouldn't listen to what he had to say.

They wouldn't care. All the public would want was the scandal . . . the gossip . . . the blood.

Peter was deciding how to break the news when Daniel came bounding up from the pool, dripping with beads of water that glistened in the morning sun.

"Heather, what a lovely sight!" He leaned over the table to give her a kiss.

Peter tried to hide the newspaper behind his back, but he wasn't quick enough. Daniel caught sight of the gesture.

"What's going on?" he asked good-naturedly.

Peter and Heather exchanged guilty looks. Then Peter extended the folded newspaper.

"You two look about ready to cry," Daniel joked, snapping open the paper. "Why—"

Daniel's words died in his throat as his eyes registered the printed words before him.

The images came in a rush. The glare of photographers' cameras; the reporters with their unending questions. The gossip. The innuendo. The end of his career. No more work—no more doing what he loved to do. No more high life. Instead he would become an outcast . . . broken . . . penniless . . . losing all he'd worked so hard for just for pretending to be something he wasn't . . . because he wouldn't be accepted for what he was.

Suddenly his whole world began to spin and he felt himself falling as a tightness began in his chest . . . around his heart . . . squeezing hard . . . making it difficult to breathe. He couldn't get any air. Blackness descended as he slumped to the ground.

"My God, he's having a heart attack!" Heather screamed, jumping from her chair.

"Call for an ambulance!" Peter cried, rushing to Daniel's side and cradling him in his arms. "Don't die on me!" he begged. "Please don't die on me!"

Diana's eyes nearly popped out of her head.

She raced across the lobby of the Fontana hotel to the newsstand, snatching up a morning paper with greedy hands.

"Yo, lady!" the vendor complained. "First you pay, then you read."

Diana plunked down a twenty-dollar bill, not bothering with the change, charging back to the elevator banks. She couldn't believe what she was reading. This was too much! Peter Fontana,

Paul Fontana's *son*, was Daniel Ellis's lover. She was positive Paul didn't know this.

Yet.

Diana smiled wickedly. It looked like the nails in Daniel's coffin were about to be hammered in after all.

She reached into her Louis Vuitton clutch, searching for her wallet. Finding a hundred-dollar bill, she used it to wave down a passing bellboy. Instantly he was at her side.

"Ma'am?"

Diana toyed with the shiny brass buttons of his uniform. "Could you have something delivered for me?"

Drew hobbled down the first-class aisle, making his way to his seat. Once there he abandoned his crutches, plopping down.

He stared morosely at the white cast on his right leg. It was covered with the signatures of the cast and crew of the mini-series he had been working on for only three short weeks. He had been thrown from the horse he had been riding in one of the battle scenes, resulting in a hairline fracture. There was no way he could continue filming, and so he had been replaced.

Now three weeks loomed before him . . . three long weeks that he had intended to spend working, using the time to push Laura out of his mind. To forget her.

The only problem was he couldn't.

He couldn't forget the way she had made him feel. Special. Loved. But when he remembered those feelings he couldn't forget the way she had abandoned him, turning her back on his feelings, ignoring his pleas for her to stay.

Drew sighed, waving away the stewardess who offered to make him more comfortable. He stared out at the Paris view.

He didn't want any comfort. He only wanted pain. He wanted to remember the way Laura had hurt him because if he forgot, he'd do something he might regret.

He might try to find her.

Because despite what she'd done, he still loved her.

"No!" He pounded his leg fiercely, drawing curious looks from his fellow passengers in first class. He ignored them, pounding his leg again, as if by the gesture he could rid himself of the love he still had for her.

"No! You'll never hurt me again, Laura. Never!"

* * *

Nico leered obscenely at Laura. "I've finally brought your surprise."

Laura huddled into the corner as far away from Nico as possible, her hands protectively drawn around her stomach.

From behind his back he revealed a white wedding gown. "Remember this?" he proudly asked.

"It's my wedding gown from when we got married," she gasped.

"Try it on," he urged, pressing the gown forward, preparing to unlock the manacle around her ankle.

"Try it on? Why?"

"Every bride-to-be needs a wedding gown."

Every bride-to-be needs a wedding gown? Laura blanched. "What are you talking about?"

"You're going to marry me, Laura. In two days. On our anniversary. And then we'll be together . . . forever."

Forever. The word chilled Laura's blood, but she had to think clearly. Rationally. For herself and her baby. "Does that mean there'll be a priest, Nico?" *Please say yes,* she silently begged. *Please say yes. Please be so demented you don't know what you're doing anymore.*

"Priest? Who needs a priest?" he scoffed. "I'm going to be performing the ceremony, Laura. We'll exchange our own vows. It's going to be such a special day."

Laura's newly sparked hope died.

He shoved the wedding gown at her. "Put this on," he harshly ordered, as he unlocked her ankle while Satan sat by his side, keeping an eye on Laura.

Laura thought fast. There was no way she'd be able to slip into the wedding gown . . . not in her rapidly expanding condition. She had taken to wearing loose clothes and keeping her hands in front of her. Keeping her knees drawn. Lying on her side. Anything to prevent Nico's attention from zeroing in on the fragile new life growing within her.

She accepted the gown from him, smiling sweetly. "You can't see me in my wedding gown," she playfully teased. "Don't you know it's bad luck?" She kept the gown draped over her arms, hiding behind the satin and tulle. "We want to make sure we do everything right this time, don't we Nico?"

"I suppose," he grudgingly admitted.

"You go take care of whatever else needs to be done." She forced herself to kiss his cheek, fighting back the revulsion she felt. "While you're gone I want to slip into this. You're so thoughtful."

When he left, Nico left her ankle unlocked, taking Satan along with him. The moment both beasts were gone, Laura threw the wedding gown to the floor, her mind racing.

"There's got to be a way out of here!" she muttered furiously. "There's got to!"

Paul Fontana was livid.

Between two crumpled fists he held the morning paper. Expecting to find a medium-rare steak when he'd lifted the silver cover off his lunch plate, he'd instead found a copy of the morning paper. At first he'd simply discarded it, more annoyed by the absence of his steak. But then the headline caught his eye: DANIEL ELLIS SLAPPED WITH PALIMONY SUIT.

Curiosity piqued, he'd skimmed the accompanying article.

Peter's name jumped out at him. Then he connected Peter's name with the other words.

Lover . . .

Homosexual . . .

Paul Fontana's son . . .

Over and over he read the article in disbelief. This couldn't be! His son couldn't be gay. It all had to be Daniel's fault. Somehow he'd managed to seduce his son. Peter was young. Impressionable. He hadn't been strong enough against Daniel.

He'd have to do something. Daniel would have to pay for this.

Paul picked up his phone, dialing a number.

"Yes?" Diana moaned contentedly, cradling the phone against her ear as a gorgeous Swedish masseur worked magic with his fingers.

"Diana, it's Paul."

Diana shivered as a drop of cold oil was dabbed on her back and massaged into her skin. The scent was heavenly. "Darling, can this wait? I'm having the most wonderful time."

"When are you flying back to Hollywood?"

"This afternoon. Why?"

"I'll be joining you."

Diana didn't dare hope it would be this easy. "Oh? Any particular reason?"

"Remember that little favor you wanted?"

The glee bubbled excitedly within her. "Yes," she breathlessly whispered.

"I'll take care of it."

Like a deadly viper, Grace was ready to strike.

She took one last look at the electrical plans for Harrison's hot tub. It was amazing the things one learned when using reference books. For instance, if two wires were accidentally miscrossed, the repercussions could be dire. A person could be electrocuted.

Grace looked around carefully as she neared Harrison's hot tub. In one hand she carried a small tote bag containing a screwdriver, pliers, wire cutter, and a pair of rubber gloves to avoid fingerprints.

After slipping on the gloves all she had to do was use her tools and recross a blue wire with a white wire. After finishing her sabotage, she tested her handiwork by turning on the hot tub, watching as the water bubbled and foamed. Throwing in the screwdriver, she was rewarded with a hissing and crackling shower as sparks flew.

Grace smiled with content and anticipation. Little did Harrison suspect he'd be joining his wife in hell so soon.

Today was the day Harrison planned on murdering Gabrielle. At this moment he was putting his plan into effect.

As was she.

After replacing her tools in the trunk of her car, Grace returned to Harrison's pool, shedding her shorts and halter top, unveiling the red string bikini she wore. Making herself comfortable on a chaise lounge, she oiled herself. Might as well work on her tan till Harrison returned.

She felt no remorse over what was going to happen to Gabrielle. The bitch deserved what she was about to get. But greater than her hatred for Gabrielle, greater than her desire for wealth and power, was her desire for revenge. Harrison had to pay for what he'd done to her. There was no way she could let him win. Did he think she was foolish enough to believe he would marry her after he killed Gabrielle?

If anything, he would kill her.

But she would beat him to it. Death was what Harrison deserved and when he was gone she would reap the rewards of what was rightfully hers. She'd already spoken to a lawyer, telling him how Harrison had screwed her. The lawyer told her she had a case . . . and her case was going to get stronger when she reclaimed her notes and drafts of *Dangerous Parties*.

She couldn't wait to see the look in Harrison's eyes as his life ebbed away and he saw that she had buried the knife in his back before he could bury it in hers.

Harrison slipped undetected into Gabrielle's dressing room on the set of "The Yields of Passion," careful not to be seen, a gift-wrapped package under his arms.

He was in disguise: dark clothes, dark glasses, fake beard and mustache. If anyone caught sight of him, he'd be unrecognizable.

Today Gabrielle was going to be cleaning out her dressing room. What Harrison had for his wife was a special farewell gift: a bottle of her favorite perfume, Giorgio. The card said the gift was from the cast and crew of "The Yields of Passion."

There was only one *small* hitch.

The bottle was indeed a Giorgio of Beverly Hills perfume bottle. But the liquid filling the bottle wasn't perfume.

It was acid.

With one spritz, Gabrielle would be history.

Naturally the cast and crew would know nothing of the perfume. Of course. It hadn't come from them. Proper credit would be given to Gabrielle's obsessed fan.

Harrison smirked as he set down the gift.

He slipped out of the dressing room and made his way outside and to the street, heading for his parked car.

Removing his disguise as he drove, Harrison turned his mind to the next matter he had to deal with: Grace. Today was the day she also became history.

"There's nothing more you can do." Heather wrapped a consoling arm around Peter, who was looking through the glass window of the intensive care unit, trying to lead him away. Yet Peter shook off Heather's arms, refusing to budge.

"It's my fault," he whispered hoarsely. "All my fault."

"Peter, you can't blame yourself."

Peter tore his eyes from the window, turning agonizing eyes to

Heather. "It's because of me that he's in there." He jabbed a finger into his chest. *"Me!* If I hadn't pushed Jaime, none of this would have happened. Now Daniel may die."

"He's not going to die. He's going to pull through this. You'll see."

"I want to believe you, Heather, but I'm so afraid I'm going to lose him. Everyone I've ever loved has left me."

Heather looked at Peter curiously. "Like who?"

"My mother. Did I ever tell you about her?" Peter's eyes became misty. "She was a beautiful woman. I loved her so much."

"What happened to her?"

Peter's eyes turned flat, his words bitter. "She committed suicide when I was three."

Heather gasped. "I'm so sorry."

"My mother was a weak woman who allowed my father to destroy her. Even though I was only a child I can still remember the way he treated her. What he did to her. I'll never forget. No matter how hard I try, I'll never forget."

"Forget the past," Heather whispered, wrapping a reassuring arm around Peter. "For now. The future is what counts."

Peter looked at Heather bleakly. "If Daniel dies I don't have a future."

"Peter, darling!" At that moment Gabrielle's voice rang out in the quiet hospital corridor as she hurried toward her brother.

"Gabrielle, what are you doing here?"

"What do you mean, what am I doing here?" She hugged Peter fiercely. "I came as soon as I heard. How's Daniel doing?"

"We don't know yet," Heather answered. "Right now it's a matter of waiting."

Gabrielle gave Heather a chilly nod of acknowledgement. "And what are you doing here?"

"I was with Peter when Daniel had his heart attack."

"Were you? Well, thanks for staying with him, but now that I'm here you can run along."

"I'm staying," Heather announced firmly. "Peter needs me."

"Peter needs his sister more than he needs white trash like you," Gabrielle flared.

"Looking for another faceful of sour cream?" Heather asked sweetly. "I'd be happy to oblige."

"Please," Peter pleaded. "No fighting. I can't handle it. Not today."

"Sorry, darling," Gabrielle apologized.

"Sorry," Heather said contritely. "Look, I'll leave you two alone. If you hear anything, please come and find me. I'll be in the cafeteria."

After Heather left Peter started pacing restlessly. Then he turned to his sister. "So it's already made the papers. I shouldn't be surprised. The press is going to have a field day with this."

"With what?"

"Daniel's heart attack."

"That hasn't made the papers yet."

"It hasn't?" Peter stopped pacing. "Then how did you know he was here?"

"One of your maids told me about the heart attack. I'd come over to see you after I'd read this." Gabrielle showed Peter a newspaper with the palimony headline. "Peter, why didn't you tell me? Why did you keep it a secret all these years?"

Peter shrugged, eyes downcast. "I didn't think you'd understand."

"Not understand?! Peter, I'm your sister. I love you. Haven't we always been there for each other?"

Peter's head nodded almost imperceptibly.

"Then why didn't you tell me?"

Peter's voice was a whisper. "I didn't think you'd love me anymore or want me in your life. I didn't think you'd be able to accept what I am."

Gabrielle flung her arms around Peter. "Darling, that would never happen! You're the only good thing in my life. You're the only person I can depend on, who accepts me for who I am. I'll be the first to admit that at times I can be a bitch, but you don't care. You see beyond that. I know there have been times when you haven't approved of things that I've done, but you've never stopped loving me." Gabrielle hugged her brother. "I don't care who you choose to sleep with or who you choose to have a relationship with. All I want is for you to be happy. That's all that matters to me."

Peter wrapped his arms around Gabrielle, hugging her tightly, needing to hold her close. "Thank you, Gabrielle. That means a lot."

Realizing Jill was right and she needed to get back out into the real world again, Kelly decided to go for a walk and get some fresh air.

Walking through the milling crowds revitalized Kelly; it made her feel better. She felt as though she could lose herself and not have to worry that the eyes of the world were upon her, watching her every move and waiting for her to slip, ready to pounce and make her private life public.

Without even realizing it, Kelly had walked down to Greenwich Village and the NYU campus. Months ago she had been a mere student, eager to make her mark on the world. Now she wished she could turn back the clock and return to a time when her life had been easier. Simpler.

But if she were to turn back the clock she wouldn't have Graham. If she were to do things over, would she do them without him? Would she surrender the memory of their love and the brief happiness they had shared?

She honestly didn't know. In fact, she felt as though she didn't know anything anymore. Her life was a mess and she could leave it that way for only so long. Eventually she was going to have to pick up the pieces. She was going to have to make some decisions that would affect the rest of her life.

Kelly stopped walking when a movie marquee caught her eye. She was in front of the Cinema Village, a revival house on West 12th Street. The theater was currently showing *Banquet*.

Of all her father's films, this one was her favorite. In *Banquet* Adam played a straightlaced lawyer in love with a madcap heiress determined to give away all her money. What Kelly loved most about the film was the emotion. As you watched her father and Iris Larson fall in love before your eyes, you honestly believed they really *were* falling in love.

Kelly hadn't seen the film that often, perhaps five or six times over the years. It hadn't been a part of their personal film library, either. She hadn't even known about its existence until she was fourteen and caught it one night on the late show.

The reason she hadn't known about the film was Diana. Her mother hated the movie. When she'd discovered Kelly had seen it, she forbade her from ever watching it under her roof again.

Kelly bought a ticket and slipped into a seat in the darkened theater. On the screen her father was pursuing Iris Larson, chasing her around a swimming pool.

Though Kelly tried to concentrate on the film, she found she couldn't. She kept thinking of Graham and remembering Jill's words. She *had* given up without a fight. She hadn't given Graham a chance to explain. Instead she had made her decision to cut him out of her life solely on the facts presented to her. She hadn't allowed herself to remember the warmth. She hadn't allowed herself to remember the love. She hadn't thought of Graham and his own feelings or what he might be going through. And she had refused to consider that *maybe*, just *maybe*, Graham *had* been telling the truth.

What a fool she had been! Now that she had time to think, why had she been so quick to jump to conclusions? To accuse Graham? Why had she been so adamant in not giving him a chance to explain?

Looking deep within herself, Kelly knew why. She was afraid. She didn't believe she deserved Graham's love and feared that was what he would tell her.

Though her heart told her that wasn't true—evoking cherished memories of Graham—on a conscious, thinking level she *did* believe it.

Because Diana said so.

Her mother had always said no man would ever love her. Not even her own father.

"She's wrong," Kelly vowed fiercely, fighting back the approaching tears. She wouldn't allow herself to cry. She wouldn't let her mother make her cry anymore. At the studio she had reacted exactly as Diana had hoped.

Kelly gazed at her father's image on the movie screen. *She's wrong. You would have loved me, Daddy. You would have.*

Like so many other times before, Kelly imagined what her life would have been like if her father hadn't died. She never would have been lonely or felt as though she had no control over her life. Like she did now.

What should I do, Daddy?

Kelly answered her own question, asking herself what she wanted. The answer was simple. She wanted to go to Graham. Now. If she didn't, especially after all that had happened between them, she might lose him forever. She'd treated him horribly in the studio parking lot, pushing him away and making it clear that she no longer wanted anything more to do with him.

But what if he confirmed the rumors? What if he *had* slept with her mother again?

She made her decision. She'd have to live with the truth. Whatever Graham told her, she'd have to accept. Maybe then they'd be able to start over. Maybe they'd still have a future. If it wasn't already too late.

CHAPTER THIRTY-ONE

"Y͟O͟U͟ ͟L͟O͟O͟K͟ ͟L͟I͟K͟E͟ you're about to melt."

"Do I?" Grace raised a languid arm out to Harrison. "Want to lick me?"

"How about if I bring you something to drink?"

"Sure." Grace wiped at her forehead. "It's a scorcher today."

"It's supposed to get as high as a hundred. Been out long?"

"Long enough." Grace propped herself up on her elbows. "Mission accomplished?"

Harrison shook a bottle of cranberry juice at Grace. "All systems go. Seabreeze okay with you?"

Grace raised her sunglasses on top of her head. "Fine. Why don't you get out of those clothes and join me? We could frolic in the hot tub."

Harrison watched as Grace went to turn on the hot tub. Acting quickly, watching to make sure she didn't turn her back, he emptied the contents of a white envelope into her glass. The powder floated until he stirred it with his finger. He'd chosen a seabreeze because the combination of vodka and cranberry juice would hide any bitter taste.

"Here we go," he announced, joining Grace with her drink. "Let's have a toast."

Grace's eyes lingered on the hot tub, then focused on Harrison. "To successful plans."

Harrison clinked his glass with Grace's. "To successful plans." Harrison sipped his drink thirstily, draining half the glass with one long swallow, encouraging Grace to do the same. She hadn't even touched her drink yet.

"You didn't join in the toast," he said, pointing to her filled glass. "It's bad luck if you don't take a sip."

"Really?" Grace stared at Harrison evenly, one finger tracing the rim of her glass. "We wouldn't want bad luck, now would we? Not today, of all days."

"No, we wouldn't," Harrison agreed, though Grace still wasn't drinking. "You know, I could use another one of these," he said, turning his back and returning to the bar. "Are you going to be able to keep up with me, Grace?"

When he reached the bar and turned around, Grace waved an empty glass at him. Sauntering over to the bar, she dropped the empty glass before him.

"Don't underestimate me, Harrison. I can do anything you can do."

"Oh, can you?"

"Yes, I can." She leaned across the bar and kissed him softly, looking deep into his eyes. "You'd be surprised at the things I'm capable of doing. Very surprised."

Harrison traced Grace's lower lip with his finger. "The same could be said about me." Now that she had finished her drink, it was time to move onto the next step of his plan. From here on it would be a snap. He rubbed a hand over Grace's shoulders. "You know, you look like you could use some more oil. Why don't you let me put it on you?"

"You're right, but I don't think I can last much longer out here." She gave him a lingering look. "Besides, I'd much rather do other things. Let's jump into the hot tub."

"Patience. Don't give up so easily." Harrison brought out a bottle of suntan oil. "I picked this up the other day. It's supposed to be the best."

Grace inspected herself. "Well, I suppose I could use a touch-up." She returned to her chaise lounge and lay down on her stomach. "But only for an hour. After this I want to take my dip."

"Only an hour," Harrison promised, opening the bottle and pouring the oil over Grace's back, massaging it in with extra long strokes.

"Mmm, that feels heavenly," she murmured. "But it smells odd."

That Grace! She was such a sharp cookie! Harrison laughed in amusement.

"What's so funny?" she mumbled, closing her eyes.

"Nothing." *Everything.* The truth of the matter was that he really was massaging oil—cooking oil—all over Grace. It was his own special concoction—three quarters coconut oil and one quarter vegetable oil. Oh well, no need to worry. Grace would be getting all the blame. Such vanity! Going to such extreme lengths for an all-over tan!

"Hey!" she shouted seconds later. "Watch what you're doing. It feels like you spilled the whole bottle on me."

"Looks like I did," Harrison apologized. "Don't worry. It can't hurt you."

Harrison massaged the oily liquid over Grace's entire body, arms, legs and back, until she glistened and glimmered in the sun.

Grace yawned. "I don't know why, but I feel so sleepy."

"Maybe you should take a nap, sugar."

"That sounds like a good idea, but don't let me stay out here too long. You know how I hate it when I burn."

"We wouldn't want that to happen. Don't worry, Grace. I'll take good care of you."

"Promise?" she asked, opening one eye.

Harrison gave her a full smile. "Promise."

Ten minutes later Harrison gave Grace a gentle shake. She didn't move. He shook her again. "Grace?" he called. No response. "Grace?" he called again, this time in a louder tone of voice. Still no response. Yes! The drink had done its job. She was definitely out cold.

Harrison took the empty suntan bottle and both glasses into the house. He rinsed them, then made a fresh seabreeze, placing it under Grace's slack hand. He added a half-full bottle of real suntan oil and in her purse he added the bottle of sleeping pills he'd stolen from her medicine cabinet, all the while making sure the pool area was clean of his fingerprints. It *was* his house, but it was better to keep his fingerprints clear of the immediate scene of the crime.

Next he went into the kitchen and returned with a roll of aluminum foil.

Harrison lifted Grace's inert form, placing it on the adjacent lounge chair. Then he opened the box of aluminum foil and covered Grace's chair with it. Replacing Grace on the chair, Harrison put her in a sitting position, placing a sun visor between her hands and beneath her chin—excellent for directing additional rays of sunshine to an out-of-the-way area.

After five hours in the sun, *basted* the way she was, Grace would most definitely be burned to a crisp. Like he had said, today's temperature was supposed to get to a hundred. The aluminum foil would most definitely speed up the process, making the sun's rays twice as deadly.

Naturally it would all be looked upon as an unfortunate accident. Poor Grace had wanted to work on her tan and had fallen asleep in the sun after too much booze and pills.

Harrison decided it was time for him to disappear—to sort of set up an alibi. As he headed for his car he passed the hot tub and turned it off.

No time for that now. Maybe later.

Gabrielle slammed into Mark's office without even bothering to knock, slamming an angry hand down on his desk.

Mark looked up at her in irritation, discarding the script he had been reading. "What the fuck is this? Since when do you barge into my office?"

"When are you getting Heather McCall to sign those contracts?"

Seeing Heather at the hospital had inflamed Gabrielle's desire for revenge against the other woman. With no change in Daniel's condition, Gabrielle had made her exit, promising Peter she would return after running a few errands. This was the first.

Never, Mark almost spat out. Instead he said, "I'm working on it. Give me some time."

"You've had plenty of time. Pay *close* attention to what I'm about to say, Mark. I want Heather McCall signed, sealed and delivered to Trinity Pictures within the next forty-eight hours."

Mark had had enough of Gabrielle's shit. Who did this egotistical bitch think she was?

"If not?" he defiantly asked.

Gabrielle leaned over Mark's desk, her heaving chest rising and falling. Her cheeks were flushed and her eyes blazed. Her lips drew back into a predatory snarl as her tongue darted out, wetting her lips. "You know what I can do."

Mark eyed Gabrielle dangerously. "And you know what *I* can do," he dared to warn as he flexed his hands. "Don't push me. You of all people know how far I'll go."

Gabrielle tossed back her head, laughing in Mark's face. "You don't scare me."

"Oh, I don't? Well, here's some *friendly* advice. Watch the kinds of games you play, Gabrielle. Otherwise you're going to get hurt."

"You don't know what you're talking about." Gabrielle tried to control the trembling in her voice. Mark wouldn't *dare* try to hurt her again.

"Really? I tried to kill you once. Want to bet the thought hasn't crossed my mind again? What about your elusive fan?"

At the mention of her fan, Gabrielle paled. For weeks she hadn't given it any thought, but now it all came back. Her fan had tried to kill her with those poisoned chocolates. And he was still out there. Probably waiting. Watching her. Getting ready to make his next move.

"You don't know what you're talking about! You don't!" she shouted, stomping her way out of Mark's office. She whirled around at the door, pointing an accusatory finger. "I want those contracts signed, Mark! Time is running out."

"For whom, Gabrielle?" he murmured softly, watching her leave. "For whom?"

Five hours later Harrison was back home, parking his silver Porsche in the carport and quite ready to find Grace dead.

He passed the hot tub again on his way to the pool. The muscles in his arms and legs felt taut and tense from the two hours he'd spent playing racquetball with some studio types who were trying to woo him. A hot shower had helped, but only momentarily. A long soak in his hot tub would make the difference.

Harrison flipped the switch on the redwood wall, watching the water start to bubble and froth. He kicked off his moccasins and pulled off his sport shirt. The water looked so inviting. Harrison knew the minute he touched the water all tension would drain from his body as he entered a level of sheer bliss. It was tempting but he held back. First he had to check on Grace. It was only fair. Then he'd allow himself the luxury of soaking in the tub before calling the police. Maybe they'd even have word of Gabrielle's death.

Harrison saw Grace's body was exactly where he had left it. Well, why not? He started to laugh aloud at the thought but then his laughter died as he saw Grace's legs start to move . . . her body positioning itself upright . . . and then her head turning to face him.

No! This couldn't be. It just couldn't be! She couldn't be alive. She couldn't! She was supposed to be dead. Dead!

"Harrison, darling!" Grace sang out merrily, getting to her feet. "Where have you been all afternoon?" she asked, waving a disapproving finger. "I should be mad as hell at you for leaving me the way you did. You were supposed to wake me up, but I guess I really don't have a reason to be upset with you." She twirled before him. "Isn't my tan delicious! That oil of yours is absolutely marvelous! You *must* give me the name of it so I can use it again." She admired her golden brown arms and legs. "I can't wait to shower and slip into something white and backless. I'm going to look *stunning!*"

"Grace?" Harrison croaked, reaching out with a hand and wanting to touch her . . . wanting to make sure she really was alive and not some figment of a suddenly guilty conscience.

"Yes, Harrison? What's the matter? Cat got your tongue?" She removed her sunglasses, perching them on top of her head, looking Harrison straight in the eye. "You look surprised to see me, sweetie. In fact, you look like you've just seen a ghost."

Harrison's mind scrambled for an answer. He didn't want her getting suspicious. He couldn't have that. But there was something in her eyes . . . something mocking. But why? *Why?*

"Harrison?" she asked. "You didn't answer my question."

"I didn't think you'd still be here, that's all," he quickly provided.

"Why not?" Grace looped her arm through Harrison's, gazing up at him with an adoring look. "You know how much I love being at your side. Just think, darling, within a few hours we'll hear that Gabrielle is dead. Then, after a reasonable amount of time, we'll be married and together till death do us part."

"Don't say that!" Harrison snapped.

"Why not? I can't wait to say my marriage vows. They're going to mean something to me, Harrison." Grace rubbed herself against him. "I promise to love only you till the day I die. Do you promise the same?"

"Let's not talk about death, Grace." Harrison was visibly sweating, trying to free his arm from Grace's iron hold, not liking her closeness. He felt as though he were talking to a living corpse.

"Why not? We could die at any time. Fate loves tossing out little surprises. You can never count on anything, Harrison, even the best laid plans. Don't you agree?"

Harrison stared at Grace in disbelief. She couldn't know . . . she couldn't! How? She'd had the drink he'd fixed . . . she'd lost consciousness . . . he'd left her all oiled. This was all too much to fucking comprehend!

Grace gave Harrison a pouting look. "You didn't promise."

He looked at her distractedly. "Huh? Promise what?"

"To love me till the day you die."

Upon hearing Grace's words, Harrison couldn't move. He couldn't speak. Why was she so fixated on the topic of death?

Grace stepped away from Harrison. "Well, did you?" When Harrison still didn't answer, Grace's face became crestfallen and crumpled under a flood of tears. "You don't love me!" she wailed.

"Of course, I do," he whispered.

"Then say it!" she demanded, tears instantly drying. "Say it!"

"Grace, I'll love you till the day I die," he said, the words barely coming out of his mouth.

Grace threw her arms around Harrison, hugging him fiercely.

"Ouch!" he shouted.

"Darling, what's wrong?" Grace asked, concern etched on her face.

"It's nothing. I'm just a little sore. I played some racquetball."

"Poor baby," she cooed. "You know what you need?"

"What?"

"A nice long soak in your hot tub. And you know what'll make your soak even better? An ice-cold drink." She headed for the bar. "You go slip into the water and I'll fix us both a seabreeze. I only hope mine are as good as yours."

"What do you mean?"

Grace gestured with her hands. "I can't explain it, but your drink seemed to have an extra added kick. Do you have a secret ingredient?"

Yes, secobarbital! Harrison's mind screamed. That was the extra kick . . . the secret ingredient. *What went wrong?* How could she still be alive? All her body fluids were supposed to have been drained by the sun.

"Harrison," Grace called, rummaging through bottles behind the bar, "don't feel as though you have to wait for me. Jump right in. I'll join you in a minute."

Perhaps a soak would do him some good. He needed to think. He needed to clear his head and figure out what had gone wrong. After that, he'd know what his next move should be. A whole new life was waiting for him and he was going to have it. Obviously his plan to murder Grace had failed. Only a temporary setback, he resolved. Given some time and consideration, he was sure he'd come up with a new plan. Right now he was going to submerge himself in the hot tub and dream of what was to come. He couldn't wait to feel the water cascading above and around him.

Harrison began running to the hot tub, building up speed as he neared until he jumped in with one flying leap.

The minute he hit the water, ten thousand volts of electricity coursed through his body, throwing him against the side of the tub. Sparks flew and soon the smell of charred flesh permeated the air. Harrison's body twisted and thrashed and there was a complete look of shock and disbelief, meshed together with a grimace of indescribable pain frozen on his face as his eyes stared sightlessly at the evening sky while his lifeless body sank to the bottom of the hot tub.

Grace calmly sipped her seabreeze while watching Harrison die.

"Burn, baby, burn," she whispered.

When the thrashing and splashing and screaming and sparks finally subsided, Grace emerged from behind the bar and headed for the hot tub. She steeled herself for the sight she was about to see, knowing it wouldn't be pretty.

The smell of charred flesh grew thicker and thicker with each step taken. As Grace neared her destination the sickeningly sweet smell of what had once been Harrison wrapped itself tightly around her, making it difficult to breathe. Covering her nose with a hand, she took breaths through her mouth, continuing onward. When she reached the edge of the hot tub she stopped and looked down into the water, seeing the now blackened remains of Harrison Moore.

Grace almost retched but she fought back the nausea, forcing herself to remember what Harrison had almost done to her today: he'd tried to kill her.

Yet he hadn't succeeded with his plan. She had beaten him to it. She'd killed Harrison before he had a chance to kill her. And it had been so pathetically easy! She'd really had him going. When he saw her sit up, he looked as though he was going to have a heart attack. And then when she'd kept toying with him, playing her little cat-and-mouse game, he *still* hadn't figured it out. He *still* hadn't realized that she knew. He'd *trusted* her. That had enraged her more than anything else! How stupid could he be? *Why* would she have trusted him after everything he'd done to her?

All along she knew he'd try to kill her—that was why she didn't drink the seabreeze he had prepared. When Harrison went back to the bar she'd poured it into one of the potted palms and then pretended to be unconscious so he could carry out the rest of his plan.

Grace still couldn't get over the brilliance of Harrison's plan. It had been perfection. Absolute perfection! If only he'd directed some of that energy into his writing. But he hadn't. He'd been too goddamn lazy even to make an effort. Instead he had to try to double-cross her. That was his big mistake.

After he had left she'd gone inside and taken a shower. Then she'd come back outside and tanned herself properly. When Harrison got back he fell right into her trap.

Grace stared down at Harrison sadly. She hadn't wanted it to come to this. She hadn't wanted to kill him. She'd loved him. She'd loved him so much! But he'd given her no choice. In the end she'd only done what she had to do—what he had forced her to do.

Grace wiped away a tear that escaped from her eye. She supposed she also owed Harrison some thanks. Although it had hurt, he had taught her a very valuable lesson, one that she would always be grateful for: the only person to think of was oneself.

Grace blew Harrison a soft kiss. Her poor darling. He'd promised to love her until the day he died. It was his own fault that that day had come so soon.

Peter had known it was only a matter of time before his father summoned him. The call arrived within hours of the newspapers announcing Jaime's palimony suit.

Now he was in his father's suite at the Beverly Hills Hotel, having come straight from the hospital. Daniel was still in intensive care. Though his condition had stabilized, the doctors said he still wasn't out of danger. Peter hadn't wanted to leave Daniel's side, but Paul had been adamant about seeing him.

"Either you get your butt over here or we have this out in front of everyone. That'd be nice fodder for the tabloids, wouldn't it?"

With Heather's promise that she would remain by Daniel's side, Peter drove over. Though he announced himself upon arriving, his father kept his back to him, hands clasped behind him as he stared out the windows, not saying a word.

Peter cleared his throat nervously. "Now you know."

"Not to mention the rest of the world. How could you do this to me? I can't even stand to look at you."

"How could I do this to *you?*" Peter asked, trying to control his anger. "It figures you'd be thinking only about yourself. What about me and the way I feel? You think I like the whole world knowing about my private life? You think that one day I just woke up and decided I wanted to be gay? Do you think I had a choice?"

"You had no trouble choosing to move in with Daniel Ellis," Paul commented dryly.

"You make it sound like the decisions I've had to make were easy ones," Peter raged. "They weren't and unless you've been where I've been most of my life, you can't begin to understand what I'm saying. Every day I wake up knowing I'm something I don't want to be. Yet I've managed to find a way to live with it, to make it a part of my life . . . because it's a part of me. I don't know why I turned out the way I did. All I know is that when I want to get close to someone, when I want to get intimate, I want it to be with a man."

"And Daniel Ellis is that man?" The disdain in Paul's voice was undisguised and he still hadn't turned to face his son.

"Yes, he is. I'm sorry if that displeases you."

"*Displeases* me?" Paul thundered, finally facing Peter, revealing his wrath. "It does more than displease me. It *disgusts* me! It *embarrasses* me, and you're not going to stay involved with Ellis any longer. Not as long as you're my son."

"Maybe I don't want to be your son anymore. Ever think of that?" Peter retorted. "Maybe I don't want to be known as Paul Fontana's son. If you can't accept me for what I am, what makes you think I can accept *you* for what *you* are?"

"And what am I, Peter?" Paul demanded. "What have I done that's made you so ashamed of me? All your life I gave you nothing but the best."

"The best," Peter repeated mockingly. "Nothing but the best for your children. You had to do something about that guilty conscience, didn't you?"

"What are you talking about?"

"I know, Papa. *I know!*" Peter cried, reverting to the endearment he'd used as a child. "I know what kind of a man you are. I've always known. You're cold-blooded and ruthless. You won't let anyone stand in your way. Not even family. You've been able to fool Gabrielle all these years but you were never able to fool me. Never! I know what you are because I saw it for myself, first hand, with my own eyes."

"Is there a point to this?"

"You're a murderer, Papa!" Peter shouted, no longer able to

keep silent about the secret he'd buried deep within himself for such a long time. "A murderer! I saw you! I saw you kill Mama!"

Paul gave his son an incredulous look. "You don't know what you're saying. Your mother committed suicide."

"Don't lie to me," Peter said in a deceptively soft tone. "Since this is the day for secrets to be revealed, let's start with some of yours. I was there. I was hiding in the closet. I saw it all. You strangled her with your bare hands and then made it look like she'd hanged herself."

Paul didn't offer any denial. "If you knew, why didn't you say anything?"

"Why didn't I say anything?" Peter repeated. *"Why didn't I say anything?* I don't know. At first I thought it was all a bad dream. A horrible nightmare. But when I woke the following morning and saw Mama was gone, I knew she wasn't coming back. That's when I knew what I'd seen had really happened."

"And still you kept quiet."

"I didn't know what to do. I was a child. Barely four. Whom could I tell? Who would believe me? I saw how angry you'd gotten with Mama. I was afraid to say anything. I thought if I did, you'd hurt me. Maybe even hurt Gabrielle. So I pushed that night out of my mind. I pushed it out of my mind and buried it as deeply as I could within myself. I tried to forget, pretending it *had* been a bad dream and accepting the story I was told. But as I got older it became harder and harder for me to forget. And it became harder and harder for me to tolerate you. Because of my silence you'd gotten away with murder. That's when I started putting distance between us, because it was then that I started to hate you."

"So you decided to get back at me by sleeping with men, is that it?" Paul concluded.

"You're unbelievable! Weren't you listening to me before? This has nothing to do with my homosexuality."

"Doesn't it? You wanted to punish me for killing your mother. Peter, I loved Marina. What happened was a tragic accident."

"Yet you made sure you covered your tracks," Peter pointed out bitterly.

"There isn't a day that goes by that I don't think of her. I'll never forget what I did."

"You sure forgot that night when you brought that blonde bimbo into your bed!" Peter shouted.

He'd been unable to see the woman in his father's bed, but he'd never forget her. He remembered her squeals of pleasure . . . her moans of delight. He also remembered her words . . . the question she had asked. It was forever branded in his mind . . . *"Did you do as you promised?"*

His father could deny it all he wanted. He could say it had been an accident, but Peter knew differently. He knew what he had heard. Paul had promised to kill his mother for his mistress. For that he would always hate his father . . . and his mistress, whoever she was.

"What do you want from me, Peter?" Paul implored. "What do you want? Your mother is dead. I can't bring her back."

"You wouldn't if you could," Peter stated sadly, "because Mama never fit in with your image. Just as I don't fit in with it."

"Peter, we can't change the past, but we can change the future. I want you to end things with Ellis. You can go away somewhere for a while and after all this blows over you can come back and we'll start over."

"Start over?" Peter sputtered in disbelief. "Are you listening to yourself? Do you think my homosexuality is going to disappear overnight because you want it to? Well, it's not. And I'm not leaving Daniel. He needs me and I want to be there for him."

Paul's voice hardened. "Peter, I'm your father. You'll do as I say."

"I'm not a child. You can't order me around. This is my life and I'm going to live it my way. If you can't handle it, that's just too bad. As for being my father, *my* father died the same night my mother did."

"Don't push me, Peter. I'm warning you. Don't make me do something I'll regret."

"Threatening me?" Peter laughed mirthlessly. "Well, I think it's time for me to go. I've got to get back to the hospital."

"You're not going anywhere. Not until I say we're through."

Peter looked at his father scornfully. "We're through. We've said everything we have to say to each other."

Gabrielle hurried through the darkened studio to her dressing room. Taping was finished for the day and the studio was deserted. Being alone was giving her the creeps, especially when she remembered Mark's words about someone wanting to kill her.

Suppressing a shiver, she took a quick look over her shoulder. Naturally no one was there. She cursed herself for allowing

Mark's words to scare her this way. Still, once inside her dressing room, she slammed the door and promptly locked it.

The first thing she saw was the wrapped package in front of her dressing mirror. Gabrielle's heart lodged itself in her throat as she stared at it, remembering the last "gift" she'd received and how she'd ended up in the hospital with a pumped stomach.

Gabrielle's eyes shifted from corner to corner, fearing she'd discover a figure preparing to lunge at her. She saw no one and started to breathe a bit easier as she warily approached the package.

Finally reaching it, she lifted the box gently, shaking it against her ear. Something inside rattled and she gave a sigh of relief, thankful for not hearing a ticking sound. A card was attached. She ripped it off and opened it with trepidation. Her apprehension disappeared. It was a going-away gift from the cast and crew.

Gabrielle ripped away the wrapping paper, uncovering the bottle of Giorgio. She uncapped the bottle, tempted to spritz herself, but held back. She was wearing Obsession at the moment and if there was one thing she hated it was mixing her scents. It always gave her the most excruciating headaches.

She recapped the bottle and tossed it into one of the boxes she'd brought by earlier to pack her things. She'd just have to wait until tomorrow to use the perfume.

"How'd it go with your father?" Heather asked.

"Don't ask." Peter headed in the direction of the ICU unit. When he got there he glimpsed through the window and panicked. Daniel's bed was empty. "Where's Daniel?" he frantically demanded, whirling on Heather.

"Calm down, Peter," she soothed. "They've moved him to a private room."

Peter tried to control his excitement. "Does that mean he's going to be okay?"

Heather managed a small smile. "The doctors are optimistic." She hooked her arm through his, steering Peter in the direction of the elevators. "Why don't we go down to the cafeteria for a cup of coffee? You look like you could use it."

"I can't leave Daniel."

"He'll be fine," Heather assured. "We'll leave word at the nurses' station so they know where to find us."

"Five minutes. No more," Peter compromised. "Anything could happen in five minutes."

"I still don't know why I had to come with you," Diana complained.

Paul wedged her into a corner of the elevator they were riding in. "Since you're the one who wants Daniel Ellis dead so much, you're going to help me pull this off."

Diana gave an exasperated sigh. "Can't you get your goons to handle this? After all, that's what you pay them for."

"I like doing things personally." He gave Diana a cold smile. "It guarantees the job gets done right."

Diana slid the dark glasses she wore down her nose. The glasses, along with the black turban covering her hair and voluminous black cape covering her figure made her unrecognizable. "So how much time do you need?"

"Five minutes."

Diana gave Paul a skeptical look. "That's all?"

"I have my methods."

The elevator doors opened and Paul shoved the floral arrangement he was carrying into Diana's arms. "Don't forget your prop."

"Lilies." Diana fingered the waxy petals. "How appropriate."

As Diana headed for the nurses' station, Paul headed for Daniel's room. He already knew the room number, along with the fact that Daniel didn't have a roommate.

Entering the room, Paul saw the slight rise and fall of Daniel's chest as he remained hooked to a number of machines monitoring his vital signs.

Paul reached into the pocket of his trenchcoat for the syringe he carried. Walking to the bed, he injected the needle into Daniel's I.V. and pressed down on the plunger.

"Are you sure Kate Steele isn't a patient on this floor?" Diana asked for the third time, using a heavy British accent as she hid behind her arrangement of lilies.

The nurse on duty, a matronly woman with steel gray hair worn in a plump bun, sighed. "I'm positive."

"Could you check again? She could be registered under her maiden name. It's Ashton."

As the nurse turned back to her records, Diana checked her watch. Three minutes had elapsed. She looked down the hallway and her heart leaped as she saw Paul sauntering her way, tilting his head toward the elevators.

"There's no Kate Ashton on this floor," the nurse said. "Maybe you should try the front desk."

"Yes, I'll do that."

Turning her back, Diana hurried to the waiting elevator. Once inside she dumped the lilies on the floor.

"Did you do it?" Her voice trembled with excitement.

"Paul Fontana always delivers."

Her secret was safe! Safe! Diana threw her arms around Paul. "How fabulous! Hollywood is having a funeral."

Paul jerked back Diana's head, tearing away her sunglasses. "And a wedding," he decreed.

"What's going on?" Peter screamed in panic, catching sight of all the white figures emerging from the direction of Daniel's room with turned-off machines. "What's going on?!?"

Heather ran after Peter as he barged into Daniel's room . . . just as a sheet was being pulled over Daniel's head.

"No!" Peter's cry was a tortured wail that scorched Heather's soul. He collapsed to his knees. "No!" he whimpered.

"What happened?" Heather asked the exiting doctor. "I thought he was going to pull through."

"So did we, but it looks like he had another attack. You never know in these cases." He gave Heather a compassionate look. "I'm sorry."

Soon Peter and Heather were the only ones left in the room. Heather knelt next to Peter, trying to wrap her arms around him, but he shoved her away, jumping to his feet.

"Leave me alone!" He rushed to Daniel's bed, tenderly drawing back the sheet. At the sight of Daniel's closed eyes, Peter's tears returned. "I shouldn't have left him. If I hadn't, he wouldn't have died."

"That's not true," Heather said.

"It is," Peter stated fiercely. "It's my fault he's dead. All my fault."

"Peter, listen to me!" Heather said. "It's not your fault. If Jaime hadn't launched that palimony suit—"

"Jaime," Peter whispered, his blue eyes darkening with hatred. "Jaime has to know. He has to know what he's done."

With that Peter stormed out of the hospital room.

Home sweet home. Drew opened the door of his beach house, sliding in his suitcase as he hobbled after on his crutches.

Sighing, he bent over to pick up the mail that had accumulated. Probably nothing more than bills.

Suddenly Drew was tired and wanted nothing more than to get off his feet. He didn't even bother with the bedroom but headed for the nearest area of comfort, the couch, abandoning his crutches as he flopped down on the cushions.

Loosening his tie and discarding his jacket, he sifted through the mail, tossing envelopes onto the glass-topped table. He stopped when he came to the envelope that had only his first name on it. There was no mistaking the handwriting. It was Laura's.

Despite himself, despite the anger he still wanted to keep alive, Drew was curious. And excited. What was in this envelope? What could Laura still have to say to him? Hadn't they said everything the last time they'd been together?

He turned the envelope over and over in his hands, a finger tracing his name until finally he was unable to resist and ripped the envelope open.

His greedy eyes devoured her words and the rekindled hope he'd kept hidden came ablaze. She wanted him back in her life!

He re-read the letter, making sure he hadn't misunderstood. She still loved him. She wanted him back and wanted to explain why she had hurt him the way she had.

Drew's first impulse was to rush out the door over to Laura's. After all, the date on the letter was three weeks ago. What must she be thinking? Did she think he no longer wanted her back?

In his mind he suddenly remembered the last time they'd been together. He'd told her how much he loved her and begged her not to go. But she hadn't listened.

Now she wanted him back. But did he want her back in his life after all the pain she had caused him? Was he willing to take a chance again? He didn't know. He supposed the least he could do was listen to her and then make his decision.

But not tonight. Tonight he was too tired. Too exhausted. He was going to sack out right here. Clutching Laura's letter possessively, he closed his tired eyes. He was sure things could wait one more day.

"One more day, Laura. One more day and you'll be my wife again," Nico crooned through the closed bedroom door. "You don't know how badly I want to see you, but I know you need your beauty sleep for our big day tomorrow."

Laura pressed her hands to her ears, trying as best she could to block out Nico's words of madness. Sleep? Did he think she could sleep? She hadn't had a decent night's rest since she'd become his prisoner.

In the mirror across the bedroom she could see how haggard she looked, with dark circles under her eyes. As always, her hands were protectively around her middle as her mind sought some way to save herself and her child from this madman.

All her hope was gone. Drew wasn't coming for her. She had no one to rely on but herself.

Out in the living room Nico continued with his wedding preparations. First he draped swirls of white crepe paper around the room. Then he sprinkled white confetti on the floor and hung paper wedding bells from the windows. In opposite corners of the living room bunches of white balloons nestled lazily against each other.

Two champagne glasses were placed next to a silver bucket. In the refrigerator, beside the three-tiered wedding cake he had purchased that afternoon, he placed a bottle of Dom Perignon to chill. On top of the cake there was a bride and groom. Nico smiled at the pair, then snapped the bride's head off. Laura would get a kick out of that.

He gave an ugly laugh. He loved the sick game he was playing with her. He had her going out of her mind and he had no qualms about what he was doing to her. She'd made a fool out of him when she'd run off for her divorce, leaving him to rot behind bars and making him lose respect in the eyes of his peers in the Family. He'd seen the questions in their eyes. How could he handle responsibility? How could he get a job done right if he couldn't control his own wife?

After tomorrow they would all know that no one crossed Nico

Rossi and got away with it. They would all know. Especially Laura.

Nico walked across the kitchen to the table where he had placed his other purchase from that day. It was a knife with a wicked twelve-inch blade. The razor-sharp steel glinted under the fluorescent lights. It was so smooth. So shiny. He ran a finger along the knife's sharp edge and a thread of blood appeared, oozing down toward the tip. Nico smiled, lifting away the blood and sucking his finger. It cut like butter. He was sure it would cut the same way through Laura's flesh.

Nico gripped the knife's handle, his knuckles turning white.

Some sins couldn't be forgiven.

Jaime delved through the pile of newspapers he had collected since that morning, relishing each and every headline pertaining to his palimony suit. At last he was a celebrity and for the next few months he'd be basking in the limelight. If he played this right he could go as far as he wanted. And the best part of all was that all of it would cost Daniel.

Jaime laughed maliciously. He wished he could have been there when Daniel had learned what he'd done. He'd have given anything to see the look on his face.

Soon the newspapers were piled at the bottom of Jaime's bed. Knowing his afternoon papers had already been delivered, he slipped into a robe and went to collect them, wondering how many more headlines he'd made.

The house phone to the downstairs lobby rang as he strolled through the living room, but he chose to ignore it. He wanted his papers.

Opening his apartment door, Jaime involuntarily took a step back, his papers forgotten as a glowering Peter barged in.

The look in his eyes chilled Jaime. Flat, empty and unseeing, they possessed an unleashed fury that was aimed directly at him.

"You're not supposed to be here." Jaime mustered his most condescending tone. This was *his* turf. "If you have anything to say, say it to my lawyer." Jaime bent down to retrieve his papers. "If you'll excuse me."

The toe of a cowboy boot slammed into Jaime's face. Blood gushed like a geyser in a rich, red stream from his nose. "You broke it," he sobbed hysterically, staring with horror at his red-stained fingers. "You broke it!"

"Fuck your lawyer and fuck you!" Peter howled in outrage, throwing himself at Jaime, his fists connecting with his face and pummeling relentlessly. "He's dead! Daniel's dead and it's all your fault! You killed him!"

Dead? Daniel was dead? Jaime's visions of a long, protracted trial with tons of publicity and media coverage disappeared. How could Daniel be dead? But he couldn't dwell on that. Right now, *his* survival was the important thing.

"You can't blame me!" Jaime croaked feebly, choking on his blood, trying to fight back as a white-hot haze threatened to envelop him. If he didn't fight back, he was sure Peter would kill him.

"Who says I can't?" Peter's fist connected with Jaime's jaw, producing a sickening crunch. "You betrayed him! If you hadn't launched that palimony suit, if you hadn't been blackmailing him, he wouldn't have been under so much stress. He wouldn't have had his heart attack."

Peter was out of control and there was nothing Jaime could do to stop him. The force of every blow and punch, magnified by Peter's agony and grief, was delivered with unfailing accuracy.

"Enough!" Jaime sobbed piteously, fearing he was about to lose consciousness. "Enough! You're going to kill me."

"No, I'm not going to kill you. Not yet," Peter declared between ragged breaths. "Not unless you insist in pursuing this palimony suit. If you want to save your worthless hide, you're going to do what I tell you."

"What?" Jaime wailed.

Peter wrapped his fists around the front of Jaime's robe, lifting him up. "You're going to drop your palimony suit, pack your bags, and slither out of town with no forwarding address. And you're going to keep your mouth shut about your life with Daniel. Otherwise, if I ever see or hear of you again, I swear I'm going to kill you."

Peter flung Jaime away from him and made his way out of the apartment.

"I'll kill you," he reminded from the doorway.

After Peter left there came the sound of running footsteps out in the hallway and two security guards crowded the apartment door.

"Mr. Barton, are you all right? Do you need any help? A gentleman barged his way past the front desk. I tried calling, but no one answered."

"You idiots! Why didn't you take longer?" he raged. "No, I

don't need you. Do I look like I need you?" He rubbed his bloody nose along his sleeve. "Just get the fuck out of here."

"Are you sure there isn't anything we can do?"

As he stared at his bloody hands Jaime remembered the cold-blooded savagery he'd seen in Peter's eyes. "Yeah, there is something you can do," he said. "Get me some boxes. I'm moving."

Graham was having a dream. In it Kelly was in his arms, letting him make love to her, telling him she was sorry and asking for another chance.

"Yes," he moaned, his fingers twisting through her hair as he brought her face close. "Yes, I forgive you."

"Then open your eyes," she whispered. "Open your eyes and look at me."

Graham's eyes opened and there in his arms was Kelly. But what was she doing in his hotel room? Was he still dreaming? Seeing what he wanted to see? He brought out a hand, intending to touch her cheek, but she caught it, resting it on her heart.

"How did you get here?" he asked.

"I asked for a key at the front desk. I told them I was your wife."

Still resting his hand on her heart, Graham sat himself up. "Are you? Or will you be filing for a divorce?"

Kelly's eyes, shining with tears, looked into Graham's. "I'm sorry I didn't give you a chance to explain. I'm sorry I treated you so horribly out in the parking lot. Seeing those pictures was a shock and I was *so* angry. It hurt so much and I wanted to lash out at someone. I wanted you to hurt as badly as I did."

Graham shook his head in frustration, jumping from the bed. "Kelly, it's over between Diana and me. Over! What do I have to do to convince you? I don't want to be skirting this issue for the rest of our lives. Your mother and I were once involved. We were lovers, but *not anymore*."

"But those pictures," she tentatively whispered. "If we have any chance of a future, Graham, you have to tell me the truth."

"The truth? You want the truth? Kelly, all I've ever given you is the truth! Those pictures are phony!" he practically shouted. "Diana set the whole thing up. They were taken in Nebraska by a photographer she had hired. She came to my trailer and threw herself at me, tearing at my clothes. Next thing I knew the photographer hurtles in. I chased after him and got his film, but apparently he'd switched rolls on me." Graham looked at Kelly's face. "You don't believe me," he said dejectedly, sadly shaking his head and slumping back down on the bed.

Kelly tried to cover her exasperation, shrugging her shoulders. "If you say that's what happened, then I believe you."

"Gee, thanks for the vote of confidence," he said sarcastically. "You don't believe me. I can see it on your face. Tell me what you're feeling, Kelly. Tell me. Otherwise we're back where we started."

"You want the truth?" she snapped. "Okay, that's what you're going to get! Your story sounds farfetched."

"It happened!" he insisted. "Don't you know by now that your mother would do anything to break us up? Why are you always so ready to believe her when you know she goes out of her way to make your life miserable? Why, Kelly? Will you please answer that question for me?"

"I don't know why! My entire life, anything she's ever said to me has always sounded like the truth."

"She's an actress, Kelly, and she's pulled you into the sick drama she's orchestrated. Can't you see that?"

Kelly slowly nodded. "Yes, I can see that. But I have to ask you something else and you have to be totally honest with me."

"You know I will."

"Have you slept with my mother since we've been married?"

Graham gave Kelly an angry look. "No, I haven't! No matter how many times I tell you, you still don't believe me. What do you want me to do, Kelly? Take a lie detector test?"

"I need to know!" She didn't care that she was raising her voice. "You wanted honesty and now you're getting it! You're my husband, Graham, and I love you. If it sounds like I'm possessive or paranoid, I'm sorry. But I need to know where we stand. I'm not going to let my mother destroy my happiness and take you away from me!"

Graham left the bed, moving toward Kelly. "You still love me?"

Kelly stepped into his arms, resting her head on his chest. "Yes, I do. Please, Graham, tell me the truth. I have to know, even if it hurts."

Graham tipped Kelly's head, gazing into her eyes. "Kelly, I love you and only you. I haven't slept with Diana since she and I broke up. There hasn't been anyone else since we've been together and there never will be. You're the only woman for me."

Kelly couldn't control her tears. The sincerity and emotion in

Graham's words, from the moment she had stepped inside this room, told her everything she needed to know. She kissed her husband fervently, locking her arms around his neck, not wanting to surrender herself from his embrace. "I've missed you so much. And I'm sorry for doubting you."

Graham scooped Kelly into his arms. "I've missed you too. Want to make love for old time's sake?"

"Yes!" she gleefully exclaimed.

With Kelly in his arms, Graham plopped down on the bed. Amidst giggles and kisses the two started undressing each other.

"Let me tell you why I was coming to see you that day besides wanting to start over," Graham said while nuzzling Kelly's ear. "What would you think of us moving to New York?"

"But your career," Kelly protested between deep kisses. "It's just starting to take off."

"There'll always be offers. If they want me, they'll know where to find me. You know the theater has always been my first love."

"Oh, it has, has it?" Kelly asked, playfully nipping at his chest.

"Uh-huh, but you're my true love, Kelly." Graham brushed back Kelly's lush caramel hair, softly kissing her lips. "You're what matters most. So long as we're together I'll be happy."

Kelly passionately returned Graham's kiss. "If we moved to New York we wouldn't be crossing paths with my mother." She smiled at the thought as Graham slowly, sensuously began entering her. "Let's do it!"

CHAPTER THIRTY-TWO

THE BODY of Harrison Moore was discovered by a cleaning woman the morning after his death. Dropping her bucket and supplies, the woman screamed like a banshee as she ran from the estate.

The police arrived forty minutes later, combing the estate and calling Gabrielle at the Beverly Hills Hotel, asking her to come down and identify her husband's body.

Gabrielle arrived within minutes of the call, wanting to get the task over with. After all, she still had to get ready for Daniel Ellis's funeral.

When she identified Harrison's fried corpse, Gabrielle's stomach turned. However, the queasiness passed when she realized she was a widow and that Harrison's death had saved her the trouble of getting a divorce.

It also gave her an idea . . . a brilliant idea.

Though the death of Harrison Moore was certainly considered bizarre (word was already spreading), it hardly caused a ripple in the Hollywood community. Attention was focused elsewhere.

Daniel Ellis's death was a Hollywood event. Anyone who was anyone planned on making an appearance at his funeral. It didn't matter if one hadn't known the deceased. The opportunity for free publicity was too much to resist. And what an opportunity it was! Cameras, reporters, and film crews from almost every leading newspaper, tabloid, and television station around the world would be there. And everyone knew Daniel's casket would have center stage for only five minutes.

The rest of the time belonged to them.

* * *

"Are you okay?" Graham asked.

Kelly was gazing out the window of the limousine bringing them closer to the cemetery . . . closer to saying goodbye to Uncle Daniel. "I'm fine." Yet as soon as the words were spoken, tears appeared. "Damn!"

"It's okay to cry."

Kelly wiped away her tears. "I know, but I still can't believe he's dead. How did it happen so fast? The last time I saw him he was perfectly fine. Now he's gone."

Graham moved closer to Kelly, his head against hers. "It's important to remember the good times."

"With Uncle Daniel that's all there was. Oh, Graham," she wailed. "What am I going to do? He was like a father to me."

"Life goes on. We have no control over it. That's why it's important to make the most of the time we have."

Kelly kissed her husband, remembering how close she had come to losing him. "That's right. We still have each other, along with a brand-new future in New York."

"Speaking of New York, when are you telling your mother?"

"Probably today."

"Think she'll be here?"

Kelly rolled her eyes. "The press will be out in droves. She wouldn't miss this for the world."

"I suppose I *could* marry you," Diana told Paul, adjusting the veil of her hat as their limousine glided to Forest Lawn Cemetery.

"Don't think you're doing me any favors. I've gotten along fine without you all these years."

"And I've managed on my own too, but I've been giving your proposal some thought. Think of what we could accomplish together if we pooled our talents." Diana's eyes glowed and she slid next to Paul. "I'm older and wiser now. I was such a fool to turn down the chance to be your wife when you first proposed all those years ago. I won't make the same mistake again."

Paul looked at Diana shrewdly. "So you'll marry me?"

Diana thought of all Paul had to offer: his studio, his casino, his money. She thought of announcing their engagement after the funeral, in the midst of all the media that would be present. What an opportunity!

She snuggled closer to him. "How could I say no?"

Though she had just become a widow and was attending someone else's funeral, Gabrielle couldn't bear the thought of wearing black. It was such a *severe* color when worn alone. Instead she selected from her closet a purple-and-black ensemble that she thought would convey just the right look: chic but sentimental.

Gabrielle was excited. Today was the day Heather signed her contract with Trinity. Once she signed, her career would be over. Gabrielle kicked up her heels with glee. More than one person was going to be buried today.

Mark stared at Heather incredulously. "How can you say no? Heather, are you crazy, turning this down?"

"Lower your voice," Heather hissed, closing the study doors. "Peter's in the next room."

"Heather, I don't understand."

"What's to understand? The contract is too limiting as to what I can and can't do. I'm uncomfortable with it."

"We can work around that. Heather, I've got the perfect project lined up for you. All set and ready to go. You sign on the dotted line and we're in movie theaters by next summer."

"Find someone else," she insisted. "I don't know when I'll be free for another project."

"What do you mean?" Panic entered Mark's voice. "You haven't signed with anyone else, have you?"

"No, I haven't. Look Mark, Peter's going through a rough time. He needs me around. I owe him and I can't abandon him."

"What about owing *me*? What about the way you're abandoning *me*? I took a chance on you, a relative unknown, and this is the thanks I get."

"Hey!" Heather flared. "I've repaid you by giving you an impeccable performance, and excuse me for sounding callous, but audiences are going to *flock* to see *Long Journey Home* because it's Daniel's last performance. Now if you'll excuse me, Peter and I have to leave for the cemetery. I trust we'll see you there."

"Yeah, you'll see me there," Mark muttered on his way out, not intending for Heather to hear the remark. "My funeral will probably be right on the heels of Ellis's."

"What's that supposed to mean?"

Mark made his decision within seconds . . . without hesitation. He had to do this. He had to clue Heather in on what was going on. She had a right to watch her back. And to be perfectly honest, he had never wanted to do this to her. He was glad she had turned down his offer. He'd deal with Gabrielle when he had to. "There's something I think you should know."

Vanessa Vought was crying her eyes out in her limousine, trying to reapply her mascara. She'd just lost her best friend and she couldn't stop the well of tears that kept pouring forth. She didn't know what she was going to do without Daniel. She didn't know how she was going to cope.

Her mascara ran down her cheeks in rivulets again.

The ceremony was anything but short and sweet. Instead it was lengthy, filled with anecdotes and stories as celebrity after celebrity recounted their memories of Daniel. There were smiles and chuckles; tears, too. After everyone had had their five minutes in the spotlight, Peter addressed those who had gathered.

He didn't try to look brave. He didn't try to hide his grief. Instead he wore it openly, without shame, as he gazed at Daniel's casket.

"I want to thank everyone for coming here today," he began in a tremulous voice. "It means a lot to me to know Daniel was so loved. Everyone knew he was a special person, but those who knew him intimately will never forget the way he changed their lives. We'll miss him and I know our lives won't be the same without him. But we will have our memories."

At this point Peter lifted his head, unaware of the tears streaming down his cheeks. He searched through the faces gathered and found his father's, defiantly locking gazes. "No matter what happens we'll always have our memories because memories can never be taken away."

Out of the corner of her eye, Kelly saw Diana detach herself from Paul and a group of mourners. Instead of returning to the area where the limousines were waiting, she moved deeper into the cemetery into an area where there were older tombstones. Curious about her mother's actions, Kelly decided to follow after her.

"Wait for me. I'll be right back," she whispered into Graham's ear, giving him an affectionate kiss on the cheek.

Hurrying after Diana through the manicured lawn, Kelly watched as her mother stepped before a small grave, placing her hands to her lips for a kiss before touching the stone and bowing her head.

Wanting to know whose grave this was, Kelly inched closer to get a look at the engraved name, stepping on a dry twig. The cracking branch shattered the stillness, but Kelly didn't hear it. She didn't hear anything. All her senses ceased to function except for sight as her eyes focused on the name on the tombstone.

It was *her* name. With the same year of birth and death—1964—the year before she was born.

Diana's eyes jolted open. At the sight of Kelly they widened with anger. "What are you doing here?" she hissed. "You have no right to be here." She jumped to her feet, protectively shielding the tombstone.

Kelly looked from the tombstone to Diana in confusion. "Why is my name there? What's going on?"

"I asked you to leave."

Kelly confronted Diana's anger, despite her trembling insides. "No! I'm not going anywhere, Mother, not until I get some answers. I've run away from you my entire life. I'm tired of running and I'm not going to do it anymore."

"You want answers? Fine, you'll get them!" Diana spat. "After all these years you still haven't figured things out, have you?"

"Figured things out?"

Diana mimicked Kelly's voice. "Why don't you love me, Mother? Why?" Diana's voice became unrelenting. "Stop it, Mother! You're hurting me! I promise I'll be a good girl. I promise. I love you, Mother." Diana laughed cruelly. "Ready for a news flash? *I never loved you!*"

It was hard for Kelly to hear what she had always suspected was true. "How could you not love me? I'm your daughter."

Those were the words Diana had been waiting to hear . . . words she had heard so many times before in the past. Those times she had been unable to say what she had truly wanted. She had had to guard her secret and privately revel in the pleasure it brought. Now she intended to unleash it. She didn't care about the consequences. All she wanted to do was hurt Kelly.

"No," Diana hissed softly. "You're not."

Kelly wasn't sure if she'd heard correctly. "What did you say?"

"You're *not* my daughter. I'm *not* your mother."

Kelly fought back the shock. She tried to remain calm, think rationally. "Are you telling me I was adopted?"

"No. Your father *was* Adam Stoddard, but I'm not your mother."

"I don't understand. How can Adam be my father and you *not* be my mother?"

"Because your mother was Iris Larson," Diana hissed, her voice dripping with scorn and hatred. "As you no doubt know, Iris had an affair with your father. What you didn't know was that Iris became pregnant with Adam's baby. You're their bastard child."

Kelly shook her head numbly. This was unbelievable! None of it made sense. The pieces weren't fitting together. If Iris Larson was her mother, then how could it be that Diana had raised her as her own daughter? She knew how her mother felt about Iris—she hated her. Why would she raise the daughter of the woman she hated so much? "You're lying. You're making this up . . . doing it to hurt me."

Diana flew into a rage at Kelly's words. "Don't tell me what *is* and *isn't* the truth. *I* should know! *I've* lived with it for the past twenty-five years. As long as I live I'll never forget what your mother did to me." Diana's eyes returned to the tombstone, then fixated on Kelly with burning malice. "No, I'll never forget what Iris did to me . . . or my baby."

When Diana first learned she was pregnant, it was the happiest day of her life. Adam and she had been trying so hard to have a baby and at last it had happened!

The sacrifice she had to make would be well worth it.

In the spring of 1964 Diana had already begun shooting her latest movie, *Banquet*. Though she was only two months pregnant, she was having a horrible time. Morning sickness and dizzy spells, and her dailies were just awful. Instead of looking svelte and sexy, she looked pale and bloated. She decided to drop out of the picture—it was the only thing she *could* do. She didn't want to give a bad performance and in all honesty, she could care less about the film now. She was finally having a baby! Nothing else mattered.

Adam had been ecstatic when she'd told him the news and that night he took her out to dinner. When they returned home they made love and fell asleep with their hands on her stomach.

Her dropping out of *Banquet* meant the producers had to find a new female lead. They narrowed their choices down to Iris Larson and another actress. Iris's career was red-hot and she knew *Banquet* could make her a superstar. Diana hoped Iris didn't get the part. Though Iris pretended to be sweet and innocent, that was only a facade meant to impress her fans. Behind the scenes she was ruthless and cunning. She wanted it all and wasn't above sleeping with producers and directors. She did that with the producer and director of *Banquet*. Together. Twenty-four hours later, Diana's part was hers.

Too consumed with her baby's arrival to think about Iris, Diana concentrated on her baby's arrival that October. She converted a spare bedroom into a nursery and was constantly shopping. With Adam off on location, she managed to keep herself busy and not think about how much she missed him.

But then the rumors started. Supposedly Iris and Adam had started having an affair. Diana decided to ignore what she was hearing. In her condition it wasn't good to get upset and she wanted to do everything right for her baby.

When *Banquet* wrapped, she was almost seven months pregnant. When Adam returned home she didn't accuse him of anything. Instead she showed him the new nursery and told him about the names she had chosen.

"Kelly if it's a girl, and Adam if it's a boy." She gave him a kiss. "I hope we have a boy. It'd be nice to have a smaller version of you around."

After three days of her pampering, coddling, and words of love, Adam broke down. Just as she'd planned. He confessed all to Diana and she chose to forgive him as long as he promised never to see Iris again. He promised.

Iris didn't take Adam's absence from her life very well. First there were the harassing phone calls at all hours of the night. Then came the hate mail—letters filled with profanities and threats of what she'd do to herself if Adam didn't come back—followed by a baby doll with its face smashed in.

Adam tried talking to Iris, reasoning with her, but she refused to listen. She swore she loved Adam and couldn't live without him.

Then came the day when she dropped her bombshell.

Diana answered the ringing phone, removing her earring as she placed the receiver to her ear. "Hello."

"Hello, Diana. It's Iris."

The silky tone of confidence irked Diana. Her own words were clipped and icy. "What do you want?"

"I was wondering if you had some free time this afternoon. We need to talk."

Adam had told her to hang up if Iris called when he wasn't at home, but instead Diana asked, "About what?"

"Adam."

Diana chose to ignore her husband's advice. She'd had enough of Iris and her games. It was time to put the desperate little bitch in her place. "I'll see you at three."

"Right on time," Iris quipped, ushering Diana into her house. "Let's go upstairs to the library, shall we? I've made tea." Iris led the way and Diana followed in stony silence.

"You're filling out. How far along are you?"

"Almost seven months."

Iris looked over her shoulder at Diana as they climbed the spiral staircase to the second floor. "What's it like being pregnant?"

"It *was* wonderful," Diana stated pointedly. "Until someone started wreaking havoc in my life."

"I wonder what kind of mother I'll make?" Iris mused. "Oh, well, we'll find out soon enough." She stopped climbing, turning to face Diana. "You really despise me, don't you?"

"I loathe you."

"I don't think that's a very nice thing to say to an expectant mother," Iris pouted.

Realization dawned on Diana. "You can't be—"

Iris smiled gleefully. "But I am! Adam's going to be a daddy again."

"You're lying! This is just another one of your stunts."

"Call my doctor. He'll confirm it," Iris smugly retorted.

"That doesn't mean a thing. Even if you are pregnant, Adam's not necessarily the father."

"If I say Adam's the father, he's the father. But don't worry, the paternity test will prove it."

"So what?" Diana hissed. "*My* baby will have Adam's name. *Always! Your* child will *always* be a bastard!"

The words enraged Iris, who lunged at Diana and pushed her. Diana lost her footing, starting to fall backwards. She grabbed for Iris, her fingers brushing the front of her silk blouse. But Iris scrambled up the steps, watching as Diana fell screaming to the bottom.

Diana woke in a hospital bed. Adam was by her side. She felt different. Strange. Immediately she thought of her baby and her hands went to her stomach. But even before that, she knew.

"Adam?"

His tired eyes were filled with tears and sorrow. Yet there was something else there. Something that scared her.

"There was nothing they could do," he croaked hoarsely.

"Was it a boy or a girl?"

"A girl."

"Kelly," she murmured. "My sweet Kelly is gone. We have to bury her, Adam." She clutched at her husband's arm. "We have to bury her! We can't let them . . ."

"I've already taken care of it."

Diana released her grip, settling back in her bed, allowing some of the tension to slip away. "There's something more. Something you're not telling me. I can see it in your eyes. Tell me."

"Maybe I should get the doctor . . ."

"Tell me!"

"There aren't going to be any more babies, Diana. The doctor says you'll never be able to carry to full term."

Diana gasped as though struck with a lethal blow. She thought of all she had done for her baby in the past seven months. She thought of all she had intended to do for her baby in the future.

She then thought of Iris doing all those things with her baby.

"We're going to get through this, Diana. We are. We're going to have a family of our own. We can always adopt."

Diana shoved Adam away from her. "*I want that bitch to pay!*" she screamed at the top of her lungs. "*I want her to pay!*"

* * *

It was Diana who came up with the arrangement after vowing to leak everything to the media and press charges if Iris didn't agree to it. Iris, thinking solely of her career, agreed.

Iris was three and a half months pregnant; Diana had been almost seven months. Both women would leave for Palm Springs. Diana would pretend to be pregnant still and claim she had miscalculated how far along she had been in her pregnancy. When Iris came to term, the baby would be given to Diana and Adam.

In January 1965 Iris gave birth to a daughter and all went according to plan. Yet when Diana held the baby in her arms for the first time, she didn't feel a thing. It wasn't the way she had imagined it would feel when she was pregnant with her own baby. She felt hollow. Empty. All she could think of was the baby girl she should have been holding, who was instead buried in a casket in the ground.

It was then that the hatred started to grow.

Hot off her Oscar win for *Banquet*, Iris was signed to a new movie with Adam in May 1965. Iris used this as a chance to worm her way back into Adam's life, wanting to know about her baby.

Soon Adam, despite all the misery Iris had caused the first time around, was back under her spell and in her bed.

This was the last straw for Diana. What Iris was doing was a direct slap in the face and she wasn't going to stand for it.

It was then that she decided to murder Iris.

What Diana did was simple. Knowing Iris's love for speed, she sawed at the brakeline of Iris's Mustang, leaving it frayed. All it would take was Iris slamming down hard on the brakes and the line would snap.

Yet Adam was the one who ended up dead behind the wheel of Iris's car.

When Diana learned what she had done after she got the phone call from the police, she almost killed herself with an overdose.

Almost.

Then Kelly began crying and Diana's anger ignited.

"Shut up!" she screamed, tossing the pills on the bathroom floor, clutching at her head, wanting to shut out the baby's wails. "Shut up!"

The baby kept crying and crying. In the nursery she picked up the red-faced, wailing infant, shaking her furiously. "Shut up! Shut up, shut up, shut up!" She tossed the infant back into her crib where she bounced on the mattress, continuing to wail. "He's gone and it's all your fault. *All your fault!*"

It was then that Diana decided not to kill herself. If she did, Iris would win. Iris would get her baby back.

That would never happen.

"I want my baby back," Iris demanded the day of Adam's funeral.

Diana clutched the cooing infant possessively, stroking the back of her head. "You must be insane. She's mine. *Mine.*"

"Adam's dead. No one will believe your wild story. No one will support your accusations. I've won, Diana, and there's nothing you can do."

Diana watched Iris head for her limousine. Then across the cemetery she could see Paul Fontana and his wife, Marina. Diana gave Paul a seductive smile as a plan began to form.

"You haven't won yet, Iris," she vowed, kissing the top of Kelly's head before stepping into her limousine. "Not yet."

"So Paul Fontana murdered your mother per my request," Diana told Kelly. "The satisfaction was delicious! I loved it, but it was so fleeting! I wanted more. Iris still needed to pay and then I discovered how to keep getting that satisfaction. Through you. By tormenting you day after day and making you pay for your mother's sins."

Kelly's mind was reeling from all she'd been told. Diana had inadvertently murdered her father; she'd had her mother killed. Her entire life had all been a lie. And it all made sense. It explained so much!

She stared at the bitter woman, no more than a stranger, standing across from her. She felt nothing for her. Yet she could see Diana had enjoyed the little scene that had just unfolded. She decided she would not retaliate with the same bitterness. To do so would only give Diana pleasure.

Her head was spinning. She needed some time alone to sort things out. But one thing she was sure of. She wasn't going to let Diana have the last word. Not this time.

Kelly spoke in a measured, even tone. "No matter what you've just told me, Iris Larson was not my mother. She may have given birth to me, but you're the woman who raised me. Do you want to know something? I feel sorry for you."

"You feel sorry for *me?*" Diana laughed hysterically. "Why's that?"

"Look at all that you threw away! After you lost your baby, Mother, you had a second chance. You could have loved me. I loved you, despite everything you did to me. I wouldn't let my love for you die no matter how horribly you treated me. I kept telling myself that you didn't mean the things you did. That one day you would realize how much I loved you and then you would start loving me. But that never happened. You wouldn't love me and you wouldn't let me love you. Do you want to know something, Mother? You've finally won." Kelly stared at Diana as though she were a stranger, a look of loathing on her face. "I don't love you anymore. You've killed whatever feelings I've had for you. Wallow in your bitterness and self-pity, Mother," she said sadly, deciding to leave. "You created it. And you want to know something else? You deserve it."

Laura canvassed her bedroom for what seemed like the hundredth time, looking for something—*anything*—she could use to defend herself against Nico.

Yet the bedroom, with its frills and flounces—its statement of femininity—seemed to mock her.

Don't panic! she told herself as her eyes noted the passing time on her watch. *Don't panic!*

At any moment Nico would be coming to get her, expecting to find her in her wedding gown. When he discovered she wasn't wearing it . . . when he discovered the reason . . .

She shuddered as she remembered losing her first baby. Nothing was going to happen to this child, she vowed. *Nothing!*

Nervously, she rubbed her hands around one of the hand-painted ceramic balls on the bedpost of the brass bed. Round and round her hands went as her mind searched for an answer.

At first she stared down at her hands without seeing. Then she stared with comprehension.

She heard his footsteps approaching. Next there came a jangle of keys, with one being inserted into her bedroom lock. There came an audible click.

And then came his voice through the still closed door.

"Laura? Are you almost ready? It's time."

Laura took one last look over her shoulder, frantically unscrewing the ceramic ball with sweaty palms as a plan began forming in her mind.

She couldn't get a grip on the ball. Her hands kept slipping and sliding.

"Come on," she urged, wiping her wet palms down her shirt-front, attempting to twist again. *"Come on."*

She heard the key being removed from the lock and saw the doorknob slowly twist. At that moment the ceramic ball spun free. Laura seized it in both hands, hiding them behind her back as she whirled around.

The door swung inward. Nico stood in the doorway, wearing an immaculately pressed tuxedo. The expectant smile on his face transformed into a frown. He smashed the bouquet of roses he held against the wall.

"Why aren't you ready yet?"

Laura brushed away the hairs sticking to her forehead with one hand. "There was a problem with my gown."

"Oh?"

"There's a horrible stain on it. I couldn't bear to put it on."

"Impossible. I had that gown cleaned."

"Check for yourself. It's hanging in the closet."

"If this is a trick to delay things, you're going to be *very* sorry, Laura," he promised with a dark scowl.

In three quick strides, Nico reached the closet, flinging open the doors. As he peered inside, searching for the wedding gown, Laura moved up behind him.

"Where's the gown?" he demanded, twisting around to face her.

"Right there!" Laura screamed, smashing the ceramic ball with all her might against the side of Nico's head.

The ball made a horrifying sound as it connected, and Nico collapsed to the floor.

Laura got to her knees, rummaging through Nico's pockets until she found his keys, knowing she would need them to get out of the house. She had just found them when she suddenly heard a jangling sound from behind.

Laura turned, catching sight of Satan charging down the hallway in the direction of the open bedroom door, coming to his master's defense. His mouth was open, fangs bared, getting ready to sink his teeth into her.

Laura jumped to her feet and raced for the bedroom door just as the Doberman's head entered the doorway. Laura threw her weight behind the door as she closed it, slamming it into Satan's neck with all her might. The dog howled in pain, struggling to pull his head back, but Laura kept pushing and pushing. The dog howled in pain, eyes rolling back in his head, snarling madly. Laura ignored his cries, knowing that the only thing preventing her escape was the four-legged beast on the other side of the door. The door dug into Satan's neck until finally he stopped struggling and his head went limp.

Opening the door, Laura stepped around the dead Doberman and ran from the bedroom that had been her prison, clutching the keys that meant her escape.

The gathering at Daniel Ellis's estate after his funeral was hardly a somber event. Daniel had always made it known that he wanted a party thrown in his memory, and that was what was going on—in true Hollywood style.

The food was catered from Arthur Simon's. Champagne was poured and the black outfits worn were no longer somber but *chic*, bright, ornamental. The Hollywood world continued to rotate on its axis.

Paul Fontana and Diana Halloway were among the very last to arrive. Standing at the threshold of the entrance, they watched as conversation dropped down to whispers.

Daniel and Diana's feud was the stuff of Hollywood legends. It was well known how the two had despised each other. Was Diana coming to gloat over her late nemesis?

Looking appropriately mournful, Diana reached for a flute of champagne from a passing tray.

"What's that line of Mark Antony's? *I come to bury Caesar, not to praise him?*" Diana smirked. "Honey, I plan on doing an Irish jig on Danny boy's grave."

"You're in an exceptionally good mood, given the circumstances," Paul commented dryly.

"Kelly and I had a chat at the cemetery."

"About what?"

Diana gave Paul a knowing look. "What do you think?"

"You told her?"

"I burst her every last bubble. Little Miss Perfect is now Little Girl Lost."

"How did it feel?"

"*Wonderful!* I suppose it compares to your private moment with dear departed Daniel. But listen, I had the most fabulous idea during our ride to the cemetery. Why don't we announce our impending nuptials?"

"Here? Today?"

"I'd love nothing better than to upstage Daniel at his own funeral."

Peter had to get away from it all—the people, the chatter, the condolences. He just wanted to be alone.

He managed to slip away unnoticed, retreating upstairs to the bedroom he and Daniel had shared for such a short time.

Everywhere Peter looked he saw Daniel—his clothes were still tossed over an armchair and in the closets and drawers; his jewelry and cologne were scattered across the dresser; his tennis racket and sneakers were in a corner—all waiting for his return. But Daniel would not be returning.

Peter laid down on Daniel's side of their bed, clutching his pillow. He could still smell Daniel's scent. The experience hurt because with his eyes closed he could *see* Daniel, *hear* him, but when he opened his eyes, no one was there.

He reached for Daniel's scrapbook under the bed. It was a thick red leather-bound volume etched in gold. The pages were filled with photos, reviews, interviews, newspaper and magazine clippings from day one of his career.

Page after page reminded Peter of Daniel's pride as he explained each item.

There was a knock at the door and Peter looked up as Vanessa stuck her head in. "Mind if I barge in?"

She joined Peter on the bed, sipping from her scotch, smiling when she saw the scrapbook. "Daniel treasured that."

"I know. You're in here a lot. Want to take a look?" He offered the scrapbook.

"Reminders of my early years? Let's not depress me." Vanessa grew quiet. "Though I can't imagine feeling any lower than I do today." She angrily rattled the ice in her glass. "Of course, you wouldn't know it from what was going on downstairs."

"What's going on?"

"*Not* a memorial. It's turned into a Hollywood party, with Diana Halloway taking center stage, as usual."

"What's she done this time?"

"Announced her engagement to your father. They're getting

married. She said that after all these years she's finally gotten him to do as he promised."

"What?" Peter slammed shut the scrapbook, jumping up from the bed. The phrase had to be a coincidence. Didn't it? Diana couldn't have been the woman in his father's bed all those years ago, could she?

"Daniel should have told what he knew," Vanessa stated bitterly. "He could have ruined her. Kelly has a right to know."

Peter's attention focused on Vanessa. "What are you talking about?"

"He would have done it the right way. Kelly wouldn't have gotten hurt. Only Diana would have suffered." Vanessa drained her glass.

"Vanessa, what are you talking about?" he asked again, wondering if she was drunk.

"I suppose I should tell you. You'll probably find the paperwork Daniel had collected and put the pieces together yourself." She drew Peter close, murmuring softly. "Kelly isn't really Diana's daughter. Diana's been pretending all these years."

"She's adopted?"

"No. Diana has been passing Kelly off as her own daughter. You see, Iris Larson had an affair with Diana's husband, Adam. The result was Kelly. For twenty-five years Diana has hidden the truth, playing her twisted games with Kelly. Daniel had planned on putting a stop to it. He loved Kelly too much. He even went to see Diana and she threatened him. Can you believe it?"

"I believe it," Peter said softly as the fragments of a memory he had chosen to ignore for the longest time returned.

"She said she had friends in high places."

Peter blanched. "Those were the words she used?" he whispered, not liking the connections he was suddenly making—not liking the parallels between Daniel's death and his mother's. That long ago scene, as he had hid in the closet, watching his father drape his mother's emerald-and-diamond necklace across his mistress's neck flashed through his mind:

Did you do as you promised?

Don't worry. It won't even look like murder.

And then with startling clarity he remembered a memory from the most recent past:

Don't push me, Peter. I'm warning you. Don't make me do something I'll regret.

Vanessa's words haunted him: *She told him she had friends in high places.*
Did you do as you promised?
Don't worry. It won't even look like murder.
Did you do as you promised?
She told him she had friends in high places.
Did you do as you promised?
Don't push me, Peter. Don't make me do something I'll regret.
Did you do as you promised?
It looks like he had another attack. You never know in these cases.
Did you do as you promised?
She said she's finally gotten him to do as he promised.
"No!" Peter shouted, blocking out the voices in his head, not wanting to believe it was true as the pieces all fell into place.

Vanessa looked up from her drink, alarmed. "Peter, what's wrong?"

"They have to pay," he vowed before running from the bedroom like a madman. "They both have to pay for what they've done!"

When Drew arrived at Laura's, he found the front door open.

"Anybody home?" He knocked once and then stepped inside.

Drew gasped. The house was a shambles. Everywhere he looked there was destruction. He stopped in his tracks as his eyes took in what looked like a bizarre wedding scene before him. "Laura?" he called, panic in his voice, afraid of what he might find. "Laura, are you here?"

Using his crutch, he proceeded deeper into the apartment. When he reached Laura's bedroom, he found a dead Doberman, along with tiny pools of blood beaded on the shag carpet, leading from the closet.

Drew hobbled to the closet, peering inside, not knowing what he'd expect to find. The closet was empty. "What the hell is going on?" he muttered.

His fear and apprehension grew when he saw the bars on the windows, the chain by the bed and the ripped-out phone.

Clutching Laura's note, Drew hobbled from the apartment as quickly as he could.

CHAPTER THIRTY-THREE

CONGRATULATIONS WERE being offered to Diana and Paul. Kelly watched the scene with disgust as she remembered what had happened between them at the cemetery. She was no longer in shock over what Diana had told her. Now she was angry.

"Are you okay?" Graham asked.

"I'm fine," Kelly murmured. She hadn't told Graham yet what she'd learned. There'd be time for that later. Right now she had some unfinished business to take care of. "Keep your eye on me. I think you're going to like what you see."

With her drink in hand, Kelly strolled over to her mother and Paul.

"Congratulations, Mother," she said sweetly.

Diana was surprised to see Kelly so well composed, considering the bombshell she had dropped. It would have been nice to see her a bit unhinged, but she seemed quite calm and collected, much to Diana's annoyance. Well, she'd have to do something about that.

"I see you're with Graham. Are you two back together?"

"Yes, we are," Kelly answered evenly. "No thanks to you."

"So you bought his pack of lies." Diana shook her head ruefully. "When are you going to wake up, Kelly? Graham's not the man you think he is. He's never going to be faithful to you. You'll never make him happy because there'll always be another woman to entice him away from you. If not me, then someone else."

"Save it, Mother, just save it, because once again you're lying. And do you want to know why? Do you want to know what your problem is? It's because you don't know how to love. You're not capable of the emotion. You never have been and you never will be!"

"You're ranting, Kelly. You don't know what you're saying."

"Don't I? All this time you've been jealous over what Graham and I have had because it's exactly what my father and Iris had. They loved each other. Adam loved Iris and he didn't give a damn about you!"

"Shut up!" Diana hissed. "Just shut up!"

But Kelly was unrelenting. She attacked Diana the way she had been attacked earlier that morning in the cemetery. "He would have left you, you know. Eventually. He would have left you and you would have been all alone, with no one but yourself. And that scares you. It scares you because when you look in a mirror you see what everyone else sees: a vain and selfish woman who'll never have anyone because she doesn't know how to love.

"Graham knew that—it's the reason he left you. You disgusted him! He couldn't stand to be around you! He loves *me*, Mother— not you! He *never* loved you and you knew that! That's one of the reasons you've tried to break us up. Shall I share the other reason?"

"You're making a fool of yourself!" Diana shouted, not liking the fact that the tables had been turned. She was aware that the other guests were watching . . . listening. "I demand you put an end to this right this minute!"

"Don't tell me what to do! You don't have the right! You never did, remember, *Mother*? I'm going to say exactly what I feel. I know why you tried to break up Graham and me. You couldn't stand to see us have what you so desperately wanted. You're pathetic! The only woman Graham will ever love is me and that just kills you. Well, nothing you ever do will be able to change that."

"I wouldn't be so sure," Diana spat. "Give me five minutes alone with your husband and I'll have him pulling down his pants."

"You can stop the crude scheming, Mother, because Graham and I are leaving Hollywood. We're moving to New York, to get as far away from you as possible. And once we do that, you're never going to hear from us again because neither one of us can stand you!" Then, before Diana could open her mouth, Kelly tossed her drink in her face. "Have a nice lonely life, Mother. You've earned it."

With that, Kelly turned her back on a dripping, sputtering Diana, giving Graham a big smile as she hooked her arm through his.

"Nice work," he complimented.

"I thought so, too. Now how soon do you think we can catch a plane to New York? I'm ready to shake this town!"

Drew drove to the nearest police station like a madman, determined to find some answers. He didn't know what was going on or how to make sense of it. The most important thing was finding Laura. Making sure she was all right. What he'd seen in her apartment had been something straight out of a nightmare.

If he was too late to do something . . .

If he'd lost her . . .

He pressed down on the accelerator, running a red light.

Heather was bustling out of the kitchen with a plate of hors d'oeuvres when she nearly collided with Gabrielle.

"My, these look tasty." Gabrielle speared a chunk of chicken teriyaki with a toothpick. "Hello, Heather. I suppose congratulations are in order."

Heather brushed by Gabrielle to the buffet table. "They are?"

"No need to be so modest. I heard Trinity offered you a five-picture deal and you took it."

"Well, they did offer me a contract, but I turned them down."

Gabrielle choked on the chicken she was chewing. "What do you mean, you turned them down? Are you crazy? I heard Mark Bauer was desperate to sign you."

"Was he?" Heather turned suspicious eyes on Gabrielle. "And how do you know that?"

"I'm only repeating what I've heard. Don't you think you're making a mistake? I mean, if Trinity is foolish enough to want to sign you, I would think you'd jump at their offer."

"Like the way you'd jump at anything in pants?" Heather demurred.

There was a chorus of laughter as Heather's remark reached nearby ears.

"You're going to regret that remark, you little slut," Gabrielle warned.

"You know what I'm going to regret? This!" Heather reached for a chocolate creme pie on the buffet, slamming it into Gabrielle's face. "That's what I'm going to regret! And here's a warning, Gabrielle. Don't ever try fucking with me again. Mark filled me in on your little scheme and I'm the one who's warning you. You ever try messing with my career again and next time you're going to find my fist in your face!"

Gabrielle shrieked in outrage before stomping away while Heather tossed the empty pie plate on the buffet, calling after her, "Next party, let's avoid the buffet. We seem to be making a habit out of this."

Laura huddled under a blanket, gratefully sipping the hot coffee she'd been handed to warm herself. No matter how hard she tried, she couldn't stop shivering. She couldn't stop her teeth from chattering, and every time she closed her eyes, she saw Nico's leering face. She didn't dare think of what would have happened if she hadn't gotten away.

A dark-haired police officer gave her a gentle smile. "Ready to tell us the rest of your story?"

Laura nodded wearily. After fleeing from the house and the madness behind its walls, she'd hitched a ride with a sandy-haired surfer, asking him to drop her off at the nearest police station. At the time all she could think of was reaching safety.

When she'd first arrived she'd been nearly hysterical, shouting at the desk sergeant that her ex-husband had been keeping her prisoner for weeks and she'd only just escaped, leaving him unconscious at her house.

After calming her down, they took her address and dispatched a patrol car while she tried to tell them her story as coherently as possible.

"We should be hearing something soon," the officer assured her.

"I want to see him in handcuffs. I want to see them lock him behind bars and throw away the key. He doesn't deserve to be free. Nico Rossi is an animal. He deserves to be locked up in a cage."

"Don't worry. If what you've told us is true, he won't be going anywhere for a long, long time."

"That little bitch!" Diana raged as she stormed across her bedroom, unzipping her dress. "If she thinks she can get away with that stunt, she's sadly mistaken."

"Looks like your daughter takes after her mother," Paul smirked.

"Don't call her my daughter! She's Iris's bastard!" Diana paraded before Paul in a black teddy, angrily waving a hairbrush. "She's going to pay for this! I don't know how, but I'll figure out a way!"

"Forget about Kelly and come over here." He reached into the inside pocket of his jacket. "I've got something for you."

"What?" she greedily demanded.

"A small token of my affection." He held out a gift-wrapped box. Diana promptly seized it, tearing away the paper and flipping back the top. Inside was an emerald-and-diamond necklace—the same necklace he'd given to her twenty-five years before and taken back after she'd turned down his marriage proposal.

"Let's make love," he growled, tossing her down on the bed, draping the necklace around her throat as he slid away the teddy.

It wasn't often that Drew pulled a star number, but he was willing to do anything to get to the bottom of this mystery.

"Do you know who I am?" he demanded in his most arrogant tone. "I'm Drew Stern. I've just told what I discovered at my girlfriend's house. What do you plan on doing about it? I want someone on top of this and I want it done *now!*"

"Mr. Stern," the desk sergeant tried to explain patiently, "if you'll just give me a moment—"

"I don't want explanations! I want answers! I want Laura found. All I want is Laura!"

It couldn't be. Laura didn't dare believe it was true. She bolted from her seat, straining to listen as the voice outside grew more and more strident.

It was! It was Drew!

She pushed past the officers, the blanket around her shoulders slipping to the floor as she flung back the closed door.

"Drew!"

"Laura?" He turned to face her with the most worried look on his face. But then the look disappeared and he smiled . . . a brilliant smile that transformed his entire face. "Laura!"

She threw herself into his arms, wanting only to hold onto him and never let go.

"Drew," she sobbed. "I thought I'd never see you again."

"You thought you'd never see *me* again? I thought I'd never see *you* again. I just came from your place. What happened over there?"

"There's so much to explain." Her words poured out in a rush. "Drew, I didn't want to hurt you. At first I thought I was doing the right thing. I wanted to protect you. I didn't want Nico to hurt you."

"Nico? Who's Nico?"

"My ex-husband. For the past four years he's been in prison and I've been running from city to city. When he was locked away he swore he'd track me down once he got out. He swore he would make me pay for divorcing him and that he would hurt any man I ever loved."

"So that's why you left me," Drew said softly.

"Nico got out of prison a few weeks ago. He managed to find me. I was so afraid, Drew. I couldn't let him hurt you. I would have never forgiven myself if he had."

"But you came back."

"Yes, I came back."

"Why?" he asked, though he suspected the answer. But he wanted to hear it. Drew Stern, who had never been wanted, never been loved, wanted to hear the reason.

"Because I love you," she exclaimed. "Because I couldn't live without you. I realized it was time to stop running. I didn't want to lose you, Drew. Or what we had. You weren't at your beach house when I got back, so I left a note. When you didn't call . . ."

Drew waved the note under Laura's nose. "I just got it. I was off in Paris filming a mini-series." He thunked his cast. "Which is where I got this baby. Some souvenir, huh?"

"A souvenir that almost saved my life. I kept wondering why you didn't come. I knew I had hurt you but you were my only hope, Drew. Every day I prayed you would come. That night when I got back to my house, Nico was waiting. He made me a prisoner." She shuddered. "He was going to force me to marry him again."

Drew held her even more tightly. "When I think of how close I came to losing you."

"I was so scared, Drew. I thought we'd never see each other again. I thought you'd never know . . ."

"Know what?"

"We're going to have a baby."

"A baby?" he gasped with unabashed delight.

Laura nodded shyly. "We're going to have a baby. Once the

police come back with Nico and lock him away, we'll be able to put this whole nightmare behind us and get on with our lives."

"You mean they've tracked him down?"

"What do you mean? I left him unconscious."

"Laura, when I got to your house, the place was deserted. No one was there."

"No! You're wrong!" Laura began trembling uncontrollably. "You have to be wrong!"

"Honey, calm down," Drew soothed.

"You don't understand! He's still out there!"

"Nothing is going to happen, Laura. You don't have to be afraid anymore. You're not alone. You'll never be alone again." He embraced her in his arms. "I'm here and I'm going to protect you. I love you. I'm not going to let anything happen to you. I promise."

Gabrielle was ready to throw a shit fit. That little bitch had made a fool out of her again!

Storming into her bedroom, Gabrielle stripped, tossing items left and right. She was absolutely sticky. What she needed to do most was take a nice long soak in her tub and calm herself down. After that she'd figure out a way to deal with Heather. And then there was Mark, that double-crossing bastard. She was so angry she was almost tempted to abandon the idea she had come up with that morning. *Almost.* But common sense prevailed. Despite her anger at Mark, there were too many advantages to the idea she had come up with.

In the bathroom, Gabrielle turned the water on in the tub, watching as the bath beads she added turned into frothy white bubbles. Then she went down to the kitchen and got herself a chilled bottle of champagne and two glasses. When she returned to the bedroom, she pinned up her hair and headed into the bathroom with her champagne.

She slid slowly into the scented water, immersing herself in a sea of white foam, leisurely sipping the glass of champagne she had poured for herself, letting the tension knotting her muscles slip away from her body.

The doorbell then rang and Gabrielle pressed the intercom in the bathroom wall. "Yes?"

"Gabrielle, it's Mark. I was wondering if we could talk?"

"Mark, I was just thinking about you," she said sweetly. "Sure, come on up. The key is under the potted palm."

Sipping her champagne, Gabrielle waited for Mark's entrance. She could hear him heading up the stairs and then he was in the bathroom doorway.

"Don't be shy," she said, waving an arm and releasing a puff of bubbles in the air. "I'm so glad you could stop by. Would you like a glass of champagne?" she asked, reaching for the chilled bottle on the floor.

"No, thank you." Mark sat himself down on the tub's marble ledge. "I wanted to see you because Heather gave me a call. She told me what happened at Daniel's."

Gabrielle waved a disapproving finger at Mark. "Naughty, naughty, letting the cat out of the bag the way you did."

Mark eyed Gabrielle warily. "You don't seem very angry."

Gabrielle gave Mark an even look, eyes narrowing dangerously. "Honey, I'm *seething*. No one pulls a double-cross on me. However, for the moment Ms. McCall's downfall is at the bottom of my priority list. I've got bigger fish to fry."

"Have you?" Mark suddenly had a sinking fear in his stomach. This scene was eerily reminiscent of the confrontation with Paul Fontana months ago in his Las Vegas penthouse. Gabrielle was about to lower some sort of boom on him and because she had him in a corner there was nothing he could do except wait and listen.

"Yes, I do," she purred, refilling her champagne glass and slowly sipping the golden liquid. "I'm sure you're aware of my recent widowhood."

"You seem to be taking it very well," he stated somewhat dryly. "I thought you'd be the bereaved wife."

"I keep a tight lid on my emotions. Anyway, I have a proposition. Would you like to hear it?"

"I'm all ears," Mark answered, knowing he didn't have any choice.

Gabrielle's eyes sparkled with excitement. "What would you think if I said we should get married?"

"What!" Mark jumped to his feet. "I'd say you were nuts!"

"Think about it, Mark. It would solve all your problems. If we were to get married my father would forget all about your gambling debt. I'd see to it. Then you'd be free."

And chained to you, Mark thought, envisioning his life as a living hell if he were to allow Gabrielle to slip a gold wedding band onto his left hand. He knew he'd have to tread carefully with his answer. *Very* carefully.

"Are you serious about this?"

Gabrielle nodded her head vigorously. "Very serious. Since I'm now a widow, we could do it whenever you want. Like tonight."

Tonight! Mark suddenly found he couldn't breathe and started hyperventilating.

"Are you okay?" Gabrielle asked in alarm as Mark started turning red in the face.

"I think I will have some of that champagne," he gasped, pouring himself a glass and quickly downing it.

"Think about it, Mark," Gabrielle said, continuing her pitch. "We'd be *the* up-and-coming couple in Hollywood. Together we could do great things."

Oh boy. How did he get himself out of this one? She certainly wasn't wasting any time in trying to get him to the altar. He felt like he was on cracking ice and about to plunge into a sea of piranha.

"Gabrielle, you know I think you're a sexy, vivacious woman. Any man would be proud to have you on his arm. And I have to admit, we have had some good times together."

"Yes, we have." Gabrielle looked at Mark suggestively, starting to rise from the tub. "Want to slip into my bedroom and start the honeymoon early?"

Mark held out a restraining hand. "Gabrielle, as tempting as your offer is, I'm afraid I'll have to turn it down."

Gabrielle sank back into her suds. *"Turn it down?"* she growled. "You're turning down my proposal?"

Mark realized he needed to do some fancy footwork. Quickly. "Gabrielle, I'm flattered by your proposal, but can't you see we're all wrong for each other? We don't stand a chance of having a future together."

"Who said anything about a future together?" She looked at him scornfully. "I don't give a fuck about a cottage with a white picket fence. This is a business arrangement we're talking about. You marry me and I get you off the hook with my father. In exchange for that you give me a film career and star billing in all your projects."

Once again it was back to square one. He hoped he'd be able to talk some sense into her. "Gabrielle, it's not that easy. I can't just *make* you a star."

"Why not? You've done it for Heather."

"Heather's a different case. She's got talent—"

Mark regretted the words the minute they were out of his mouth. He'd just made a *big* mistake.

"What are you saying?" Gabrielle screeched, waving her arms left and right, bubbles flying in the air. "Are you saying I don't have any talent? Is that it? *Is* it? Answer me, Mark!"

"Gabrielle, calm down. You're getting excited."

"Don't tell me to calm down, you bastard! I gave you a chance and you threw it away. You're history in this town. History!" She stood up, about to climb out of the tub. "Out of my way. I've got some phone calls to make."

Mark reached for Gabrielle, wanting to shake some sense into her so she'd listen to what he had to say. "Gabrielle, please don't do anything rash. Please don't do anything you're going to regret. I'm willing to talk. I'm willing to compromise."

"Don't touch me!" she screamed, suddenly afraid. "Don't you dare lay a hand on me." Gabrielle reached behind her, grabbing for a bottle of perfume from a shelf of toiletries and cosmetics behind her, flipping off the top with her thumb.

As she brought the bottle up, she saw it was the Giorgio she had been given as a farewell gift from the cast and crew of "The Yields of Passion." She felt her only hope was to squirt him in the eyes with the perfume so she could get past him and out of the bathroom.

Gabrielle pressed down on the plunger.

Mark released a howl of agony as the mist sprinkled his face. Gabrielle watched in horror as his flesh began to blister and turn raw.

"My eyes!" he howled. "My eyes! I can't see! He started stumbling around blindly. "I can't see!"

Gabrielle stared in stunned horror at the bottle of perfume she held in her hand, suddenly realizing that it had been meant for her. She dropped the bottle of perfume in horror, jumping from the tub and running from the bathroom.

"The police said they'd send a patrol car by every hour. Just to check things out. Don't worry, Laura. They'll catch him."

The police officers who'd returned from Laura's house had found nothing. An all-points bulletin was issued throughout the state, along with a sketch of Nico.

After leaving the police station, Laura was taken to a hospital, where she was thoroughly checked and released. The only advice given was that she relax and take it easy, which Drew promised to see to.

Now they were finally alone at the beach house. Drew was starting a fire, while Laura huddled on the couch, knees drawn up.

"Do we still have a chance?" she asked solemnly. "I mean, if it weren't for the baby . . ."

Drew abandoned his kindling. "Laura, how can you ask that?" He came to her side, joining her on the couch. "You came back, didn't you? I came looking for you, didn't I? This was before either of us knew about the baby. I think that should tell us something—don't you? Laura, I love you." He placed a gentle hand on her abdomen. "This baby only makes our new beginning extra special. Let's put what happened behind us and concentrate on the future, okay?"

Laura didn't know what she'd do without this man she loved. How she had missed him! But now they had the rest of their lives to spend together. "Okay."

"How about something to eat? Hungry?"

"Famished. In fact, I have this strange desire for vanilla ice cream sprinkled with Bacos."

"A craving!" Drew stated with excitement. "You have a craving! My first official Daddy duty." He gave Laura a kiss before bounding into the kitchen. "Be right back."

Moments later he returned empty-handed. "My cupboards are bare. Look, why don't we run down to the supermarket? We can stock up on lots of goodies, anything that might catch your eye."

"I'm a big girl, Drew. I can stay by myself."

"After what you've been through? Uh-uh." Drew shook his head adamantly. "No way. You're not leaving my sight."

"I'll be fine. Really," she insisted, snaring his leather jacket off the coat rack and tossing it to him.

Drew caught the jacket and rehung it. "Nico is still out there. I'm not leaving you alone."

"Drew, I'm not going to be afraid anymore. Suppose they don't find him? Am I supposed to spend the rest of my life in fear? Are we supposed to remain joined at the hip? I lived my life that way for far too long. I'm not going to live that way anymore."

"Are you sure?" he asked somewhat reluctantly.

"We'll check all the rooms and we'll check the locks on all the windows and doors. After you leave I won't open up for anyone and the police will be checking on things. I'll be fine. Honest."

"All right," Drew grudgingly conceded. "Let's check things out. I'll try not to take too long."

Peter had watched Kelly throw her drink in Diana's face. He had watched his father try to calm Diana down, following as they'd left the memorial and returned to Diana's estate.

He'd watched as his father gave Diana the necklace that had once belonged to his mother. And then he'd watched as the two made love.

Now he was going to watch them die.

He clutched the gun he'd retrieved from Daniel's study. It was a .44 caliber. Sleek. Powerful. Deadly.

Peter slipped into the bedroom, approaching the foot of the bed.

"Rise and shine," he whispered.

Diana jumped up in bed, clearly surprised, clutching the sheet to herself. Paul only looked at him in annoyance.

"What do you think you're doing here?" Paul demanded. "We said everything we had to say to each other."

"Not quite. I had to bring something."

"What?"

Peter brought up the gun. "Justice."

Diana's eyes widened in fear. "Paul! He's got a gun!"

"You think I don't have eyes, you stupid bitch?" he snarled. "I can see he's got a gun! So what? He hasn't got the guts to use it."

"Haven't I?" Peter released the safety. "Would you like to die before or after Diana?"

"Before or after?" Diana squeaked. "Why do you want to kill me? What did I ever do to you?"

Peter turned to her, eyes narrowing with hatred. "You did plenty. You made him kill my mother! You made him kill Daniel! *He did as he promised!*"

Diana shook her head vehemently. "I don't know what you're talking about."

"Don't lie to me. I was there the night my father murdered my mother and I was there when you showed up hours later, though I never knew who you were. You asked him if he'd done as he promised and he told you not to worry. He told you it wouldn't even look like murder. He strangled my mother, gave you her necklace, and then made it look as if she'd hanged herself."

"I didn't know anything about your mother's death, Peter. I

swear," Diana implored, ripping the necklace away. "What we were discussing was something entirely different."

"Was it? Well, you're still involved with Daniel's death. Are you going to deny that? Vanessa told me what happened. She told me how you'd threatened Daniel." Peter waved his gun wildly, turning to his father. "How could I have been so stupid? How could I have not figured it out? Especially after that last conversation we had . . . You have to pay for what you've done," he vowed. "You both have to pay."

"Paul, do something," Diana begged. "I don't want to die!"

"Will you stop your whining!" Paul snapped. "Give me the gun, Peter." He held out an open palm to his son. "We can talk."

"No," Peter refused. "There's nothing left to talk about. It's my fault Daniel is dead. I should have been able to protect him. I knew you were a killer. I should have known you'd try to kill him." Peter shook his head regretfully and lifted his gun. "I let you both get away with murder once. I can't let that happen again. It's all over. For both of you."

Peter aimed the gun at Diana.

"No!" she shrieked as her life flashed before her eyes. There was no way out of this. No escape. She was about to die. "Please don't kill me!"

Peter pulled the trigger and a bullet ripped into Diana's heart. She collapsed against the headboard as her blood began to seep through her negligée and onto the sheets. Another bullet followed.

Peter then aimed the gun at Paul.

"Your turn."

"You can't do this to me," Paul said, still unperturbed, his voice filled with confidence. "You can't kill me. You won't. I'm your father. Doesn't that mean anything?"

"Yes," Peter commented, watching as his father's face relaxed. "It means shit."

He squeezed out another two shots.

Drew drove to and from the supermarket in twenty minutes. When he got back to the beach house, he cut the engine and clambered out of the Jaguar while reaching into the back seat for his crutches.

"Hey, how about giving me a hand?" he called. "There's a jar of Bacos with an expectant mother's name on it, not to mention a few other goodies. Come on out."

The sound of Drew's voice was welcome relief. Laura had to admit she had been scared being left alone. Every little noise had made her jump. But she'd done it and now Drew was back.

Unlocking the front door, she stepped out onto the front deck with a smile.

Drew had just opened the trunk and lifted out two bags, preparing to hand them to Laura when he heard a sound, like the approach of rushing footsteps, from behind.

But Drew was too late to do anything. When his crutch was whacked against the side of his head, he grunted once in pain before slumping onto the sand and slipping into unconsciousness.

Laura's scream came too late as she watched Drew collapse.

"I told you I'd be waiting in the bushes, baby," Nico said, tossing the crutch away. "So you've got a bun in the oven, do you?" One side of his head was crusted with dried blood. "You're just full of surprises, aren't you?"

Laura ran for the beach house, slamming the door behind her and desperately trying to turn the locks. But before she could, Nico was barreling his way inside.

She fell backwards onto the floor but quickly scrambled to her feet, running for the sliding doors leading to the back deck, not daring to look back as she undid the locks with fumbling fingers and escaped outside.

Drew groaned, awash in a sea of pain. His head was throbbing and a cloud of welcoming darkness promised to carry him away.

But then he heard a scream—Laura's scream—rip through the night.

Drew fought back the blackness, struggling to his feet, reaching for a crutch and dragging his bad leg behind him as he headed for the beach.

Footsteps pounded behind her as she headed for the shoreline and then a body crashed into her, tackling her to the wet sand.

Nico flipped her onto her back, roughly seizing her face. "Did you really think I'd let you get away from me?"

"Nico, please!" she begged.

An incoming wave rolled over them, drenching them in cold water. Laura choked on the water, struggling for air.

"You don't deserve to live, Laura. And neither does your bastard!"

He pulled her farther out and shoved her head under the water.

Drew saw Nico holding down Laura . . . drowning her . . . and staggered as fast as he could.

Laura tried holding her breath but couldn't. Nico was relentless. He kept pulling her head out of the water, only to push it back under.

Her fingers scrabbled in the wet sand. They closed around a round stone. Hefting the stone, she was about to bash it into Nico's head when there came the sound of gunfire. The next thing she knew Nico had released her, slumping into the water.

Laura saw the dark water surrounding her in a daze. Blood was oozing from the holes in Nico's back. Pushing his dead weight off her, Laura splashed through the water and ran for the beach. Sobbing, she threw herself into Drew's arms. Behind him she could see the two police officers from the watch patrol, both reholstering their guns.

"Looks like we got here in time," she heard one say to the other.

"Are you all right?" Drew asked.

She nodded. "Fine."

"Are you sure?" he asked worriedly.

"Yes, honest. I'm just a little shaken. But Drew, I've still got my craving," she confessed. "Were you able to get the Bacos?"

Drew, kissing Laura passionately, laughed all the way back to the beach house.

EPILOGUE

THE DOUBLE MURDER of Paul Fontana and Diana Halloway, following on the heels of Daniel Ellis's death *and* the bizarre death of Harrison Moore, allowed many in Hollywood, particularly the older legends, to breathe a collective sigh of relief. Whenever anybody who was anybody died in Hollywood, two more deaths were sure to follow—Hollywood deaths *always* came in threes. And now the quota was filled. At least for the time being. Or so the superstitious believed.

Long Journey Home was a box-office smash once it opened in December and garnered rave reviews. When Oscar time rolled around, the picture snared eight nominations, including Best Picture, Best Actor for Drew Stern and Best Supporting Actress for Heather McCall. Critics expected the film to sweep every major category.

When the envelope was opened, *Long Journey Home* didn't win one award.

Believing her "fan" would eventually kill her, Gabrielle abandoned her acting career in Hollywood and relocated to Italy. With her portion of her father's estate, she bought a villa on the Adriatic and equipped it like a fortress, complete with armed guards and pit bulls.

After six months of boredom Gabrielle decided to test Italy's acting waters. She starred in a number of soft porn films and instantly became an overnight sensation.

* * *

Kelly and Graham were blissfully happy in New York. After abandoning the bright lights of Hollywood, Graham answered the call of Broadway, while Kelly gave up her acting altogether, deciding to turn her hand to writing. The finished product was a Hollywood glitz novel entitled *Hollow Legend*. It told the story of a Hollywood legend, her husband, his lover, their daughter, and her husband. The book was also chock-full of sex, drugs, murder, and Mafia kingpins.

Hollow Legend was offered by Kelly's agent in a blind auction and sold for one million dollars. Aaron Spelling Productions bought the television rights for a mini-series, with Vanessa Vought to star as the legend. *Hollow Legend* debuted on the *New York Times* Bestseller List in the #1 position and spent twenty-six weeks on the list. Kelly was already starting work on her second novel and was being hailed as the new queen of glitz.

When asked if her mother had been the inspiration for the divinely bitchy Solange, the Hollywood legend of her novel, Kelly would always cagily respond, "Write what you know."

After his beating from Peter, Jaime needed to have his nose fixed. Which wasn't a bad thing since he decided to have a major overhaul done on the rest of his face—a nip here, a tuck there, one or two implants. The results made him look five years younger and with his new face, along with a new name, Jaime headed for New York and a modeling career.

Within a month of his arrival, Jaime was the lover of an aging fashion designer. Dropping in on his lover one day during lunch, Jaime found him being serviced by a Puerto Rican delivery boy. A gold Rolex managed to smooth Jaime's ruffled feathers. A month after that he found his lover in their bed with a Greek waiter. A diamond pinky ring helped Jaime to forgive the relapse into promiscuity. A week later he found their chauffeur giving his lover a blow job. This time Jaime was *not* forgiving and packed his bags.

Four months after the relationship ended Jaime discovered his ex-lover had tested positive for HIV.

* * *

Vanessa Vought was written onto "The Yields of Passion" to replace the deceased Diana. The fans loved her and after a week on the show she began an affair with the virile young Frost Barclay.

With the publication of her autobiography, *Totally Vanessa*—topping the bestseller lists for six months—and the starring role in the *Hollow Legend* mini-series, Vanessa was riding high. She hoped Diana was watching, wherever she was.

Mark was fortunate enough not to lose his eyesight after being squirted in the face with acid. He was even more fortunate when Gabrielle decided to leave Hollywood. With her no longer breathing down his neck, he was able to create some semblance of order in his life.

Peter somehow managed to get him out of his contract with Trinity and also saw to it that his gambling debt was paid off. When Mark learned he was off the hook with the Mafia, he pledged his eternal gratitude to his former assistant.

The first thing Mark did once he was a free agent again was to follow Kelly's example and put pen to paper. The result was a hot new screenplay that every studio in town was after. He called it *Golden Boy* and it was all about an up-and-coming Hollywood producer/director who suddenly finds himself working for the Mafia.

Bidding for the screenplay was fierce; favors were called in; anybody who was anybody wanted a role and instructed their agent to do whatever was necessary to make them a part of *Golden Boy*.

Mark, Hollywood's reigning golden boy, was still on top.

After Grace claimed rightful ownership of *Dangerous Parties*, all rights to the screenplay reverted to her and Harrison's contract with Trinity Pictures became null and void. Though Trinity offered to pay Grace the same amount of money they had intended to pay Harrison, along with perks and bonuses, Grace promptly took her screenplay to another studio. The reason for Grace's defection was simple. Not only did the other studio offer her a three-picture deal, but it also cast Heather McCall as Melanie Dalton. Though Trinity's offer for *Dangerous Parties* had been tempting, Grace was unable to resist screwing Gabrielle over. She felt she owed Harrison that much.

* * *

Peter pleaded temporary insanity to the murder of his father and Diana Halloway. When the circumstances surrounding Peter's state of mind were revealed at the trial, he was found not guilty of all charges brought against him and was ordered to see a psychiatrist twice a week for a year.

The running of Trinity Pictures fell to him and he managed to pick up the pieces of his life. He no longer hid his homosexuality and started dating an actor he'd met at a party. They were a tender and affectionate couple, but they delayed going to bed just yet—Peter wasn't ready. It would be some time before he got over Daniel.

Heather decided to accept *Playboy*'s offer of a layout and it was the smartest move of her career. Within twenty-four hours of hitting the newsstands, the issue was sold out.

When her nomination for Best Supporting Actress was announced, it was predicted that Heather would be a shoo-in for the award. Then her pictorial appeared and critics announced that although she still had a good chance of winning, what she had done could cost her a few votes with some older members of the Academy. Heather told the members of the Academy exactly what she thought of their priggish attitude while presenting an award during the Oscar telecast.

She gave them the finger.

The audience gave her a standing ovation.

After that night the country was hit with Heather fever. Her career soared to new heights and the offers poured in.

Drew and Laura were married, and six months after the wedding Laura gave birth to a baby girl, which they named Victoria Danielle. Drew decided to take a year off to be with his new family—not only to play Daddy, but also because he and Laura wanted to give their daughter a little brother or sister.

One year later Andrew Michael Stern was born.

"So this is happiness," Laura said, beaming at Drew as she cradled their newborn son in the delivery room.

Drew touched his son's dark head and then kissed Laura.

"This is happiness," he affirmed.